BELL OF
THE DESERT

Bell of
the Desert

A Novel

Alan Gold

YUCCA

Yucca Publishing books may be purchased in bulk at special discounts for sales promotion, corporate gifts, fund-raising, or educational purposes. Special editions can also be created to specifications. For details, contact the Special Sales Department, Yucca Publishing, 307 West 36th Street, 11th Floor, New York, NY 10018 or yucca@ skyhorsepublishing.com.

Yucca Publishing® is an imprint of Skyhorse Publishing, Inc.®, a Delaware corporation.

Visit our website at www.yuccapub.com.

10 9 8 7 6 5 4 3 2 1

Library of Congress Cataloging-in-Publication Data is available on file.

Cover design by Yucca Publishing

Print ISBN: 978-1-63158-007-9
Ebook ISBN: 978-1-63158-023-9

Printed in the United States of America

This book is dedicated to all of the astonishing, outstanding, and brilliant women of the past who have been dismissed, discounted and obliterated from the annals of history, simply because men were in charge of keeping the records.

ONE

Baghdad, April, 2003

In the beginning, there was shock and awe. The American president promised the world the greatest fireworks display in human history, a minimum number of civilian casualties, and a brief but merciless engagement with the Iraqi Republican Guard. The mission was to eliminate weapons of mass destruction and to replace a genocidal dictator and his sadistic sons with a democratically elected Iraqi government of the people, for the people and by the people.

In the beginning, it all went well. American troops met no resistance from Saddam's vaunted army of a million men. Pilots of B52 bombers flew unopposed through the air over Iraqi towns and villages, dropping laser-guided bombs onto garish palaces and government buildings, destroying in seconds the hubris of a dictator whose monuments for decades had symbolised his people's suffering. Tomahawk and Cruise missiles, F-14 Tomcats and F/A-18 Hornets screamed over a terrified populace and skimmed above rivers and deserts, steel birds of prey in Iraq's ancient skies.

And when the air was again silent, clean, and breathless, dozens of 70-ton Abrams tanks began rolling towards Baghdad, shaking the dust of eons from ancestral monuments. Iraq's million-man army disappeared like a desert sandstorm in the time it took to change TV channels. A world watched in amazement as huge tanks, once engines of warfare, became elephants pulling down ostentatious statues of the great dictator. The Colossus of Baghdad was no more.

In the beginning, the Iraqi people welcomed the Americans. They danced in the streets on top of portraits of Saddam which had once adorned the entire sides of buildings. They tore at them with their fingernails and defaced and mutilated them until satisfied that they had humiliated the man hated and feared by so many. They jumped on top of his images and spat at his statues. They hit them with mallets and hammers, and shot at them with rifles and machine guns. They searched everywhere for him and his insane sons so they could vent their wrath.

And then, where earlier there had been the fury of war, silence descended as news began to circulate that Saddam and the entire command structure of repression and evil had disappeared from their command bunkers, and now there was nobody in control of Iraq. Like so much of the nation's ancient history, Saddam had buried himself underground, and it would take foreigners to dig him up again.

Singing and dancing and kissing soon gave way to irrepressible greed as the looting began. Shops, factories, warehouses were denuded by a people suddenly released from the chains of tyranny, no longer petrified of Saddam's secret police, his army and his torture chambers.

A huge building dedicated to the country's past was emptied with an almost maniacal sense of mischief. It was the National Museum of Iraq. This museum, which housed some of the world's finest collections of antiquities, some dating back five thousand and more years, operated in conjunction with the British Museum even during the most oppressive days of Saddam.

First Lieutenant Michael Jennings Rourke led his twenty man scouting patrol along the western banks of the Tigris River, near to the course of the Old City Wall, following tanks which were clearing the way and ensuring no machine gun nests would pose a problem for his troops.

Before him loomed the walls of the compound which housed the Iraqi National Museum. From a distance, they looked like animals scurrying around in a nest, but as he led his patrol closer, Lt. Rourke could see that men and boys were swarming throughout the compound, running away with priceless vases and statues and pottery and idols and other objects of inestimable value. He shot an M16 round into the air to scare them off. By the time he and his men entered the broken building, it was already empty both of the Baghdadi looters and of their country's most prized possessions, precious objects from the dawning of mankind's earliest civilization in Mesopotamia, the Land between the Rivers Tigris and Euphrates.

Lt. Rourke gave terse orders for his men to search the building, warning them of the dangers of snipers who might be hiding in the upper balconies and levels of the building.

There was dust and shards of glass everywhere, both from the initial collateral damage caused by the American bombardment in the earliest days of the battle for Baghdad, and from the looting which had followed when the Iraqis determined that they wanted to benefit from the war. But every display case, every article, every idol and statue and stele and frieze which had once made this one of the greatest monuments to mankind's earliest genius, had been taken. Nothing was left other than dust and destruction. He shook his head in disgust. Having majored in History from Syracuse University, he had a fair idea of what should have been here, a collection gathered together over a hundred years by archaeologists from around the world who had come to the cradle of civilization to uncover the record of the people who had first taught humankind how to write, to record, and to narrate myths in explanation of the natural phenomena which governed their lives.

He heard his name called. Turning, he saw one of his younger troopers, a nervy black kid from Harlem, not more than seventeen years old. Dwayne or Duanne or something.

"What is it?" he called.

"Over here, sir. Dey lef' sumpin.'"

Michael Rourke walked over, his army boots crunching over the glass and splintered wood. He joined the young trooper, and together they looked at a marble bust of a severe-looking woman, hair tied back in a tight bun. From the neckline of her dress it was obvious she was no ancient, but from a much more recent age. Probably Victorian or from early in the twentieth century.

3

"Only one dey left. Muthafucka cain't be no value? Y'all know what it is?" asked the trooper.

Michael shook his head. He had no idea why it was the only object left behind. He cleaned the inscription with his fingers, blowing away the dust which obscured the carved dedication. It was both in Arabic, and in English. It said,

Gertrude Bell. A Woman of Iraq.
First Director of the National Museum.
Presented by a grateful King and People.

"Who dis lady?" asked the trooper.

Michael looked carefully at the middle-aged woman. He'd never heard of her. And neither did he have time to wonder. The building had to be secured before he and his men could move on.

He turned to the young trooper. "No idea," he said, and moved deeper into the building.

When all this was over, he thought, he might Google Gertrude Bell and try to find out something about her. She might be interesting . . .

~

Windsor Castle, October 1888

The young woman standing in line before Gertrude was nervously arranging and re-arranging the curls in her hair which cascaded beyond her neck and over the bodice of her flawless white ball gown. Her gleaming black hair partially hid the pearls embedded within the delicate Irish silk embroidery and organza lace which suffused the dress's neckline. The girl's father, the plump and pompous Duke of Rawlthone, whose orotund voice was strangely muted for the occasion, stood beside his daughter, whispering in her ear to stop fidgeting. Immediately obeying her father's instruction, the young woman moved in procession with the long line of precisely-arranged debutants as they stepped a single pace forward to advance towards the Throne Room for each successive candidate to curtsey before Queen Victoria.

Hugh, Gertrude's father, glanced at his daughter. Unlike the other debutantes who could barely contain their fear at approaching Victoria, Gertrude was calmly looking around the room, taking in its vaulted architecture, the Gainsborough, van Dyke and Reynolds masterpieces hung on the walls, and the resplendence of the princes and princesses, the dukes and duchesses and the marqueses and marchionesses clustered in the vast auditorium watching the latest contingent of eligible young women from noble families about to be released onto the marriage market.

Hugh never ceased to be amazed by his marvellous daughter's ability to take command of whatever situation in which she found herself. Since her earliest days, she'd always seemed more adult than child. She was both sister and mother to her younger brother Maurice. After Hugh's marriage since the death of his beloved Mary, Gertrude had willingly accepted Florence as her stepmother, and had done her very best to be a glorious daughter.

When she went up to Oxford as one of the University's first women students, she'd refused to be cowed by the young men's chauvinism and bullying or the disdain she'd experienced from the dusty old professors. Indeed, she'd taken a first in history in only two years, some sort of University record, he was told. And now, just as she was about to come out in her presentation to Victoria, Queen of England, its Colonies and her Empire, Gertrude just stood there, tall and regal, auburn hair aflame, yet cool as a cucumber, as though she was about to be introduced to the new parish vicar. Amazing!

"Aren't you in the least daunted?" he whispered.

"Daunted? Why?" Gertrude asked quietly.

"You're about to meet the Queen of England," he said.

She didn't reply, but only looked at him oddly and frowned. "You seem more nervous than me."

Her father shook his head. "Too much Oxford, m'girl. That's your trouble."

Gertrude looked round at her father, and frowned. "Frankly, these other girls need a bit of Oxford to stiffen up their spines."

Before her father could respond, the equerry's stentorian voice called out, "Your Royal Highness, may I introduce in attendance His Grace the Duke of Rawlthone, who approaches your throne to present to you his daughter, the Honourable Eugenia."

Gertrude watched as the pompous man grasped his daughter's arm and almost pulled her forward, her jellied legs struggling on the long walk from the corridor, passed the hundreds of assembled nobility in their brilliant gowns and jackets. Gertrude watched as they approached the foot of the throne and the young Eugenia perform a perfect curtsey, genuflecting to the Queen while her father the duke bowed low from the waist. Only when Victoria nodded, smiled and raised her left hand a fraction, did the father straighten up and was the daughter permitted to rise. Then, wordlessly, and by the merest dismissive flick of the equerry's finger, their time before royalty was up, and they walked uncertainly backwards towards the assembled throng of nobility, never once committing the ultimate social gaffe of turning their backs to the queen.

~

The Queen's equerry glanced at the father and daughter now at the head of the queue and waiting at the end of the corridor for admission. He looked at his list and appeared to sneer when he realized the next candidate to present his daughter for coming out wasn't a prince or a duke or even a lord, but a mere *honourable*, some industrialist from up north of the country.

Emphasising Hugh's lack of title to ensure the man's debasement in front of the nobles gathered before their monarch, the equerry said, "Your Royal Highness, may I introduce in attendance the Honourable Hugh Lowthian Bell who approaches your throne to present to you his daughter Gertrude."

Gertrude walked towards the throne, one pace ahead of her father. Having been well tutored all day by a succession of Ladies in

Waiting, Gertrude curtseyed low to the ground as her father bowed in deference to Victoria. While close to the polished oak floor, she sneaked a look up at Victoria's dress. It was the customary pitch black silk worn because she was still in mourning for her beloved Albert who'd died twenty-seven years earlier, but there were pearls sewn into the hem, which indicated Victoria was now accepting some adornment, some relief from the burden of her grief.

Sneaking a further look upwards, against the strict instructions of the Ladies in Waiting, Gertrude saw that Victoria was whispering to her equerry, who was furiously searching his notes in order to answer the queen's question. But he shook his head and whispered something back, then he bowed low and retreated.

Her voice was deep and gravelly, but instantly silenced the muffled chatter in the audience hall because the queen rarely spoke during these coming out occasions, and only then to the daughter of a duke or above personally known to her. Sensing that something sensational was about to happen, the assembled nobility listened with mounting expectation.

"You're the gal who's just been at the University in Oxford, aren't you?" asked Victoria.

Gertrude stood immediately to respond to the queen. There was a gasp at the unprecedented impertinence of her action, throwing centuries of protocol out of the window. Nobody, but nobody, and especially not a young girl coming out, ever stood before the queen had said "rise," and never engaged in conversation as though she were a familiar.

"Yes, Your Royal Highness. I took a degree in history. One of the few degrees open to women."

"And what was it like? You were one of the first girls there, I'm told."

"It was very enjoyable, thank you, Your Majesty. And very challenging."

"And what bit of history did you study?"

Gertrude smiled. "Actually, Majesty, I studied your family's history from the time your ancestors were in Hanover to your late uncle William."

Victoria nodded and masked her smile. The hordes of nobility in the room could barely believe their ears, especially when Victoria continued the conversation. "Ah, yes, the four kings George. And what aspect of their lives did you find particularly interesting?"

"Well, they were participants in a most fascinating time of Britain's history, but what I found really absorbing were the relationships between the monarch and the next in line to the throne. I could never properly understand why there was such intractable hatred between father and son. Such unhappy relationships. It's not particularly unusual for there to be jealousy between monarch and the successor, after all, British history is full of it, but your recent ancestors . . ."

She felt a sharp pinch in the shoulder as Hugh tried to stop his daughter from talking. But contrary to what the entire shocked audience was thinking, the queen smiled and said, "We'll have to forego this discussion, my dear, for I have a lot of young women to welcome. And you're not quite right about all my predecessors. I was very close to my dear late uncle, King William. Perhaps, Miss Bell, we might meet after the formalities, and share a cup of tea, and you can tell me more of what you learned about my ancestors."

Hugh bowed, Gertrude curtsied again, and they walked backwards into the assembly of nobility. When they were absorbed and cordoned off from the throne by the crowd, Gertrude turned to her father, and said quietly, "Well, that seemed to go quite well, didn't it."

Ashen-faced, her father hissed, "I . . . how could . . . you mustn't . . . you can't be that familiar with the queen. After all, she's the queen . . ."

Gertrude frowned and asked, "Father, I wasn't being familiar; Her majesty was engaging me in conversation."

"She was being nothing more than polite."

"And I was being polite. And she's not quite correct. You see, whilst the queen was certainly close to her uncle, William hated Victoria's mother, the Princess of Saxe-Coburg, and if the stories are true, banished her from his palace and it's said that he used to constantly berate her whenever they were in public for the way she kept Victoria from him. Victoria's mother wanted to rule after his death as co-regent with her lover. What's fascinating is that the Hanoverian disease of parent-hating offspring seems to be continuing to this day. It's said that Victoria detests her son, the Prince of Wales, and blames him for the death of Albert."

Horrified that she might be overheard, Hugh said, "Silence, child! This isn't the right place, nor is it one of your university tutorials. I'm your father, not—"

"But it's true and all the gossip in London, which is why the prince to this day has so little to do with the palace. Apparently when Edward was a young man, he behaved appallingly and Prince Albert was forced to ride on horseback, all through the night and in the middle of winter in order to rescue him from some scandal which could have damaged the crown. As a result, he caught a cold and died of typhoid. Victoria has never forgiven Edward. But I don't think I should raise that topic when I have tea with the queen. It might upset her."

"Gertrude," whispered Hugh, increasingly irritated by his daughter's unrestrained enthusiasm. "You may be factually correct, but you're being socially inept. There's a time and a place and this is neither. You've just come out. This is a ball. The queen traditionally disappears before the music begins. She's not going to sit down with you and have a chat. It was just a passing remark. And God only knows what you've managed to do to the family's reputation by addressing the queen directly in such a moralising way, especially when you were specifically ordered by the Ladies in Waiting just to say 'yes Ma'am' and 'no Ma'am' on the flimsiest chance that Her Majesty might deign to speak to you."

Before she could answer, the crowd around them parted as a tall and rotund man sporting a huge beard and moustache, bemedalled and dressed in a frock coat, walked towards them. Hugh tried to remain calm, recognising him immediately.

"Lord Salisbury, Mr. Prime Minister, this is a great honour," he said.

"Mr. Bell, Miss Bell. How d'you do? Miss Bell, I couldn't help but overhear that you'd read history up at Oxford. As you may know, history is one of my few relaxations from the burdens of office. I wonder whether you'd care to take tea with me tomorrow at Downing Street. You seem to be an interesting young woman, Miss Bell, and I'd very much appreciate the views of somebody of your tender years concerning this movement determined to give women the vote. Shall we say four o'clock?"

He turned and left. Now it was Gertrude who was astounded. It had all been such a whirlwind of experiences since she'd graduated with first class honours earlier in the year. She'd assumed that her just rewards for all the hard work in studying and taking her finals a year earlier than all her friends, would be the coming out balls in the season, but to take tea with the Prime Minister of England was, well, she could think of no better word than extraordinary.

After they'd retreated from her presentation to the queen, she and Hugh had stood in a bubble. The surrounding nobility didn't want to come too close in case Gertrude's inexcusable lapse of protocol had caused the Bells suddenly to become social pariahs, unacceptable in British households. But now that the Marquess of Salisbury, the Prime Minister of England, had not just acknowledged them, but had invited them to tea at Downing Street, it was obvious that they were celebrities, and like waves breaking on a shore, Hugh and Gertrude were inundated by handshakes and introductions and invitations.

The crowd of well-wishers quickly parted again as Victoria's imperious equerry approached, nodded curtly to Hugh, smiled at Gertrude, and said, "Miss Bell, Mr. Bell, Her Majesty has asked whether you would care to accompany her to her private apartments before the ball begins and take tea with her."

~

The Honourable Eugenia Mary Louise, daughter of the Duke of Rawlthone, looked over at where the assembly had gathered around Gertrude and saw her follow Her Majesty's Equerry towards the back of the Audience Chamber. She couldn't understand how this could happen when this Gertrude girl didn't even have a noble title. Eugenia scowled in anger at all the fuss and bother on the other side of the room. Why couldn't her father do something like that for her, she wanted to know.

~

Bucharest, Romania, Two Years Later

Gertrude Bell was a girl when she came down from Oxford but she knew for certain that Bucharest would make her into a woman. In Oxford, she'd been bookish, haughty, and intellectually voracious, but since coming down and especially after her coming out party, and her two seasons of balls, two years of numbingly boring social gatherings and dinner after tedious dinner with wearisome guests where she did her best to attract some young man to be her husband, she was now disillusioned and frustrated.

She knew she was startling to look at. Her height, her slim and athletic body and mass of red hair made her stand out from all the other young debutants desperate to ensnare the second son of some Duke or Baron. Some girls even had pretensions for a liaison with the son of a prince and did everything in their power to flaunt themselves whenever a princeling happened near.

Gertrude was quickly bored by such nonsense and sought other means of distraction, mostly involving books or arranging discussions when she was in the city house, with men in London who were leaders in the fields of politics, arts, science, or diplomacy.

The young men she met at the coming out balls seemed to lose interest in her after a first encounter, possibly—no, certainly— because she showed her disdain when they didn't want to discuss the subjects which interested her. She was even given to think that she was attractive, not only because the mirror reassured her, but

11

also because young men initially flocked around her. It was only after she began trying to find a topic of conversation which would be mutually interesting that they tended to drift away, attracted by any one of the dozens of other pretty young women who were, like her, trying not to end up as old maids at the age of twenty two.

Unlike her friends, she'd found snaring a husband far more difficult than society made out, despite having been a debutante before the queen and attending a dozen balls and twice as many parties. In the two long and desultory years between Oxford and Bucharest, years in which she'd come to realize that her intellect was an encumbrance in the marriage market, she had grown in maturity and stature, but her intellectual and social growth had been with her father and his friends, and not with a young man by her side. She prayed that the diplomatic season with her uncle Frank Lascelles would prove positive for her morale and perhaps lead to her finding a husband.

~

Watching her become increasingly dispirited at the conclusion of each ball and party, her father hoped that Romania would be a suitable place for her to learn the art of diplomacy, sadly lacking in a girl who turned discussion into energetic conversation, vigorous conversation into heated debate, and debate into a furious argument which must be won on the basis of superior knowledge, regardless of the effect it might have on the young man trying to make an impression.

Hugh had lost count of the number of eligible sons of the nobility, some of them both handsome and from ancient families, whom she'd inadvertently managed to demolish between the dance floor and the buffet when she failed to hide her obvious disdain for their stories about hunting or holidays and instead set about trying to discuss some arcane political issue which the youths often didn't begin to understand. She didn't mean to be arrogant or rude, which was how she seemed to come across, but

12

she had gained an unenviable reputation for being conceited, over-confident and haughty. She was none of these things with older men, who found her delightful and refreshing company. Most welcomed her challenging their traditional views with the voice of youth.

He'd begged her to veil her intellect and temper her knowledge, at least until she was married, and then she could do whatever she wanted. Until she was walking down the aisle, her father advised her to defer to the young men's interests in country life or fishing or sport, feign interest in their tales of jolly escapades like stealing policemen's helmets when they were in a drunken rampage after a party. But she could only be true to herself and told Hugh that she was incapable of pretending to be impressed by what she called 'their mindless infantile frolics, their total lack of interest in anything beyond themselves.' And so she remained husbandless while plodding down the aisle as bridesmaid at an increasing number of her friends' weddings. Bucharest, Hugh agreed, was an ideal place to send her to be chaperoned by his wife's brother, Frank Lascelles, Britain's Minister in Romania.

Father and daughter kissed goodbye in the choking smoke of the Gare de l'Est in Paris and as Hugh walked back along the platform, Gertrude shed a tear as the train began the twelve hundred mile journey from Paris to Strasbourg, then onto Vienna, Budapest, Belgrade, and finally Bucharest. After her aimless and frustrating time in London, she was eagerly anticipating spending time in the ambassadorial circle. There she would meet men of stature and worldly experience, provided her aunt didn't insist that she sit with the women, and discuss fashion, food, and the domestic help.

Why couldn't she find someone willing to marry her? She had enjoyed the occasional romantic escapade, escaping from the ballroom to the back stairs where she'd kissed a boy and laughed and been sporty. But more usually, after the initial introduction, the marking of her dance card, and then opening up topics of conversation to find a common interest, the boy had typically just smiled and indulged her with a single dance, and then made an excuse to return to his party. What was it about her that turned young men's initial interest into artless apathy causing them to seek the relief of distance? She knew she was gaining a reputation as a joyless blue stocking, but it seemed only to be with young men. Their older brothers and fathers found her delightful, even though their mothers often found her odd and different. But she couldn't, and wouldn't, camouflage her brain and feign interest where there was none. She'd studied damned hard at Oxford, learned a lot, and all she wanted was somebody whose mind was at least equal, if not a lot better, than hers.

Even the dinners to which she'd been invited had invariably turned out to be painfully dull, mainly because she'd been placed at the end of the table reserved for the sons and daughters of the guests. She knew that she attracted the attention of the assembly with her cascades of burnished red hair and her piercing blue-green eyes, and she knew she was fashionable in her beautiful clothes from Paris' finest couturiers; and she always took pride in dressing in her late mother's exquisite jewels. But when she sat at the table, the older men and women discussed topics which she found interesting and in which she was keen to participate, whilst the young men and women around her laughed and giggled at the silliest things, like knocking over the salt cellars or surreptitiously flicking food at each other.

She hated her reputation as a stick-in-the-mud, somebody who talked about subjects such as science and history and politics. But what could she do? How could she change? And why should she change? Hopefully, she'd find some young unmarried British diplomats in Uncle Frank's embassy with whom she could gain companionship.

She looked out of the windows as the train gathered speed through the eastern suburbs of Paris. The books about Bucharest said that it was a meeting place between East and West, the closest point of contact between Europe and the Ottoman Empire. This, surely, was the sort of adventure for which she was born. Suddenly, those young men and their juvenile japes didn't seem relevant any more. She sat back, picked up a newspaper, and realized that she was smiling.

~

"You told the Prime Minister that!" shouted Frank Lascelles, spluttering on his early morning cup of coffee. "And how did old Salisbury react? He must have been utterly mystified."

"Well," said Gertrude, "I simply said that I didn't believe that women should be given the vote, no matter what colonies like New Zealand were planning." Her hair suddenly burned red as the horizontal rays of the rising sun burst through the windows to illuminate her face. She, her uncle Frank, her step-mother's sister Mary and their son Billy were sitting in the loggia as the sun rose above the distant Black Sea. It was her second morning in Bucharest, and they'd risen early so the family could ride north out of the city to the foothills of the glorious Carpathian Mountains where they would spend a week walking, talking and relaxing.

But when she saw that Mary was looking at her quizzically, surprised that a young woman like Gertrude could possibly be against a measure which might ensure the elevation of her sex, she explained, "Look, it's simply this. I told His Lordship that whilst all people should be allowed to vote for their governments, it should only be on the condition that they understand the grave issues which are involved in a general election, and that, unfortunately, is where most of Britain's women are *de facto* disqualified. I'm against all this suffragette nonsense. You wouldn't give the vote to a man who didn't know what he was voting for, now would you? Just because somebody has reached a certain age and owns property, shouldn't be a qualification for voting for a government and participating in a democracy. Frankly, and loathe as I am to criticise dear old Pericles of Athens, I have real doubts about the very underpinnings of egalitarianism earned without merit.

"So I told the Prime Minister that whilst ever women are slaves to their husband's requirements in the bedroom and tied to the scullery sink, they cannot be considered as having a mature understanding of the policies for which the parties are asking for their vote to be the government. I don't really understand why he was so shocked."

Frank chortled, while Mary said softly, "My dear, the Prime minister is in the grand old conservative mould. He would hate the idea of electoral change. He rejected Mr. Disraeli's bill which gave the vote to working class men. The idea of women voting would be anathema to him. The reason he invited you and your dear father to Downing Street was to find out what was in the minds of young people so he could find a countervailing argument. Now you've almost certainly turned his world topsy-turvy. Knowing him, I doubt whether he knows what to think."

The ambassador's butler coughed softly, entered the loggia and gave Sir Frank his morning's post on a silver salver. Frank looked though the letters quickly, saw that there was nothing to engage the mind of the British Minister and nodded to his butler, an instruction for him to give the post to the Embassy's Second Minister, Frank's deputy.

After breakfast, they readied their horses for mounting and prepared to set off on the long ride to the foothills of the vast horseshoe-shaped distant mountains which cut a massive swathe through Central Europe. Their servants had already left hours before in the darkness before dawn in order to lay out a picnic for their mid-morning refreshments. Lunch would be taken in one of the many inns which were on the road between Bucharest and the mountains and they would spend the night in the private holiday residence of King Carol I, a good friend both of the ambassador and of Great Britain.

When Frank told Gertrude they were to be guests at one of the king's country estates, she was excited. "What a shame he won't be there. I've been reading all about him. Interesting man from an interesting family," she said. "I do hope I'll get the chance to go to a dinner at the palace. I'd love to hear his *major domo* introduce him as Prince Karl Eitel Friedrich Zephyrinus Ludwig

16

of Hohenzollern-Sigmaringen . . . what a mouthful; by the time his name's been called, the party will be half over."

Frank burst out laughing, but turned in surprise when the bell at the gates to the embassy's courtyard was sounded. He steadied his horse which took fright at the sudden noise. A gardener ran to open the entryway, and as he did so a huge man was revealed, dressed in the clothes of a desert Arab, sitting astride a blindingly white horse. The sun was behind him, and it was hard for Gertrude to make out his face as he appeared to be shrouded in a halo of light. But as he patted his horse's neck to steady the beast, Gertrude saw a tall swarthy man with a glistening black beard, a keffiyeh of red and white check, a gleaming white *thoub* which covered his whole body, and a massive scimitar which hung on a jewelled strap from his chest to his knees.

"Good God, I didn't know he was in Bucharest." hissed Frank. "What the deuce does he want?"

Gertrude looked at the lone Arab, waiting at the gateway for the entry to be wide enough for him and his horse to pass through.

"Who is he?" asked Gertrude. But Frank didn't have time to answer as the Arab urged his horse forwards into the embassy grounds towards where the Lascelles and Gertrude were about to mount and start their journey. The man bowed, kissed his hand, and then touched his forehead in a gesture of respect.

"Greetings, English Lascelles," said the Arab.

"And greetings to you, Abd al-Rahman ibn Faisal ibn Turki ibn Abdullah ibn Muhammad of the great tribe of Sa'ud from the limitless deserts," said the ambassador. "To what do I owe this immense honour of your visit to my humble home?"

"I am here to seek your counsel and your wisdom," he said, dismounting in a single fluid movement. Gertrude was impressed by the large man's aquiline grace as he slipped from his saddle-less horse and onto the ground just in front of her uncle. A head taller than Sir Frank, the Arab moved as though he were one with his horse.

Abd al-Rahman turned and bowed towards Mary, nodded curtly to Billy, and stared fixedly when he came face to face with

17

Gertrude. She was about to extend her hand towards him, but suddenly remembered her manners and gave the briefest of curtseys.

"English, you will walk with me in your garden," said Abd al-Rahman.

"Sir, on any other day, it would have been my heart's desire and greatest privilege to have walked with you, but on this day, I and my family are about to ride to the mountains. My niece, Gertrude, has just arrived in Bucharest and it is my desire to show her the beauty of Romania. Can these great matters of state which occupy your mind be spoken of on another occasion?"

The tall Arab breathed deeply, and said, "I would be forever shamed if I was the cause of any delay in your journey. I will ride with you, English, and talk on the way. There are matters concerning my country, stolen from me by the sons of apes and pigs called Rashid. I must reclaim what is mine, but this can only be accomplished with the help of the English and their rifles and cannon."

Gertrude was suddenly absorbed. She'd assumed that she'd simply be riding and seeing the sights, but now she was embroiled in a political situation and was fascinated. She'd studied the history of the Ottoman Empire as part of the first year of her degree at Oxford, and would be riveted by an insider's understanding. But when she looked at Frank Lascelles, she saw him breathe deeply, and his face furrow in concern.

"Of course, Excellency. It would be an honour and a privilege for you to accompany us, but as to the help which Her Majesty's government can provide, well . . ."

In silence, Frank, Mary, Billy, and Gertrude mounted their horses, as did Abd al-Rahman, and together then rode out of the British Embassy onto the busy streets of Bucharest.

For the first half an hour after leaving their embassy, they rode in silence as their horses clopped over cobblestones, then gravelled roads and finally, as they left Bucharest's walls, the houses disappeared to the north of the city and they found themselves trotting beside fields of corn and orchards of apples. More types of apples than Gertrude had ever seen, not planted in neat rows like an English country garden, but seeming to grow haphazardly, wildly, unstructured and natural. She rode away from the party and into the nearby field and soon was tugging different apples from different trees and testing their taste.

English apples came to dining tables in only a small number of varieties. She regularly ate the Cox's orange pippin, the Granny Smith, and the russet. But here the varieties were vastly different in colour and shape, and the sizes and flavours of the different apples staggered her. Some were bright red and tiny, little bigger than a walnut; others were deep green and so sour they were inedible, yet others were mauve and golden and tasted as sweet as honey. It was a Garden of Eden as she trotted from tree to tree, sampling as she went, feeling a frisson of guilt as though she was a latter day Eve. Suddenly she heard a horses' whinny just behind her. Abd al-Rahman had also left the party and was close to her side.

"In Arabia, such a garden would truly be paradise," he said.

She smiled, and replied, "As it would in England, Eminence. And I was just thinking about the Garden of Eden. Tell me, Excellency, does your Koran speak of the Garden of Eden and Adam and Eve?"

He said, "Yes, there is mention of Adam in the Koran, our holy book, which is the word of Allah given to Mohammed, peace and blessings be upon him."

"Adam was such a clever invention of the people who wrote the Old Testament, wasn't he."

Abd al-Rahman looked at her in bemusement. "As Muslims, we believe that all of the Holy Books came directly to man from Allah. Man did not invent them. But the Old Book of the Jews was corrupted by man, as was the New Book of the Christians, and so in his love and wisdom, Allah gave us the Koran which is the unchanged and perfect word of God. From the day that Mohammed, peace and blessings be upon Him, received the words of the Koran, to this day, not a single letter has been changed. It is perfect as is His messenger."

Gertrude plucked a large blue-green low-hanging apple from a tree they rode by, and handed it to Abd al-Rahman. He took it and smiled in gratitude.

Softly, she said, "But neither the Christians, nor the Jews, would agree with you. The Jews believe that their religion was given to them on Mount Sinai by God through Moses, and that they were the Chosen People because it was their burden to receive the Ten Commandments, which are the basis of all great and civil societies. And Jesus Christ is a prophet and the son of God.

"Doesn't it therefore follow that if God gave the Jews the law by which mankind must live, but to the Christians, he gave His only son, surely that's a much greater religion than any. I don't want to sound disrespectful, Abd al-Rahman, but Mohammed was only a prophet and a messenger. Unlike Jesus, he wasn't a deity. And he was very much a human being, with wives and offspring. I believe that one of his wives, Aisha, was only a child of nine, which is pretty unsatisfactory and medieval. Hardly the sort of thing that one would expect from God's messenger, is it? So by any logic, Judaism and Christianity are more perfect religions than Islam. Wouldn't you agree?"

Never having been spoken to in this manner by anyone, and especially not a strange girl whose face and body he could clearly see, Abd al-Rahman tried to decide whether to answer or draw his sword and execute her on the spot.

Knowing she'd gained his attention, Gertrude added, "And another thing I don't understand about Islam, Excellency, is that the Jewish bible, as well as that of the Christians, is considered the revealed word of God, but Jews and Christians accept that it was written for a time and place. That's why over the millennia there have been wise men who have interpreted it for their societies. So long as the basic message about Allah and all that stuff doesn't change, what's wrong with modernising the Koran and making it relevant for Muslims today. I mean, stoning and amputation of the right hand and all that sort of barbaric stuff."

Before Abd al-Rahman could silence her, Gertrude continued, "For instance, in the Jewish Old Testament, the punishment for not observing the Sabbath was death. Well, if that were carried out today, half the Christians and Jews in the world would be stoned to death, wouldn't they? It doesn't work for modern times, don't you agree?"

Angered, he said, "It is given to our leaders, to our great religious men, to carry out the work and obey the words of our Prophet Mohammed, peace and blessings be upon him, who was given these words by Allah himself. Are you saying that men should not follow the word of God?"

Gertrude responded, "But Thomas à Kempis said that man sees your actions, but only God sees your motives. Not being divine, I can only judge your society by its actions, such as stoning women who commit adultery. Pretty beastly, if you ask me. But maybe God sees things differently."

Before he could answer, Frank Lascelles rode up quickly, both as a chaperone for Gertrude, and because he was well aware of her forthrightness and was afraid that she'd say something undiplomatic. The moment he saw Abd al-Rahman's face, he knew his niece had behaved true to form and he would need to do some rapid diplomatic fence-mending.

"We have a long journey ahead of us. Perhaps we should continue," he said. "Gertrude, will you re-join your Aunt Mary and Billy."

"Your child, English, believes that Islam is only the third most important religion, after Christianity and Judaism, and she has said other things which insult the Faith. In my country, she would be buried up to her neck and then stoned to death. Her words, ambassador, are an offence to my ears," said Abd al-Rahman curtly. "She has disrespected our Prophet. She must be corrected."

"Oh, dear," the ambassador replied, knowing what the Arab meant by correction. "I'm afraid that Gertrude is somewhat more outspoken than most other girls. She's been to Oxford, and speaks and thinks like a man. In England, Excellency, it is not customary to punish people for their opinions, I'm afraid. But I certainly will speak with her about her attitude and require that she has more respect for the glories of Islam."

Abd al-Rahman shook his head in amazement. "Is her attitude the same as other English?" he asked.

Gertrude was about to respond, but Frank said curtly, "Gertrude. Go! Ride back to Mary and Billy. Now!"

"But . . ."

"Go! Now!"

As Gertrude rode away, she felt stung that Frank hadn't supported her. She thought that he, of all people, would engage in the discussion.

"I beg your forgiveness for my niece, Your Excellency. And please don't think that she is typical of other English girls her age. She is highly educated and knowledgeable."

"She has education? This is not the way of women in my country. No woman must be learned."

"In England . . ."

"Your Chatrude is knowledgeable of books, but she knows nothing of life," Abd al-Rahman said curtly. "You will punish her. Yes?"

"No. I will not punish her. I will advise her. Were she in Arabia, she would know not to say what she has said. But she is in my protection, and England will not allow somebody to be punished for his, or her, thoughts."

Abd al-Rahman rode slowly, silently beside Frank. Then he said, "This is not a world I recognize, English. Perhaps I am too quick. Our worlds are different. If we Arabs have to live in your world, we must learn how you do things. But will you learn how to respect us if you come to my world?"

Frank said cautiously, "Excellency, Islam is respected in my country, and even though no Englishman worships Allah, I assure you that we only have the warmest and most considerate attitude towards the Faith of the Prophet, just as our empire respects the religion of the Buddhist and Hindu in India and those who revere Confucius in China. We must learn to live with each other in these modern times, to respect the faiths of others, just as their faiths must respect ours."

He looked at Gertrude as she rode towards the others and frowned. What was he going to do with her, he wondered. He just prayed she hadn't ruined relationships between England and the Arabs.

Abd al-Rahman smiled and nodded. "I think, English, that much damage was done to the Faith of Islam when the Ottomans from Constantinople came north and tried to conquer Europe. Your niece shows the work Islam must do to reassure all that we are a religion as great and holy as that of the Jews and the Christians. We are a peaceful and loving religion, no longer warlike. Many years ago, our warlikeness was like that of the Crusaders; but as your Chatrude says, that was of a time and a place. Now our wars must be fought against those who believe in Islam, but who are unfaithful to the true word of the Prophet.

"But between us, this is a time of peace and understanding, not a time of war. My people were great and will be great again, but for now we are servants of the Turks and must live in the desert around our oases and smoke our hookahs and dream the dreams of our poets. Perhaps that is what I should be telling people such as English Chatrude. I now think that my meeting of you was foretold by the Prophet, for you and I will speak of matters of state, while in the days ahead, I will tell English Chatrude the truth about Islam."

They urged their horses out of the orchard and back onto the path, where the roads were rutted with the tracks of carts. Despite the dangers of snakes, it was easier for their horses to ride on the grasses and fields through which the pathways ran and they made good time. As they rode, Frank and Abd al-Rahman held their horses back from the others so they could talk about the need for England to assist the Sa'ud family in ridding the Arabian peninsula of the Rashid family who had taken residence in Riyadh and now commanded much of the surrounding countryside.

Gertrude reined in her horse and cautiously dropped behind her aunt and cousin so she was in earshot of what the two men were discussing. Apparently, this Rashid person was a former vassal and servant of the Sa'uds, but he'd used the quarrels between the Sa'ud family members to advance himself, and had managed to conquer a city called Riyadh. Abd al-Rahman had come secretly to Bucharest to ask Uncle Frank to write to the Prime Minister of England and get him to send an army to Arabia to drive out the Rashid family and restore the Sa'ud family to their lands.

It was all so exhilarating to listen to. It was real and exciting politics. It meant actual people, battles where people were hurt and even killed. And, as though a brilliant light had suddenly illuminated the world around her, Gertrude knew that this was the life to which she'd been born. The world of the society hostess, married and raising a family, going to balls and the theatre might be distracting, but she knew at her age it was probably out of reach. And anyway, such a lifestyle paled in comparison to immersing herself in the realism of politics, where decisions could alter history and cost the lives of countless people.

~

It took them a further five hours to ride slowly to King Carol's lodge deep in the heart of the foothills of the Carpathian Mountains. There was room available for everybody, but Abd al-Rahman asked whether he might stay the night, sleeping outdoors under the brilliant canopy of the stars.

After dinner, Gertrude walked outside and stood beyond the umbra of light cast through the windows. Shrouded in darkness, she lit a cigarette, lay on the ground, and stared up at the enormity of the night sky.

Sensing that somebody was approaching her, she lay still, until Abd al-Rahman said softly, "Truly, the skies of the desert show infinitely more stars than are here. It is possible to see the distant horizon, even on the darkest of nights, by the light of the stars."

"It must be very beautiful," she said softly.

"The desert is different things to different people. This is why Islam is so important to us. Without submission, without obeying those who have wisdom far beyond our understanding and lay down decrees, we would all die in the wilderness. You see, to you, the desert might be beautiful and to me it is home, but to others, to infidels and adventurers, it is a place of death. When the sun is highest and the wind whips the sand into your eyes and nose and tears your flesh, when the nearest water is three day's distance, when the heat sets aflame the very skin on your hands and face, then not even you, Chatrude Pell, could find beauty in the deserts of my country."

She smiled at his pronunciation of her name. "Then why does Your Excellency continue to live there?"

"Your home is where you are born. You may move many times, but you will always return to the place of your birth. And I have much work to do in order to reclaim my lands."

"Why is there so much disputation between your tribes, Excellency? Your people seem to do nothing but fight. Can't you somehow learn to live together?" she asked.

Abd al-Rahman said, "Each of our tribes, and there are many, wishes to be the leader of our nation. To take the place of Saladin. But except for me and my sons, there are no great men of Arab tribes any longer. That is why I wish to destroy the Rashids. Because when they are gone, I shall rule and I shall bring all others to bow to my leadership. That is why I am here and why I speak with English Lascelles."

Gertrude remained silent. She was desperate to continue the conversation, but her Uncle Frank had warned her in no uncertain terms that she mustn't discuss anything to do with politics with Abd al-Rahman, on pain of expulsion from the country and certain imprisonment and beheading in the Tower of London. What Uncle Frank failed to understand was that as a student of politics and history, and one who was now passionately interested in the Ottoman Empire, she put these threats to her life secondary to her desire to know.

"In England, Excellency, our kings used to fight for their kingdoms. But those were the ancient days. Today, our kings are anointed because they are first-born. Our monarchs become ruling families because of their blood, not because they win battles and destroy those who hold power. That's why ours is a nation at peace with itself."

"Then how do you change kings if a king is cruel or stupid?" he asked, walking closer and laying down beside her. She felt his presence and the warmth of his body. It was somewhat unnerving, as he was old enough to be her father, yet he was providing her with what she'd always sought in much younger men—somebody who spoke to her and listened to her views as an intelligent adult.

His question had unbalanced her. Having studied the Hanoverians, and especially George III who was insane for a part of his reign, having learned of the unbridled hatred of father and son, it wasn't a question she could easily answer.

"We trust the blood of our monarchs. And since the time of Charles I, whom we beheaded because he was a tyrant, we've vested power in our Parliament instead of the monarch. So even though we bow and scrape and call our monarch Your Majesty, it's only a title. The person who holds real power in our country is the prime minister."

"And if your King is angered, he can behead your prime minister?"

Gertrude tried not to laugh aloud. "No, Excellency. It doesn't work that way."

"But if a prime minister is angered, he can behead a king?"

"Er . . . no."

"But this Charles. He was beheaded by your prime minister. Yes?"

"Sort of. It's very complicated."

Abd al-Rahman remained silent for some moments. And then he said, "I know that your king is a queen."

26

"Yes, Queen Victoria."

"And her dead husband, he was king?"

"Her husband, Albert, wasn't a king, but a prince."

"A prince is the son of a king and queen. Did she marry her son?"

Gertrude reacted in shock, "No, she didn't marry her . . ."

In the moonlight, she saw that Abd al-Rahman was grinning. "Your Excellency is making fun of me."

"You are a clever woman, Chatrude Pell. I have never met a clever woman. But like a man, it is easy to make fun of you. You will learn not to be so serious."

She burst out laughing. Abd al-Rahman liked her laugh. "Yes, I know I'm too serious."

"Why are you not a wife?"

"Because I'm too serious," she said. And as an afterthought, said softly, "And I'm too educated."

"In my country, we do not allow our girls to be educated. They marry. They are happy."

"I don't know how a girl can be happy unless she's educated," said Gertrude.

"If she is educated, then her mind will be troubled by what is going on around her. Without education, she will obey her husband because he knows all. That is why our women are happy."

Gertrude remembered Sir Frank's injunction, and remained quiet, until Abd al-Rahman asked, "Is Victoria happy ruling England without her husband?"

"Nobody could say that Victoria has been happy since Albert died. But you wanted to know why Albert remained a prince when they were first married. It was because the Parliament didn't like the fact that some minor German noble had married the greatest queen in the world, and so they refused to grant him a title. It was really very poor."

"So he was not of her tribe?"

"No! Albert was German. They had many children together."

"How is it, to be ruled by a woman?" asked Abd al-Rahman.

"I don't know, because I've never been ruled by anybody but a woman."

Again, there was a long silence. Eventually, Abd al-Rahman said, "In my country, no woman could become a king. Our women remain in their homes, and take no part in our business. It is men who rule, both the country, and the household. It is another reason why our women are happy. They know their place. They are cared for by us and in return they provide us with children, with food and with silence."

"How can you be so certain they're happy?"

"Because I know."

"If I were to show them what we women in England do, how we work in factories and in the professions, how we travel to distant lands and participate in the life of our nation, do you think they would still be happy with their lives in your nation?"

Abd al-Rahman burst out laughing. "Why would our women want to work in factories? I have seen photographs of your factories and of your young children who work in darkness under the ground digging filth in mines to make men rich. Is this what you want for our women and our children?"

"Excellency," she said, "there is much wrong in my country. But there is much right. Soon women will be able to vote. I hope that one day all women will be educated so that they will understand what it is they're voting for. But you cannot suppress half your nation by forcing them to remain at home to do service to their men. Can't you see the terrible waste of capacity when half of your country cannot contribute?"

"Are you always so free with giving advice, girl? You have not lived many years, yet you feel free to tell me about my religion and how my lands should be governed."

"It's easy to advise others, Excellency, even though I would be very hesitant before taking my own advice. I see the situations of others quite clearly, but my life is somewhat tumultuous, I'm afraid."

He sighed long and hard. "Ah, Chatrude Pell, you are much like the whirlwind in the desert. You cause confusion and there is much sand and dust flung into the air whenever you speak, but in the end you disappear as though nothing had happened. And the desert returns to the way it had always been, and always will be."

She was hurt by his dismissal, but countered, "Sometimes, Excellency, a strong wind is necessary to blow away the dust of ages and reveal what treasures lay buried."

Abd al-Rahman laughed. "And are you that wind?"

"Perhaps."

"Then you must change your sex, because no woman will ever be able to rule the men of the desert. Not even you, Chatrude Pell."

TWO

Teheran, Persia, May 1892

It was two years from the moment she'd set eyes on Abd al-Rahman until Gertrude was able to fulfil her heart's desire and visit the land of the Arab. During that time, she'd traveled around the world with her chaperone and devoured everything she could about Arabic culture, language and traditions. She'd now come close to mastering the language and had gained a greater appreciation of the role of women in Arabic society.

She and Billy Lascelles had already come close to Arabia when they'd enjoyed a brief holiday in Constantinople, explored its Blue Mosque, its Hippodrome and Hagia Sophia, boated on the Bosphorus and sailed the Hellespont. She'd determined to learn more Arabic, especially the classical underpinnings of the modern language as soon as she arrived in Jerusalem, but now she was in Persia and was determined to come to grips with ancient Persian.

Gertrude revelled in her freedom, of movement and thought, and was delighted to be away from fusty fussy old England. She now knew that at the age of twenty-four, her chances of snaring a husband were growing more and more limited by the hour. She'd had years of coming out balls and parties, and it was generally acknowledged by English societal rules that a few seasons was all a girl was entitled to strive for marriage before retreating to the sides of the room where wallflowers became faded blossoms who inevitably were disparaged by society as withered and lonely old maids and decrepit aunts.

There were times when her body overwhelmed her mind, and she ached for a man to hold her, hug her, enter her, make love to her. But all she had available were books which were a poor but necessary substitute for the real thing. She knew the opening lines of Jane Austen's Pride and Prejudice by heart: "*It is a truth universally acknowledged, that a single man in possession of a good fortune, must be in want of a wife."*

What sublime irony, both for Jane's Regency readers and Gertrude's modern reality. She was in possession of a good fortune and was in want of a husband. Her family was immensely wealthy but no matter how much she tried to attract a suitable young man, none had stepped forward and proposed. Were she Miss Elizabeth Bennett, she would have grabbed the hand of Mr. Darcy the moment he asked her to marry him, and not spent the entire book rejecting him, until slowly coming round to see his better points before finally saying yes.

At her age, even though she had never felt more vital, alive, and vibrant, society determined that she no longer be viewed as eligible. She knew she was a curio, bright, intelligent, attractive, yet rejected by England's eligible young men, whose eyes glazed whenever she began to talk about what interested her, and not feign interest in what they'd done the previous Saturday night.

Gertrude had become all-but invisible in England, and even in her own heart, she was coming to terms with a life of sexual frustration and loneliness. So instead of partnering a husband and supporting him in his career, instead of being a splendid hostess at the centre of sparkling soirees with her own clique of artists and scientists and philosophers and politicians meeting regularly at her house to engage in the most spirited of conversation, she would now have to make her own way in the world. Like Mr. Keats, she would make a virtue of being alone and palely loitering. She would have to become a somebody and not a somebody's wife.

And she'd determined that Persia, mysterious and exotic Persia, was the place for her to become someone, to make society appreciate her difference, and not exclude her because of it. Since meeting Abd al-Rahman with Frank and Mary in Bucharest, she'd studied Persia and Farsi, Arabia and the Arab society, becoming more and more involved in learning the politics and customs of the area. It was virtually unknown to Englishmen, yet it was utterly absorbing.

She and Mary had left England, joined the Orient Express train in Paris and journeyed to Constantinople where they took a boat to join Frank Lascelles, who'd recently been appointed the British envoy to Shah Nasser al-Din Shah Qajar, the King of Persia. Nasser was an interesting man who'd ruled the land with an iron hand for fourteen years since he succeeded his father at the age of seventeen. Very close to Britain and keen to import modern technology and business methods, Nasser had returned to Persia from his state visits to Queen Victoria, enthused by the progress England had made, and determined to enlist the very best inventions for the improvement of his country. It was the reason that an ambassador of Frank's seniority had been appointed to advise the Peacock Throne.

As they journeyed by carriage along dusty and pitted roads from the Caspian Sea towards Teheran, Mary kept fanning herself, still finding it difficult to acclimatize to the heat of the desert. Gertrude reached into her bag and pulled out a bottle of *eau de toilette*, which Mary gratefully accepted. She splashed some on a handkerchief, and wiped it over her neck and forehead. The dusty air of the carriage was immediately transformed into a Parisian *perfumerie*.

"Frank tells me the Shah has eleven sons. Perhaps you'll find a suitable husband amongst them," Mary said.

Gertrude burst out laughing. "He also has ten daughters, and so I'm sure many of the suitable young men have already been accounted for."

"Good heavens, you don't mean that Persians are like the ancient Egyptians do you, and marry their sisters?"

"No," said Gertrude. "I was being facetious. But they marry their royal children off early for political reasons, just as the English monarchs did in the Middle Ages. Anyway, can you seriously see father accepting a Persian for a son-in-law?"

"Doesn't he like Arabs?" Mary asked.

"Persians aren't Arabs. They're Shi'ite Muslims of the tribe of Qajars. They were originally of Turkman origin."

"Well, they're all Arabs to me, I'm afraid."

~

When they arrived at the embassy, a large party of officials had gathered outdoors to greet them. Every counsellor, attaché, secretary, official, and supernumerary lined up outside the vast portico to pay his respect. Frank greeted his wife with a hug and kissed Gertrude on both cheeks. He took them along the line, introducing them to each of his staff. Towards the end where the lesser officials stood waiting was a tall and ruddy young man, who kept staring at Gertrude as she neared his station.

"Gertrude," said Sir Frank, "this is Mr. Henry Cadogan, my Third Secretary."

Cadogan shook her hand. Unlike many of the other hands she'd shaken along the line, Cadogan's were warm but dry. His handshake lingered a fraction longer than was necessary. She looked up at him, surprised. Was there a glint in his eye as he looked at her? He was an attractive man, slightly too lean for her taste, but he had a pleasant and accommodating face and a delightfully playful grin when he let her go. It was almost as though he were daring her to continue looking at him, throwing protocol and convention to the garden's perfumed wind.

As they continued to move down the line nearing the front door and food, drink, and rest, Cadogan peremptorily called out, "Ambassador, I wonder if I might seek your permission to be privileged to show Miss Bell the more beautiful parts of Teheran."

Surprised at his presumption, Frank was about to make a curt remark, when Gertrude said quickly, "How kind . . . if that's acceptable to you, Your Excellency."

Frank shrugged and continued to introduce his wife and niece to the servants who would see to their every wish. As Gertrude continued to walk behind her uncle, she sneaked a quick look back at Cadogan, who was staring regimentally ahead, but wearing a large grin.

~

It was a journey of nearly 500 miles through empty broiling deserts and past encampments of black tents and wildly excited children who'd never seen a large party of nobility and their servants before, let alone two white women with unveiled faces, riding side-saddle on their horses. As they rode, husbands ordered their wives back into the tents, but despite commanding their children not to approach the party, the little ones screamed in delight as the English people threw sweets and coins onto the roadways.

Gertrude, Mary, Henry Cadogan and a dozen servants traveled directly south from Teheran towards ancient Persepolis. She had been in Persia for two weeks, luxuriating in the fragrances of the vast gardens of the embassy, walking with Henry around the centre of Teheran and thrilling at the extraordinarily delicate yet imposing Islamic architecture of the palaces of Saad Abad, Golestan, and Niavaran. But ever since Henry had described the wonders of Persepolis, city of Darius the Great and his son Xerxes, built five centuries before Christ, she'd been itching to see it. He'd warned that it was still buried underneath two and a half thousand years of sand and debris, but she'd brought along spades and brooms, and was determined to expose some of the city.

She and Henry had shared memorable experiences since she arrived at the embassy. He was attentive, polite and, most attractively for Gertrude, knowledgeable. Whatever she asked him about art, architecture, history, or the culture of the Persians, he seemed to know immediately, or he admitted his ignorance, and promised to have the answer for her by the time she appeared for dinner that night.

It took a mere three days for her to feel fondness and affection for him, and to eagerly anticipate their rides, picnics and times together. Another three days, and she was seeking him out wherever he was within the Embassy, finding excuses for interrupting his work and asking him questions. And by the end of the second week, before setting out for Persepolis, her heart was aflutter whenever she saw him. And she knew, with absolute certainty, that he felt the same towards her. They'd held hands, he'd put his arm around her and had kissed her several times on the hand saying goodnight. She eagerly anticipated this long ride south to the ancient city, to see where their conversation and affection would take them.

They continued to ride inexorably onwards, Mary finding the horses much less comfortable than Gertrude, who'd spent her childhood on the back of a horse riding around the grounds of her estate. Mary looked in envy at Gertrude's skills as a horse-woman. She seemed to be born to a saddle. As the sun began to sink low into the western desert, without warning, five of their servants suddenly spurred on their horses to disappear ahead of them down the road. It was to enable the party of English people to ride at their leisure until dusk fell. When it did fall, it came on very quickly in the desert, and when the air rapidly changed from stiflingly hot to cool, with a freezing clarity on its way as the sky blackened and a galaxy of stars suddenly appeared, a warm fire, hot food, and comfortable tents would already be prepared and waiting for them.

~

Wrapped up snuggly against the freezing night, Gertrude lay on her back, far from the tents and the fire, enshrouded in the blackness of the desert, and gazed directly upwards. She'd done it every night since leaving Teheran and entering the vast wasteland which was Persia. No matter how long she stared at the profusion of stars, their brilliance always brought her to the brink of tears. The enormity of the stellar canopy made her feel tiny, made her problems seem insignificant and trivial.

The Persian sky was so different from the English sky, confined to a ridiculously tiny number of stars struggling to be visible through the smoke and grime, even in the North England countryside where she lived. Rarely did she have a clear, cloudless night to observe the firmament. Yet in the desert, there were rarely clouds to cover the heavens and looking upwards at nature's miracle seemed to put everything into a more profound perspective. And she thought back to a night in a king's hunting lodge in the Carpathian Mountains, when an Arab named Abd al-Rahman had challenged her sense of understanding of the nature of womanhood.

As she gazed heaven-wards, she heard a noise of somebody approaching. "Am I disturbing you?" asked Henry.

"No. Actually, laying here and looking up with somebody else will make me feel less small."

He lay down beside her, close to her, and together they gazed upwards, silent for some time, lost in the wonders above them. Softly, he said, "When I was at the embassy in Peru, I climbed the foothills of the Andes, and the stars were very dramatic there. But here . . ."

"Every time I gaze upwards," she said, "my mind flies back to Moses and Jesus and Mohammed and I can clearly see who they were and what they did from the perspective of their times. Today, with our Anglican churches and Catholic cathedrals and Mosques, it's all too easy to see the buildings as representing the prophets, but when you step into their shoes and walk in their paths and see the same sky they saw, it's so much easier to connect to the reason they needed to invent a deity, isn't it?"

"But think back before Moses, to the days before monotheism," said Henry. "Think of the Hittites and the contribution they made to our ways of understanding the natural phenomena. How terrifying lightning and thunder and drought and hailstorms must have been to minds which were pre-scientific. How else to explain swarms of locust or earthquakes or volcanos erupting suddenly? No wonder they invented all those fearsome and angry gods to explain whatever catastrophe was happening around them."

She remained silent for what seemed an eternity, echoing the stillness of the night, adrift in the warmth of her thoughts. In the freezing night air, wrapped underneath a blanket, Gertrude could feel Henry shivering. "Would you like to share my blanket?" she whispered.

Wordlessly, he moved closer to where she was laying. He thanked her, and she felt the cold skin of his arm touching her warmth, their legs now together. It was the closest she'd been to a man in . . . she tried to remember the last time. She discounted her momentary closeness to Abd al-Rahman in the Carpathians. No, the last time she'd been this close to an eligible man was at a dinner party at Lord and Lady Russett's house on Sloan Square in London where a young and silly lad had held her knee under the table. When she'd turned to tell him not to touch her, he'd given her the most ridiculous wink. Instead of being cross, she burst out laughing at his dismal attempt at seduction, but he'd taken it as encouragement, and she'd spent the whole night trying not to be groped.

But her closeness to Henry was altogether of a different complexion. He was a young man of erudition, of warmth, and of respect. Like her, and from the way he was speaking, he was an atheist, completely unbothered by the pretence of worshipping a deity, but accepting that natural phenomena had created all things on Earth and in the heavens. And he was well-read, knowledgeable, sophisticated, and delightful company.

"Miss Bell, Gertrude, I wonder if I should be under a blanket with you? It's not exactly the done thing, is it?"

"You're right, Henry. It's one thing to kiss my hand, but entirely another to lay on a bed of sand where anything could happen. I shall call over to Mrs. Lascelles and ask her to come between us as chaperone."

He burst out laughing and moved his hand fractionally to hold hers. "Sir," she said, "I do believe you're touching me!"

"Ma'am," he replied, "I crave your forgiveness. I thought I was grasping the hand of the Goddess of the Sand."

"But that would mean I'd slip through your fingers."

"Not while you're in Persia."

"And when I return to England? What then?" she asked softly.

He sighed. "May I speak frankly?"

She remained silent, and felt her heart beating rapidly. She'd only known Henry two weeks, yet in that intense and contracted time she felt increasingly drawn to him. He was the most delightful companion and she felt a delightful and growing closeness. Not since she was at Oxford had she enjoyed another person's company as much. She revelled in their riding together, reading books of Persian poetry, sharing picnics and sampling the delights of the *shuks* and street traders and market salesmen following them around the streets of Teheran importuning them to buy whatever knickknacks they were desperate to sell. They'd been into Mosques and Synagogues and Churches together. And even though many of their trips had been alone, unchaperoned, he'd behaved like the perfect gentleman, attentive, respectful, but quite obviously admiring her in every way. She was keen . . . more than keen . . . for his affection.

"Gertrude, I know I'm only the third secretary and I earn a pittance. But I have great hopes of advantage in serving the crown in a future capacity as an ambassador. We've only known each other a short while, Gertrude, but I want to assure you that my prospects are good, and my—"

"Henry? What are you saying? Is this a proposal of marriage? My dear, we've only been intimate this once, and you're telling me about your future. You're a sweet and dear man, but we're nearing the twentieth century, so don't you think you ought to kiss me before you go down on your knees and ask me to be your wife?"

"Oh!"

She turned towards him, and put her arms around his waist, drawing him closer to her. She kissed his lips, his forehead, his nose and his lips again. His face was still cold from the night air, but he drew closer and kissed her again, this time more passionately.

"Mr. Cadogan, I do believe you're trying to seduce me," she whispered into his ear.

"Would you permit it?"

"Shouldn't we wait until we're married?"

"Then you'll marry me?" He dared not raise his voice in his excitement, fearful of waking the others nearby.

"We've only known each other for a moment, but it's been a glorious moment. But yes, dear Henry, with my father's permission, I'll marry you. But not yet. Not until you've improved your position and become a first secretary or an ambassador. You must understand that I have a position in society, and being the wife of an ambassador will be completely acceptable to my circle, whilst being the wife of a third secretary, no matter how fond of you I am, will be a problem. Oh, I know you'll think I'm a frightful snob, but when one's been presented to the queen and taken tea with the prime minister, one has a certain . . . how can I say this without sounding insufferable . . . a certain standing. Does that sound awfully snobbish, my dear?"

"Yes, but I understand what you're saying. You come from a very wealthy family, and your position in society means that like must marry like."

"Of course we can marry, but not until you're elevated in the service of the crown. And that means we must have a long engagement, both to give you time to secure your position, and also to ensure that we're not making a mistake."

"But that could be years."

"Perhaps, but with my connections in London, you might not have to wait nearly that long for advancement. A word in the foreign secretary's ear, and you might find yourself helped up the ladder. Anyway, we've hardly got to know each other, so it'll be wonderful plumbing each other's depths. I think it's probably best to give each other a period of time. The last thing I want to do is to make an error when I've finally met a man I want to marry. What about a situation where either of us can retreat from our understanding if we find the other objectionable after . . . oh, what shall we say . . . twelve months?"

"Dear heavens, Gertrude, you sound like you're a lawyer drawing up some agreement. I've just asked you to marry me. You should be overwhelmed."

"I'm whelmed, Henry darling, but I never allow myself to be overwhelmed. It's just not in my nature."

He laughed, and snuggled closer to her, touching her breast. It sent a surge of desire through her body, but she smiled as she slowly removed his hand, delaying several moments more than was necessary.

"Wasn't it you who said that we're nearing the twentieth century. Haven't times and conventions moved forward?"

"Times might have advanced, Henry, but on issues of morality, the clock is still running slowly."

"So I can't seduce you?"

"Not with my Aunt Lascelles so close at hand. What would she say if she were to see this blanket suddenly bobbing up and down like a trampoline?"

Henry laughed, and snuggled closer. She was becoming excited by his obvious enthusiasm, despite the freezing night air. She felt his strong arms and pulled his body closer to hers.

"Good heavens," she suddenly said. "Is that your . . ."

"Yes. Should I apologise?"

"No. Please don't do that. Apologise I mean. Good heavens."

"Have you never . . ."

"No. Have you?"

"Once, but it was with a Peruvian llama."

She looked at him in horror, and his straight face in the starlight made the moment even more excruciating for her.

"I'm kidding."

She banged him on the shoulders. "You rotten thing," she said, and they collapsed in each other's arms muffling their hysterical laughter.

An hour later, when they were sure the rest of the party was asleep, they made love. The first time was cautious, quick and passionate. The second time, an hour or so later, was slow and loving and tender. It was everything Gertrude had ever hoped for.

The following day, Mary Lascelles couldn't understand why the normally boisterous and quick witted Gertrude seemed like a dullard and why she was yawning throughout the day.

~

During the next four weeks, Gertrude and Henry spent an increasing amount of time together. While they were intimate in their private moments, kissing when they were alone, hugging in corridors and holding hands underneath the ambassador's table, they maintained an outward propriety when they were in public. Increasingly they found excuses to leave the embassy and travel unchaperoned to locations where Henry knew they could lay together and make love. Sir Frank asked his wife Mary whether it was appropriate for the young couple to be alone together, and she put him firmly in his place.

"Unless Henry marries Gertrude, at her age, she's likely to spend much of her life alone and without the company of a man. Frankly, my dear, she needs all the experiences she can accumulate now in order to keep her warm on long cold nights alone."

"Do you think Hugh will allow Henry to marry Gertrude?" her husband asked.

"He's a lovely young man but without a penny to his name, he's not in her class. No, I can't see Hugh allowing the wedding."

"She wouldn't do anything stupid, would she, like running off and eloping?" he asked. "After all, I'm *in loco parentis*, and Hugh would blame me."

"Times are changing, Frank, and I just don't understand what's in the minds of young people these days. But I doubt that Gertrude would elope. She's fearless and intrepid, but she's got a wonderful mind and I'm certain she's destined for great things. She'd think twice before doing a rash act which might destroy her prospects and expunge her from our society. No, let her and Henry have their fling, let's keep our mouths shut, pretend we don't know and hope for the best."

Sir Frank smiled. "So you want me to act like a diplomat?"
Mary said, "Just be true to form, my darling."

~

What excited both Gertrude and Henry as much as their physical
relationship was their exploration of each other's minds. Gertrude
revelled in Henry's excitement when she told him things about
history which he didn't know, and she was his willing and grateful
pupil when he explained to her the intricacies of Middle East
politics, culture, and traditions. He introduced her to the original
text of the poems of Omar Khayyam, not FitzGerald's *Rubaiyat*, a
thin interpretation at best. Instead, he read her the original words
in ancient Persian, whose beauty and elegance, whose profound
insights and depth of feelings made her weep.

At Mary's instigation, Frank Lascelles called Gertrude aside
one morning and suggested that while he neither approved, nor
disapproved of their closeness, it could become the subject of
gossip and urged them to be less public in their private affection.
But when Henry told his ambassador that he would be writing to
Gertrude's father Hugh to request his daughter's hand in marriage,
Frank knew that this particular horse had bolted, and cancelled
his cunning plot to send Henry on some spurious exploratory
mission to the far east of the country.

Gertrude also wrote imploring Hugh to give his consent
to their wedding. And while they waited for a response, they
continued to read together the great works of medieval Persian
literature, especially the poet Hafez. With her amazing ability to
learn the intricacies of the ancient Persian language, she was able
to begin translating with the intention of launching his elegiac
verse on the British public.

Gertrude used the long delay in her father's response to learn
more about the condition of women in Arabia. Little was known
or written about how women were treated. It was as though an
entire half of Arab society didn't exist. Aside from the wives of
Mohammed and his followers, women were a vacuum in Arab

culture, history, and society. On a bicycle ride to a mosque on the outskirts of Teheran, Henry told Gertrude about the status of women before the advent of Islam.

"Before Mohammed, women in Arabia had no rights at all. They were sold into marriage by their fathers or guardians for a fee and after the husband had his way with her, he could simply end the marriage. The woman left the marriage with no property or rights and was often abandoned or shamed into the outskirts of her society. It was terrible."

"But isn't that still the situation today?" asked Gertrude. "I had long conversations some time ago with the leader of the Sa'ud tribe, and he said to me that women in his tribe, and in the rest of Arabia, had no rights, other than to stay at home, cook, and perform their bedroom duties."

"It's a terribly tribal society, but not nearly as bad as it used to be," said Henry. "Mohammed, when he created Islam, laid down rules. Before him, if a woman gave birth to a girl, the father was shamed, buried his face, and often had the girl-child killed. Mohammed put a stop to all that, and insisted that women were accorded respect and some rights. He was quite advanced for his age, especially when you think of the condition for women in Europe at the time."

"Perhaps," said Gertrude, "but it's a shocking indictment on Arab society that it does nothing for its women, except enslave them in something like a domestic prison. Something needs to be done to bring these pathetic women into the 19th Century. It's disgraceful that women should be treated like chattel to be bought and sold without their will, and that half of Arabia should be invisible."

Henry looked at her and winced. "My God, Gertrude, you sound like some of the women *The Times* reported demanding the vote. Suffrage, they call it. Are you one of those?"

"No, not until they've earned the right to vote by understanding the issues. But this situation with women in the Arab world isn't just about equal rights and voting. It's about the dignity of the human being. And frankly, I can't see much dignity being a woman in Arabia, where you're expected to follow some role laid down for you by men a thousand years ago, and you have no voice, no say, no rights."

Henry interrupted her, "But darling, when John Stuart Mill published *The Subjection of Women* twenty something years ago he was talking about English women. He said that our Christian civilization has been claiming that they've restored rights to women, and he said that was all bunkum. He said that the wife is the bondservant of her husband with fewer rights than the slave. So what you're saying, surely, applies to English women as much as their dusky sisters in the desert."

"Which means that British society is just as regressive as the Arabs? Of course it doesn't Henry. We have a long way to go before we're able to claim equal rights, but the Arab woman hasn't even begun to tread the path we've started down."

"Alright. What's needed?"

She thought long and hard before she answered. Henry knew from experience that you didn't interrupt Gertie when she was in one of her deeply reflective moods.

"Saladin."

He turned to her in surprise. "Saladin? But he was a vicious bloodthirsty tyrant. He'd be the last to give women—"

"On the contrary. He's the perfect model. He was a fair-minded, decent, honourable, and just leader. He only had one wife, not the four to which he was entitled, and it's said that he listened to her advice and respected her very highly. She, apparently, played a role in his court. And as a warrior, he was almost never unjust and fought fairly."

"But he was a Kurd."

"Precisely. If change is to be brought to the Arab world, then the impetus for that change has to come from outside, and not within. People like the Sa'uds and the Rashids and all the other tribal leaders are fixed into an almost unbreakable mold. It's going to take hundreds of years to transform Arab society from within for the benefit of women. But an outsider can bring in sweeping changes, and that's what we need," she said. She shook her head in determination.

"We?"

"Yes, we. They can't do it themselves, you know."

Taken aback, Henry remained silent, looking at Gertrude.

She was pondering the difference between her society, and that which lay to the south. And she realized how much work there was for her to do.

~

They continued to wait achingly for Hugh's reply. But the longer they waited, the more concerned and certain Gertrude became that her father would reject Henry as a suitable life partner. Sir Frank and Lady Mary knew what the answer would be, but refrained from telling her what they saw as a reality. Better that she should live in hope for a week or more.

The delay in her father's response was at first painful, and as the days wore on, heartbreaking. For she knew her father intimately, and understood that he would respond immediately if his answer was going to be positive. When eventually his letter arrived, Gertrude already knew its contents, but still she howled as she read the letter alone in her room.

As she read, and re-read his letter, she was in turns furious and resentful. How could he be so blind to her needs? He knew her age, and must realize that this was her last chance at marriage. Her father explained that despite Gertrude's obvious affection, and her understanding that the couple must wait until Henry was more advanced in his career, her young man was not a suitable match for a girl of Gertrude's fortunes or position in Victorian society. He was impecunious and even if he did rise to be an ambassador, it was insufficient without a private income to keep Gertrude in a lifestyle to which she'd been born. Further, he wrote, he'd checked the young man out with others who knew him and the family and was reliably informed that young Henry was not only very poor, but his father was virtually bankrupt, and that the young man was said to be argumentative and a gambler.

Furious, indignant, and determined not to let Henry slip through her fingers, she kissed him a fond farewell without revealing the depth of her father's concern in his letter, explained that she was going back to England to change her father's mind, and left Persia within the week. She promised that she and Henry would be married, even if she had to wait ten years for him to be made an ambassador. As she departed, bidding a loving and fond farewell to Frank and Mary, she whispered to the ambassador, "Uncle, I'm begging you not to believe that this is a flight of a young woman's fancy. I love Henry. I've never loved any man as I do him. I know he has his failings, but he complements me more than any man I've ever known. I know in my heart that I can spend my entire life by his side. Please support me."

Frank kissed his niece, and said, "Be assured, Gertrude, that your best interests are in my heart."

And as she mounted the carriage to travel to the Caspian Sea port to return to London, she said to Henry, "I swear to you, my love, by all in which I believe, that I will return to you and we will be married." He could barely speak as he watched her leave, but as she closed the door, through the open window, Henry handed her an icon of the Hittite Sun Goddess, Arinnitti which they'd dug up together in Persepolis. "Return her to me when you come back to be my wife," he whispered, kissing the idol.

~

Gertrude Bell's life changed forever two months after she returned to England. Try as she might, she couldn't persuade her father to change his mind about her desire to marry Henry. She tried logic, then pleading, then attempted to use her step-mother Florence to intervene, and finally informed her father that while she would never marry without his consent, she would continue to be Henry's partner in all but name. He was shocked at her assertion, but she assured him that there had not been, nor would there be a physical partnership without a wedding ring, even though she determined to define for Hugh just how much she loved Henry and why he was so right for her.

And every night when she went to bed, she took out the idol Arinnitti, a tiny white marble figurine with exaggerated pointed breasts and a swollen belly, and kissed the goddess on the lips, whispering a request to keep her Henry safe and sound, his love for her constant and faithful.

She would ride with the goddess inside her bodice and close to her breast. She would go to sleep with the goddess underneath her pillow, and when she rose and dressed for breakfast, she would place the goddess on the windowsill of her bedroom looking south-east towards Persia in the hope that it would keep her Henry safe.

Yet for some reason, a feeling of doom was beginning to creep into her mind. She couldn't put her finger on it, nor explain it logically, but for the past two weeks or so, the clouds had been thick and hidden the stars, the air had been chilled, and nothing which she tried to do could elevate her feelings. It was as though a veil had been placed over her face, and she found it difficult to breathe. Riding, fishing, and reading no longer held out the distractions she'd once found in them. Neither did writing letters to friends or family. And inexplicably, she hadn't written to Henry for a week.

Then the letter arrived from Frank Lascelles. A letter in an envelope with a black border.

It was steeped in sympathy, profound regret, but his sentiments couldn't alleviate the shock which shook her very marrow. *"Your dear Henry, waiting every day for your return, and in consolation at your departure, took some pleasure in fishing in the River Lar, high in the Alborz Mountains on the shores of the Caspian Sea. He insisted on going alone, despite his colleagues offers to join him.*

"I deeply regret that during one of his fishing trips, he slipped on some rocks and fell into the waters of the river, icy with the melt-water from the nearby peaks. Returning to the embassy and

still chilled to the bone, he took to his bed, but his cold became pneumonia. Try as we might and with great medical attention for his health, your young man passed away last night. His light has been extinguished. We are all darkened by his loss. I beg you to be consoled by his last dying word . . . Gertrude."

No matter how many times she read her uncle's words, nor what combination of meanings she ascribed to them in order to alter their construction, in the end, her Henry was no more. His knowledge and joy had been extinguished, like blowing out a brilliant candle. She would never see him again. They would not marry. Gertrude would not be his bride.

Hugh tried to console her by taking her to the seaside, by having friends visit her constantly, and by asking her for help with a speech he was to deliver the following month. But she recognized the transparency of what he was doing, and it drove deeper the immense sense of loss she'd suffered. Wherever she looked, at a flower or a cloud or a distant hillside, she saw his face. Never again would she lay underneath the desert stars with his body beside her, enveloped in his gentle love.

Gertrude knew herself well enough to know that were she to stay in England, grief for Henry would overwhelm her. She would become a Queen Victoria and never dress in anything other than black. She would be a figure of pity and retreat to her study to lose herself in her work.

So she determined to take herself to foreign shores, to push herself and her body to the limit in order to expunge the heartache she knew would consume her, and be her end. Life, when she'd left Oxford, had been so open, so full of promise, so inexpressibly exciting. She was rich, attractive, intelligent, vigorous, and aching to take on any challenge which life presented. But after the enriching intellect of Oxford, she'd suffered a series of frustrations, of the mind, the body, and especially of her expectations of what she would do with her life. In just a few short years she'd transmogrified from an open, cheery, and vivid girl into somebody in danger of becoming intellectually and physically dowdy. She felt frustrated, depleted, and depressed, as though all the expectations to which she was entitled had been pulled away from her by some malicious sprite who was manipulating the strings of her life. Nothing, now, gave her pleasure. Not riding horses, reading, talking, food . . . nothing.

Six months after Henry's death, she knew she had to regain her control of life, or she'd be buried by a mountain of trivia and for the rest of her days, deal in nothing but irrelevancies. She had to get out, leave the mausoleum of her life. She had to travel, to see more of the world, to go places where adventure was the everyday currency of life. And the more she thought of where she should go and what she should do, the more she thought back to an orchard in Bucharest and a mysterious Arab. What was it about him and his people that fascinated her? Why did he radiate a light in her otherwise bleak existence?

THREE

Switzerland, August 1901

Since Henry's death, Gertrude had traveled around the world for a second time, improved her proficiency in Arabic for what she called her great mission, and taught herself the new science of archaeology. She wrote and published her first travel book, Persian Pictures, to great critical acclaim, the reviewer in *The Times* calling it "an outstanding explication of this mysterious region's culture." It was dedicated to Henry.

Determined to uncover the vast treasury of hidden civilizations buried for millennia in the sand, she set out to travel to Arabia. She booked her passage to the south of France, but a week before she was due to leave, an article in *The Times* caught her eye. In January, Queen Victoria had passed away, the longest-serving monarch in British history, and to mark her reign after the proper period of mourning, the newspaper had challenged its readers to think of ways in which they, as individuals, could commemorate the queen's sovereignty. The newspaper asked red-blooded men to exercise their imaginations, to push their bodies to the limit in breaking records and to perform previously impossible tasks as a way of ending one great era in British life, and beginning another under King Edward.

Gertrude, shrewdly reading between the lines, realized that the editors of the newspaper were poking Edward in the ribs. Whereas his mother had been a model of propriety and rectitude, and her consort Albert had been the figurehead for British innovation in science and industry, King Edward was seen as pampered, self-indulgent, excessive, and morally fallible. So they had decided to show the new king that Britain had become great because of the greatness of its people, and that if he wanted to be a ruler, then he had to change his ways.

And Gertrude decided to take up the challenge by breaking a mountain climbing record. She'd always been a climber and since her childhood had scaled the peaks on her property at Rounton Grange. She'd climbed in the Lake District, in Scotland and in Wales, and although Swiss mountains were far higher and more challenging than anything she'd previously climbed, she felt up to the task.

She didn't tell her family, because she knew they'd object at her endangering her life in such a fashion. But Gertrude knew herself well enough to know that only by testing her mind and body to the limit would she be able to succeed with her dream of making Arabia into one great nation. All her life, she'd been surrounded by the benefits of civilization and she knew with certainty that her great adventure meant her spending years in the worst deserts on Earth, the Nefud and the deserts of Arabia, uncharted, and uncivilized landscapes compared to England's green and pleasant land. So it was important for her to understand the limits to which her body and mind could be pushed. And what better place than in the unfamiliar domain of the gods of the mountains, maybe even winning a mention in *The Times*?

Out of the bedroom window of her hotel outside of Berne, Gertrude, now thirty-one, stared at the magnificence of nature and the distant lofty Finsteraarhorn. Still strikingly attractive with her red hair and tall carriage, she'd packed a lifetime of adventures into the time since Henry's death. She'd travelled wherever her fancy and interests took her. But whether she was in Palestine, in Syria, approaching Hong Kong through azure seas or lying beside a brook in her beloved home of Rounton Grange in Yorkshire, she was always at one with nature. And when she saw nature, she saw Henry's face. Everything seemed to remind her of Henry. She no longer cried and withdrew when she thought of him. Time and experiences had dulled the despair his death had caused, but she still strove to fill the aching void which his death had left in her life.

For the past few years, she'd traveled all over the Middle East, gone to places never before seen by an Englishman, learned their

51

languages and sat cross-legged drinking coffee and eating sheep's eyes with Bedouin chieftains.

Because of her growing intimacy with Arabia, when she returned to Great Britain, she was sought out by the government for her understanding of local events and her insights into Arab politics. The British government, partly because of the growing expertise of people like Gertrude, was beginning to appreciate the strategic importance of the Arab area, both because of the Suez Canal as a route to India, and because of the discoveries of vast quantities of oil.

As a result, Gertrude had written major reports for the British government on the disposition of the Ottoman military forces in Arabia, Southern Turkey and the Levant, and had twice been mentioned in the Westminster Parliament as an asset to the British Crown.

Despite her father's concern at the way she was continually pushing herself and her body, Gertrude's voluminous letters home continued to reassure him that she knew precisely what she was doing, and it was the only way she could retain her sanity. But this time, because she wanted, no, needed to scale the magnificence of Switzerland's mountains, she'd written to her father telling him that she was merely visiting friends.

Looking beyond her reflection, she stared up at the peaks and saw in the distance the Engelhorn, the snows of the insurmountable caps of the Wetterhorn, the Mittlehorn, and the Rosenhorn. The mountains were outlined in vivid contrast against the clear black night by the brilliance of the full moon, whose radiance overpowered the cold light of the invisible stars, so different from that night in the deserts of Persia only eight short years ago when the stars shone on her and Henry, and seemed to give approval to their love.

Gertrude was daunted by the height of the mountains, but her inner compulsion drove her to scale, to achieve, to conquer. She rose at 3:00 the following morning and by 4:00 was already dressed in her blue climbing suit, made especially for her by Hegrés of Paris. She placed the tiny statuette of the goddess Arinnitti in the specially made inner breast pocket, and descended the hotel's staircase in order to meet her guides outside the hotel for the assault. They were two Swiss brothers, Ulrich and Heinrich. Tall, fair-haired, muscular, and utterly devoid of a sense of humor. She asked playfully, "Will I be safe in your hands, a single woman on a Swiss mountain in the company of two rugged young men?"

Ulrich replied laconically, "Is danger, yes. Stay close to me and you be alright. Some peaks are unclimbable and you will not attempt, yes? Others we will attempt. You will be third. One Heinrich, two Ulrich—me—three you, Gertrude. Understand?"

She shrugged and wondered how demoralizing the three day journey ascending the foothills would become with the brothers grim. At first, the scree was loose and slippery and she found struggling up an incline with a heavy backpack, her feet constantly slipping backwards on the loose stones, to be nearly impossible. But Ulrich and Heinrich were manfully storming ahead of her, and she was determined not to have them wait. So she ran upwards, slipped, ran more and eventually reached them. They were hardly out of breath and she fought to get air into her lungs, gasping in shallow pants and trying to remain inaudible so they didn't turn and realize she was in distress.

Soon the scree gave way to large, perpendicular boulders, worn smooth by eons of erosion. The two men clambered over them as though they were pebbles, but Gertrude eventually found her centre of gravity and learned quickly how to position her body low to the rock so she didn't fall backwards.

And then came the snowline. They climbed higher and higher, the top of the mountain disappearing and reappearing as they traversed arêtes, saddles, and ridges on the way up. As the ascent became steeper, Ulrich turned, and said, "Here is to get difficult. Now to turn back if you don't wish to go up. Nor I nor Heinrich have climbed beyond this."

"We will ascend. I didn't come this high to be a tourist. I climbed to get to the other side."

Both men nodded and Gertrude wondered if she saw a glint of emotion in their eyes, possibly admiration? They began to clamber up the almost vertical sides of an arête which linked two deep valleys. Only by climbing to the top of the arête and somehow walking along its length could they reach the upper part of the saddle which would lead them to a pass between the two peaks. One slip, one false move, and, although roped together, they would all plunge a thousand feet to their deaths. This was no longer a time of physicality or testing ones resolve, Gertrude knew. It was a moment of life and death. It was what she'd come to Switzerland to face. Meeting such dangers was the only time she felt truly alive. Now, as she stared upwards at the sheer cliff, which had never before known the feel of human feet on its unconquered crags, she felt a sense of paralysing fear, but at the same time, relished how far she could push herself, desperate to know how her mind would cope.

When they reached the vertical snow and rock wall, Heinrich positioned himself like a statue at its base and readied himself for his brother's weight. Ulrich climbed onto Heinrich's shoulders, but despite balancing and feeling with his gloved hand, couldn't find any indentation on which he could lever his body upwards.

Against the increasingly banshee howling of the wind, Gertrude screamed, "I'll climb onto Heinrich's shoulders, and you climb onto mine."

She gripped the young man's shoulders and hauled herself up his back until her waist was level with Ulrich's feet. Grasping his ankles to let him know that he had to move aside to let her transplant herself into his position, Ulrich now looked to the side for somewhere to stand. Reaching as far over as he could, he hammered a pin into the ice and rock, from which he hung a carabiner, securing the rope which held him so he could swing away while Gertrude climbed onto Heinrich's shoulders.

The Swiss seemed to hang there, high above the ground, watching Gertrude carefully reach upwards, handhold over handhold until her feet were placed firmly on Heinrich's shoulders.

"Are you alright?" she screamed down to him, her words disappearing in the gale.

He shouted back a muffled "Ja!", and Gertrude dug pins into the wall as handholds so she could position herself more safely.

Now it was time for Ulrich to swing back and begin to climb up Gertrude's body until he stood on her shoulders. He was unbearably heavy and Gertrude was terrified that he'd dislocate her shoulder. His weight pressed down on the soft parts of her shoulders, but there was nothing she could do. Any movement, any adjustment of her position to try to make herself more comfortable, would likely see them all plummet downwards into an icy grave. He was hurting her badly, but she was determined to show no signs of weakness. In the game of life and death she was playing, the pain felt strangely comforting. It told her she was alive. She felt him adjusting his feet on her shoulders until he was on tip-toe, but was despondent when he called out loudly against the wind, "Are no handholds. I feel not secure. I could fall. Then we all die. I will come down."

"No!" Gertrude yelled. "I'll raise my arm. You climb onto my hand and get more height. You must be near the top of the ridge."

Against the weight of his body, she lifted her arm and felt his leg leave her left shoulder and reach upwards until his toes found her extended gloved hand. Heinrich's body started to sag under the weight of the two on top of him. Suddenly the wind had picked up even more sharply, and flurries of icy snow were blowing onto her body and face, making her both wet and freezing cold, a cold which cut through her fleece-lined clothes and touched her naked flesh. She began to shiver, but fought to stop any movement which might be transferred upwards and make Ulrich even more insecure. She felt the outline of the tiny idol Arinnitti pressing into her breast as she strained every muscle in her body against Ulrich's weight. Even the slightest unbalancing of the man standing on her hand could see him plummet.

Ulrich's weight was incredible, and she was certain her arm would bend and he'd plunge screaming downwards, pulling the two of them with him into the bottom of the valley and certain death, far below.

"How long can you hold?" he shouted. She could barely hear his voice above the banshees which were screaming from the top of the mountain.

"Can you get a hand-hold? Don't worry about me. I can stay like this forever," she said, biting her numb lip against the weight and cold.

"Is nowhere."

"Ulrich, come down" screamed Heinrich, whose body was about to collapse like a concertina. The sudden freezing cold was sapping him of strength and he could feel his body weakening to the point where he could no longer remain standing. The combined weight of Gertrude and his brother were forcing his knees to bend. He didn't know how to stop it happening.

"No!" screamed Gertrude again. "No, stay and try to find a handhold to pull yourself up. If you come down, we'll never make it across."

She began to count the seconds to see how much longer she could remain supporting Ulrich on her single outstretched hand. She'd never in her life felt under so much strain. Her muscles were shrieking, her bones bending. She was beginning to feel faint from the unyielding pressure of the weight of a big young man standing on her one up-stretched hand. She began to whimper, but silently, so neither of the men could hear.

And suddenly, the massive downward pressure on her arm ended as Ulrich yelled out an exultant cry. He'd found a grip in the ice and rock, and was able to haul himself up and off the two of them. The sudden removal of his immense weight from her shoulders and hand caused a rush of blood to her arms, face and chest. She felt warm and suddenly secure, even though she was still perched precariously on Heinrich's shoulders and could fall to her death at any moment. But she was suddenly suffused with joy at Ulrich's advance.

"Yes!" she shouted. "Yes, you've done it. Oh, well done, Ulrich."

She heard him hammer pins into the rock, splinters of ice falling down on her face. But after a few moments, she felt the rope around her waist and shoulders suddenly become taut and pull upwards as Ulrich, now sitting on top of the ridge, hauled first Gertrude, and then Heinrich upwards to a sitting position. They had ascended nearly thirty seven vertical feet and managed to do what had, for all times, been impossible. They had ascended the pass. Now they had to struggle inch by inch along the upwards trajectory of the arête in order to reach the relative security of the saddle between the middle and the upper part of the mountain where they could rest, have a warm drink and regain their energy before continuing their climb upwards and over the pass.

An hour later, the three of them lay in the lee of an overhang out of the path of the wind and snow, drinking warm chocolate and eating biscuits to give them an immediate energy boost.

"I not believe," said Heinrich. "Till today, this pass never climbed. Now we are over it. You are brave Englishwoman," he told her.

Ulrich nodded while Gertrude, still aching from the stressed muscles in her arm and shoulders, basked in their praise.

"Please," said Ulrich. "May I kiss you? I wish to kiss the lady who climbed Gertrudespitze."

"You're calling a mountain after me?" asked Gertrude in shock.

"Of course. To you goes the honor."

"But you two . . . ."

"We are guides only. This is why you will kiss me. Yes?" said Ulrich.

"Certainly," she beamed. She kissed the two young men on their frozen cheeks, and without them seeing, took the idol Arinnitti out of her inside pocket, and kissed her Henry, thanking him for protecting her yet again.

The idol, whose face and features she knew better than anything on Earth, looked back reproachfully at her, the mournful eyes, pouting breasts and swollen belly seeming to say, *enough of this cold. I need to be back in the warmth of the desert.*

"And so you shall, my love," said Gertrude, putting Arinnitti safely back into her jacket. She surveyed the vista before her, still dazed by the brilliance of the snow despite her dark goggles. But soon she would be back in her hotel room, and there she would write to the editor of *The Times*, informing him that Miss Gertrude Bell had taken up his challenge, succeeded, had a mountain pass named after her, and pointing out the fact that she wasn't a red-blooded English man, but an English women.

~

Jerusalem, 1905

There were times when she didn't think of Henry. Times when she was so overawed by the biblical surroundings, so overshadowed by the precipitous depths of the wadis, so enamoured of the antiquity of the buildings, that Henry, her father Hugh, the Swiss mountains, Rounton Grange and everything else in her European life faded into the distance, as though there were two Gertrudes. One was the Gertrude setting out to explore Jerusalem, Petra, Palmyra, Syria, and the Druze nation, the woman gaining a reputation as an adventuress, daring and resourceful, negotiating with tribal leaders and informally representing England as no other ambassador was able to do.

The other Gertrude, the one who returned regularly to England to renew her soul with intimate dinners with friends, visits to museums and galleries, parties, lectures, writing her books and articles, was the daughter of Hugh, a woman alone who had lost her fiancée in the most tragic of circumstances, a perennial widow in perpetual mourning for her long-dead lover. She was becoming something of a Queen Victoria mourning eternally for her Albert, and knew she must stop it, or she would lose her identity.

In London she was a curio, regularly invited to dinners just so hostesses could say that they'd had the extraordinary Gertrude Bell to their soirees. Rather like a circus freak, she knew that when she'd departed, the hostess and her coterie would talk about her mannishness, her lack of a husband, her childlessness, and especially the eccentricity of traveling to all these dangerous places instead of living the life of a British society lady.

After only a few short months in London or at Rounton Grange, the leaden weight of the country and the memory of her love seemed to crush all enjoyment out of her. And that was when there came a time, inexplicable but ever present, when she knew she had to leave England within a week. Her peremptory withdrawals, with profuse apologies for not attending pre-arranged dinners or social functions, were now accepted as doing a Gertrude. It might suddenly come on her when she was watching a play, and one of the characters said something which transported her back in time to another place or circumstance. Or she might be at a social gathering, laughing and joking with the assemble or the coterie of young men gathered around her, when one of them would look at her in a certain way, and she'd see Henry standing in the young man's place, smiling and nodding that everything was alright.

It was then she felt the heat of the desert on her skin, smelled the purity of the air, saw the incalculable density of stars in the heavens. It was then she knew she had to leave England and wander again, to feel the limpidness of sand in her fingers, relish the luxurious taste of water, and breathe in the perfumes of roasting goat or lamb cooked beneath the brilliance of the firmament.

She would write to her father and friends, send them apologies, beg their forgiveness and understanding, and get her maids to pack her trunks, book passage to the south of France, spend a week in Marseilles or Monte Carlo allowing the sun to revive her spirits and acclimatize her skin, and stock up on her favourite Russian special reserve Sobranie black cigarettes, unavailable in London. Then she would find a ship which was sailing east towards the ports of Tyre, Bodrum or Haifa. She would pack her maids off back to England and once in the Levant or Palestine, she would hire servants and discuss with the Ottoman port authorities where she could travel under her Carte d'Passage.

Which was why she had begun this, her latest exploration of Arabia, in Jerusalem. She'd been to the ancient city of the Jews twice before, but only as a visitor. Now she wanted to spend at least a few months here, learning about Solomon's temple, the mosques on the holy mountain and the Christian churches and especially learning more about the Druze community and their hatred of Muslims.

She realized from the very beginning that the key to improvement of the women of Arabia lay in the Arab rise from tribal obscurity to a place at the table of the nations of the world. Once a great Arab leader arose, melded the tribes together as one grand nation, and became a figure of respect in the corridors of American and European power, he would have to improve the lot of the women of Arabia. For a dramatic transformation to occur, which might take several generations, it would have to start with Arabia feeling itself as an equal with Europe. In the old days, Saladin could have traveled to London or Paris or Rome and he would have been accorded the respect due to a national leader. But nobody in government or bureaucracy in Europe, and especially in America, would give a moment's consideration to some minor Sheik or Emir who asked for an appointment.

Nor did Gertrude think a national leader whom she could support and sponsor in Whitehall, would come from any of the tribes. Men like ibn Sa'ud or ibn Rashid or the other tribal leaders of the Bani or the Howeitat were little men in the bigger picture. For years, she'd been searching for a leader, a Muslim like Saladin, who could rise up from outside the tribes. And her search continued in Jerusalem. Perhaps the Druze would provide such a man.

She viewed these holy places in Jerusalem as a scholar, not a tourist or a believer in their spirituality. Whenever she was in a building which others defined as holy, while respecting their beliefs, she retained her objectivity. At times it wasn't easy to be objective, especially when she was in Constantinople and overwhelmed by the Blue Mosque or Hagia Sophia. But all she had to do to bring herself back to Earth was to remember the countless numbers of men, women, and children slaughtered throughout history for their belief in one god or another, one dominant theology or its heretical blood brother.

She hated religion as much as she loved its architecture. She detested the pomposity of its spiritual leaders, be they Muslim, Christian or Jews. Whenever she spoke to them, she was outraged by their confident certainty that they were right and all others were wrong, their self-righteousness, haughtiness and aggrandizement. The art and architecture of religion had been amongst mankind's finest achievements, but its inspiration had brought destruction to countless millions. Even the ancient artefacts she'd personally uncovered in the desert, monuments to humanity's earliest attempts to come to terms with spiritual explanations for natural phenomena, had been exquisite, but etched into their stone or marble were the blood and bones of those who believed differently.

And now she was in Jerusalem, the most ancient and mystical city of them all. High in the Judean hills, she thrilled as she wandered the streets of King David and King Solomon, of the prophets Elijah and Elisha, of the Maccabees and the Roman Emperor Vespasian, of Saladin and King Richard the Lionheart, of Umayyad Caliph Abd al-Malik, and now a virtual cascade of Jews fleeing the pogroms and anti-Semitism of Eastern Europe. What a hodge podge of humanity, of architectural styles, of history and culture. And why had this amazing city been allowed to devolve into a stinking hovel because of the absentee landlords and nepotistic Ottomans?

Once she'd explored every inch of Jerusalem, of Jericho and Bethlehem, of the Dead Sea and the coastal city of Jaffa, she would slowly make her way into the nearby desert and visit the amazing Nabatean ruins of Petra, then travel north to Syria, from where she'd go to Aleppo or Damascus and enjoy the luxury of a good hotel, servants to attend to her every need, and perhaps, just perhaps, meet some exciting gentleman and have an illicit and very private liaison. She loved and relished such liaisons and was still sufficiently striking to have men buzzing around her in an hotel lobby or bar. She had had her fun in many cities around the Middle East, and had enjoyed the minds and bodies of diplomats, novelists, journalists, adventurers, dilettantes, rich wastrels and those who had been expelled from their lands because of some sexual scandal. She went by various names so that she could never be identified, the most exciting being Miss Byron, claiming to be the great granddaughter of the notorious poet. It was fun, foolish, disgraceful and she loved it. Perhaps in Jerusalem, she'd find some divorcee who might take her fancy.

But before she could allow time for her own bodily pleasures, she had to see what was so mystical about the Druze religion and whether a leader might emerge, her main reason for coming to Jerusalem. The Druze had been persecuted by the Muslims ever since the religion had been founded in 1017, and Gertrude wanted to find out why. And she especially wanted to understand the role of women in the Druze religion. She knew from close friends in Jerusalem, that Druze women were more than equal with men. Indeed, many of the learned and wise members and leaders of the religion were women who were respected for their knowledge and wisdom, and not disadvantaged because of their sex.

~

She was fussing in the bathroom of her hotel in the old city of Jerusalem longer than her maid, Fatima considered necessary. She was a strange one, this English woman. Were she not so generous, both to Fatima by paying her more wages than she'd ever before earned, and to Fatima's children in buying them presents, her maid would have left her employment. She didn't like all the mystery, all the strange and guarded conversations. She'd served visiting English and French and German ladies before, many times before, but this English was different. She wasn't nearly as interested in seeing the tourist sites of Jerusalem and the Dead Sea and Jericho, even though she visited them once or twice in the three weeks since she'd first taken up residence at the hotel. But this woman kept bringing men back into her room, and closing the door. All sorts of men. Englishmen from the embassy, Egyptians who worked in the money houses, Frenchmen who worked in importing institutions, and Arabs. Arabs from all over the Middle East came to her room. It was unseemly, undignified. What was she doing with all these men behind the closed doors of her suite? And why was an English talking to so many Arabs? Tall Arabs from the desert country, fat Arabs from the south, old Arabs who were tribal leaders, young Arabs who were Imams to a religious community. Was there no end to the men this English would entertain?

And now she was in the bathroom for what seemed to be hours. Fatima had cleaned the room, opened the windows to let the cigarette smoke out, and prepared the lady's evening meal. But why was she so long in the bathroom?

It wasn't until Gertrude emerged that Fatima got the biggest shock of her life, and determined this would be the last minute she'd work for this ridiculous English. She was supposed to be a lady, but she emerged from the hotel's bathroom wearing a galabeya and an Arab headdress, with a red cord around the middle and a sword dangling from her waist. She was dressed like a man, like a rich Egyptian. And worse, she had glued some black hair to her face as though she had suddenly grown a beard and a moustache. She was mad. No, this was worse than dressing like a man, this was a blasphemy against Allah. A woman dressed as a man. Fatima spat on the floor to ward off the servants of Satan, and screamed as the English approached her.

Fatima threw up her hands, and shouted. "No, lady. I go. I no stay here with you. Satan's demons will eat your eyes before the night is ended."

And with that, Fatima spat twice over her left shoulder to ward off any evil spirits sitting there, left the hotel suite with a string of foul Arabic curses and swear words, and ran down the stairs into the street.

Amazed by her reaction, Gertrude wondered what on Earth was wrong with her maid. She'd paid her well, treated her with respect, spoken to her in faultless street Arabic, bought presents for her brood of children, but despite all that, the woman had been lazy, indolent, and resentful. Gertrude was stunned by Fatima's swearing at her. It would never have happened in London, but now that she was alone, she realized she'd been saved the trouble of firing the woman in the morning. She intended to leave Jerusalem tomorrow, and had bought Fatima and her family some lovely presents which she intended to give to her when she returned from her observations of the Druze mystical religious rituals, a ceremony which could only be seen by a man. Women had their own special service, but she wanted to see what the men were up to, and in this particular service, women were *haram*—forbidden. Which was why she'd been forced to buy an Arabic man's outfit from a Jerusalem clothier and a beard and moustache made from leftover hair from a local barber. She would give the gifts intended for Fatima's children to the hotel's manager, to donate to the poor of Jerusalem.

Gertrude walked downstairs into the hotel's reception, where she met her guide for the night, Lieutenant Colonel Lionel Sonter of the British Consulate's signals section, one of Jerusalem's most knowledgeable residents concerning the Druze and their customs. Lionel had lived in Jerusalem for six years, and was now trusted by the Druze community, so much so that they allowed him to observe their religious rituals. Because of their faith in him, they'd allowed him to bring along a friend of his, an Egyptian Coptic Christian gentleman called Gamal.

"You look splendid, Gertrude," he told her as she entered the lobby bar, but might I remind you that you will be killed if the Druze suspect you're not a man. This particular service is for men only. So I'd most strongly advise you to remain silent, and not draw attention to yourself."

"I've faced much greater dangers, Lionel, and it's Gamal, if you don't mind, effendi, not Gertrude."

Lionel smiled, and said "That's your first mistake, Gertrude. 'Effendi' is a Turkish honorific, which I doubt an Egyptian would use, now that Britain has taken back Egypt."

"Wrong, Lionel. An Egyptian who hates the British and is still loyal to the Ottomans, even when addressing Muhammad Ali

Pasha, would continue to use "effendi." I was in Egypt two months ago, and so I know I'm right. Anyway, we'd better get going if we're not going to miss the show."

They walked out of the hotel and into a network of narrow interconnected laneways, each built of the pure white Jerusalem stone. Even at night, with just a few street lights dimly identifying the laneways and paths, the pale stone from which the buildings were constructed seemed to glow and illuminate their way. The Old City was the most biblical place in the world, smelling of centuries of perfumed cooking and aromatic drinks like peach and pomegranate, of ancient rugs and burning incense. The men and women were almost exclusively Arab, with the occasional Jew dressed in black leggings and a fur hat walking back from the Wailing Wall in his Hasidic costume dating back to 17th century Europe.

Lionel directed her along the narrow streets until they came to a house guarded by two burly men, one in a turban, the other in a fez. "This gentleman is with me," said Lionel, his Arabic still retaining an overtone of his English upbringing.

Silently, Gertrude nodded to the two Druze guards and followed Lionel through the door. She was nearly overpowered by the smell of smoke from the candles and the incense burning. In the dimly lit room were, perhaps, fifty men, all sitting on rugs, their hands upturned on their laps as though they were cupping them together to drink water.

On a raised dais at the other end of the room, was the Druze religious leader.

"That's the Uqqal," said Lionel quietly. "He's the religious leader, or the sage. The people praying here are the Juhaall. They're just the ordinary people. They're not allowed to read the holy books of the Druze, because they're considered insufficiently educated."

She listened for a moment to what the Uqqal was reciting to his followers. It was familiar to her. In a lowered voice, trying to speak like a man, she whispered to Lionel, "but they're reading the Koran. I thought they had their own books."

"They do," said Lionel. "But they consider the Koran to be just the outer shell of their belief, the inner being of their faith is the text known as the Kitab Al Hikma, or the Book of Wisdom. Druze are monotheists and view Adam and Noah and Abraham and Jesus and Mohammed as their prophets. They believe that at death, one's soul is instantly transformed and reincarnated, and if you've been good, you'll get into a better person, but if you've been bad, you're next incarnation is downhill."

Gertrude nodded. "I know how they feel. But if they use the Koran, and if they believe in Mohammed, why are the Muslims persecuting them?" she asked.

Lionel thought for a moment before he whispered. "I'm afraid the Muslims will persecute anything and anybody who doesn't follow their particular ideology. Mohammed was a pretty rum chap, all those centuries ago. He slaughtered his way out of Arabia and his followers have conquered by causing fear and mayhem. They issue fatwas, virtual death sentences, at the drop of a hat. I know you have a liking for them, m'dear, but I have far more experience with Muslims than you do, and I'm afraid I have a very different opinion of the blighters. The Druze are alright, because they're followers of many different prophets, and they're against involving themselves in wars and politics. But the Muslims! No, I'm afraid I have very little time for them. And I foresee them causing enormous trouble for the British Empire. I can't quite put my finger on it, but I think they're going to be a big problem for us. You mark my words."

Gertrude hoped that Lionel's words weren't a forerunner of difficulties ahead.

~

Mesopotamia, 1910

Tall, elegant, windswept, Gertrude Bell was dressed in a fur coat, cloche hat, trousers, and long boots to protect her against the freezing early morning of the desert. Riding as majestically as her camel made possible, she and her entourage sauntered away from the camp and the dying embers of the breakfast fire as they entered the final stage of their journey to see what the Englishmen in the desert were up to.

Famous in England for her travels and revered as a writer and translator, Gertrude's reputation now preceded her. She could no longer be anonymous walking the streets of Jerusalem or Cairo or Damascus without some local coming up to her with a copy of one of her books and begging to touch the cheek of the English lady who was making Arabia known to the West.

And so she set her mind to travel through the wastelands of Arabia, usually sleeping alone, and eating with her faithful servants who treated her like a monarch. And no matter how she adjusted her body, the mean-spirited, spiteful, spitting and growling camel reminded her that English people were born to ride horses, not these implausible beasts of burden.

She rode onwards, whipping the camel's flanks to encourage the stupid beast to pace more quickly. But its spindly legs trod the ground at its own pace, unimpressed by her imprecations. It was both the ship and the captain, and she was merely its temporary voyager.

It would take her another day of travel before she arrived at her destination. Then she would spy the glistening waters of the Euphrates and, after satisfying the thirst of her camels and her servants, she'd wash herself in its sparkling waters and order an immediate continuation north until she reached the dig site.

Ancient Carchemish. It was so exciting that Englishmen were digging in Carchemish, kingdom of Shalmaneser and Sargon and the site of the most famous battle of the ancient world when, six hundred years before Christ, Nebuchadnezzar expelled the marauding southerners and put an end, once and for all time, to the glory of Egypt. All history was at Carchemish. All was to be revealed by the archaeological dig. She could barely restrain herself from seeing what was hidden beneath the whispering sands of time, listening to the now-silent voices of the ancients and finding out what would be revealed when the stones were uncovered.

In her explorations of Arabia, she'd developed her interest in the new science of archaeology to such an extent she'd given an occasional address to her old college at Oxford where, she was delighted to find, there was a sizeable number of women students. Many years earlier, she'd seen what was beneath the sand when she was with Henry Cadogan riding to Persepolis. They'd dug and revealed massive stone walls, but the more they exposed, the less adequate she had felt revealing the hidden truths of ancient civilizations. So she'd studied books on archaeology and undertaken digs in the desert until she was now considered one of the most able archaeologists England had ever produced. Her papers on ancient cities and peoples had been published extensively in *The Times*. Now she was interested in two Oxford men who were apparently digging in the middle of the desert.

On returning to Constantinople the Beys had laughed at the idea of Englishmen burrowing below the sands of the desert until she reminded them of the fortune uncovered by Mr. Schliemann not forty years earlier in Hissarlik on the Asiatic coast of Turkey. He'd sold Helen of Troy's jewellery to the Germans for a king's ransom, and when she told them precisely how much Schliemann's find would be worth in gold today, the Beys had stopped laughing and, in between their cups of coffee, hawked their spit into the ground in contempt.

The following day, after fitful sleep, she sensed they were close to Carchemish. It had been rediscovered after two millennia only thirty years earlier, and been largely forgotten until the damned Germans began to build the Berlin to Baghdad railway—a danger to British influence in both trade and the oil of Persia. This monstrosity had now reached the Upper Euphrates and the area was, she was certain, soon to be overrun by sightseers or amateur part-time archaeologists incapable of comprehending the difference between a pile of stones and a rare and beautiful monument. So the haste to uncover the miracle of Carchemish and to protect it from amateurs was all the more urgent.

Riding over a crest she saw, down in the valley, the unmistakable constructions of an archaeological dig. Her heart pounded as she recognised the mounds of discarded sand and gravel and earth, the reinforcement walls which were needed to prevent collapse of the exposed trenches, the tents which the archaeologists used to store their finds, the living quarters, the crudely made toilets, and the enclosure for the animals. She took out her binoculars and looked carefully. There must have been a hundred Arabs scurrying around the site, climbing into and out of pits, pushing wheelbarrows, carrying panniers full of rubble and dumping them onto huge mounds.

Gertrude felt a tingle of delight, the same excitement she'd felt beside Henry all those years ago when they'd reached Persepolis. Today, she had found another ancient city, Carchemish. She looked at the mounds of earth and sand, and saw that they had yet to be sifted for any further treasures. Gertrude continued, and eventually came to a halt at the edge of one of the channels which had been carefully dug into the ground.

Crouching in the trench were two white men, one slouched over a mound of stone, the other on his hands and knees, scraping away at the earth to reveal what it concealed.

The camel belched and growled, and both men looked up at the unexpected noise to see a lady high above them, dressed in what appeared to be the latest fashions of London or Paris, yet seated on a camel and staring down at them.

"Good God," said one of the men.

"What the devil . . ." said the other.

"Good morning. My name is Miss Bell. Miss Gertrude Bell. I've come to see what you're doing."

They remained silent, just staring up at the apparition until the kneeling man said, "Well I'm damned!"

The men stood, and adjusted their clothing. One, incongruously, raised his hat in greeting.

"Good morning," he said, his refinement absurdly out of place.

"Good morning. I am Miss Gertrude Bell. I've ridden here to see what you gentlemen are digging. May I ask you to introduce yourselves."

"Thomas Edward Lawrence, madam," said the younger of the two. He was fair-haired, with extraordinary piercing blue eyes, of thin face and slightly built with a fey expression. He had a high-pitched voice which made him seem somewhat effeminate. By his look, he was a born-and-bred Englishman, more suited to the cricket pitch at Marlborough or the banks of Cowes than the oven of Mesopotamia. Yet Gertrude was instantly struck by something about him. It was as though the desert was made for him, and he for it; as though by some unaccountable association, it had become a part of his being, in his sand-yellow hair and his sky-blue eyes.

The other man looked particularly out place in an Arabian desert. He was rotund, sweating profusely, and unlike Mr. Lawrence who had a wonderful tan, had developed a ruddy, rough, and sand-blown complexion. He raised his hat, and said, "Mr. Campbell Thompson, ma'am. At your service. Miss Bell? Well I never! I assume that you are *the* Miss Gertrude Bell?"

She smiled at the recognition, and declined to answer. The two men straightened their backs, and adjusted their clothing, climbing out of the trench as Gertrude dismounted.

They met at the edge of the excavation, and shook hands solemnly.

"Miss Bell, may I ask what you're doing in Carchemish? In the middle of the desert? An Englishwoman on her own."

"Mr. Lawrence," she said, "I'm not on my own. My men have temporarily deserted me, following their camels to the river after the long journey from Aleppo. They'll return soon, but in the meantime, I wonder, after I've rested, if you could explain more about this excavation of yours."

Campbell Thompson again raised his Panama and shook her hand for a second time.

"I just can't believe that you're here. The famous Gertrude Bell? The famous mountaineer, the translator of the poems of

70

the Divan of Hafiz, the author of Safar Nameh and the woman who wrote that marvellous work *The Desert and the Sown*? I've read everything you've written, and all your articles in *The Times*. I just can't believe we have the honor of entertaining you in our camp."

She smiled again; Campbell Thompson was sounding like a sycophant for some ancient Mesopotamian Tyrant, and when he realized it, he flushed an even deeper red. He looked her up and down as though inspecting a mare he was considering purchasing. His jaw was slack, and Gertrude wondered if she was inappropriately dressed. Yet she had dressed carefully for the desert just that morning, a long and divided royal blue skirt in the form of trousers for riding, a brown linen jacket and an Arabic Keffiyeh headdress to protect her from the sun on top of which was a cheeky beret from the new Parisian fashion house of Chanel. She was pleased that her appearance had bemused them and couldn't help but smile. Having lived so long out of England, having traveled around the world and sojourned in Arabia for so many years, she was only vaguely aware, and indeed, largely uninterested in the reception her literary outpourings had received and who might know of her.

"Despite your amazement, I am Gertrude Bell," she said modestly, "and yes, I wrote those works." She carefully manoeuvred between the camel and the excavation trench, assisted by Mr. Thompson, and stood close to him. Like so many men, she was considerably taller than he was.

"Good grief," said Thompson. He turned to Lawrence. "Good God! Do you realize in whose presence we stand, Lawrence?"

Lawrence smiled at her and interrupted the older man. "Thompson. Stop blathering. You're sounding as if you've just stepped into a Buckingham Palace Garden party. I've read all of Miss Bell's works like you, and she was in part my inspiration for coming to Arabia."

"Gentlemen! I'm becoming embarrassed by all this praise. I've ridden halfway across the country to see what you're doing here.

May we at least proceed to an explanation of the dig, and what you've achieved so far? Is this dig undertaken by just the two of you and natives?"

Thompson smiled. "No, ma'am, this is a British Museum archaeological site, though I'm an assistant at the Ashmolean Museum at Oxford. We're merely the first of a dozen members of staff and volunteers from London. We're preparing the ground so in a month, when the heat is less fierce, the others can come out and assist us."

He turned to explain the dig, but was interrupted by Lawrence. "Where are your manners, Thompson? Miss Bell has just arrived after a long journey, and being in Arabia, it's incumbent upon us to offer her hospitality. Come away from the trenches, Thompson, and assist me in entertaining her. Might I offer you a cup of coffee, Miss Bell? A cup of tea?"

She smiled at the attractive young man as he clambered out of the trench to join them. She noticed he was wearing a red tasselled sash as a belt, the Arabic sign that he was a bachelor. He was a strange, yet somehow magnetic fellow. In any other circumstances, she would likely ignore him, but here, in the desert, his yellow hair and flamboyant blue eyes were fascinating her. He seemed to be examining her, inspecting her, almost piercing her, rather than just looking at her. She knew of him by repute, even though he was only twenty-three years old. He was some sort of Oxford man, educated in medieval pottery. But something about his looks fascinated her. Initially she wondered whether it was because he was dressed so garishly in Arab slippers and an eclectic mix of Middle-East and Western dress. She instinctively felt that Mr. Lawrence would turn out to be less of an Englishman than a traveler through space and time. Like herself. But more than just his attire, there was something about him, some intrinsic quality which she picked up immediately, which made her look at him again and again. Others might see an effeminate and delicate individual, but Gertrude looked into Lawrence's very being and thought she caught a glimpse of a leader.

They took tea before examining the site, and although she kept it to herself, what she saw didn't impress her. There was a lack of professionalism, and most certainly a lack of discovery. Whole areas seemed to have been overlooked, obvious formations below which must be walls and pathways left uncovered, and trenches made where it would have been apparent to a more professional archaeologist they would only find a dead end. And the lack of artefacts after so many days of digging, was surprising. Her first task would be to go through the mountain of rubble and extract what priceless relics had been tossed away with the rocks and dust and sand.

She slept very well that night, and during the following couple of days, worked with them in establishing timelines for the artefacts and survey lines for future dig directions.

Gertrude particularly enjoyed being in their camp during the few days she helped them with classification, with digging, and with interpretation of their finds. During this time Thompson and Lawrence showed her all the artefacts which they'd so far uncovered and Gertrude, although dismayed by the quantity, was impressed by the importance of what they had so far discovered. But simply by going through the mounds of rubble, she was able to treble the number of statues, idols, jewellery, shards, and inscriptions.

She examined numerous clay tablets and seals, a bulla used for storing records, idols of gods and goddesses, stamps, unidentifiable figurines which could have been idols of unknown gods, exquisite jewellery, and much that it would not be possible to categorize without reference to the collection at the British Museum. She'd wandered the trenches, helped them uncover further walls of houses, and ordered her men to assist those employed by Lawrence and Thompson in carting the earth and debris from the site.

After the better part of a week in the camp, it was time for her to return to civilization. She had much to do. As the sun was setting over the Syrian Desert, descending into the distant Mediterranean, she spent her last evening sitting by the banks of the wide and

73

slow-flowing Euphrates river, sluggish in the heat of summer, resting her feet in its cool waters. She had brought with her a book, and was reflecting on whether she should alter her timetable and stay here another few days or journey back to Damascus and perhaps take a train to Constantinople. Earlier in the day, she'd told Thomas Lawrence and Campbell Thompson that she was thinking of moving on, but now she had to determine when would be a suitable time. Lawrence had done his best to dissuade her, but she was determined to leave, although in the short time she'd been at the camp, she'd built a very real friendship with him. Despite his often girlish mannerisms and his fey appearance, he had a superb mind and was happy and willing to learn from her. Had he been considerably older, she'd have been attracted to him, but she felt certain his tendencies lay in other directions.

Since Italy looked as though it would declare war on Turkey at any moment, and since the Moroccan crisis looked as though it was going to escalate, it was almost certain the damned Italians would attack Tripoli and Benghazi, making the whole area of the eastern Mediterranean fraught and dangerous. She'd risked coming here, but after a few months in the wilderness with little information and almost no up-to-date intelligence, Gertrude had only a scant idea of how things lay to the west.

Perhaps she should take her camels directly north, out of reach of the Italians, and head over the mountains for Turkey's Turquoise Coast? Or perhaps she should head directly south, down the Euphrates towards the Gulf, risking the dangers inherent in traveling through the land of the Marsh Arabs, and if she survived, take a ship out of Umm Qasr or Al-Basrah or even Abadan, back to Constantinople.

Her musings were disturbed by an elongated shadow which appeared beside her. She turned, and looked upwards. The figure's features were dark against the setting sun, but by its grace and slimness, she immediately recognised it as Mr. Lawrence.

Without a word, he sat beside her, took off his shoes, and his feet joined hers in the river.

They sat there, looking at the opposite bank at least a mile away, as the torpid water slowly flowed over their ankles and toes.

"I can't tell you how pleased I am that you came to our little excavation, Miss Bell. These few days have been quite the most marvellous I've spent since leaving England."

"And they've been very enjoyable for me as well, Mr. Lawrence," she said, resuming her interest in the book.

Lawrence remained silent, but the silence was of such a nature Gertrude realized she had to give him her attention, like a mother gives to a child.

She closed the book, placed it in her lap, and jiggled her feet in the water. "Mr. Lawrence, are you here to pass the time of day, or is there intent in your unexpected appearance?"

It took him some time before he admitted "Intent, I'm afraid, as well as to pass the time of day with a charming and intelligent companion. Thompson's busy classifying and the men are clearing, and my back's about done in with the bending, and I just needed some time to reflect."

"Reflection is normally an act accomplished on one's own, often with a vanity mirror."

"Would you like me to leave?"

She looked at him. He was a pretty man lacking the muscular physique of the Arab or the dusky hues of the Mediterranean, but pleasant for all that. But his way of dressing! Having washed up from the day of digging, he was now dressed for the evening in a gray flannel blazer with pink piping and white flannel shorts as though he was about to step out onto a cricket pitch or engage in a game of tennis.

Yet for all his mannerisms, he was interesting to look at and be with. Not, of course, that Gertrude was in any way entertaining the idea of a liaison with him, because there was a twenty-year age gap between them, and at forty-two, she was certainly old enough to be his mother. And anyway, she was so busy with her archaeology and her writing and numerous other pursuits that any time she had for her own personal life couldn't be squandered on romance.

Those days, she knew, were starting to be behind her, brightened by the occasional illicit and thrilling romance with a middle-aged gentleman, sometimes with a journalist in some hotel, more often with one of the British or European diplomats with whom she came into contact. Marriage may have provided her with much more physical satisfaction, but the societal strictures it would have imposed would have driven her insane. But even the physical nature of marriage was uncertain. While Gertrude was free to travel and explore, to meet and greet whomsoever her fancy desired, many of the women friends in England for whom she'd been a bridesmaid now lived their lives like shrivelled fruit in an arid desert of a home, spending every day alone with their children while their husbands were gallivanting around the fleshpots of Soho entertaining mistresses or actresses in some sordid atelier in London.

And if the truth be told, after her conspicuous failures to attract suitable men and the disappointments of seeming to have desultory affairs only with older, married men, she was growing more interested in minds than in bodies.

"No, Mr. Lawrence, I don't want you to leave. I've enjoyed our many conversations. I hope I shall continue to enjoy them in greener climes, such as England on your return."

Again he remained silent, and out of embarrassment, Gertrude was about to speak when he said, "You know, Miss Bell, for a man as young as myself, it's a privilege to be so intimate with a woman who has such a considerable knowledge of the Middle East, and archaeology and pottery . . ."

"Intimate?"

He flushed. "Intimacy of mind and purpose. Unlike good old Thompson who is little more than a librarian, you've lived and breathed the desert. You're what I've always imagined for myself—at one with the sand and the impossible sky, dressing in the clothes of an Arabic Sheik, and riding a white horse alone through the dunes and into the sunset."

76

She smiled. "I'm afraid you've been reading too many of those dreadful penny romance novels, Mr. Lawrence. I've ridden through the desert, and it's far more painful than beautiful. Talk to a desert Arab about the beauty of the desert, and he'll think you're mad. He'd exchange it at the drop of a hat for some of Britain's verdant pastures, for Blake's green and pleasant land."

He swirled his feet in the water and splashed her legs. Their feet, magnified slightly by the water, created gentle eddies as the river flowed over them. Their bodies were hot, but the water below the surface was cold, fed by the melt-waters of the distant mountains of southeastern Turkey. As she looked at her ankles and legs in the water, she was transported back to the moment she'd read the letter from Uncle Frank about dear Henry who'd frozen in the River Lar. She sighed in remembrance of what might have been.

Breathing deeply, she said, "Anyway, Mr. Lawrence, you're a young man, and the desert is no place for somebody like you to settle down. There are many dangers here for young men, solitude being only one of them. At your age, you should be enjoying the full benefits of English society."

"I'm not all that young, Miss Bell. I've lived more of a life than many men my age who remained in England and did little but attend school, university, and enter a profession."

Gertrude looked at him quizzically. What was he trying to say? "You indicated that there was intent to your coming to join me here. I wonder whether you'd care to reveal it?"

Lawrence cleared his throat. He struggled to say something, but changed his mind.

She took pity on him. "Is it something to do with Mr. Thompson? Or perhaps something about me? Something of a personal matter you wished to discuss?"

He nodded.

"About me?" Again, he nodded. "My travels? My life?"

He shook his head.

"Come now, Mr. Lawrence. We could spend the rest of the day in thrust and parry. What's on your mind?"

"I wanted to . . . not that you need to tell me . . . but if you were of a mind, perhaps . . . although I realize that it's of a personal nature . . ."

"Oh, for God's sake, Thomas! What?"

"I wanted to know whether you . . . if there was a gentleman to whom you showed a particular fondness."

"Several. I am familiar with a number of gentlemen in London and in Constantinople and in Cairo." She thought for a moment. "And in Jerusalem and Damascus. Oh dear, I do sound promiscuous, don't I, but I travel a great deal, and when opportunity arises . . ."

"Have you never thought of marriage?" he asked.

She smiled. "The opportunity didn't present itself, I'm afraid. But the German philosopher Nietzsche said that there are many more unhappy marriages than unhappy people. It isn't lack of love which makes for unhappy marriages, Thomas, but lack of friendship within the marriage. I value my friendships greatly. Many men say they've fallen in love with me, or what they told me was love, but there were very few with whom I was friendly. Friendship is far more demanding than marriage, which is, after all, only a contract dealing with property and inheritance. That is of no interest to me. But friendship! True and honest friendship! Ah, now that's where a man and a woman can truly be lovers . . . of the mind, if not the body."

He nodded, and remained silent for some time. She knew he wanted to talk to her about some physical or romantic matter and could have helped him out of his embarrassment, but decided that if he was to succeed with the process of finding a suitable mate, he really must develop the vocabulary. But after an interminable wait, she gave up on him finding his own voice, and said, "Are you discussing this with me for a particular reason?"

Slowly, warily, as though he had suddenly come upon a coiled snake, he said, "I have grown fond of you since you arrived at the dig. I know it's only been a matter of days, but . . ."

"As I am fond of you, Thomas."

"No! No, I don't mean that kind of fondness. I mean . . . I mean the other kind of fondness . . ."

She reached over, and touched his knee. "Mr. Lawrence. I'm old enough to be your mother. I thank you for the compliment, but the difference in our ages . . ."

"That's why I'm fond of you," he said softly.

"Ah!"

The sun continued to sink lower on the horizon, casting longer and longer shadows. The sky turned from turquoise to a darker blue. "Do you not find yourself attracted to younger women?"

"I find them feckless and silly."

She thought back to her own three years of misery and disappointment, her coming-out seasons straight after Oxford, three years of uncompromising embarrassment as her parents had paraded her like some article in a shop window, her father and mother frantic in their efforts to find her a husband. They couldn't understand why it was so hard, she was tall and very attractive and as rich as Croesus, but despite the dozens and dozens of eligible young men, she found them all, without exception, to be vapid and stupid and utterly unexciting.

To her shame and horror at the time, but now far more understandably, she too found the fathers of the feckless young men far more interesting than their sons. And why was it that when a man was forbidden to her by the bonds of his marriage to another woman, even a woman he detested, she was so often attracted to him? Did she have some sort of romantic death-wish, she wondered.

Mr. Lawrence continued, somewhat diffidently, "I find I lose interest in young women very quickly. They're so unworldly and unwise. They blather and say silly things and when I try to talk to them about something in which I'm interested, I can tell that all they're doing is feigning interest, but I can see that they're waiting for me to change the subject and to talk about empty things like holidays and plays and visits to the seaside. Yet I seem to find their mothers of much greater interest. And more exciting."

"Believe me when I say that I completely understand what you mean. But do you also find you have more in common with these young ladies' brothers? Are you more interested in a physical relationship with them?"

He looked at her in shock. She smiled, and stroked his face. "My dear Mr. Lawrence, you may try to hide your persuasions from yourself, but you hide nothing from me. Perhaps more than any other English woman you will ever meet, I am a woman of the world. Nothing which I have seen, and I've seen many extraordinary things, shocks me anymore. I knew from the first moment of our meeting that you were ambivalent about your sex. As you grow older, you may find yourself drawn either to women or to men, but to whatever and to whomever you are attracted, you must obey the dictates of your body, and not be forced into a loveless and painful relationship just to conform to society. Remember the horror which Mr. Oscar Wilde suffered at the hands of the insufferable Marquis of Queensbury, and you'll see the dangers of living a lie."

Lawrence shook his head in amazement. "You're extraordinary. I've never met a woman like you," he said.

"And it's unlikely that you ever will again. Yes, Mr. Lawrence, I've enjoyed the company of a number of very elegant and intelligent gentlemen. I've loved some of them to distraction, and have given myself to a number of them, even those who were married, but whose marriages were disastrous. Because, you see, I don't look on some church aisle as a sacrosanct passage to eternal fidelity. Good God, Lawrence, I'm on Earth for a good time, and I'm determined to have one. But that's me, Thomas. That is my choice, and the knowledge with which I live daily. You, Mr. Lawrence, must make your own choices."

She smiled, removed her hand from his knee, opened the book, and began reading again. He sat there, looking glum and disconsolate. She took pity on him, and undid the top two buttons of her bodice. Putting her hand into an inside pocket of her blouse, she withdrew the tiny idol which she'd carried with her since the day Henry had given it to her.

80

"My dear, many years ago, a young man with whom I was deeply in love, gave this to me. Do you recognize it?"

"It's a Hittite goddess. I don't know which one without comparing her with other figurines. Aserdus, Hannahanna, Inara?"

"She's the Goddess Arinnitti," said Gertrude

"Ah, the sun goddess," said Thomas.

"She's looked after me for many years, but I feel she's probably more suited to a young man such as yourself than to a middle-aged lady like me. A young man who still has to find his way around the tortuous pathways of Arabia, and one who has to determine in which direction his body will take him. My sun is fading, whilst yours is in ascendance. It's time for me to pass on her good fortunes to one who will make better use of her, so I'd like you to have her, in the hope that she fulfils your expectations and guides you to an accommodation with life."

Before Gertrude handed the goddess to Thomas, she kissed it, just as Henry had kissed it as they'd left each other all those years earlier in Teheran. Thomas took the idol, and kissed Gertrude on the cheek, thanking her.

"Now," she said, "why don't you return to the camp, so I can continue my reading."

He stood, and she glanced at him surreptitiously as he walked. Not that she was sexually interested in him, but for the first time she noticed that his gait had a slight limp. Odd that she hadn't noticed it before. That sort of limp often came from childhood accidents, and she determined to ask him about it at an appropriate time.

He was a fascinating young man, yet one who exhibited all the hallmarks of a reject. But not to her! There was something about Thomas Lawrence which drew her in as a fascination, one of those inexpressible, even obscure ambiguities which could see him either as a footnote to history, or one who overcame all obstacles and succeeded beyond his wildest aspiration. Somehow, and she had no idea how, she was betting that in the coming years Mr. Lawrence would be the agent of her triumph.

~

Central Arabia, Towards Hayil, February, 1913

For the journey across the fearsome Nejd desert, the world's harshest and most merciless wasteland, a boiling anvil of rock and baked sand, Gertrude had employed a veritable legion of servants. Fearsome armed guards, cooks, camel drivers, and porters, her entourage consisted of more than forty people, hired from the western edges where vegetation and trees still grew. Everybody in her party privately thought the English woman was mad to attempt such a journey, and made their thoughts known the first night around the camp fires until she responded in fluent Arabic that her purpose in traveling to the south of Riyadh was to interview Abdul Aziz ibn Sa'ud, who was camped there, and who Gertrude believed was intent on storming the city and reclaiming it for the Sa'uds and for Wahhabism. It had been twenty years since Abdul Aziz' father, Abd al-Rahman, had been with her in Bucharest and sparked her interest in Arabia and the need for all the tribes to come together under one Saladin-like leadership if they were ever to throw off the shackles of being a conquered people. The father had failed to be a modern Saladin, but his son, Abdul Aziz, was spoken of in the most extravagant terms, and Gertrude was determined to meet with him. Not just to spend time in his company, but to attempt to explain to him the benefits of a friendship with Great Britain. If he was as extraordinary as people were saying, then she could and should be his conduit to Whitehall and Buckingham Palace.

"But ibn Rashid is in control, Lady," said one of her guards. "He is in Hayil. He will kill us for trying to see ibn Sa'ud. They are blood enemies."

"I know that, but I'm trying to gain information on what's going on in Arabia for my government," she said.

"But you are a woman. You must not do this," he informed her.

"Arabs treat women as possessions. In England, we are almost equal to men."

The entire party of men shook their heads in amazement. Several hawked spit into the fires. "What a terrible place this England must be," they commented.

The following morning, they continued their slow progress towards Hayil and then on the long journey through the Arabian Desert southeast to Riyadh. As the camels were lumbering ever onwards through the rocks and sand, the guard who had spoken to her the previous evening drove his camel forwards until they were riding side by side.

"Lady," he said. "You are a great English?"

She smiled. "No, I'm just an ordinary woman."

"You are not Sultana?"

"No. Not royalty. Just an English lady."

"There are many like you?"

"No, not many. Most are content to be wives and mothers. But I'm driven to see the world."

He nodded and remained silent for some time. Then he asked, "Why are you going to Hayil? The Emir is a boy. All his family has been murdered by all his family. Blood flows like milk on the ground of the Rashids," and he hawked a gob of spit onto the sand at the mention of their name.

"You support the al Sa'ud family?" she asked.

"I support nobody. All are thieves and murderers. Allah will curse them and dogs will lick their balls. But why seek out Rashid and Sa'ud? We don't understand. What can you learn from these sons of pigs?" he asked.

"Information about what they intend to do. It might affect my country one day."

The moment she said this, the Arab burst out laughing. All the others laughed aloud, even though they hadn't heard the joke. "But you live far away. You live in an oasis. How can what we do in the Nefud or the Nejd be of interest to you in your England?"

"The world is a small place, and what happens in Arabia can affect what happens in my country which lies far across the sea."

Mystified, he reined back his camel and re-joined his companions. He softly told them what she'd said. They burst out laughing. The woman was truly stupid. But so long as she paid well, they didn't mind.

~

Three days later, the entourage ascended a granite plateau and saw the mud walls of Hayil far ahead. It was getting late, and they decided to make an encampment and finish their journey the following morning.

As dawn rose and they shook off the freezing night air, Gertrude mounted her camel. She'd employed the guards to protect her from brigands and Bedouin thieves in the desert, but knew that if she were to ride towards Hayil with a large contingent, it would be too threatening, and would mean a battle. She told her men what she was about to do, and with money and gifts she set off to ride the three miles to the city gates. Knowing the protocol, Gertrude waited two hundred yards from the closed gates until they opened, and three riders came towards her.

They circled her, came close and then retreated until they were assured she bore no arms. Then they came near her. She gave them gifts to present to the Emir until he was satisfied she was no threat. Then she waited alone, sitting on a camel in the heat of the desert. Behind her was her entourage, but she knew with absolute certainty that except for one or two loyal servants, if an army came out of the gates, they'd disappear into the desert like a mirage. In front of her was a small city with a massive wall behind which could lay her death or imprisonment or freedom, depending on whether the ruler accepted her gifts. What a world!

It took half an hour in the rapidly heating air for them to ride back, and escort her into Hayil. She made the strangest sight the men of the city had ever seen. Dressed in blue linen trousers and a silk blouse, a thick fur coat and brimmed feathered hat which was covered by a silk *keffiyeh*, she was escorted through the narrow streets to a large building in the centre of the city. She entered the building, and was immediately impressed by the huge height of the ceiling and the colonnade around the walls. Dazzlingly colourful carpets of immense technical and artistic merit covered the floor and Islamic writing which she recognized as verses from the Koran were inscribed around the cornices and along some of the walls. Divans, on which lay bejewelled men and women, were positioned like carriages of a train. All were watching this extraordinary vision walk from the doorway to the foot of the throne, on which sat a bald and grotesquely fat man. She knew him to be Ibrahim, uncle to the sixteen-year-old Emir who was off fighting a battle in the north.

"Your journey to us has been known for many days," said Ibrahim.

"What can be kept secret in a desert which has the eyes and ears of Rashid?" she asked.

"You are known to me, English. You have traveled the lands of Arabia for many years. You have been in Al Quds."

"Jerusalem is a great and important city, Excellency," she said, refusing to use the Arabic name for a place as holy to Christianity as it was to Islam. "It is also known as Zion by the Jews, whose claim and ancestry goes back fifteen hundred years before the birth of the Prophet Mohammed, peace and blessings be upon him."

"The Jews are newcomers to Al Quds, English. They have no place in the land conquered by our Prophet. We will drive them out. Now, why are you here?"

"I am here, Excellency, to present you with gifts from my master George, fifth king to bear that name in the past two hundred years, and to ride beyond your city to speak with Abdul Aziz ibn Sa'ud. I need to find out what is in the minds of the Sa'uds and the Rashids. It is of interest to my king."

Ibrahim looked at her suspiciously the moment she mentioned the name Sa'ud. Barely able to contain his hatred, he hissed, "The Sa'uds are a dry and withered fruit, woman, full of bitter poisons. They are a band of dogs. wild with hunger. They bark fiercely, but

85

they have neither teeth to bite nor courage to fight and they cower in dark corners."

She heard a murmur of agreement from the dozens of princelings and other hangers-on lying on their divans, and immediately realized that she had just made a grave tactical error. Such errors in Arab society could prove deadly. Trying to recover, she said, "I have brought you gifts, Excellency, to show you my respect."

"Are these gifts for me, or for my Emir ibn Rashid?" he asked. It was a trick question, and Gertrude knew she had to be wary of the answer.

"How two great men divide my king's gifts is a question for the two great men, and not for me."

He nodded, and asked her, "And have you brought the same gifts for the dog ibn Sa'ud?" he asked.

"It is not my custom to discuss what gifts I will give to him, just as I will never disclose what gifts I give to you and your Emir," she said. She didn't like the way the conversation was going.

Ibrahim continued to look at her for some time. She knew that by custom, an Arab woman had to avert her eyes when a man who wasn't her husband looked at her; but she was damned if she was going to be cowed by the uncle of the Emir Rashid. She knew she had to stand up to him, or she'd be robbed of everything, and she and her men would probably be killed.

"You will be my guest until His Majesty the Emir ibn Rashid returns. He is in the north, fighting the Shammar. When he sits on his throne, he will allow you to leave."

Suddenly frightened, she said, "But I have . . ."

"You have to leave here to visit Abdul Aziz ibn Sa'ud? No, you will stay until my Emir returns. Then we will decide what to do with you. Death, English, will be a merciful reward for those who seek to visit ibn Sa'ud. And your men beyond the gates will be treated to the hospitality of ibn Rashid."

He grinned. She began to say she was given authority to be here by the Turks, but before she could utter a further word, Ibrahim rose from his throne, and walked to a rear entrance, leaving Gertrude standing there, alone and impotent, facing an empty chair. As he left, the dozens of princelings and other followers, scurried out after him until she was in the room with just three huge Nubian guards, who surrounded her, and led her to prison.

For every day of the two weeks she spent in the prison in Hayil, she dreamed of London—foggy, fussy, but delightfully safe London. She wondered what her friends were doing. Were they having dinner parties and discussing plays and concerts and things? As she sat in the roasting and airless heat of her cell, was anybody asking about her, she wondered? Would she ever again sit at a London dining table and regale politicians, writers, editors and her friends with her stories of Arabia, she wondered.

And what part would she now play in her grand plan to unify all of Arabia as a future great and modernizing nation when it allowed the sort of medieval barbarity she was experiencing, to exist? How could Arabia ever unite under a new Saladin when such primitive malevolence as she was suffering, was the norm? It had taken England hundreds of years to modernize from the cruelty of its kings to the emancipation of today. But the world couldn't wait that long for Arabia to modernize. Its resources would soon be under siege, its people confronted with the prospect of freedom from serfdom, its women seeing life from the other side of the veil, and then all hell would break loose unless a strong leader held the nations together.

She could have accomplished so much! But now she'd have to wait for ibn Rashid to return and for the 16-year old to decide in a fit of childish pique whether to dispatch her and her men to their deaths. And if he did, would anybody in London know what had happened to her?

FOUR

London, 1914

The moment she saw it looming out of the London smog, her heart sank. It was a great moment in her life, yet the very building itself, supposed to define England's solidity and permanency, was gloomy, melancholy, and fussy, a stolid construction of red bricks and chimneys and architraves. The feeling it imposed upon her as her carriage drew close was that of a building full of pomp and circumstance and self-importance, so very different to the ethereal, creamy, light-as-air architecture of Baghdad and Constantinople and the dozens of other cities of the Near East where she was truly happy.

The new headquarters of the Royal Geographical Society at Lowther Lodge in Kensington Gore overwhelmed the smaller houses beside it and diminished the charming park opposite in both stature and importance.

A shudder of despondency surged through her body as she stepped from her carriage and looked upwards to take in the enormity of its massive chimneys, its clumsy frontage and ridiculously delicate Queen Anne windows which were at odds with the ponderous weight of building. Despite herself, she couldn't help but compare it to the delicate and deliciously ornate tents in which she lived when she explored Mesopotamia and traveled through the deserts of Arabia, or to the soaring gleaming monumental walls of Jerusalem, or the blinding white palaces of Damascus or Mecca or Medina which from afar looked like mirages of heaven. But that was an unfair comparison, because this was cold and gloomy England and the pure and breathless deserts were another time and another world away.

As she stepped onto the pavement, she shuddered at the thought of all those men who would be inside the building. All gathered there to celebrate her bravery, her adventures, and to congratulate her on achievements which no other woman had accomplished. Yet the setting was so very wrong. To properly appreciate what she'd achieved, this presentation should be made in a Sheik's citadel in his desert domain, or some Caliph's sandy kingdom or the Ottoman Sultan's vast Topkapi Palace overlooking the Bosphorus in Constantinople, somewhere delicate and light and unearthly, something which looked like a wedding cake . . . not this red brick eyesore, a monument to the permanence of Rule Britannia.

Instead of driving through London's parks with their stately poplars and elms and oaks, their tulips and daisies, she should be wandering amid palm fronds and date trees and fragrant orange groves, the air warm and sweet and heavy with the perfumes of frankincense and atar and roses and myrrh.

Rather than Londoners enshrouded in scarves and tweed coats and wraps to protect themselves from the unseasonably cold night air and ubiquitous smog, she should be walking amongst beautiful dusky women meandering through the *shuks* or the narrow ancient streets. And the men! Lean and tall and magnificent in their jet black beards, their faces burnished like bronze by the desert sun, walking majestically with leonine steps, supremely confident in their long *galabiyahs*, their swords and daggers swinging freely, their place in the world secure.

Unlike walking through the streets of London as merely another Englishwoman, she should be noticed and talked about, just as she was whenever she appeared in public in Arabia . . . glanced at covertly and in amazement by admiring Arabic women through the slits which showed only their eyes, or stared at in anger by the men because of her Paris outfits and because she dared to reveal her face and the shape of her body and look them confidently in the eye. Yes! That's where she should be . . . in Arabia where she was able to be herself, and not a product of a society whose young men had rejected her.

She'd been back for three weeks, yet she couldn't get London's stench out of her nose. The city streets were piled high with rotting brown mounds of reeking horse dung around which unwashed people stepped with caution, its air laden with the fumes of coal fires and chimney smoke and soot and fog and the cloying stench of braziers burning coke to keep night watchmen warm or to enable hot chestnut sellers to ply their trade.

This was the London in which she'd spent much of her young adulthood, but since those days, the capital of Great Britain had become even more pestilential, as though Hell itself had opened its gates in London and emitted a sudden effluvium of fug from motorcar and omnibus exhausts. All the combined reek of coal and coke and dung couldn't begin to equate to the choking pall of filth which hung at head-height as these new motorized vehicles belched their thick black smoke into pedestrian's eyes and mouths. Blake's green and pleasant land may exist beyond the borders of its capital city, but London was more Dante's vision of Hell.

Hugh, her father, grasped her arm, and with his free hand, burrowed inside his cape to take some coins out of his purse to pay the driver.

"No need, m'lord. I've already been paid by the Royal Society. Thank you, m'lord, and I might I say, ma'am, that it's been a privilege to have met you," the cabbie said, and whipped the flanks of his horses which trotted off into the night, their iron shoes clattering over the cobblestones. Gertrude Bell looked at the carriage in astonishment. She hadn't said a word to the cabbie since he'd picked her up at the hotel, yet he seemed to know about her. She immediately knew what was going through her father's mind, when he whispered, "You're something of a celebrity, dearest. Everybody's talking about your exploits."

Alone in the crowded London evening, Hugh put his arm around his marvellous daughter and whispered into her ear, "Look at the sign."

She glanced towards the entrance foyer, and saw a billboard close to the street railings announcing the evening's entertainment

Involuntarily, Gertrude smiled. She was being recognised and rewarded for something which she had done merely because of

> *Their Excellencies,*
>
> *the Governors*
>
> *and Hon. Members of the Committee*
>
> *of the*
>
> *Royal Geographical Society of Great Britain and Her Empire*
>
> *proudly announce the granting of their prestigious Gold Medal*
>
> *to*
>
> *Miss Gertrude Bell.*
>
> *Society Members Only. The public will not be admitted.*

her love for Arabia, for its archaeology and history, its isolation from the rest of the world, but especially for the ancient culture of the people. It was a great honour, but she wondered whether the Society would have awarded the Gold Medal had they known her real intention was not to explain Arabia as it was, but to change it to what it should be.

She drew closer to her father, and whispered into his ear, "It appears as if I'm a celebrity, father. This is all a bit strange."

"You deserve being celebrated, my darling girl," he said as they began to climb the steps. And as if to reassure her, he said, "they've all read your books. They know you were imprisoned by that bounder Rashid. We all know how hard it must have been for you, a woman, in a place like Arabia. They know . . ."

"Do they, father? I wonder . . ."

She thought back to her narrow escape just the previous year. She'd been isolated, terrified, threatened and for the first time in her life. Her will and resolve had nearly broken. Only when she herself had threatened that the British would send an army of a million men to rescue her had they begun to listen, as well as giving the Emir's uncle her pair of Zeiss binoculars and a purse of gold.

Suddenly, as if on cue, the entire Board of Management of the Royal Geographical Society emerged to stand like a phalanx in the dusk and formed a line of honor in the entryway. They were enshrouded by the warm yellow light which flooded out the hallway, yet Gertrude could clearly see their faces. Each man was dressed in top hat, white silk scarf and tails, and looked very elegant. She immediately recognised the president, the Earl Curzon of Kedleston. Beside him stood Colonel Sir Thomas Holdich and to his left Sir Francis Younghusband.

Lord Curzon opened his arms in an embrace as Gertrude and her father walked through the gates and towards the entryway.

"My dear Gertrude. My dear girl. I can't tell you how wonderful this is for all of us. It's about time we recognised a woman. This is one of the proudest moments of my life."

"Now George," she said, chiding him gently, "I rely upon you to ensure this doesn't all to go my head. I only did a bit of archaeology and exploration, nothing like your achievements."

She embraced him, kissing him on both cheeks. The others bowed in mock reverence, as though she were royalty, and shook her hand as Lord Curzon introduced them in turn. Hugh basked in the esteem these brave men showed towards his daughter as Curzon introduced him to the Committee of Management. As he shook each man's hand, he wondered how he, a simple industrialist, could have given birth to a girl as brilliant, adventurous, and extraordinary as his Gertrude.

They escorted her through the tiled vestibule of the Society with its red carpet, velvet curtains, and green leather furniture and into the large meeting hall, built like a tiered university lecture theatre, as imposing and awesome as any Greek amphitheatre of the ancient world.

As they walked in, five hundred members of the Society stood as one, and began their applause. The sudden rush of adulation made her breathless in a tide of apprehension and delight. Should she wave? Should she acknowledge their applause? Should she turn and bow?

Instead, she continued to walk in procession to the front of the lecture hall and out of the corner of her eye, she saw her father being shown to a reserved chair in the front row. She followed Lord Curzon and the others and sat in the centre of the raised dais in front of the lecture theatre. To be so honored by the Society was an explorer's greatest accolade, and her presence in this room made her feel as though she was on hallowed ground. In the place she now occupied had stood some of the world's greatest explorers, men such as Colonel Godwin-Austen, Sir Douglas Mawson, Commander Scott and the redoubtable Dr. David Livingstone. And now Gertrude Bell was to take her place before the assembly of the members of the Royal Society and receive the highest tribute which it could offer.

Lord Curzon banged his gravel on the oak desk and called for order. The members stopped their clapping and resumed their seats. Gertrude glanced at her father, and saw him trying to suppress his beaming smile.

"Gallant Lords, and most valiant members of the Royal Geographical Society. Tonight marks the beginning of a new era. Just over two decades ago, in 1892, Miss Isabella Bishop was elected as the first ever woman member of our Society. We have all read the remarkable exploits of Miss Alexandrine Tinné, the lady from Holland who first crossed the Sahara Desert in 1869. And who can forget Lady Stanhope who left the shores of England in 1810 to explore the unknown Middle East, never to return to her native land.

"But tonight's recipient of the Society's Gold Medal, Miss Gertrude Bell, is altogether of a different ilk. Indeed, it would not be an exaggeration to say that she stands proudly in a different league to all and any of the remarkable women who have gone before her. For unlike these other women, who were romantics and untutored in the ways of exploration, Miss Bell has defined her own category. The other women who indulged in some form of exploration, or were dabblers in adventure, had they been men, might have been called dilettantes, well-meaning amateurs setting out for their own vicarious pleasures. But not Miss Bell. Indeed, Miss Bell has crafted the mold for women for all time to come. She has broken barriers once thought impassable. She has crossed borders once thought impenetrable. She has set a standard to which other women, and indeed men, must now aspire."

Gertrude couldn't help herself, but looked up at George Curzon in bewilderment. Was he talking about her? Were these words about a woman who considered her own achievements as merely advancing knowledge of Arabia, and not much more? Were her achievements so vastly different to those of many of the men in this room? Would George, a most famous and celebrated politician and explorer himself, speak in this way about a male member of the Society? And if not, were her achievements of greater quantum merely because she was a woman?

Lord Curzon continued to define and expound upon Gertrude's travels through Mesopotamia, her mapping and discovery of archaeological sites, the way in which she had created a demographic and cultural compendium of information about the previously unknown tribes of desert Arabs between the Tigris and the Euphrates in Mesopotamia, the dangers she'd faced, her recent imprisonment by an Arab bounder, and the fact that she had earned the unique title of Daughter of the Desert from patristic Arab chieftains and tribal leaders.

But Curzon didn't merely outline her exploratory skills; he reminded them that she had enjoyed an outstanding academic career at Oxford University, that she had written the most brilliant and well-received books about her travels, which had the reviewer for *The Times* waxing emotionally about her literary skills. He also told the members how she'd given vital intelligence to the British government about how England could benefit in Arabia from the downfall of the Ottoman Empire, a crumbling nepotistic and diseased empire which was on the verge of collapse.

Curzon even conspired to talk about Gertrude's mountaineering adventures and there was a further round of applause when he told the audience she'd taken up the challenge published in *The Times* and that previously unconquered peaks and passes in the Swiss Alps had been named after her.

And he finished with a particularly generous rhetorical flourish, when he said, "Gentlemen, had I been speaking of one of our sex, I am in no doubt that you would rise to you feet and carry this brave member shoulder-high into the dining room. But I speak not of a man, but of a woman . . . a very attractive woman . . . a woman of great intellect whose first class degree in history from Oxford university was earned in a mere two years, the first time such a feat has ever been accomplished.

"My lords, Honored Members, and Gentlemen, I have the utmost pleasure and great privilege of presenting the Gold Medal of the Royal Geographical Society to Miss Gertrude Lowthian Bell."

The applause resumed, this time with a thunderous stamping of feet. Everyone had known Gertrude Bell as a woman of splendid achievement, but none, other than her father and her friend George Curzon, knew of the extent of her extraordinary life. At the age of forty-six, she had achieved what most men could only have achieved in a dozen lifetimes.

She stood to receive the Gold Medal, proffered by Lord Curzon, who had arranged for it to be ribboned so he wouldn't embarrass her by having to pin it onto the bodice of her gown. She wore it as she walked the few steps to the lectern, and waited for the deafening applause to die down. She knew some of the faces in the crowd personally, others she recognised from engravings in *The Times*. She wondered how many would be invited to the special dinner in her honor that night.

Few had met her personally, and the men in the audience were surprised by her appearance. For some reason, many had expected a portly matron, all tweeds and fox furs, yet before them stood a tall, thin, ram-rod straight, superbly elegant middle-aged lady, dressed in the most stylish of fashions, with luminous skin, a shock of red hair piled high on her head, and the greenest and most innocent eyes which somehow cut through to a man's soul.

Had they not been seated in the Royal Geographical Society, they could have been cheering the appearance of a famous actress walking on stage in Shaftesbury Avenue.

Gertrude cleared her throat, and the audience quietened to hear what she was about to say.

"My Lord Curzon," she began, her voice clear though deep from her constant cigarette smoking, "Members of the Executive Committee of the Royal Geographical Society, my Lords and Gentlemen. I would much preferred to have begun my address in reply, 'Ladies and Gentlemen', but there are no ladies present tonight, save myself," she said. The audience roared in appreciation.

"Arabia is a land of great mystery. Its limitless deserts, its shifting sands, its ancient people, its immense antiquity defining mankind's ascent from primitive farmer subsisting in the marshes between the Tigris and the Euphrates to today's nomadic warriors, are all virtually unknown to us. We in England, this blessed land of grass and trees and orchards, can have no conception of a land so barren that a refreshing cup of water could be two hundred miles distant. And yet, Gentlemen, it is a land of almost unimaginable beauty and potency. Let me tell you a little something about my Arabia . . ."

~

Rounton Grange, North Yorkshire, Two Weeks Later

She was happy at Rounton Grange. It was a place of serenity and certainty, the anchor which secured her in time and in place. She enjoyed its link with the indolent world of her childhood, she loved roaming in the iconic English countryside of Yorkshire's North Riding, she adored the certainty and timelessness of the gently undulating hills and meadows which in the spring were dizzying with the spray of color . . . yellow buttercups in the meadows, bluebells in the forests, tulips and daisies and marigolds and the emerald green of the grasses of the fields, and wherever she walked in her childhood, there seemed to be pink and white blossoms of fruit trees and berry bushes.

To recover from the exhaustion of her years traveling throughout Arabia, negotiating with potentates all over the Middle East, traveling to the remotest parts of Mesopotamia and living in places where only Muslim women were allowed, Gertrude spent the days after her presentation by the Royal Geographical Society in recuperation. Because the weather was particularly cold and miserable, an altogether horrid June, she spent much of her time indoors. She read Mr. Joyce's rather unseemly book called *A Portrait of the Artist as a Young Man*. She read *The Times* from back to front, she wandered over the hills and called in to see those people whom she'd known when she was a child on her father's estate.

She wrote long and detailed letters to the First Lord of the Admiralty concerning her views on the necessity for English battle fleets to be present in the Gulf of Persia. She wrote to diplomats and friends in the Lords and Commons about the great danger to English interests should the political situation deteriorate. She wrote to friends in Cairo and Alexandria and Bucharest, to diplomats and ambassadors and scholars and school friends. When she was not walking or riding, wrapped up against the cold, she was never without a book or a pen and paper in her hands.

An observer might have said this was a middle-aged spinster, a woman of high birth from a family of position and wealth, filling in her days because she had failed to find a husband all those years ago when other young women were on the marriage market at coming out balls and galas. Some might have blamed her intellect and the universality of her knowledge for the fact that she was husband and childless in her mid-40's. Some, still, might have considered her life to be that of a Bohemian, utterly un-English, racing hither and thither around the world of the fuzzy wuzzies and doing heaven knows what in the tents of Arabs.

For Gertrude, the only things which mattered to her these days were the brilliance, bravery, and knowledge of those in whom she devoted her friendships, and by far the vast majority of these were men. Though she enjoyed being back in England, in the forefront of her mind Gertrude Bell yearned to be in the desert. She ached for the vistas, the eternity, the mystery of the tribal kingdoms. Even after a mere few days away from the desert, she began to need it again, as though it was some medicine on which her life depended, the nectar which nourished her body.

There was so much to do over there, so much to see and experience and explore, so much for her to change. Deep within her, she felt an irrepressible obligation to be the instrument by which Arabia entered the twentieth century, and enabled its women to be released from their servitude. Just as William Wilberforce a century before her had freed black slaves from Africa, so she knew her mission in life was to free Arabia from its tribal primitiveness and unite the people behind a great national leader.

So many reasons to return. There was archaeology which she was desperate to commence before some German or American adventurers uncovered ruins which should, by rights, be hers to discover. Then there was her political work on behalf of England, the importance of which only she seemed to be able to fully comprehend. Certainly there were talented men in the British Foreign Service, but only she thought out the problems of the area from both sides and attempted to come to an accommodation which worked in the interests of all parties. This had led to the tribal leaders trusting her more than any other English diplomat or viceroy.

But she also wanted to get back for a particularly pressing and personal reason. Always in the back of her mind was Mr. Thomas Lawrence, the young, fair-haired, blue-eyed Oxford man who had turned up in her life one day quite unexpectedly, and who had fascinated her. Not in a sexual way, of course, for women didn't attract him and she wasn't in the least bit interested in any physicality with the young man, but there was something about Mr. Lawrence, something which the others, who were busy ridiculing him for his short stature, his limp, his effeminacy, his garish dress sense, simply hadn't seen. She had great hopes for Mr. Lawrence. Of all the Englishmen who had come within her circle, those who came out from the Foreign Office or the Indian Office to Egypt or Palestine or Mesopotamia, only Mr. Lawrence had impressed her as being totally at one with Arabia. He was a very interesting young man, passionate for the tribes and utterly desirous of seducing them away from the Ottoman Turks. Yes, she thought, Mr. Lawrence was a man of Arabia, and she had an inkling that he needed her guidance, or he would be led astray. She even toyed with the idea that he might be the catalyst for her great adventure, the agency through which she might accomplish the changes she knew must happen if Arabia was to succeed.

Her thoughts were interrupted by her father who entered the dining room in order to eat breakfast. Since returning to Rounton, Gertrude had made it a habit of deliberately waiting for him to rise in the morning before she ate her own breakfast, even if it meant going horse-riding for an hour or two in the early morning. She knew how much he liked to begin his day by eating with her, especially before her stepmother and her sister and brother rose. Sometimes it was difficult to wait, for she had a ravenous appetite, and the smells which came from the salvers heating on the buffet were always delicious. Smells of kipper and kedgeree and lambs fries and bacon and eggs and porridge. But she forced herself to wait until her father was seated before she put on her napkin.

"Morning, Gertrude, my dear," he said as he paced into the room and kissed her fondly on the cheek. He was still a handsome man, though the years had aged him since she'd last been home. They had always been close and loving, she and Hugh.

"Morning father," she responded, and stood to join him at the buffet.

They ate and talked about what the day held, before the butler came into the room carrying two copies of *The Times* on a silver tray, one for each of them.

It only took a moment of reading before, as one, they both said, "Good God!"

"Sarajevo?" asked her father.

"It's the capital of Serbia," she said, still furiously reading about the assassination in the middle of Europe.

"Archduke Ferdinand?" he asked. "Isn't he next in line to the Austrian throne?"

"He became heir because of the death of the real Crown Prince, Rudolph . . . well, he was mad as a meat axe and shot himself actually, along with his sixteen year old mistress . . . but that was years and years ago. The next in line was the old Archduke, Carl Ludwig, but he died a few years after Rudolph. That put Franz Ferdinand in line for the throne, and a less likely heir you'll never meet."

"You sound as if you've met him."

"I have," she said. "Many years ago when I was staying in Berlin with Mary and Frank Lascelles during Frank's ambassadorship over there. The Archduke—everyone had to call him that, nobody was allowed to call him Franz Ferdinand—attended one of the embassy balls. Even though was he was very stuffy and middle-European, all starch and clicking heels, he impressed me as a reformist and wanted to modernise the Hapsburg throne, even though he held a passionate hatred of the Serbs. He was keen to reorganise the Austro-Hungarian Empire from a dual monarchy into a triple monarchy, giving the Slavs an equal voice in the empire, but the Serb nationalists hated the idea of having the same footing as the Magyars and the Germans. They formed this awful group of terrorist and assassins called the Black Hand, and Lord only knows whether they're behind this outrage."

She continued reading the story to delve deeper into the details, not realizing that Hugh was marvelling at her knowledge of politics. He had steeped himself in world events, but he felt like a dullard compared to Gertrude. She seemed to know the minutest details about everything.

When she came to the end of the newspaper article, she looked up at her father and said, "obviously I feel sorry about this assassination, but I have to be honest and admit that I didn't take to him at all. He was arrogant and silly and brooding when

I met him, and all night, he acted like a spoilt child. He was so demanding and vain with neither elegance nor charm and he has no social skills whatsoever."

Hugh looked at his daughter in astonishment. How on Earth had he been graced with a daughter who was so knowledgeable, so worldly, so exquisitely sensible, and such a consummately brave person? In comparison, and despite his wealth and position, he felt provincial.

"Well," he said, "unfortunately, like his late brother and father, he's no more. Shot in a motor carriage. What's the world coming to?"

But his daughter failed to answer. Instead she was again reading the article carefully, but this time between the lines of the newspaper's report.

"Gertrude . . .?"

Still she failed to respond.

"What's wrong?" he asked.

She put down her paper. There was a look of deep concern on her face.

"What is it, my dear?"

"On reflection, I'm afraid this could turn out to be a lot worse than the newspapers are making out."

"For England, you mean?"

She nodded.

Her father smiled. "Surely not. This incident occurred in the middle of Europe. On the border of Russia. Too far away from us in this part of the world to be of any concern, surely!"

Gertrude shook her head. "I'm afraid I have to disagree with you, father. Now I think about it, this could affect France and Russia and England very badly. Indeed, this could be just the excuse Austria-Hungary has been looking for. No doubt there'll be a strong move to crush dissent in Serbia—that'll involve Russia, which has borders very close, but the politics are very complicated. Germany will most certainly want to become involved on Austria-Hungary's side. With Germany involved,

France will want to join in the fray as revenge for the humiliation of the Franco-Prussian armistice agreement in Versailles, and with France and Russia involved, and the Triple Alliance in force, England will be dragged kicking and screaming into the fray, and will probably have to mobilise. And this is just the excuse Turkey needs to win back its empire. The Young Turks who have the ear of the Sultan won't want to stay out of the action. They'll insist that Turkey joins with Germany because these Young Turks want to re-establish the supremacy of the Ottoman Empire and quash British advances . . ."

Her father looked at her in amazement. "Are you quite mad? You're talking about the whole world getting involved because of some minor assassination in some marginal part of the East of some minor princeling of whom nobody's really heard. I'm sure it's all a storm in a teacup, and it'll be over in a week. These middle Europeans are always assassinating each other. And why on Earth do you think Turkey will become involved? The Ottomans are on the other side of the world. This has nothing to do with them. Do you really think half of Europe will go to war because some character out of a Gilbert and Sullivan operetta goes and gets himself shot?"

She looked at him, and shrugged her shoulders, almost in apology. "What's that expression, father, 'large oak trees out of tiny acorns do grow'. Half the people who run half the countries of Europe are itching for war. The Kaiser wants to show who's boss, the French want to give the Germans a bloody nose, everyone knows that the Ottomans are on their last legs and Young Turks won't stay in their barracks much longer. They'll have some kind of revolution, and to avoid it the government in Constantinople will rattle its sabres because the Balkans are on their northern borders. And of course, the poor Tsar is so overwhelmed by this hideous priest, Rasputin, that he's allowing the country to go to rack and ruin . . . the serfs are up in arms and there's been gunshots heard in St. Petersburg and Moscow. And after what Karl Marx and his friend Friedrich Engels have written in their manifesto for the Communist League about revolution, and the Russians' hatred of the Tsar . . . its more than likely that Russia will explode.

"I tell you, father, that in Europe today, things are so agitated that the assassination of Franz Ferdinand will be like throwing a lighted match into a barrel of gunpowder."

Hugh shook his head. "I pray to God you're wrong. But if you're right, I pray to God that Mr. Asquith is wise enough to keep out of it."

"I'm afraid he might not be able to. We have treaties, you see, and we're committed to going to the aid of countries like Belgium if they're attacked. We might be forced to enter the fray, if one arises."

"Belgium? Good God, surely you don't really believe that England will go to war to defend Belgium? Didn't we learn enough from Waterloo?"

He sighed deeply, and continued to eat his breakfast.

FIVE

Whitehall, London, Geographical Section,
General Staff Headquarters, 1914

There was a bit more hustle and bustle, a bit more concern on peoples' faces, but aside from these minor differences, there was little else which had changed to inform the British public that they were now in a state of war with the Austro-Hungarian Empire. Judging by the behaviour of the citizens of London, Great Britain could just have easily been involved in a cricket match as in a war. But closer to the buildings from which the war effort was organised the signs of war were more obvious. Men dressed in their khaki uniforms stood guard, sailors in their dress whites and the occasional army nurse wrapped in her red cape walked hurriedly and urgently. Military flags, vehicles, and motorcycle couriers weaved in and out of traffic with an earnestness normally reserved for motorcab drivers and eager young swains on their way to a weekend in the countryside.

But the reality of war was more prominent the closer citizens came to the military headquarters building in Whitehall, the Admiralty, and the roads occupied by the residencies of the Prime minister and the chancellor of the exchequer.

Certainly there were posters on almost every street corner portraying the stern and uncompromising face of Lord Kitchener pointing at the consciences of young men and reminding those who hadn't yet enlisted that their country needed them, and the night-time newspaper vendors shouted out the headlines from *The Star*, *The Evening News*, and *The Evening Standard*, announcing the most recent details of the dastardly doings of the Kaiser. But aside from that, London was London. There was no perceptible air of tension, no tortured look on the faces of passers-by, no torment in people's attitudes, and no appreciable deviation from the way in which Londoners went about their business yesterday, last month and last year.

The cabs continued to ply their trade, motor cars and omnibuses were increasingly ubiquitous and fume-laden, the theatres continued to disgorge their silken patrons onto the streets at the end of a performance, diners still flocked to the hotels and restaurants of the nation's capital, prostitutes in absurd black lacquer hats adorned with garishly colored paper flowers still stood in the demi-lit recesses of street corners. The costermongers and barrow boys plied their trade from side-roads, coke braziers cooked chestnuts, and everybody went about their business.

Almost everybody. Because for the particularly observant witness there were additional military personnel standing rigidly at attention on the pavements, bayoneted rifles in their hands, carefully scrutinising those who entered the Headquarters building. Groups of middle and upper-class women dressed in long woollen coats and hats to protect themselves from the cold of the streets gathered at intersections and on corners with collection boxes, chiding passers-by who failed to donate to the war effort. The windows of some of the larger department stores no longer carried their normal displays of dresses or cigarettes or cigars or hats and gloves, but had donated some of the space to dummies dressed in military uniforms with patriotic messages like, *Support our gallant fighting lads,* and *Let's all fight for King and Country.*

As she stepped down from the taxicab which had fought the pedestrians all the way from St. Pancras railway station to Whitehall, Gertrude Bell was more aware than most people of the changes which had taken place in the three months since she'd last been shopping in London. Perhaps because she was more knowledgeable of the realities of the rapidly-spreading European war, or perhaps because she wasn't living on a daily basis in London, she found the subtle differences quite surprising and worrying. Although she had been born a decade after the hideous Crimean War which had dragged the Ottoman Empire into a confrontation with Russia, she knew the horrors of conflict better than most and wasn't blinded by the nationalistic zeal spreading through Great Britain. She understood all too well that a Londoner's fervent patriotism became a Cardiff boy's hideous death on a foreign battleground.

The war in the middle of the previous century should have warned all politicians of the dangers of confrontation. Because of the skirmish in the Crimea, England had gone to war against the Russians and Austria-Hungary had postured and posed. It could have blown up into a global confrontation, though, mercifully, because Russia was so backward and weak, it had managed to remain a localised incident in the far-flung recesses of Europe. But now the same nations were doing the same things fifty years on, and she wondered where it would all end.

And as she saw military men passing her on the street, and talking and laughing animatedly, she shuddered when she remembered the evil of the Boer War which had ended only twelve years earlier, and which had claimed so many British lives because of the damned intransigence of the stiff-necked Boers in the Orange Free State and the Transvaal.

Wars! They were portrayed as such glorious enterprises, yet while the generals and admirals sat in their luxurious offices dictating the disposition of forces as thought they were playing some kind of universal chess game, it was flesh and blood men— young men—fathers and sons and brothers—who died in agony or who lay mortally injured on the front line, wounds festering in the blistering sun, waiting for the relief of a sip of water before their life ebbed away.

She forced herself to put these thoughts out of her mind as she paid the cabbie, and walked towards the entrance of the General Staff Headquarters. It was a white marble building, stark and unforgiving in the late-Georgian, early-Victorian mold of London's official edifices. Like the empire, it was grand and huge and glorious and sturdy and eternal. And like the empire, those inside it would defend Great Britain's interests against all-comers, regardless of how many men had to die in order to do so.

The soldier on guard duty saluted as she pushed her way through the heavy brass doors. She walked across the carpeted vestibule to the reception desk, where another solider was seated. He was reading some sort of list, and continued to read, head bowed in ignorance of her presence as she stood there, waiting for some acknowledgement from him that she existed.

After an annoying time, she said, "What's your name?"

The soldier looked up, and frowned. Officers and gentlemen walked straight in to the building and went to their designated places of business. Tradesmen and journeyman and messengers came to his desk, and he had no compunction but to keep them waiting. He hadn't realized a lady was standing there.

"What? Beg yer pardon?" he said.

She gave him a withering look, and said softly, "I see from your insignia that you're a Lance Corporal in an engineering regiment, so I assume you have the capacity to understand the King's English. I asked for your name. In my report to the Prime minister, I shall make special mention of your penchant for reading instead of examining the credentials of everybody who enters such an important building as this. Your name please, Corporal."

The Sapper immediately stood at attention and saluted. "Who did you want to see Madam?"

"Whom! The expression is 'Whom did you wish to see'. I'm here because I have a ten o'clock appointment with Lieutenant General Dowling. It's now five minutes to ten. Kindly inform the general that Miss Gertrude Bell is waiting to see him. And King's Regulations say nothing about saluting a civilian."

"Yes ma'am, certainly ma'am," he said. He called over a private and instructed him to escort the lady up to General Dowling's office.

But she didn't move. She stood there, staring at the Sapper.

"Is there something else, ma'am?"

"Do you know me?"

"No ma'am."

"Yet you would allow a complete stranger to enter the most important building in London where top secret plans for the war effort are being drawn up. And you haven't even asked me for any identification."

The Sapper flushed and coughed in embarrassment. "Might I have you name please, ma'am."

"Oh don't be so ridiculous," Gertrude snapped as she turned and walked towards the stairs, intent on making a serious complaint about security to General Dowling.

It was a long climb up the central flight of stairs, then around into the Western Wing, then around the mezzanine balcony before climbing another flight which brought her to the floor on which was housed the General Staff, England's most senior military men. The corridors were alive with men in uniform walking hastily from room to room carrying sheafs of papers and reports. There were men huddling in groups across the landing, talking urgently. An imperative atmosphere of quiet and restrained activity infused the air.

A military officer in dress uniform was stationed, like some Cerberus or Chiron, at the entryway to the Senior Officer's floor, ready to ferry some poor hapless individual into a darker realm. The officer was a young and very attractive Second Lieutenant and was sitting at a desk which had a telephone placed centrally. He was writing a report, but snapped to attention when the private and Gertrude arrived. He'd obviously been informed by the guard in the lobby that some harridan was on her way up.

"Miss Bell?" he asked, "How very nice to meet you. General Dowling is expecting you, ma'am. Please follow me. That's all, Private," he said.

She followed the younger man down the corridor, and couldn't help but glance into the walnut panelled offices of the senior military planners. Each office was decorated in precisely the same way—maps on the wall, the pink swathes of British Empire dotted with pins and small flags, huge round globes of the world, all fixed on Europe, papers sprawling across desks which pointed to late night discussions—it was an organised bedlam of activity and serious intent.

They turned to the left into another corridor, and the atmosphere suddenly changed from that of a practical factory floor into a deeper, calmer, and somehow more purposeful environment. Instead of walking along an inexpensive floor covering, she suddenly found herself walking on a thick blood-red carpet. Even the walls had changed and were festooned with paintings of former Chiefs of the General Staff, of Admirals of the Fleet, and Generals of the Army, all resplendent in their uniforms and ribbons and decorations. Halfway down the corridor, the young officer stopped, and showed her into an anteroom. It was a place where people waited while the great General Dowling finished one conference and readied himself for his next. The room was utilitarian in its furnishings. There was a round mahogany table on which were copies of *The Times*, *Tatler*, and *Country Life*, and leather chairs around the walls. It smelled of tobacco, and even though Gertrude was a heavy cigarette smoker, she couldn't abide the cloying stench which lingered long after a cigar had been smoked.

Discomforted, and still unsure why the foreign secretary had asked her to meet with General Dowling this morning, when the war against the Kaiser had been declared three months earlier in July, she sat, picked up a copy of *The Times*, and began reading about the success of the 5th Cavalry Division of the British Expeditionary Force in a battle at some Godforsaken place in Belgium called Mons.

She was three paragraphs into the news article, when someone entered the room, and a high-pitched and somewhat quavering voice she knew from the past said, "Good God. Gertie! What are you doing here?"

Gertrude couldn't help but beam a smile of delight when she saw him. She hadn't set eyes on him in years, yet he didn't seem to have aged a bit. As he walked over, he bent down to where she was seated and kissed her on both cheeks. He sat beside her, and held her hand, stroking it and delighting in their reunion, equally pleased they'd found each other again. He was such a precious boy!

"My dear Thomas. How unexpected and glorious to see you here, dear boy. Never mind about me! What are you doing here? I haven't seen you since we dangled feet in the rivers of Babylon."

"Gertie, I heard just this morning that some very important person was coming in to see the boss, but I never imagined you would be the Grand Pooh Bah. They said it was some expert on Arabia, and I couldn't think for the life of me who it could be. And it's you. Oh, this is just too wonderful. I feel like it's my birthday. But what are you doing here? Why are you seeing the top brass? Have you met General Dowling before? He's pretty fearsome, so I understand, not that a lowly officer like me would even be noticed by one such as him. And then I received a summons from on high, and here you are."

"And here we are. Oh, Thomas," she said, grasping his hand and holding it, "I've thought so often about seeing you again. I've missed you, dear boy. I've really missed you very much indeed."

She hadn't answered his questions. Deliberately. He was always full of questions, and the best way to handle his curiosity was to ignore the questions he asked initially. When he re-asked a question, it meant that it was important, and that was one she would answer.

She breathed deeply, and smelled the lavender and pomade he put in his hair. She remembered the scent from when she'd first met Mr. Lawrence in Arabia. Even then, despite the strangeness of their first meeting, she'd been attracted to his easy-going way, his lack of pretension, his keen sense of the wonders of the desert, and his passion for Arabic history.

They continued to hold hands and speak animatedly. It was so very good to see him again. She'd corresponded with him since their first meeting in the desert, and had enjoyed his honesty, his valour, and his knowledge. Under her guidance and advice, he'd educated himself about the politics of the Middle East, and was now quite familiar with both its landscape and its peoples. But in the last year, with all the confusion and turmoil in the world, they'd lost touch. She was thrilled they were together again.

"So what are you doing in uniform? Second Lieutenant, isn't it?"

"Temporary Second Lieutenant-Interpreter, to be precise. I'm here doing maps, and stuff. There's great concern that a fresh front will open up should Turkey enter the war . . ."

"Should? I would have thought it was a case of when rather than should. Constantinople is bound to want to take advantage of the British and French distraction in their involvement in Europe."

"Do you think so?" he asked. "We're all rather hoping that Turkey will have enough sense to keep out of it. After all, aside from the Berlin to Baghdad railway, there's precious little trade between Germany and Constantinople. Not like Britain and France who do a lot of business with the Turks. Surely they'll realize on which side of the bread there's butter?"

"Don't you believe it, dear boy. The Turkish War Minister, Enver Pasha is just itching for a reason to involve his government. He sees it as his great opportunity to revive the fortunes of the Ottomans. Oh, there's opposition to him in his government, people who think Turkey should stay out of the engagement, but I'll bet they'll be overruled because of pressure from the Young Turks in the army, and their involvement in this war will begin in the Black Sea. You mark my words. They've let the German Navy in there, and that's the underbelly of Russia, and Turkey hates Russia with a vengeance. You'll see. They'll be shelling Odessa and Sevastopol before the years out."

Before he could respond, the door of General Dowling's office suddenly opened, and a group of uniformed military men walked out talking urgently to each other. The general appeared framed in the doorway, and walked over to where they were sitting. Lieutenant Lawrence immediately stood and saluted, a gesture returned by a curt nod from the general. Then he turned to Gertrude, and shook her hand.

"My dear Miss Bell. I've heard so much about you."

He turned, and acknowledged Lawrence's presence once more with a curt nod. They followed him into his office. The air below the ceiling was tinged blue with the cigarette smoke from the previous meeting. There was almost no oxygen in the room.

"It was very good of you to travel down to London to see us. Not too arduous a journey, I hope," the general said. He was a portly man, tall but with a middle-aged spread which made the buttons of his drab brown uniform strain to hold in his girth. Another door suddenly opened, and a batman walked in with a silver tray holding cups, a teapot, another pot for hot water, a dish with lemons, a jug of milk, and the ubiquitous tin of Fortnum and Mason's mixed assortment biscuits. Thomas Lawrence eyed the large chocolate biscuit in the middle of the tin, and wondered whether he had the courage to take it before the others.

While the batman was setting it down on the buffet, the general continued, "I've asked Lieutenant Lawrence to join us, because he's working on maps of the Middle East. The point is, Miss Bell, and this must remain top secret, our military advisors believe that Turkey will almost certainly enter the war in the very near future, and we have to protect British interests in Egypt, in the Suez Canal, and elsewhere. As I'm sure you'd be the first to appreciate, we have to protect our route to India. For that, we have to have intimate knowledge of how the local Arabs will react when we call on them. Will they side with the Turks, or will they side with us?"

She began to speak, but the general hadn't finished. "I'm aware you've been flooding the Foreign Office with letters and reports about what we should be doing, so we all thought it was time for you to come in and meet with us."

She saw her report on his desk, a document she'd written to the Director of Military Operations in Cairo, about how Great Britain should respond in order to protect its Suez route to India and its developing oil interests in the Persian Gulf. Both of these would be under threat if Turkey and Germany joined forces. Its appearance on General Dowling's desk meant that the Director in Cairo had passed it on to the British foreign secretary, who in turn must have given it to the War Office.

Her report was based on her extensive travels through the region in the previous few years and outlined what she understood of native attitudes and dispositions in Syria, Egypt, Palestine, and other parts of Arabia. She'd heard that her report had been studied with great interest at the War Office and the Foreign Office, as well as at Military Intelligence in Egypt. Her advice was that the British must motivate and organize the Arabs into a unified army to revolt against their Turkish masters. She'd begged Military Intelligence to let her travel her back to Cairo so she could be on the spot. This, she assumed, was her call to serve.

General Dowling continued, "The foreign secretary himself decided it was about time that we on the General Staff listened to you. You seem to have an expertise in the area. How'd you feel about working with Lawrence here, and drawing up the disposition of the area?"

Surprised by the minimal nature of the request, she composed herself, waited a moment to ensure he'd finished talking, and said, "Frankly, General, much as I admire Mr. Lawrence, I would better serve the interests of the government if I was on the spot. I need to be at Military Headquarters in Cairo, not in London. I have an expert knowledge of the tribes of the deserts. I know their leaders, I know how they think. I can influence them when they're pressured by the Turks to join them in the struggle. You have to understand the Turks are thinking precisely what we're thinking at the moment, and their method of persuasion is handing out *baksheesh* like it was confetti at a wedding. They'll pay a fortune to keep the desert Arab sheikdoms on their side. But if I'm there, I know I can prevail on them to see the importance of fighting for Britain, perhaps even at a lower cost than the Turks. I've been given the greatest compliment of hospitality in their tents by the very people we have to influence to join us. I speak their language, I'm an intimate of their wives and families, they seek my counsel and trust me and call me the Daughter of the Desert . . ."

"But they imprisoned you . . ." interrupted General Dowling.

She looked at him in surprise. "How on Earth did you know that?" she asked.

"We have pretty good intelligence, you know. Apparently you were going to try to see some blighter called ibn Sa'ud, and his mortal enemy ibn Rashid thought you were a spy, and according to reports I've received, locked you up in some town called Hayil."

She nodded.

"Were you in danger?" asked Lawrence, who knew nothing about it.

"I have to admit I was pretty frightened. For the first time in my travels, I honestly didn't think I was going to get out of there alive. The Turks and the British had withdrawn any permission for me to travel to the area because it was so dangerous, and so I was completely on my own. Still, I talked my way out of the situation, and I'm still alive to tell the tale.

"But that's the point, don't you see? I know these people well enough to save my own skin. I've lived with them and understand them. They've spoken to me about an Arab revolt. The King of the Hejaz held a very private meeting with Lord Kitchener last year asking him what Britain would do in Arabia if the desert tribes revolted against the Turks. They're on the cusp of either siding with us, or those who will soon be our enemy. The decision could go either way. The moment is crucial, General, and I can assist in the process of persuading them. There are dozens of tribes, some small, some large, and I know them. They trust me. I'm useless here, but I could be of inestimable valuable over there."

She looked at Dowling, but by his attitude, she knew her words were falling on deaf ears. She became annoyed at his patronizing manner and his supercilious smile.

"Look, General, there are lots of people here in England who can draw maps and make assessments, but I would venture to say that nobody has the experience or knowledge of Arabs that I have. No, General, I need to be in Cairo, or Baghdad, or Damascus to be of real use. I insist that the British government send me out there."

The general shook his head in amazement. "Send a woman to a sector where there are hostilities? Are you insane? There's no possibility whatsoever of that happening. I'm not sending you into the front lines. The area's far too dangerous."

"That's ridiculous. Nurses like Florence Nightingale were in a battle zone in the Crimea. Stop thinking of me as a woman, General, I'm an expert in Arab affairs. You're being negligent in your duties if you don't send me."

Lawrence looked at her in astonishment. Nobody spoke to a general like that. But Dowling merely shook his head, and said softly, "You're not going. Sorry, Miss Bell, but women don't serve at the front."

"I see," she said. "Perhaps if I was to go and speak to the foreign secretary . . ."

"You'll be given the same answer. He and I have spoken about you at some length, and we're both of the opinion that you're of more use, and much safer in England."

Thomas Lawrence unexpectedly spoke, "General, if I may be permitted. I've worked with Miss Bell in Mesopotamia. I've seen her interactions with the desert tribes. She's extraordinary. She speaks Persian and Arabic fluently . . . she's done one of the best translations of Persian poetry ever. She's written wonderful books about her adventures in the desert. She's an explorer, an adventurer, an archaeologist, and a linguist. She's—"

"Lieutenant Lawrence," the general said sternly. "My decisions are not to be questioned, and certainly not by a junior officer. Now, kindly take Miss Bell to your office, and show her what you're doing, so she can assist you."

The general looked at Gertrude, and said simply, "Maps, Miss Bell. That's where you'll be of most use to Great Britain. Maps."

Then he sat down at his desk, and started signing papers. They left the general's office in silence.

"Damn him," she hissed once they were in the corridor. "Pompous arse of a man. I'll go above his head and speak directly to the Prime minister. Don't you see, Thomas, I have to be in

Cairo or Alexandria. I have to get back into the desert to speak to the tribal leaders. There's not a minute to lose."

"Gertie, this war has only just begun. People are saying it won't last beyond Christmas, but my guts tell me that it's going to be long and drawn-out and bloody. If you rush things, it'll just rebound in your face. Look, I know it's frustrating, but stay with me for a while, work with me in Intelligence, and we'll do something useful. And we'll have a pretty good time to boot. I'll take you to the theatre and we'll go to one of the motion pictures? Just wait it out for a bit, and when the generals have made a pig's ear out of their negotiations with the Arabs, you can ride in on a big camel and save the day."

She smiled. They walked along the corridors and down the stairs towards the bowels of the building. But as they descended deeper and deeper, Gertrude wondered whether there would be a day left for her to save.

The room which he occupied was the diametric opposite of the general's suite of offices on the uppermost floor of the Staff Headquarters. Lawrence was stationed at a small rickety wooden desk, one of a dozen such desks which surrounded a massive central table in the basement of the Headquarters building. The room was window-less, airless, and gloomy, even with electric lighting shining in the middle of the day. Yet despite the conditions, it was frantic with activity, all centered around books and old maps and intelligence assessments, mounds of reports, and sheafs of papers.

The huge map table in the center of the room was covered with large rectangles of cloth-backed paper, all glued carefully together to appear joint-less. Gertrude recognized it instantly as the land through which flowed the Tigris and the Euphrates. To the left was the barren Nefud Desert. Northwest was Syria, northeast Persia, and south were the great deserts of Arabia. But what captured her eye were the two great rivers of Arabia, both sourced within a couple of hundred miles of each other in the snowy mountains of Asiatic Turkey. Both of them flowed southwards to the Persian

Gulf, nearly meeting at the place when the ancients of the Abbasid dynasty had built their capital, Baghdad, on the sparkling waters of the River Tigris.

All over the map, from Mosul in the north to Basrah close to the Gulf, were pins and small flags and markers which gave what the cartographers believed were the dispositions of the Arabic tribes and geographical formations such as mountains, rivers and valleys. It took merely one glance to show Gertrude that the mapmakers were hopelessly inaccurate in their demographic data.

Before he could introduce her to the others, she scrutinized the map, and asked of one of the orderlies, "Why is the flag labelled Anazzah on the eastern side of the Tigris and just to the north of Al Amarah?"

The hapless man looked at her in astonishment. Not knowing who she was—she could have been a well-dressed char lady as far as he was concerned—he replied peremptorily, "Because that's where they are."

Others in the room looked up to see the diminutive Lawrence in the company of a tall, fashionably dressed middle-aged lady. But more than being interested in her clothes, they were listening intently to what she was saying.

Gertrude walked over to the map, and said, "That's not where the Anazzeh are to be found. Their traditional land is the western border of the Euphrates. You've placed them close to the territory of the Marsh Arabs."

Now everyone else in the room looked up from their maps and pieces of paper to listen to the incident. One stood, and walked officiously over to the map table.

"I gave him instructions to place it there. They're nomads, madam, and the location on the map is based on latest intelligence from our sources. And who the dickens are you to tell me where to place a flag?"

Gertrude bridled at his arrogance, but decided to restrain herself. "Might I respectfully suggest that your intelligence is inaccurate? The Anazzeh are nowhere near the location you've been given."

"And you'll forgive me, madam, but that really is no concern of yours. Our intelligence is a mere week old, and that's where the Anazzeh live," he said, pointing to the spot near to the Gulf.'

"No it's not. It's totally inaccurate. Just last year, I was in their tents. I lived with them for a week. I befriended the latest wife of their leader Fahad Bey. I tell you, sir, that your position is inaccurate."

"And I tell you, madam, that it's not."

Furious, Gertrude said, "The Anazzeh are Sunni Arabs. You've got them within a day's march of the Marsh Arabs at the confluence of the Tigris and the Euphrates. The Marsh Arabs are Shi'ite. They hate each other, each calling the other apostate, and if they were as close as you've got them now, there would be war, and one of them would be wiped out. You really don't understand the culture or the people, let alone the geography, gentlemen."

She looked carefully at the other flags giving the disposition of the Arab tribes of Mesopotamia.

"These other tribes are hundreds of miles from where they should be. This is just too bad," she said, picking up a long wooden pole, and beginning to shift the positions of the flags.

"Look here, you can't do that. Who the deuce are you? Damn it, Lawrence, did you bring this woman in here? What's she doing? This is a war room."

Lawrence looked uncomfortable, but Gertrude wasn't in any mood to banter. The arrogance of the captain dismissing her intimate knowledge had made her mad. "My God, all of this is grossly incorrect. The whole map will have to be re-drawn. It's woefully wrong. You have desert where there's arable land, mountains where there are plains and you've got flowing rivers which haven't run for a millennium. What idiot constructed this, anyway?"

By now, all the cartographers and intelligence officers had left their desks to defend their work against the assault of the unknown woman and walked towards the central mapping table. As one, they joined their colleague in decrying her arrogance and presumption.

Before Lawrence could jump to her defense, Gertrude looked at all the irritated men gathered before her, and held up her hand for silence.

"Be quiet! All of you! Answer me this . . . has anybody here been to the Arabian desert?" Nobody answered.

"Has anybody been to Baghdad or Mesopotamia at all?" Again silence.

"Has anybody been out of England?"

They all began to argue with her, until one man's voice rose above the others, "We don't have to go there to be able to draw a map. We're not explorers, you know. We're bally intelligence officers, and we rely on our men out there for the information which we piece together. That's how you make maps, in case you hadn't realized it. What the bloody hell gives you the right to just come in here and tell us how to do our work, anyway?"

Lieutenant Lawrence shouted over the hubbub, "Gentlemen, this is Miss Gertrude Bell. Miss Bell has traveled for years through the entire area of the Middle East. She knows the towns, the cities, and the people like she knows the back of her hand. The foreign secretary invited her to speak with General Dowling, and Miss Bell has kindly consented to assist us with mapmaking and intelligence work. Miss Bell was the recipient of this year's Royal Geographical Society's Gold Medal."

Not one of the other officers had heard of Gertrude, and their faces showed they weren't impressed by what he had said.

"Frankly, Lawrence," one of them told him, "I don't give a tuppenny worth of tar who this lady is, or what bally medal she's won. But for her to come in here and start criticizing months of painstaking work is just too . . ."

"Oh don't be so stupid," Gertrude snapped. "When it's finished and printed, this map will be the basis for British troop movements and disposition. Thousands of British service men will be using it to determine lines of communication and for the purposes of military maneuvering. What if they make decisions based on a map which is hopelessly inaccurate? What if they travel fifty miles eastwards to meet up with Sheik Fahad Bey ibn Hadhdhal of the Anazzeh and instead, thanks to your map, they come over a hill and find themselves face to face with the Rwallah or the Juheina or the Harb or the Billi or the Beni Sakhr, any of whom could side with the Turks tomorrow? Where are those tribes on your map, gentlemen? They're not, because you've never even heard of them. Yet between them, they can provide a million fighting men against the Turks if we negotiate the right price. One of our most pressing strategic objectives in the coming engagement is that the Arabs rise up on the side of Great Britain, yet you have no idea who they are, or to whom they're currently loyal, or their current positions. One million men unaccounted for, gentlemen. That's enough to win the coming war in the Middle East and protect British interests, or, if we can't find them, to allow them to join the Turks and inflict upon us the greatest losses ever suffered by the British Army. Yet your intelligence sources haven't deigned to supply you with the details of their existence for your map?

"Now, instead of complaining about my criticism of your months of painstaking and useless work, let's start doing things properly, shall we?"

She forced an alleyway through the cluster of fuming officers, took off her coat, and claimed an empty rickety desk near to the map table. It was going to be a very long couple of months.

~

The Royal City of Jeddah,
Port City of the Kingdom of the Hejaz, July 1914

He read, and then re-read the advisory note from the British Foreign Office about how he should conduct this interview, what the Arabs might require, and the maximum which should be offered. He was glad the person who'd written it, some female called Gertrude Bell, hadn't used the sort of Whitehall diplomatic jibber jabber which was too cautious and ambivalent to state an opinion, and said ridiculously unhelpful things like "on the one hand . . . but then on the other hand . . ."

Instead, her report was precise, focussed, direct, and perceptive, not only giving him the background to the people whom he'd be meeting, but instructing him on their strengths to circumvent and the weaknesses he could play on. He didn't know who she was, but this Bell woman had made his life much easier for a task in which he felt unprepared and unqualified. Negotiations weren't his strong point. He was a man of dedicated action, a man more comfortable leading an army rather than parlaying with kings and princes, but he'd been given the job of delivering news, and deliver it he would.

Dressed in his crisp white dress uniform, beribboned and bemedalled, General of the British Army and unwilling Diplomat Plenipotentiary, Sir Alistair Waverley Booth walked stiffly behind the slow-moving servant of Sharif Hussein bin-Ali of Mecca, the King of the Hejaz. The general's footsteps, which normally echoed off the walls wherever he walked, were today uncharacteristically silent. Whenever he entered a mosque or a palace, he found walking in his stocking feet difficult and unusual.

The building was only an average Arabian palace, unspectacular in design and ordinary in execution compared to other Arabian bastions he'd been in. This one had no more than twenty or thirty rooms, and must have been erected in the seventeenth or eighteenth century by some wealthy merchant. Alternatively, it could have been built more recently by some distance cousin of the Hashemite ruling family, someone who lived in Jeddah because he wasn't of sufficient prestige to build a palace in the holy cities of Mecca or Medina.

Yet like other edifices in this extraordinary part of the world, this palace was a masterpiece of Arabic ingenuity. In the cornices between every ceiling and wall was an inscription in flowing Arabic writing from the Koran. Ceramic tiles and the marble floor kept the rooms cool from the fierce heat of the outside world, and the coolness was enhanced by fountains of playful water in every room. But what most impressed Sir Alistair was the way in which the lattices in the upper parts of all the rooms concealed hidden mezzanine corridors and suspended galleries and spy holes which enabled a thousand curious eyes to see and hear what was happening on the floor below.

As he walked through the rooms to the central part of the palace where Sharif Hussein was waiting, he was impressed by its lightness of weight, as though the entire construction was made of sugar and cream to form a wondrous meringue. It was remarkable that such a large building could seem somehow so flimsy, and yet at the same time portray such solidity.

Booth understood very well why the Sharif Hussein bin-Ali insisted on this meeting in Jeddah. As a Christian, he wasn't allowed to set foot in Mecca, or there'd be a riot. And as a descendant of the Prophet, the custodian of the Ka'aba, Islam's most holy shrine, Hussein could not possibly be seen meeting an infidel on such holy land.

But there were other, altogether more devious reasons for this meeting being held in the port city on the shores of the Red Sea. The Sharif knew better than anybody that Abd al Aziz, the leader of the Sa'ud family of the lands in the eastern part of Arabia, a murderous warlord who was in bed with the Ottoman Turks, had spies everywhere in the eastern kingdom of Hejaz, and this was a conversation which must be kept top secret. The other reason was that Jeddah was one the few places left in the Hejaz kingdom where the fanatical followers of the Wahhabist Islamic sect hadn't yet gained a particularly strong footing.

One room of the palace flowed into another, each decorated in distinctly different color to signify their usage—rose rooms for the women to gather, rooms with dark brown cushions for the men to use after they had eaten, others with blue furnishings and cushions and drapes on the walls for use when the men had returned from a sea voyage and needed to rest before seeing their wives. Each room was a masterpiece of design and sensibility.

The servant ushered Sir Alistair into a room which seemed no different from any previous room and without pausing suddenly stepped to one side, allowing the Englishman to enter unannounced. In the centre of the large room, its gauze curtains fluttering in the gentle breeze which came in from the inner garden courtyard, was a huge divan, on which he saw the ruler of the Hejaz, Sharif Hussein bin-Ali. In traditional Arab manner, he reclined on the couch, reading papers and sucking on the pipe of a huge hookah, water bubbling, and the smoke rising like a cloud beneath the ceiling.

On another couch sat Faisal, third son of the sharif. Sir Alistair was surprised Faisal was permitted in the room. He'd rather expected that he would be greeting by the Sharif's advisors, and at the very least Faisal's elder brother Abdullah. He knew little about Faisal, other than he'd been educated in Constantinople, and was, according to the note written by this Gertrude Bell woman, an intelligent young man.

Sir Alistair stepped forward, removed his plumed helmet and bowed in respect to the king. While still abasing himself, he placed the fingers on his right hand on his forehead, then he kissed them, and then he rested them on his heart in the traditional Arabic greeting.

"Good morning, Sir Alistair. I don't know whether or not you've met my third son, His Highness Prince Faisal? I think you've met my son Abdullah, but not Faisal, is that correct?"

The Englishman nodded and looked at Faisal. The young man, who couldn't have been older than his late twenties, stood and walked over to the representative of Great Britain. Faisal was tall and slender, and hardly looked robust, but when he shook hands, Sir Alistair noted that his grip was firm and masculine. But by the look of him, Sir Alistair thought he could use a couple of boxing lessons. It was almost as though he'd been a strange and sickly child who had somehow come through, but suffered from the effects of youthful malnutrition or disease. He was slightly built and somewhat effeminate looking, but there was an unmistakable inner strength. He looked like an interesting young man, somebody possibly worth cultivating. Bell's advisory had mentioned this Faisal chappie as a person of interest to be noted, but even though he'd read her notes before entering the Palace, Sir Alistair couldn't for the life of him remember whether she'd said he was a force in the family, or just some hanger-on, like so many of the other minor princes and princesses in the Arabian Gilbert and Sullivan dynasties.

"Delighted to meet you, Your Royal Highness," said Booth.

"And to what do we owe the honor of your visit?" Faisal asked.

Sir Alistair had two choices. The first was to ask for a private meeting with the Sharif, thereby insulting Faisal who could be useful to the British government in the future. The other was to include him, and hope he had the sensibility to keep the contents of the meeting in the utmost of secrecy.

"Your Royal Highnesses. I bring you the very warmest greetings from His Majesty's government. The Prime minister has instructed me especially to pass on his personal regards to you and your family."

"And," said the Sharif, "please tell Mr. Asquith that all Arabia and all Muslims wish him a long and contented life with nothing but peace and prosperity."

"I shall pass on your greetings, Majesty. Sirs, I am here to speak to you of a very delicate situation which has recently arisen in Europe, and to ask . . ."

"You speak of the assassination of the crowned prince of the Austro-Hungarian Empire," interrupted Faisal.

Astonished that the news had already reached the desert kingdom, Sir Alistair looked at the younger man. "I do indeed, sir."

"You're surprised that I know of the reason of your call. Don't be, Sir Alistair," continued Faisal. His father was looking at him, smiling with pride and pleasure, and Faisal knew it was because he'd managed to out-fox the fox of Britain.

Faisal continued, "Anybody who is a keen observer of world politics knows the consequences of the assassination of Franz

Ferdinand. This will lead Austria-Hungary to invade traditional Serbian lands. Russia will react adversely, but because of the Triple Entente will be forced to side with France and Great Britain. Germany will be brought into the war, though this will hardly come as a surprise, because the Kaiser has been looking for any excuse. And then all Europe will be at war. Am I correct, Sir Alistair?"

"Indeed you are, Your Highness," said the British emissary. He was motioned to a seat and sat down beside the Sharif. Settling himself, and accepting a cup of coffee from the servant, Sir Alistair continued, "Your assessment of the situation in Europe is very much along the lines which His Majesty's government believes events will happen. But a crucial element of your evaluation is missing . . ."

Again, the younger man interrupted. "The Turkish Empire? The Ottomans? Naturally, I assume we're all in agreement that Constantinople will act in its own interests against the widening interest of Great Britain and France in this area. The Turks will look upon this as an opportunity to re-establish their flagging empire in Egypt and the rest of the Middle East. The desert kingdoms have long been struggling to throw off the shackles of the absentee landlords of the Bosphorus. With Europe distracted in a war, what better time to attack the colonial interests of Britain and France, and side with Germany and Austria-Hungary?"

Sir Alistair sipped his coffee. He'd come here prepared to explain the immensely complex situation to a desert tribal leader, and suddenly he was faced with a sophisticated young man who knew what was happening in the world.

"Your Highness is very astute," he said.

"Perhaps, Sir Alistair, I can be even more astute by foretelling the purpose of your visit. You are here to ensure the Kingdom of the Hejaz joins the Kingdom of Great Britain in any future fight which you might have against the Turks. Your visit is to ensure we don't join forces with Constantinople, and thereby create an even greater army for you to fight against. Am I correct, Sir Alistair?"

"You're correct, sir."

Having proven himself a match for the wily old army officer and diplomat, Prince Faisal withdrew from the fray, bowed respectfully to his father, and regained his seat on the divan.

"My dear Sir Alistair," said the Sharif, sensing the General's growing discomfort, "my son Prince Faisal was merely assuring you that, although we are people of the desert, and although we are what might be loosely known at present as a client state of the Ottoman Empire, we are not a people disconnected from the rest of the world. Faisal's display of his understanding of our situation was merely to assure you that any decision which we come to will be based on our own perception of where our own interests lay."

Sir Alistair stiffened. "Does that mean you might not join with Great Britain should the Turks enter the coming war and side with German?"

"It doesn't mean that at all, Sir Alistair," said the Sharif. "It merely means that for most of the past millennium, the Arabs have been the subject to foreign occupiers, and that if the whole world is turned upside down by this assassination, it's only right that we Arabs should look after our own interests."

Sir Alistair began to argue, but the Sharif put up his hand to tell him to remain silent. "We have been a people subservient to others for too long, Sir Alistair. Even before the occupation of Arabia by the Seljuks, we were not allowed to be ourselves. After them came the Ayyubids, then the Monguls, then the Mamluks and then the Ottomans. I can't even remember how many conquerors we had in between. And now suddenly Europe is interested in the Middle East, with the French and the British trying to exert their influence over our Arab lands. How long before Germany and Russia look with envy upon our access to the Far East, and our warm waters. And what if these reports about oil being found underneath our sand are correct? What then, Sir Alistair?"

"Oil is of little interest to Great Britain, Your Majesty," he said. "Our ships and our industry run on coal, of which Britain has an infinite supply."

126

The Bell advisory note had instructed him to play down what would become increasingly important to Britain, and that was Arab oil, so he dismissed what the Sharif said out of hand.

"Yet Mr. Churchill is set upon the path of converting all of your war machines and your industry to oil, Sir Alistair," Faisal interrupted.

Sir Alistair started to explain, but the Sharif continued, "But please don't think all this means that we will fight against you. Better the enemy who can advance your interests and modernise you, than the enemy who will keep you in chains. Eh, Sir Alistair?"

"Great Britain is not your enemy, Highness," he insisted.

"Perhaps not, Sir Alistair, but is it our friend?"

The conversation lasted another half an hour, and Sir Alistair took his leave. He emerged satisfied from the palace and walked to his carriage. He had been briefed only the previous morning by a top secret diplomatic telegram from the Foreign Office, and to have arranged an interview at such short notice in Jeddah with the Sharif had been a singular feat. As to the *double entendres* which both father and son had so gleefully been uttering, well, that was something which either the British government in India or the British Egyptian Office would have to consider. He, thank God, had done his duty and now as a Senior British Military Advisor in the Middle East, he was going to return to his office in Cairo, and have a drink. The journey northward up the Red Sea to the Gulf of Suez would relax him and the one hundred mile drive by motor-car from Suez, across the desert into Cairo, would put him in dire need of a whisky and soda. He was particularly looking forward to the camaraderie of the Senior Officer's Mess after the enforced abstinence from alcohol in the Kingdom of Hejaz.

But before he managed to walk to his waiting vehicle, Prince Faisal suddenly emerged from one of the side doors of the palace, and paced across the ground.

"A moment more of your time, Sir Alistair."

The general stopped, and waited for the young man.

127

"Perhaps we could drive together to the docks. There's a matter I need to discuss with you."

Sir Alistair felt himself compromised. "Sir, I must respectfully remind you that I came here as advisor to His Majesty, and not to His Majesty's son."

Peremptorily, Prince Faisal stepped into the automobile. Sir Alistair was given no alternative but to follow. Seeing two passengers in the rear seats, the driver rotated the starting handle beneath the radiator, and when the car rocked on its axis and then coughed into life, immediately ran around from the front and jumped into his seat, depressing the accelerator so it didn't falter.

Faisal slid the glass partition closed so the driver wouldn't be able to hear what was being said, and the car jerked forward on its journey towards the dock.

Sir Alistair remained silent, deciding it was up to young Faisal to compromise himself. The less Alistair said, the better.

"Tell me," asked the young man. "What would Mr. Asquith and the British government do if we in the Kingdom of the Hejaz followed the family of the Sa'uds, and fought alongside the Turks against your country?"

"Nothing."

"Nothing?"

"Nothing! Our fight is going to be with Germany. If the Ottoman government in Constantinople is impelled into the war by these Young Turks, so be it. We have enough men in this area to deal with such an event, and vast numbers in India which we'll call upon. Don't forget, sir, that the British government in India sees this area, the Middle East, as coming under its control. They're not going to stay out of the war. Not by a long shot."

Faisal remained silent for some moments. "But don't you understand what would happen if British troops from India came into this arena. It would cause you all manner of problems on the Sub-Continent. India would erupt, for it would be a signal to the Indian Independence Movement to rise up and revolt against British Imperial rule. Your foreign secretary himself warned of that possibility with diplomats in London not two weeks ago. And it's not just the Indian Hindus with whom you'll have a problem if you send your armies into this region. The millions of Indian Muslims look towards the Ottoman Sultan as their spiritual leader, so how could they possibly refuse to support their brothers in Constantinople if Great Britain went to war against the Turks? Their revolt against the British would act as a match on gunpowder when the Hindus see their English masters distracted, and they, too, would rise up and revolt against you. The whole of the subcontinent would become revolutionary, and you certainly couldn't afford to show weakness and lack of resolve at a crucial moment such as this. You wouldn't risk losing India, just for Arabia, would you? Isn't that right, Sir Alistair? You wouldn't send your Indian army here to fight the Turks if there was a danger of your losing India? Or is the oil of Persia actually far more important to you than you were prepared to admit in front of my father?"

"Your Royal Highness seems to forget that we have millions of young men in Great Britain who would join up in moments to fight for the empire. My government's decisions aren't based on what is done in Mecca or Medina. This war, if there is to be a war, will be fought in Europe by the nations of Europe. The Middle East is merely a sideshow."

"A sideshow? But what about Persia's oil? And the real prospect that we have vast amounts of undiscovered oil beneath our desert? The early results are looking very encouraging."

Sir Alistair grinned. "Might I remind you of what I said to your father, sir. Great Britain runs on coal. That's been the source of our wealth for centuries, and we have limitless supplies beneath our earth. And remember also, Prince Faisal, that for over a hundred years, since the beginning of our British industrial revolution, we have stood resolute and alone. And we are now the most powerful empire the world has ever known. Persia might have oil, sir, but we have British ingenuity."

Again, Faisal remained silent. The car continued towards the dock. Suddenly, the young prince said, "You will need this area's oil, Sir Alistair. If not today, then certainly tomorrow. And to secure it, you'll need my help. What if I was to persuade all other Arabic rulers, here and in Mesopotamia and Syria and Palestine to rise up against the Turks—to join together for once as a united Arab nation, and to fight with Great Britain and throw off the shackles of the Turks which have been restraining us for hundreds of years? This could be the moment when all Arabia comes together as one. Then we would truly be a great nation. What about that, Sir Alistair?"

The general looked across at the young man. "Sir, the chances of your being able to convince all of your brother sheiks and chieftains and emirs to join with you are extremely remote. Unity has never been a part of the Arab mind. At heart, you're a nation of individuals, of nomads, of wanderers. You have no heart for pan-Arabism. You and your people have never developed beyond the level of the tribe. You know as well as I do the Arabic nation is a fiction . . . that you're only a collection of families and clans and groups. That doesn't make you a nation.

"Look, Prince Faisal, for the time being, why not just simply agree to join with us, and we'll look after you. Then, when the war's over, you can . . ."

Suddenly Faisal leaned forward, opened the partition, and said to the driver, "Stop here. I'll get out now."

The young man opened the car, and said to the surprised British officer, "Don't worry about my father's decision, Sir Alistair. We will give Great Britain six hundred thousand men to fight the Turks. We people of the desert have a saying. *An army of sheep led by a lion will defeat an army of lions lead by a sheep.* You're right, we are an undisciplined and isolationist people, and for a thousand years, we have been led by sheep. We will easily be defeated by the Turks if we alone rise up against them and we will be demolished by the British if we fight for the Turks. But if a man was to rise up and show the Arabs the value of nationhood, of fighting the Turks and being led by the British lions . . . well, Sir Alistair . . . isn't that something to contemplate? Provided, of course, that eventually the old lion returns to its lair and leaves us alone after the kill."

And with that, he left the astonished general and disappeared into the crowds of the *shuk*.

SIX

General Command Headquarters
Military Intelligence Office
Ismailia, Egypt, November 1915

Exhausted after an entire day in the office working closely with maps and writing reports, Gertrude returned to her suite in the Hotel Continental in Ismailia on the western banks of the Suez Canal, and eighty miles to the northeast of Cairo. Despite of the beauty of the hotel, or the delightful green zone which had been created for Western residents, Gertrude was too tired even to remove her shoes. She fell onto the bed, lit a cigarette, and swore at the ceiling. They weren't the words a lady could ever say in public, but shouting "shit shit shit" at the fan was an outlet for her frustrations and usually made her feel much better.

Reaching for a wet towel, she cooled her face and then drank a glass of whisky and soda which had been prepared for her by her servant. Then she lay on the bed watching the ceiling fan slowly undulate back and forth, pulled by unseen hands far below her, and creating a gentle breeze which gave her relief. Even in the month of November, Ismailia was still oppressively hot and clammy.

But the humidity and the workload weren't the reasons she returned to her empty room every night in a state of anger and frustration. She'd done everything in her power to warn the British government that the coming war was likely to produce the most horrific results, but because she was a woman, she'd been patronized and forced to suffer the condescension of men who held government office and military rank. Some, certainly, were excellent, perceptive and wise, but so many, from generals down to majors, from government ministers down to parliamentary private secretaries, listened to her with a knowing smirk on their faces and ignored almost every word of advice she gave. And why? Because she wore skirts and scarves and blouses. Once, she'd turned up to a meeting with the First Lord of the Admiralty in trousers, just to see if it would make any difference. But he pretended to ignore the modern fashions and she felt as if she were a ghost sitting at the table.

While she was still in London waiting to be of service to the empire, she'd weep at the sight of the Zeppelins bombing the dockyards of the Thames and at the German planes flying over Finchley and Hampstead Heath on their way to obliterate munitions factories in the north of London, knowing that her letters about the need to put all efforts into building up a strong air force as well as a navy, had been ignored. Somehow, the idiotic generals thought the battle would be won against the Hun using men on horses doing cavalry charges.

Just before she left London, when the dirigibles from the Zeppelin and Schütte-Lanz factories droned overhead, huge, monstrous balloons which made her feel violated and vulnerable, she had begun standing on the balcony of her home in Kensington, looking up at the sky, and screaming out swearwords. She had hoped the din of the dirigibles would drown out her intemperate language, until an Able Seaman passing beneath her balcony had shouted up, "You tell the fuckers, darling." Laughing, he'd walked beyond her, not seeing how mortified she was that he'd heard her.

For the most part, and especially in England, she'd managed to hide her frustrations and retain her outward composure and positive demeanor. To her friends with whom she dined in the cafes or purchased things in the shops on Burlington Arcade or the Strand, Gertrude Bell looked as though she had everything. She was working on hush-hush military and government things to do with the war, and consorting on vital issues with the most influential people in the land. She was the guest of honor at literary and political dinner parties. She was recognized in fashionable theaters where her entrance into a box was occasionally applauded by the audience and, even more remarkably, Gertrude was given a standing ovation when she walked into the dining room of Claridges where only the very top people in England dined. But despite her growing acclaim by the British people, Gertrude knew that to the people who mattered, to senior military and government men, she was being marginalized because of her sex, and it was making her increasingly furious.

Sexual frustration also, at times, overwhelmed her, and when it did, when she was alone at night and her mind sank into its usual melee of loneliness and abandonment she found herself in a state of despair, the relief for which was a drugged sleep. She was desperate for somebody with whom she could share her concerns. Yet for reasons she could barely fathom, her emotions annoyed her. She felt that she should be above them at her age.

But now that she had forced the government to allow her to go to Egypt, and the armchair generals were thousands of miles away drinking brandy and smoking cigars in their clubs in the Strand or Piccadilly, she had hoped her advice would not be discounted because she was a woman. Frustration, though, was her constant companion, and while she knew she must control these emotions, she swore one more time for good luck and decided to dress for dinner with her fellow intelligence officers.

As she sank into the warm bath, she wondered how England would cope in the future now that so many wonderful young men were lying on the shores of Gallipoli. Killed. Murdered by the bloody Turks. When she learned of the landing at Gallipoli, she implored her friend, Lord Curzon, the Secretary of State for Foreign Affairs to allow her to go to the Middle East. She adored George Curzon and with him had instigated the Anti-Suffragette League, and because of their closeness, he was particularly sympathetic to her needs at this most pivotal of times. He realized that, despite the dangers, Gertrude had to be out of England and working hard for the good of the country.

Within a matter of weeks, she found herself in Egypt, beavering away for Military Intelligence in their Arab Office, and being accorded far more respect than she'd ever enjoyed in England.

But even though she saw things with greater clarity and knew far more than her male colleagues, somehow, the generals seemed to prefer their assessments to hers. She always had an uphill battle getting her assessments accepted.

It was nearly 8:00 and she and her colleagues dined at 9:00, so she'd have to get out of her bath and get ready, and stop indulging her silliness. As she wrapped herself in a dressing gown and walked back into the lounge-room of her suite in the hotel, she lit another cigarette. They were such a consolation to her frustrations. And then came a knock on the front door. Surprised, and assuming it was Thomas Lawrence who had appointed himself as her fashion advisor and never allowed her to dress without his approval, she walked in bare feet across the carpet.

Her servant, Farouk, was downstairs ironing her dress, and so she checked her face in the mirror, walked to the front door, and opened it. Gertrude was surprised to see a tall and magnificently-dressed Arab. By his clothes and the red and white *shemagh* on his head she realized he wasn't Egyptian, but from somewhere in Arabia.

He stood straight, eyebrows arched at having to address a woman without a veil and asked in guttural English, "You are Chatrude Pell?"

To save him further pain, she replied in faultless Arabic. "Yes, I am Miss Gertrude Bell," she said, stressing the way in which her name was pronounced in English. "And who are you?"

"You will come with me," he said. He turned and began to walk away from the door.

She closed the door, and returned to her bedroom to continue getting ready. Egypt wasn't a safe place at the best of times, certainly not with an imminent Turkish invasion and going somewhere with a complete stranger was the last thing she would do. A moment later, there was again a knock at the door.

When she re-opened it, the tall Arab was looking bemused. "You did not follow me."

"Of course I didn't. I am not in the habit of following strange men."

135

"But you must do as I command," he told her.

"I do not follow the Arabic custom of obeying a man unquestioningly, unlike your wives and your daughters. If you want me to follow you, you had better tell me why and where."

He looked at her in astonishment. "I cannot disclose these things."

She began to shut the door, saying "Then I will not go with you."

He immediately said, "Wait. Do not close the door. I am the servant of His Highness, Prince Faisal of Hejaz. I am commanded by His Highness to bring you to his presence. You will follow me immediately. His Highness is waiting."

"The prince is here?" she exclaimed loudly. "In Egypt?"

The tall Arab put his finger to his mouth. "Silence. It is a secret. He has come to see Chatrude Pell. Only his father, His Highness the King knows of this visit. Come immediately."

The man turned and began to walk away. This time, Gertrude decided to follow, even though she was in a bathrobe. "Where are we going?" she asked. But before he could answer, the servant had already stopped at the suite two doors down the corridor from hers, and was gently knocking on the door.

"Good God," was all Gertrude could say, as the door quickly opened, and standing in the doorway, she saw Prince Faisal, third son of the King of the Hejaz.

She entered the room quickly, not knowing whether to bow or to shake his hand. He was a tall if slight man, effeminate looking, despite his glistening and pomaded black beard and Savile Row clothes.

He held out his hand, and said, "Thank you for coming, Miss Bell. I appreciate you giving me your time."

"The pleasure is mine, Your Majesty, and I apologize for the state of my undress, but your servant said it was urgent. Why are you in Ismailia?" she asked.

"Before I tell you, let me say what a pleasure it is to meet you. I've heard so much about you and your travels through our lands. When you were last in Hejaz, in the land of the Prophet,

136

peace and blessings be upon Him, I was in Europe, and the time before that, I believe I was in Constantinople. But at last we're meeting, although I apologize if the circumstances are, shall we say, unusual."

Was he trying to charm her? She had to be careful in her dealings with Arabic ruling classes, because she was here to protect British interests in wartime. She was no longer the free spirit, able to wander where she wanted or meet with whomsoever she decided seemed interesting.

"Majesty, when I was traveling in Arabia and Mesopotamia, I was an independent woman. I visited your domain, though as a Christian, I was unable to see for myself the glories of the main cities of the Kingdom of the Hejaz, the wondrous Mecca and Medina, the centers of the life and death of the Prophet, peace and blessings be His. But that was then, sir. Today, I am a mere servant of the British government, undertaking work for our war effort. With respect, I feel I ought to know why you wanted a private meeting with me . . . and why your presence in Egypt has been kept secret."

The Prince smiled. He'd been told she had a fearsome intellect, and that she was very direct and to the point, but he was unused to the ways of Western people, and especially of Western women, and hadn't anticipated she would come to the matter in hand as directly.

"Business . . . always business. Why can't we sit down and enjoy a coffee together, and some pastries, and then, when the circumstances are appropriate, we'll talk about why I'm here?"

"Sir, I feel constrained at meeting alone with someone of your august standing. I fear I must advise General Gilbert Clayton of my presence in your company. You must understand that I will be compromised if I don't."

The Prince sat down on his sofa, and invited her to sit opposite. She did so, waiting on his response, but thinking to herself how odd it was that she was naked save for a bath robe, and he was dressed for a night at the opera.

The Prince considered his next words very carefully because he knew time spent alone with Gertrude Bell was the equivalent of sitting at the feet of somebody of great knowledge and wisdom. The last thing he wanted was to dilute his future relationship with her by filtering her through some senior army man. "It would be a great pity if you were to involve General Clayton in this matter, because even before he arrived, I would disappear into the desert like a spirit in the night and deny that we had met."

She looked at him strangely. What was all this about?

"You look disconcerted, Miss Bell. Surely you, who have traveled so often in our lands, are familiar with the Arabic way of doing things. We are a people without trees, yet despite this arboreal disadvantage, we have learned over the millennia of the advantages of beating around the bush."

She burst out laughing. She was beginning to feel more comfortable in his presence and starting to enjoy the way in which things were going.

"And we, sir, are a people whose land contains many forests, yet somehow our history has taught us to walk in a straight line. Why do you believe that you can't talk with the more important people here? I'm merely a person who is assisting with the work of intelligence gathering and recording. Why is it you wish to see me, and not the commanders of the British forces?"

"There are many commanders, but only one Gertrude Bell. Your knowledge of our people, our history, and our language sets you apart from all others. Your commanders come and speak with us as though we are children. Yet people in my country, and in Syria and Palestine and the land of the Druze and in Mesopotamia still speak of Gertrude Bell as the Daughter of the Desert, as a woman who understands the way in which we think, and the needs we have, caught up in a world not of our making."

She felt overwhelmed by the praise. "I'm not used to flattery, Highness," she said, "and my advice is not listened to with the same favor as is that of my male colleagues, so this interview might not work to your advantage. I hate to have to admit it, but

138

you might be better off with a man present. However, if you feel a private conversation might assist to clarify matters in your mind, then I give you my assurance that it will remain private until such time as you give me permission to discuss it with others. But having said that, I must also let you know that I will not and cannot compromise Great Britain's interests."

He nodded and smiled. "You see, Miss Bell, as soon as I explain why my presence has to be kept secret, you will understand why I wish to sound you out for advice, rather than your commanders. We both know that Britain and Turkey will each require Arab armies to fight on their sides. The British want the oil which we are informed is underneath our deserts in order to ensure a continuous flow to British ships and motor cars, while the Turks want our strength to maintain what he has, and hopefully to reclaim what he has lost.

"In the end, however, it is we of the Hejaz who will make the decision as to the side on which we fight. It is a decision for my father the king. Last year, my father, Sharif Hussein bin-Ali, was visited by General Sir Alistair Booth, and we gave him the assurance that the fighting men of the Hejaz, six hundred thousand men in total, would side with the British. He seemed very pleased. But on a later visit to the lands to our north and east, the lands of Sheik ibn Rashid and Sheik Ibn Sa'ud, he received a very different reception. These men will lead their people to the side of the Turks," he said.

Gertrude shuddered when the Prince mentioned the name Rashid. Faisal saw her react. He was aware of her imprisonment and the danger she'd faced. The story was becoming legend in the desert.

"I am aware, Prince Faisal, of the temperaments and the dispositions of these two desert leaders, though I have not met either in person," she told him. "Many years ago, I met ibn Sa'ud's father in the Balkans, but I doubt he would have told his son of my existence."

"Then you will know that ibn Rashid and ibn Sa'ud are only interested in how much the Turks will pay them, and ultimately in independence for our nation from all overlords, Turks and British and French alike."

His servant poured a glass of rose water, and gave it to the Prince. At a nod from his master, the servant poured a second glass for Gertrude and handed it to her. She took it without acknowledgment, as was her right for a woman who sat in the presence of the prince.

"Sir, while this is very important, I'm afraid I still don't think I'm the right person for you to be discussing this with. You need a commander who can transmit your enquiry to higher levels. Visiting from England is Mr. Mark Sykes, who is a diplomat of considerable experience. He'll . . ."

"On the contrary, Miss Bell. For me to discuss such a delicate matter with your Mr. Sykes or with General Clayton will make it official. My purpose in secretly visiting Ismailia is to sound you out as a friend of Arabia, as one who has intimate knowledge of both ourselves and those who wish us to join them. I seek your assistance in formulating a convincing argument which I can use when my father is on the point of making his decision. At the moment, he is being mercilessly pressured by ibn Sa'ud . . ."

"But I thought your father had already given his decision," she said urgently.

"In times of war, Miss Bell, decisions are made today and changed tomorrow. The pressure to join the Turks is very great. My father is in a cleft stick, thanks to other desert leaders."

Her next words, she knew, could affect the conduct of the war. "Sir, you would know that ibn Rashid is a blood-thirsty youth who will sell his mother for a gold piece," she said, surprised by her own vehemence. Her imprisonment and closeness to death in the lands of ibn Rashid impelled her to continue, even against her own better judgement. "And from what I understand, ibn Sa'ud is little better. You know what he did when he took back Riyadh from ibn Rashid. It was a bloodbath. Ibn Sa'ud's intention is the control of all of the lands of the Arabian people, and I fear he also looks towards your lands. He's—"

"We know he's a man who undoubtedly has his eyes firmly focussed on the Kingdom of the Hejaz, and on ownership of Mecca and Medina and Jeddah. Now that he has retaken those of his former lands from which his family was exiled, and beaten back ibn Rashid, I'm sure he's intent on spreading westwards and making the whole of the peninsula into the Sa'ud's Arabia. Because he wants to become the pan Arabic leader, he needs the legitimacy of controlling the holy places of Islam. Both my father and I are well aware of this, and despite the fact that my father is the guardian of the Holy Cities, as well as a descendant of the Prophet, that will count as nothing to the ambitions of ibn Sa'ud.

"Yet even with this knowledge, bearing in mind the overall weakness of the Turks, but also taking into account his sudden encouragement at the British disaster in the landing at Gallipoli, my father has just begun thinking that if he was to join with ibn Sa'ud in a confederation against the British, this act of camaraderie might sway ibn Sa'ud from attacking us."

Gertrude looked at him in grave concern, for this was seriously dangerous information for Britain and could alter the entire course of the war. Neither she, nor anybody else in the Arab Office had any inkling that Hussein was considering joining ibn Sa'ud or ibn Rashid in fighting on the side of the Turks. Yes, this was very serious news indeed.

Noting her surprise, the prince continued, "My question is, if we side with the British, will the British protect us after the war, not from the Turks, but from our Arabic brothers?"

He sipped the rose water and looked at her. Gertrude realized immediately the overwhelming gravity of the next few moments and of the consequences for Great Britain in her answer.

Suddenly, there was a loud knock on a door farther down the corridor. They remained silent, listening. Then they heard a voice calling, "Gertrude? Gertie, are you there? Are you alright?"

The prince looked at her questioningly.

"It's a certain Mr. Lawrence. He's a colleague. He's come to my suite to advise me on my dress . . . it's a long story. But I have to go

141

out and see him, or he'll send for the manager to open my door, thinking I'm in distress."

She cursed Lawrence's timing. This was an utterly crucial moment, and she couldn't afford for him to endanger it. The prince nodded, and Gertrude stood to leave the room. The moment she appeared in the corridor, she saw Lawrence, looking anxiously at her door. He turned when he heard the nearby door opening, and was surprised when Gertrude emerged, dressed in a bath robe. Without her knowledge, the prince's servant followed her out of the suite, and stood guard, arms crossed, in the doorway to prevent Lawrence's entry.

"Dear boy," she said, "I'm not coming to dinner tonight. I'll have something in my room. You go down and enjoy yourself. Give my apologies to the others."

Lawrence frowned. "What's going on, Gertie? Why are you dressed like that? And who's this?"

She turned, and to her annoyance saw that the prince's servant was standing behind her guarding the door. She snapped at him, "Go inside. Nobody told you to follow me."

"I remain," he said laconically.

Lawrence walked towards her, but instead of addressing her, he looked up to the huge servant and said in fluent Arabic, "Who are you? Whom do you guard?"

"Thomas," she said in irritation, reverting to English, "I'm meeting somebody in this suite, and we're going to be dining together. Now be a good dear, and go away. This doesn't concern you."

"Good God, Gertie, you're in a bathrobe and having an assignation? My dear girl, that's marvellous. Very Bohemian. And I'm not in the least bit jealous. You need somebody to cater to the personal side of your life."

She began to protest, but garrulous as ever, Lawrence continued, "So there's life in the old dog yet. I think you're absolutely right to do so, just so long as you don't exclude me from your life. Tell me, is he rich and handsome? I assume he's an Arabic gentleman from the manner of his rather hefty and terrifying servant here. Egyptian? Syrian? Or an Arabian like his servant?"

"Stop being so silly, Lawrence. It's nothing like that. He's merely a gentleman I met and we're sharing a few moments together before he returns home to his wife and children. Now don't be tiresome. Go downstairs and let me get on with things."

"Dressed in a bath robe. You've been doing dirty business, haven't you? Oh well."

Lawrence shrugged, and winked. He walked away to the stairs, and Gertrude and the prince's servant returned to the suite. But before she had even sat down, there was a sharp rap on the door. The servant sprang to attention, and opened it. Lawrence was standing there on tiptoes to see above the servant's shoulders and to look deep within the room.

In Arabic, he said, "I'm so sorry to bother you, but could I possibly have a quick word to Miss Gertrude—Good Lord."

Lawrence spotted Prince Faisal sitting on a sofa near to the window.

"Highness," he said from the corridor, bowing.

The prince said urgently to his servant, "Don't allow the gentleman to remain outside in the corridor. Bring him inside immediately before he makes a fuss."

Lawrence was pulled into the room by the guard, and summed up the scenario in seconds.

"This really is too bad, Lawrence. How dare you commit such a breach of etiquette?" she hissed at him.

"I'm sorry, Gertie, but I simply returned to inform you that there's a game of bridge after dinner. I had no idea you were with royalty." He turned to address the prince, "Your Highness, this humble servant of the English king greets you and begs you to know that I am honored to be in your illustrious presence."

"How do you know me?" asked the prince, still startled at being recognized. And then he realized. "Oh yes, the damned photos in your British magazines when I was in Zermatt skiing last year."

Lawrence nodded. Too late for remedy, Gertrude said, "May I be permitted to introduce you to a colleague of mine. This unworthy and disgraceful man is Captain Thomas Lawrence, who should know better than to do what he did. However, more than any Englishman I've ever known before, Captain Lawrence is Arabia. For all his faults, Your Highness, Mr. Lawrence is a man of the desert. Although he is English, there is sand in his blood. While I might have been of assistance to you, sir, between the two of us, I'm sure we can answer your needs, without the English generals or the Prime minister needing to know of your visit. Mr. Lawrence and I are very good friends, and we work closely together for the British Intelligence Service. I can vouch for his knowledge, and I will ensure his discretion."

Too late for him to do otherwise, the prince gave his assent, and it took Gertrude only a matter of minutes to brief Lawrence on why he had come to Egypt to seek out Gertrude.

With a bow, Lawrence said, "Highness, it is a privilege of the highest order to be called upon to assist you in this urgent matter."

"You are a flatterer, Mr. Lawrence. We should always beware of flattery. We are told that flattery looks like friendship, just like a wolf looks like a dog."

Lawrence laughed; the prince was bemused by his high-pitched, girlish giggle. The Englishman said, "If I may be permitted to respond, sir, one of the greatest writers in the English language, Jonathan Swift, wrote a wonderful and amusing poem. If my memory serves me right, it goes

It is a maxim in the schools,
That flattery is the food of fools;
Yet now and then your men of wit,
Will condescend to take a bit.

"Therefore, Highness, I treat Your Majesty not as a fool, but as a man of wit."

Gertrude looked at Lawrence in astonishment. Was he going too far? His impertinence could imperil the situation! But the prince burst out laughing, and said, "You are good with words, Captain Lawrence. A thousand years before the renaissance of your Queen Elizabeth the First, when you English were still grovelling around in the mud and wearing blue paint on your skin, we people of the desert were writing the finest poetry and dealing with the most complex mathematics man had studied since the time of the Greeks."

"And will again, Prince Faisal," Gertrude told him. "You were once a great people, living in great cities. In Damascus and Baghdad, you made the desert bloom and you excited the world with the most breathtaking of dreams. Your nights were lit by street lamps while the English were scurrying around like rats in the dark, and your astronomers were lighting up minds with their mapping of the skies. And yet, Prince Faisal, you have allowed yourselves to become the slaves of barbarians and like the slaves of Africa who worked on the tobacco and cotton plantations of America, you are shackled and your impoverished dreams are no longer the dreams of free men. You need a great man to rise up and unite your people."

"Gertie!" Lawrence hissed. "How dare you speak to His Highness in that way? This is gross impertinence."

"It is the truth, Mr. Lawrence," said the prince. "However uncomfortable it might be for me to hear, Miss Bell is merely telling us all the reality of our situation. If I wanted to deal in flattery, I might as well present myself at the Topkapi Palace of the Sultan in Constantinople, for he would tell me how important I and my people are to the future of Arabism and Islam. And the Turks, once they had their agreement, would continue to treat us like slaves. I came here because my people need to face the urgent reality of the modern world, and they look to their leaders to guide them. Which is why I and my father who lead the people of the Kingdom of the Hejaz, the very home of the Prophet himself, peace and blessings upon him, look to you both for your advice. For I know I will hear from Miss Bell, the Daughter of the Desert, and now from her friend, Mr. Lawrence, a friend of Arabia, words I can trust when my father and I make our decisions."

Lawrence sat down, and told the servant to fetch him a glass of rose water, which he did immediately. It was a gesture noticed with annoyance by Gertrude. She had spent half her life traveling in the most masculine-dominated place imaginable, in the homes and palaces and tents of rulers where she was treated with respect. Yet earlier, when she had asked for a glass of water, the servant had looked to his master for permission before acquiescing to her wishes. It was so typical of the chauvinism of Arabic society, but it was an irritation which she would have to bite back.

"So," said the Prince, "now you know my position, what should I advise my father the king to do? Side with the Turks, and defer the assault by ibn Sa'ud at least until this war is ended, which might not be until next year, or side with you British and incur not just the wrath of the Turks, but also of his brother Sheiks who see Great Britain as just another colonial master?"

"Your Highness already knows the answer," said Gertrude. "Your father's only option is to be part of the British assault against the Turks. The Ottoman Empire is on the point of collapse. This war is a preposterous adventure, a moment of triumphalism, merely the last hurrah. Your people must be part of the winning side, or in the peace which inevitably follows, you will be crushed by empires whose size Your Highness cannot imagine. France and Great Britain alone could carve up the Middle East and if you had fought them as their enemy your father, his sons, and their children's children will long remember the time when you could have been great, if only . . ."

"So you think the Turkish Empire is on the verge of collapse, do you, Miss Bell. Then what was Gallipoli."

"Gallipoli was a miscalculation by the War Office, sir," she said.

"A miscalculation which cost the lives of tens of thousands of young British and Australian men, I think."

146

"Errors always happen in the heat of battle," said Gertrude. "In wartime, decisions are made without possession of all the facts. How, for instance, were we to know that the Turks was waiting for our lads in the hills and that they'd be mown down like dogs? And how does your Highness know that by joining with ibn Sa'ud to fight us, he won't suddenly turn on you in the heat of battle? The fact of the matter is, Prince Faisal, that while Great Britain is undoubtedly imperial, and looks towards spreading its empire into new lands and new continents, we will do so in partnership with local rulers. The days of Victoria, Empress of India, are long gone. A close relationship with Great Britain will afford you security and independence. And from that independence, sir, I feel certain a leader will emerge who can, who will, create a great Arab nation, not just a collection of small tribes all feuding with each other."

The prince smiled and shook his head. "If anybody should be the leader of all the Arab people, Sunni and Shi'ite and all the rest, then it is my father, for he is guardian of the holiest sites of Islam. But we are a tribal people, Miss Bell, and tribes by their very nature will always fight and squabble. I was told this by your Sir Alistair."

"I hate to disagree with Sir Alistair, but if you think back almost a thousand years, things were different under Saladin," she said.

"True, but a man such as Saladin arises only once in a thousand years," said the prince.

"So now is the time for another Saladin to arise. This is your moment, Majesty. You and your people are ready for such a man."

"My father is no Saladin. He is cautious, worried, and elderly."

"But Saladin wasn't an Arab, Highness," she said quietly, barely daring to utter the words. "Those such as your revered father and ibn Sa'ud and ibn Rashid are not men who the leaders of other Arab tribes will follow. They carry too much baggage. Perhaps you need somebody from beyond the Arab people . . ."

Thomas Lawrence looked at her again in astonishment. This presumptuousness was as close to treason as anything he'd ever heard. She was talking as though she were the Prime minister of England. "Gertie dearest, while this is a very private conversation for the prince's benefit, I would urge you to remember that you're a servant of the British Crown. You aren't entitled to talk to his Highness about such issues as leadership and especially not about partnerships or such like."

"On the contrary, Thomas," she said, sipping her rose water. The prince looked on in bemusement as a quarrel began to develop between them. "If the Arabs are ever to be a great nation again, they must learn to come together as one people under a wise and fatherly ruler, and not as underdogs to some empire from over the sea, be that empire Turkish or British. Arabic history—"

"Never mind about Arabic history. You're a serving British official, and this disloyalty does you no credit." he said sternly.

"But what does you both great credit is your painful honesty," said the prince. "From what I have heard, you both wish the same—that Britain's interests and the interests of Arabia must be as one. This is what I came to hear. I am not so naïve as to think that supporting Britain to conquer the Turks will result in Britons returning to their home once the war is over. Mr. Churchill talks in the corridors of Whitehall about the need for oil to run the nation's ships and his factories. He is young, but far from naïve. He will, I'm sure, persuade the rest of the British Cabinet to his point of view. The oil from Persia is all well and good, but another supply in Arabia will be better. Two oil supplies are more secure than one. So after this war is over, we will entertain a partnership with Great Britain in oil and other mutual interests.

"I shall now return to my home, and advise my father that he should negotiate the signing of a treaty in which we of the Kingdom of the Hejaz will fight alongside our British friends, and that a part of the negotiations of that treaty with Great Britain will be an undertaking to protect us from our brothers who might seek to destroy us when this war is over. I thank you both for clarifying the issue. It was as I thought, but I needed to hear it from you. Now I need your joint assistance on the way in which I should frame the argument which will persuade my father to do so."

~

Cairo, Egypt, November, 1915

Sir Henry McMahon's home in Cairo was a former Ottoman palace, large, airy, and ornate. His wife detested it with a vengeance, telling her friends she'd rather live in a Wimbledon two-up two-down bungalow than in the middle of a wedding cake. But as the British government's resident in Egypt, his standing determined the home in which he and his wife would live until they could return to their country estate in verdant England.

A passionate ex-smoker, Sir Henry was becoming increasingly irritated by the fact that the woman sitting opposite him in the second withdrawing room of his private apartments—one of the few places in the palace where there was no possibility of his servants overhearing any conversations—was puffing like a train on one cigarette after another.

"Shall we go for a walk in the garden?" Sir Henry suggested pointedly to Gertrude and Captain Lawrence. "It's such a beautiful day, and I feel the need for some fresh air."

They walked in studied silence through the labyrinthine corridors of the palace until they left through the rear and entered the delicately constructed gardens full of scented trees and flamboyant bushes. They meandered along and around the pathways until they came to the central fountain which was surrounded by marble tables and stone benches. They sat, and Sir Henry breathed the air deeply to clear the fumes from Gertrude's cigarettes out of his lungs.

"Let's recap for a moment, shall we, so we're all in complete understanding of the picture," he said. "You know I've been in regular correspondence with the Sharif Hussein of the Hejaz about rising up against the Turks, yet you insist that I now send over another delegation to offer him support against ibn Sa'ud.

And with them I send a lot of money to assist him in convincing his people to side with us?"

"Yes," said Gertrude.

"But you also insist at the same time as I'm paying those in the Hejaz, that I negotiate with ibn Sa'ud and offer him another lot of money to ensure that he joins with us against the Turks?"

"Yes," said Lawrence.

"And yet you both know that the Turks are putting a fortune into ibn Sa'ud's pocket."

"Yes," they both said at once.

"Isn't that rather a lot of money to gamble with? I mean what if they pocket the money and stay out of the war. They both know the Turks are intent on attacking the Suez Canal and expelling us from Egypt. Surely these Arabians would be better off waiting six months and determining which way the wind blew . . . wouldn't they?" asked Sir Henry.

"No," insisted Gertrude. "That's not the way they think. Look Henry, it's vital that the Arabs revolt against the Turks, or we're in real trouble."

Sir Henry looked at her in amazement. "Have you forgotten that the British Army from India has taken the city of Basrah on the Gulf from the Turks and is, as we speak, fighting its way northwards towards Baghdad. The way our lads are going, I'm not all that sure we're going to need the help of the Arabs. I really think you might have underestimated the ability of our lads in khaki, and overestimated the fighting skills of the tribesmen. I know them, Gertie, and they're an undisciplined lot. Most of the buggers are nothing short of cutthroat villains who'd take money one day and stab you in the back the next. So what makes you think that even if they do side with us, we'll be able to turn them into an army?

"Sir Henry," interrupted Lawrence, "the Arabs won't ever be a spit and polish army marching four square in ranks. Desert warfare is an entirely different thing. It's hit and run and hiding behind sand dunes and attacking the enemy when he's bedded down for the night. Nobody has written a manual for desert warfare, yet warfare in the desert has been conducted for millennia. Think about how Mohammed and his followers managed to take a rag-tag group of tribesmen and conquer all of Arabia, all of North Africa and then cross into Europe, taking Spain and damn near the rest of Western Civilization. And there are no fighting men in the world who can fight in the desert better than the Arab."

Henry McMahon looked in distaste at Lawrence. He'd taken an instant dislike to him, viewing the young man as effete and pompous, yet he was accorded both prominence and respect by the redoubtable Gertrude Bell, whom Sir Henry knew well from London, and who's reputation as a woman of knowledge and wisdom meant that if she respected this Lawrence person, then of necessity, so must he.

"Be that as it may, Lawrence, I still think you're overestimating the importance of this Arab army you're talking about."

"No he's not, Henry," said Gertrude. "You underestimate both the Arab and the Turks at your own risk. The latest intelligence is that our boys are doing well despite the marshes and the lack of roads, but that the Turks have massive forces in Baghdad, and are just waiting for the British army to get within firing range. Then all hell will break loose," Gertrude said, her voice vehement and strident.

"That's as may be, but you have to understand the political realities." Sir Henry took a sip of water, and continued, "The big brass in India have overtaken responsibility for Persia and Mesopotamia and all the land between Palestine and Turkey. We, in the Arab Office, have been given Egypt and Africa and the Sudan by our Lords and Masters in London. That's what we have to deal with, I'm afraid. Decisions made about Arabia and Palestine and Syria are those of Lord Hardinge in the Sub-Continent, as well as the Foreign Office, and the Viceroy of India himself isn't in favor of an Arab revolt. He thinks it's a dangerous thing, and it'll just lead to the creation of a whole bevy of independent Arab kingdoms in Mesopotamia and Syria and elsewhere and British interests will go to pot."

Captain Lawrence laughed. "Our noble Viceroy, Lord Hardinge, doesn't know his arse from his elbow."

Sir Henry McMahon bridled at the impertinence of the young man. "May I remind you, Captain Lawrence, that Charles Hardinge is a friend of mine, and was nearly assassinated in the service of the British Crown. He deserves more respect, if you don't mind."

"I apologize, Sir Henry," the young man said quickly, especially as Gertrude had given him one of her looks, a raised right eyebrow which told him he'd gone much too far.

Sir Henry continued, "You might not fully appreciate the problem which Lord Hardinge faces. It's an unquestionable fact that Great Britain's empire currently encompasses a vast number of Muslims. India has tens of millions of Sunni Muslims who look towards the Sultan of Turkey as their spiritual leader. Hardinge is terrified that the non-Arab Muslims of India will never accept it if Great Britain supports an Arabic revolt against the Turks. So after winning Basrah, he's pushing northward towards Baghdad, and . . ."

"Pushing northwards recklessly, Sir Henry", said Lawrence. "That's the problem. We in the Arab Bureau know the difficulties our poor blighters are going to face. Lord Hardinge is in India, and has no idea of the terrain or of the numbers of Turks on the ground which face him. There are almost no lines of communication between Cairo and Delhi, just the occasional terse and intemperate telegram. He has no understanding of which side the Arabs will decide to fight for. I'm sorry, sir, but right now, Hardinge is doing all of this on his own for King and Country, but . . ."

Gertrude interrupted Lawrence, terrified that his lack of subtlety would imperil their mission. Looking at Captain Lawrence sternly, she said to Sir Henry, "I'm afraid what Captain Lawrence is telling you about the intelligence we've received is quite correct. Word came yesterday about the difficulties which Hardinge's troops are experiencing, Henry. The British Indian army is pushing northwards up the Tigris valley towards Kut and Baghdad and even though they had a lot of victories after they took Basrah on the Persian Gulf, they're beginning to encounter very real difficulties. They're bogged down in the marshes of the Shatt al Arab waterway, they've got insufficient equipment, and a shortage of boats to navigate up the Tigris, and the Arabs are taking pot-shots and stealing their food and equipment. Taking Basrah was fairly easy because it was largely a sea-born assault. But right now our boys are in the land of the Arab . . . sand and salt and marshes . . . and they're going to find that things will soon start to go very badly for them."

Sir Henry frowned, and shook his head. "But I don't understand. Taking Basrah was a triumph. Hardinge said it was the turning point in the war. Why should we suffer a reversal?"

"You have no idea of the dangers of what lies ahead for them," Gertrude replied. "You see, Hardinge's men are experienced fighting in the mountainous terrain and jungles of India, not in the deserts of Mesopotamia or in the marshes of the Shatt al Arab waterway. They're heading into disaster marching northwards up the Tigris towards Baghdad. The Turks are encamped in huge numbers along the way. By the time they reach their destination, the Turks will be in plague proportions south of Baghdad. I pray that my fears are unfounded, but I feel it important that you advise Lord Hardinge of this immediately. Tell him to halt any forward march northwards from the Gulf of Persia to Baghdad until they're fully reinforced and they have sufficient boats and horses and even medical people on the ground. If they go northwards half-cocked just because they found Basrah easy pickings, they're heading into the jaws of a terrible battle. My information comes from an extremely reliable source," said Gertrude.

Sir Henry listened carefully, but said, "While I might accept your information, and pray that you're wrong, I'm afraid Charles Hardinge isn't about to listen to any information from you Arabists here in Cairo. I've just received a copy of a letter he's sent to the Foreign Office, saying that the creation of an Arab revolt is detrimental to British interests in the Middle East. He's put the cat amongst the pigeons, I'm afraid."

"Why the hell did he do such a stupid thing as that?" asked Gertrude. "We're on the spot . . . we're the ones who know what's happening . . . he's in India, for God's sake. Oh, this is really too much. What did the Foreign Office say in response?" she asked.

"They haven't formulated a response yet, but the point is more what this will mean for our participation in the war effort."

A servant, dressed in a long striped *galabiyah,* appeared as though from nowhere, and deposited tall frosted glasses of fresh lemonade on the table in front of them. It was a welcome relief from the heat of the day and the tepid water which had been there on their arrival. And it was also a relief from the tension in the air. They all waited in silence for the servant to bow and then disappear back into the house.

"Look," Sir Henry said after seeming to consider his words with great care, "I've been having a lot of communications from the War Office in London. They're sending out a chappie called David Hogarth to run the Arab Office here in Egypt . . . well, I suppose it's alright to inform you that they're changing the name from Arab Office to Arab Bureau to impress people with how much importance they place upon the future of the Arab revolt against the Turks. But chappies I know in Whitehall tell me that London's decision will be to fight Hardinge tooth and nail. And knowing him, he'll see it as an attempt to diminish his empire . . ."

"His empire?" asked Lawrence.

"You know what I mean, Captain Lawrence. The point is the British Government of India wants to annex Mesopotamia and claim it as its own. Right now, and I don't want this to go beyond the two of you, we in Cairo and Hardinge in Delhi are at loggerheads. It's not just intemperate telegrams, Gertrude; it's nasty reports back to London. I told you Hardinge was my friend. He once was, but now we've become bitter rivals instead of fighting for the same cause. Hardinge and the Indian government are perfectly happy for us to be in charge of Egypt and the Sudan, but they're insistent on keeping control of all the emirates and sheikhdoms in the Gulf. They seem to think Arabia can be run from the Sub-Continent and that they should control and rule the Middle East . . ."

Gertrude gasped. "But that's insane. That's just boneheaded stupidity. What does Delhi think it knows about the Arabs? Absolutely bloody nothing. Nothing at all. They're only doing it because they want to control the wealth which will come from Persian and Arab oil."

"I know," Sir Henry insisted. "But that doesn't stop them wanting to control it. They want to annex Mesopotamia, which will cost London an absolute fortune. They'll have to station a huge permanent army there to keep the Arabs down, and have all the infrastructure of government and the civil service.

"We in the Arab Bureau, on the other hand, want an affiliation in an Arab kingdom which extends from Arabia to Mesopotamia and over which we can exert a sort of covert and well-concealed control. Hardinge says that unless we annex Basrah and Abadan and Baghdad, we'll lose control of any oil which might be found, and then our ships and armed forces and industry will be subject to the will of an Arab leader."

Thomas Lawrence put his glass down, and stood to straighten his back. He walked over to a pomegranate tree, and smelt the fragrance. "Does Lord Hardinge seriously believe that a hundred and fifty million Arabs can once again be annexed against their will? Does he think that after centuries of Ottoman repression, the Sheiks and Emirs will just meekly accept one ruler in place of another?"

"It's up to us to persuade Lord Hardinge otherwise," said Sir Henry. "We might think he's wrong, but he is the Viceroy of India, and his voice is very powerful in London. And it's made even stronger by the fact that his troops, the India Expeditionary Force, have just succeeded in taking Basrah and are about to travel up the Tigris to take Baghdad. I'm afraid what Lord Hardinge needs is to listen to the voice of reason, to hear firsthand why it would be

155

such a terrible mistake for India to try to rule Arabia. I know you came here to talk about payments to the Sharif of the Hejaz, but this, I fear is a great deal more important. What Hardinge needs is to listen to a subtle voice, one which understands the complexities of the Arabic mind, one which is fluent in the language and customs of the people and has lived in their tents and knows how they'd react."

He glanced over to Gertrude, who was sitting there, nursing a glass of lemonade. When she looked at him, she reacted in horror.

"Me?" she shouted. "Go to Delhi?"

Sir Henry said nothing, but merely nodded. Then he turned to Lawrence.

"And you, Lawrence, will go to Arabia and carry our message to Prince Faisal and his father."

SEVEN

Approaching Basrah. Mesopotamia. 1916

For almost the entire journey back from India to the Middle East, the Englishwoman had been driving Gertrude crazy. As the Sub-Continent disappeared into the mist-shrouded immensity of the Indian Ocean, the woman had been firing off a mindless barrage of thoughts, observations, and prejudices, almost without respite. Be it the state of the ship, the ocean, the war, fashion, or whatever, the woman had an opinion and insisted Gertrude be made aware of her judgements. Because there was virtually no escape within the confines of a troopship, Gertrude had decided to be polite, to smile, but not to respond or confirm the woman's narrow-mindedness or even support her prejudices by acknowledging that she was listening.

She was the wife of a Catering Corps officer, who, presumably because he could cook a roast beef without burning it, had been elevated to some dizzy rank in the British Army. The fussy Englishwoman took great pride in explaining tirelessly to Gertrude that because her husband had once cooked a meal for the late King Edward, he had been specially selected to be stationed at Headquarters in Hyderabad where all the action was, and without him and the men in his command, the whole of the Indian Army would collapse.

The major's awful wife had been in India for two years, and was now catching the troop transport across the Indian Ocean to Suez, where she'd take a passenger liner through the Mediterranean to reach Southampton and home. Lucky cook, Gertrude kept thinking, to be free of this awful woman for at least a couple of years.

Between Bombay and Karachi, perennially over-dressed in fashion which was at least three seasons old, with strings of pearls around her neck and an absurd hat adorning her head even at breakfast, the damnable woman had insisted on seeking out Gertrude morning, noon, and night as the only other lady on the ship. The excuse was always for them to go on a 'perambulation' around the decks in order to get away from the 'dreadful and distressingly crude' enlisted men and non-commissioned officers who were swarming over the ship bound for the Middle East to support the British Indian Army's Expeditionary force in the assault on the Turks. And when she wasn't complaining about the troops, she was defaming the quality and quantity of the food served on board . . . food which her husband wouldn't serve to pigs.

So oppressive was she, Gertrude had taken to staying in her cabin, or getting up late and missing breakfast in order to avoid the boorish snob, but regardless of how she crept around the ship to avoid the major's wife, the buxom Home County's woman always seemed to find her.

After a number of excruciating days sailing, they were at last entering Middle East waters, approaching the head of the Gulf where the Shatt al Arab waterway emptied into the sea. The watercourse resulted from the confluence of the Tigris and the Euphrates as the two great rivers emptied the snows of Asiatic Turkey into the Gulf of Persia. They would put in there, unload the troops who would then go by barge to Basrah, and the ship would continue on its way to end its journey in Port Said.

Gertrude had been away from the Middle East for several months, negotiating on the orders of Sir Henry McMahon in the hope of resolving the deep-seated antipathy between the two commands in Egypt and India. And because of her practical skills as a negotiator, her visit to Delhi had been wonderfully successful. With her knowledge of the peoples of Arabia and Mesopotamia, with her understanding of the politics of the region, and with the very real concerns of the Indian Viceroy that there could be an uprising of Indian Muslims if his army sided with the Arabs against the Turks, Gertrude had convinced Lord Hardinge to support a more co-operative working relationship between Delhi and Cairo.

She'd also persuaded him that Mesopotamia could supply the British Army with vast quantities of grain, cotton, dates, figs and much more, and, when it was eventually proven, vast supplies of oil if the early geological reports were confirmed. It could be a virtual treasure house of riches, and now that she'd finally got him to understand the potential of the area for the Empire, Lord Hardinge was sending her to Basrah to be a spy for Britain's Indian Government, his eyes and ears for Britain in the Middle East.

So excited was Gertrude at returning to the area that as the troopship left the Gulf of Oman and entered the turquoise waters of the Straits of Hormuz and then into the Persian Gulf, she had made the mistake of allowing her excitement to overcome her judgment, and stood by the railings on the upper deck, watching the nearby land glide past. And that was where the damnable woman found her.

"Ah, my dear, I see you've surfaced. I've been looking all over the boat for you." she said coming up behind Gertrude who was surveying the huts, palm groves, and oases on the distant shore. The cook's wife looked at what it was that was fascinating Gertrude.

"Ugh! Such a pity you emerged from your cabin after so long, only to have to look at those hovels. How can any respectable person live in a place like that," she commented.

Gertrude had made a real effort to be polite to the major's wife, if only by absenting herself from the woman's presence, but this latest obscenely stupid outburst made Gertrude snap. She was furious with the comment. Something—she had no idea what—erupted inside her and an irresistible urge demanded she teach the woman a lesson. After days in the company of the dim-wit, having to listen to her tireless drivel about the importance of her cook-husband and her social standing being the wife of a major, Gertrude had forced herself to remain uncharacteristically silent until now. But being back on her home territory, her self-restraint came to a regrettable end. She turned slowly to the major's wife, and asked simply, "Are you, by any chance, talking about those huts over there?"

"Yes, my dear! Those simply awful dwellings over there," the major's wife said, pointing to an encampment. "They're hideous. They shouldn't be allowed. I mean, really. You know, I'll bet they're full of flies and vermin and men and women in filthy clothes. Really! You have to wonder how they can bring their children up in those hovels."

"But people have been living like that in this area for thousands of years . . ."

"That's the whole point, my dear. They haven't progressed. They're still as primitive as they ever were. Dirty, filthy people."

Gertrude forced herself to nod and smile. She knew she should remain silent, but a malicious sprite within her forced her to ask softly, "Would you prefer that there were zero huts like that?"

"Oh, absolutely. None at all."

"No," insisted Gertrude. "I asked specifically whether you'd prefer that there were zero huts like that."

The major's wife looked at her strangely. "Yes, absolutely. Zero huts."

"Interesting," Gertrude said, softly enough to be close to a whisper. "You see, we English, and indeed the rest of the world, wouldn't have understood the concept of the zero had it not been for these people, ancestors of those filthy dirty people in those very huts over there. And without the concept of zero, mathematics couldn't have advanced to the point it has today, absolutely central to modern scientific discoveries. It was the Arabs, living in this part of the world, in huts just like those, who invented the concept of zero, which is a dramatically difficult concept to begin to comprehend. It's a concept which requires a huge imaginative leap, and these people did it thousands of years ago."

"Did they?" she responded, not sure where this conversation was going. "And is that particularly important?" she asked.

"Only if you want to be able to understand the concepts of higher mathematics and any form of modern science. Oh, and another thing," said Gertrude, "Do you think there's a signpost with the name of that village on it?"

"I should think so."

"So would I," said Gertrude. "You see, without those people's ancestors, we wouldn't have signposts or words. Thousands of years ago, while our ancestors in what we today call Great Britain were painting themselves with woad and living in wattle and daub huts and foraging around in the ground for nuts and berries like feral animals, this wonderful civilization invented the alphabet and the written word. In fact, this area gave rise to the most imaginative and inventive people the world has ever seen. These people were the source for most of the great myths of humankind. From here came the progenitors of Judaism, Christianity, and Islam. From here came the stories of Adam and Eve, the Tower of Babel, the Garden of Eden, Noah's Ark. Out of these sands grew the civilizations of Babylonia, Sumer, Akkad, and others of which you might not have heard. From living in huts like these and sitting underneath date palms and thinking great thoughts, not recipes for roast beef, poets wrote the most sublime lines, mathematicians created concepts to explain the order of the world, chemists discovered the nature of matter, geographers shaped the Earth and astronomers mapped the stars in the heavens. Indeed," said Gertrude, looking now directly at the astonished major's wife, "The man who thought up algebra might very well have come from that village over there. So first appearances can be deceptive, can't they?" she asked.

She was about to walk away, when she couldn't resist saying, "Britain might call itself Great, but remember the words of Sir Isaac Newton. He said, 'If I have been privileged to see further than other men, it is because I have stood on the shoulders of giants.'"

Gertrude pointed to the distant shoreline. "Over there, madam, in those huts with flies and lice, might have been born some of the giants on whose shoulders Sir Isaac stood."

Gertrude excused herself, and returned to her cabin. She sat on her bed, furious with herself for embarrassing the woman.

It was intellectual snobbery at its very worst, but the major's wife—she couldn't even remember the damn woman's name—was everything Gertrude detested about the British. They were so smug and self-satisfied in their arrogance at being the greatest empire the world had ever known. Yet how smug were the ancient Egyptians and the Akkadians and the Sumerians and the Mesopotamians at the height of their existence? All were the masters of the world until some other warlike tribe began flexing its muscles, or some natural phenomenon like drought or earthquake destroyed the center of government, and the periphery drifted away, to be absorbed by some other fast-rising power.

And then how great were the great civilisations when their empires began to erode? She recalled Shelly's Ozymandias, a brilliant poem about hubris in which a traveller finds the plinth of an ancient statue, on which are written the words:

My name is Ozymandias, king of kings;
Look on my works, ye mighty, and despair!
Nothing beside remains,
Round the decay of that colossal wreck,
Boundless and bare, the lone and level sands stretch far away.

Great Britain was in the process of fighting the Ottoman and hopefully beating him out of Arabia, then Arabia would become a British possession, ruled by the Arabs but run by the British. So where would it stop?

Of course, nobody was for one moment predicting the decline and decay of the British Empire. But while the sun might never set on Britain's possessions, it had grown vast and imperious and strong and smug, despite men and women like the idiot lady on deck, and not because of them. She, and probably her husband and their friends, were typical of why Gertrude had been so unsuccessful with all but the most intellectual and high-minded of British society. She only ever felt comfortable with the rulers of the empire—with Prime ministers and Cabinet Ministers and the most senior diplomats and officials of the Ministries, with judges

162

and politicians and writers and journalists, with brilliant men from the Universities or with Lords who had gained high office because of their minds, and not because of the place to which they were born in society. She mixed comfortably with all and any of them, drinking their whiskeys and smoking their cigarettes and conversing at the level of great and enduring concepts.

She never swapped recipes or discussed fashion—though she spent a fortune on clothes whenever she was in Paris—and she never indulged in gossip. Yet when all was said and done, the major's wife was just that . . . a major's wife and a mother of five children and woman who was probably more acceptable to British society than Gertrude with her first class honors degree from Oxford and her gold medal from the Royal Geographical Society, and with Swiss mountain passes named after her, and her explorations and her literary successes. Gertrude sighed and became angry with herself as she felt tears welling up and frustration started to get the better of her.

When she worked hard, she somehow managed to keep control of her emotions, her aggravation, but when she had long days of solitude, the loneliness welled up, and she felt desperately unhappy about the way her life had been shaped.

Gertrude lay on her bed, thinking of how she'd upset the major's wife, thinking about the fact that only married and ineligible men were attracted to her these days, as she was to them, that the only men she ever wanted were brilliant and brave and worldly and unavailable, other than for an illicit but glorious romantic interlude. And despite her anger at herself for being so weak and female, she began to swear softly under her breath as the ship carried her towards Basrah.

~

Basrah, Mesopotamia, 1916

"I fear, Gertie, that your view of the noble Arab on a white charger, as pure and unsullied as the desert sand, might change from what it used to be," Sir Percy Cox told her over dinner at his residency in Basrah. "You're working towards the unification of all the petty tribes under the banner of a single Saladin-type of leader, but recent events have shown just how far the Arab has to go before he puts aside his petty jealousies and can think on a broader scale.

"Unlike your Indians, or your Africans, our recent experience of the Arab is that he's a liar, utterly untrustworthy, duplicitous, traitorous, and cowardly. It grieves me to say this, but although I recognize that we probably need them to fight the Turks, I wouldn't give them an inch of slack as a part of the British Army."

Sir Percy, the brilliant and normally temperate chief political officer in Mesopotamia, had the job of overseeing the new administration now that the Indian Expeditionary Force of the British Army had gained a foothold in Arabia and was driving north towards Baghdad. Gertrude had known Sir Percy and Lady Cox socially, meeting them once when she was traveling in India in 1902 and again several years later in England, but now that he was in such a senior position, she was answerable to him.

She didn't know how to respond to such a diatribe. He knew of her love for Arabs and Arabia, and she felt inclined to respond to him in defense of those hundreds of Arabs with whom she'd dealt in the past dozen or so years, people of the highest caliber of decency and integrity. Like the wife of the Emir of Hayil who had saved her life when it was most imperilled during her imprisonment and threat of death by ibn Rashid. Like Fattuh, her faithful Armenian-Arabic servant who would lay down his life for her, and like so many others whom she had grown to admire. But she was in a war situation, and these generals and political officers didn't want to hear her defense of the people who had been so much a part of her previous life.

But she couldn't resist a small jab, "Liars, utterly untrustworthy, duplicitous, traitorous, and cowardly? Really, Percy? I didn't know we had so many newspaper and magazine reporters in Arabia."

The room erupted in laughter, and some of the men began to clap. She looked around the table, and acknowledged their appreciation. It was an interesting assembly of guests, for also at the dinner in the hot and uncomfortably humid dining room were the other political officers, St. John Philby and Captain Arnold Wilson, as well as the generals from the British Army's Indian Expeditionary Force, General Lake, General Cowper, General Money, and General Offley Shaw.

~

Gertrude had been in Basrah for two days, acclimatizing herself, setting up her shoebox office, and beginning the job of creating a gazetteer of Arabia and Mesopotamia so the latest dispositions of the Arabic tribes could be identified, catalogued, analysed, and determined. In this way, her office could ensure the most up-to-date information was given to the field commanders. She also set in motion a series of meetings with Arab leaders, Sheikhs, Emirs, and local potentates, to enable her to determine the mood of the area—who would side with the British, who would stay loyal to the money paid to them by the Turks, and who would require additional bribing to change sides. In this way, she could report back the true disposition to Lord Hardinge in India, and that would surely show him the impossibility of trying to rule Arabia from so far away.

Even though it had only been a few days since Gertrude's arrival, she already knew firsthand from conversations that one Sheikh, Ahmed bin Ibrahim Faoud of the Zahawi tribe had refused outright to back the British. He informed her that unless she paid him a quarter of a million American dollars, he would put his support behind the Turks, a fact she'd relayed to General Lake, who'd turned crimson with fury and told her to tell him to go to buggery.

Another chief, Ajaimi Sadun, who claimed to control the disposition of four thousand of his tribe currently serving in the Turkish army in Mesopotamia, was initially tempted to tell his men to decamp and fight for the British, but after meeting and being singularly unimpressed with some of the generals, had changed his mind, convinced Britain would undoubtedly lose the war.

What she was experiencing now, and what she'd begun to think since she was a young woman and Arabia had entered her bloodstream, was that this most extraordinary part of the world would never develop its true potential unless it was united. Dozens of different tribes, little more than extended families, ruled by an omnipotent and often dangerously ignorant and self-indulgent sheik fervently following an unreconstructed medieval religion, jealously guarding their territory, meant that Arabia would remain divided. She hoped and prayed that a good outcome from this terrible war would see the situation change and that, with her guidance, a leader would emerge and Arabia would become another Switzerland, a wonderful and rich land, divided into the Arabic version of cantons, but united under a central government and a wise ruler.

The entire High Command was in a state of utter disgust with the Arabs, and Gertrude knew she had two major campaigns to fight before the British could win their own battles—to convince the Arab sheikhs and chieftains to side with Britain, and to convince the generals that the Arabs were worth having on their side. Their typical British disgust with the Arabic way of being loyal to the nation which paid them the biggest bribe bubbled over into dinner, both because of Sir Percy's outburst, and in spite of her flippancy. Her great plan, of being the catalyst which brought all the Arab tribes together under one leader, seemed to be slipping further and further away as the horror of the war progressed, and layers of civility and past relationships were stripped away and greed became the sole reason for action.

"I know you've got some sort of special relationship with them, Miss Bell, but I'm afraid that Sir Percy's absolutely right," said General Cowper as he lit his cigar and sipped a particularly fine Rhine wine which had been appropriated from a now-closed German produce shop in the port of Basrah. "For the past three months, the bally Arabs have been causing us all manner of problems," he told her huffily. He looked at Lady Cox, and hastily added, "Begging your pardon, ma'am."

"General, I'm sure both Miss Bell and I are quite used to the word *bloody*. It's so much more adult than *bally,* don't you think."

General Offley Shaw commented, "What Cowper says is something of an understatement. The Arabs have been robbing us blind. They steal from our stores, loot our camps, murder our wounded, strip our dead of their rifles and ammunition and personal effects before we've had time to get medics to carry them off and perform some sort of decent Christian burial rite, and they're like hyenas around our troops as the poor buggers march northwards. They wait for one of our troops to drop behind, too exhausted from the heat and the flies and mosquitoes and as soon as he stops to catch his breath, they're on him. They slit his throat and strip him half naked before his mates realize what's happening and come to rescue him. They're bloody brigands, Miss Bell, bloody rotten evil brigands. They have no understanding of the rules of civilized warfare. I know they're your best friends, and you've spent a lifetime ingratiating yourself with them through your articles and your books, but now we're beginning to see the real side of the Arab, and it isn't nice.

"General," she insisted, "I haven't ingratiated myself with them. I've merely translated some of their great writing into English. But I don't just speak their language, General, I understand their customs. And while I have intimate knowledge of why they do the things they do, it doesn't mean that I approve of murder and theft and brigandry. You see that, don't you General?"

General Money hesitatingly continued, "I'm afraid, Miss Bell, that you might have convinced Hardinge in Delhi of the need for liaison between India and Egypt, but we're on the ground, and we need a lot more convincing than just his letters introducing you. Your being here has caused us problems, not to put too fine a point on it. I'm afraid that some of the chaps you're going to be working with will resent you a bit. They consider themselves the experts, and don't take kindly to having a woman working alongside them."

The room descended into silence.

"I see," she said softly. "And what am I expected to do about that? Pretend I don't know ten times more about Arabia than any of the men under your commands in Basrah? Pretend I've never travelled the length and breadth of the lands of the Abu Muhammad, or the Bani Lam, or the Bani Rabiah, or the Sadun, or the Anazzeh? Pretend I'm just a jolly English woman who's here to support her officer husband and ensure I wear the correct hat to the viceroy's tea parties? Is that it, General? Is that what you'd like me to do?"

"Of course not. When Hardinge wrote to introduce you, he said that you've got the brains of a man. But many people here think you're an Arab lover, and . . ."

"No, General Money. I'm not an Arab lover, nor an English lover, nor a French lover. I love no tribe or race or religion. I only love people who are knowledgeable, worldly, honest, and decent. I'm sorry if my being here causes you problems, General, but I'm here to do a job, and I'll prove to you I can be of great assistance in your efforts to win this damnable war." Gertrude sipped her glass of wine, and looked around the room.

She'd kept her temper, which is all that mattered. She'd given well of herself. Now it was up to them to learn to live with her.

General Offley Shaw was the first to speak. "Point is, Miss Bell, we're in a real pickle at the moment. We told Hardinge. We said we couldn't embark on an expedition to push northwards from Basrah to capture Baghdad without proper logistical support, but our victory in Basrah went to his head, and he insisted we push on with all speed. Now we've got thousands of British troops dropping like flies at the mercy of Arabs and Turks, and no way to rescue them. These bloody Arabs . . ."

"They're not bloody Arabs, General," said Gertrude, trying to restrain herself. "They're an ancient people who have been slaves of the Ottoman Empire for four hundred years. And they see the British as yet another interloper in their lands. A useful interloper, certainly, because we can rid them of the Turks; but a trespasser nonetheless. They want their land back . . ."

The entire table suddenly went quiet as she sat up as straight as a ramrod, her green eyes had narrowed and her lips were pursed.

She was on the verge of saying more, but instead, she stubbed out her cigarette and looked at each of the military men in turn. What she'd said could be considered as treason. She noticed that Percy Cox closed his eyes, unsure of what she was going to say and do next. One of the generals twirled the ends of his waxed moustache

"With the greatest of respect, you gentlemen are making the timeworn and classic mistake of judging one people by the standards and behavior of another.

"Bribery to an Englishman is a criminal act, yet in Arabia it is considered a quite acceptable way of telling a person how important he is. Nepotism is frowned upon in certain classes of society in Great Britain, yet the Ottoman Empire successfully ran on nepotism for most of the past four hundred years. Killing someone who has offended your honor in England will see you dangling at the end of from a noose, yet you'll be considered a hero in Italy and Spain and in many parts of South America. And I might say that if you're a stranger who's travelled a distance and seek out a refreshing drink at the door of an Englishman's house, he'll more than likely set the dogs on you, but even the most humble Arab will invite you into his tent and share with you the most generous hospitality, and that's even to his worst enemy, provided he's a genuine traveller.

"Look, please understand my position. I'm an English woman through and through. I've dined at Buckingham Palace. I've come out at all the social balls. And you must understand I have no fondness for Arabs who take money from the Turks and hold out for a better bribe from the British. But you must also learn to appreciate that it's a part of their way of life. To the Arab, the more money you pay him is a sign of your greater respect for him and his tribe. And trying to change their way of doing things is as useless as missionaries telling brown-skinned South Sea Islanders to cover their nakedness with shirt, trousers, and a tie."

Lady Cox burst out laughing. It broke the strained atmosphere. Even one of the Generals laughed.

Sir Percy intervened, "So what do you advise, my dear? You're the expert on Arabs and Mesopotamia. I know we've got supposed experts here, but frankly we're in a mess, and there doesn't seem to be any way out of it."

"Oh yes there is, Percy. I know I've only just arrived in Basrah, but I'm not new to this area by any means. I've spent the past fifteen years traveling from north to south, east to west. Give me a month, and I'll have a majority of them understanding the danger of siding with the Turks against us. Give me two months, and I hope to be able to deliver you a million or so men, armed to the teeth, to fight on our side."

There was a protracted silence, as the generals looked across the table at each other. It was broken by General Lake. "I'm afraid we might have neither two months, nor two weeks. I've been receiving reports from my commander that several thousand of his men have been forced to retreat to Kut al Amara."

She looked at him in astonishment. "Kut? Surely not, General. The battle for Kut was our great victory. After Basrah and Qurna and Shaiba and Amarah, we stormed the city and took Kut. It was in September last year. I was in India, but we heard about it. It was a great—"

"Forgive me for interrupting you, Miss Bell," said General Lake, "but you obviously haven't yet heard what's happened at the Battle of Ctesiphon—"

"Ctesiphon?" she shouted in surprise. "I've dug there. It's an archaeological wonder."

"It was a terrible battlefield, I'm afraid," said General Money.

"My God, no! Not Ctesiphon. Don't tell me there was damage. The archaeology . . . it's priceless."

She held her breath in dread of the devastation a battle could do to a place as delicate as Ctesiphon, the ancient ruins where she'd undertaken some initial exploratory archaeology. She loved its romance, the gigantic temples, and the antiquity of the place. It was built at the very beginning of mankind's climb to greatness. Ctesiphon was one of the greatest cities in all of Mesopotamia. It was the capital of the Parthian and Persian empires for nearly a millennium. In 200 AD the emperor Septimius Severus sacked the city and killed tens of thousands of its inhabitants. Since then it had been hidden by the sand from prying eyes until archaeologists had begun to uncover it, and the ruins were priceless.

"My God," she whispered, "we have to do something to protect the temples . . ."

Astounded, Sir Percy said quietly, "Gertrude, may I remind you that British men are laying dead in Ctesiphon. Have some thought to them, rather than some long-forgotten empire and its pile of stones."

Realizing her gaffe, Gertrude nodded, feeling chastened, and said, "I do apologize, Percy. I shouldn't have said what I did. It's just that I love Ctesiphon very dearly. But I do, sincerely, apologize for what sounded like my lack of concern for our lads. I've only just arrived, and I don't yet feel a part of this damnable war. Do go on, General Lake."

"You're right when you say the Battle of Kut was a resounding victory for us. The commander, General Townshend, deserves great credit for it. But he was worried afterwards about pushing on and asked to be allowed to consolidate his forces. His supply route was horribly over-extended far up the river. We were four hundred odd miles from the sea, and supplying him was very difficult. We took on over ten thousand Turks who were under the command of General Nur-Ud-Din. It was quite a scrap, I can tell you! We killed over five thousand of their men, and captured all their heavy artillery. But then Townshend was ordered to continue pushing northwards to Baghdad. He told us it was folly. He told us he'd prefer to wait for reinforcements, for supplies, for boats and airplanes. But our lords and masters in Delhi were flushed with his victories, and ordered him to push on. And then he encountered Ctesiphon . . ."

"What happened?" asked Gertrude quietly.

General Lake looked uncomfortable. "Townshend kept sending back dispatches reminding us how dangerous his supply situation was. He demanded extra transportation and trench warfare equipment, the most basic requirements when you're going to battle against the Turks. But Viceroy Hardinge and the Indian Government thought we were on a winning streak and that the Turks were in full retreat. We told them the truth of the situation, but they didn't listen. Hardinge told him just to push northwards. They looked on a map, and saw that he was only about 20 miles from Baghdad, and they thought he was being too cautious. They didn't listen to him or us about the fact that the Turks would throw thousands of fresh men at the front line to defend the city. We went behind Delhi's back, and appealed to Whitehall. Even London disagreed with Hardinge, but for some reason, the mandarins in the War Office went along with the Indian Government. In the meantime, the Turks had learned from their series of defeats, and especially from their disaster at Kut. They retreated and prepared defensive positions in the ruins of Ctesiphon."

Gertrude refrained from saying anything out loud, but silently hoped there was no damage to the site.

"The Turks decided to make this the forward defense line for Baghdad. General Nur-Ud-Din had constructed two deep lines of trenches on either side of the Tigris. He brought in eighteen thousand experienced and fresh troops from the North, all of them raring to go and committed to reclaiming the honor of their Army after the ignominy they'd suffered. Townshend had eleven thousand exhausted men. He rallied his men magnificently, and breathed spirit into them. He tried to repeat his successes at Kut and issued orders for night-marching in order to surprise the Turks defenders and out-flank them from the rear.

"But his damned army got lost in the dark. All element of surprise was gone, and the British attack became a rout. We couldn't provide naval support along the Tigris because the Turks had deployed mines in the water and heavy artillery along the bank.

"The next day, the Turks launched the most ferocious attacks, and Townshend's men dropped like flies, though they fought like warriors. Four thousand five hundred English men, good and true, were killed in that one day alone. It was as bad as Gallipoli . . ."

Gertrude bit her lip as she thought of all those dead young men, their lifeblood soaked up by the thirsty sands of the desert, their lifeless eyes staring at the eternal stars. She struggled to restrain her emotions.

General Lake continued, "Nur-Ud-Din suffered double our casualties, but he had access to countless reserves in Baghdad, and this was his last-ditch stand.

"Townshend knew it would be a slaughter if he continued, so he ordered a retreat and as our men fought their way south, through the marshes and God knows what other difficulties, they were set upon by Turks and Arab alike. They altered one of the larger boats on the river to create a makeshift hospital craft to ferry the dead and wounded back to Basrah, even knowing that there were submerged mines, and Townshend began to create a defensive position. We're trying to send up reinforcements, but he's in a terrible pickle, I'm afraid."

"Dear God Almighty," Gertrude whispered. "What's happening to us? I just don't understand anything any longer. Two years ago Turkey attacked Odessa and Sevastopol and closed the Dardanelles. People were talking about the war lasting six months. They said the Ottomans were diseased and decaying imperialists and would crumble at the first sight of our fighting men, but now you're telling me, General, that the Turks are a valiant fighting force . . ."

The generals looked at Sir Percy waiting for the political officer to say something. He finished his glass of wine, and said softly, "We all miscalculated, both here and with the Kaiser's armies in Europe, and I'm afraid millions—tens of millions—of men on both sides are dying as a result. It's the greatest slaughter in the whole sorry history of humanity, I'm afraid. It makes all the previous wars in all of history seem like local neighborhood scraps. It even makes the Crusades pale in comparison.

"Since this damnable war began, Russia has mobilized twelve million men, France has mobilized over eight million, Britain nearly nine million, and Germany and Austria-Hungary between them claim to have nineteen million. We've got no idea how many the Turks have sent into battle, but in all we're talking about figures of . . ." He did a quick calculation in his head. "Probably sixty million men if you include Italy and the smaller nations, fighting with and against each other in all the theaters of the war. There's never been anything like what we're seeing now. I wouldn't be surprised if ten million men weren't killed before this damnable thing in Europe and here in the Middle East is over."

Gertrude felt her jaw visibly drop at the sheer unimaginable quantity of humanity, fighting a war whose cause she had almost forgotten. "But that's an entire generation . . ."

"Ten million, Percy? Surely not," exclaimed General Money. "That's staggering . . ."

Sir Percy looked at him and shrugged.

"And I wonder how many of those will perish as a result of miscalculations?" Gertrude asked.

Again the room fell silent.

"What's to be done about our lads in Kut-al-Amara, Percy? We're talking about the lives of thousands of men. They can't be wasted. What are we doing to bring them back home again?"

"That's why I've asked these generals to dine with you and me," Sir Percy said. "You see, trying to get them back to Basrah will result in further unimaginable losses. The Turks smells victory and he's reinforced himself with thousands of fresh troops from the north. We can't retreat by river, because he'll blow us out of the water with his artillery on either bank. We can't fight our way out of Kut, because we're surrounded. We're trying to send up reinforcements, but we haven't got enough, and what we do send are repelled by the force of arms. Which means we can be certain of two options only, I'm afraid. Surrender . . ." He lapsed into silence, seemingly unable to say the alternative.

"Or pay the Turks a massive bribe?" asked Gertrude.

"Precisely, my dear."

"And since I'm an expert on how the Arabs will react, you want to know if there's a third way. You want me to tell you whether I can get the Arabs to change sides and fight the Turks to drive him off. Am I correct, Percy?"

The generals all looked at her in amazement. They hadn't before met a woman with such an acute and strategic mind.

"Correct, Gertrude."

Slowly, she looked at everyone sitting at the table. "Do I have a week?"

General Lake shrugged.

"Can I call for an assistant?" she asked.

"Whom?" asked Sir Percy.

"A certain Mr. Lawrence. Captain Lawrence, to be precise, although he might be Major Lawrence by now, maybe even Colonel Lawrence. Right at this moment, I think you'll probably find him somewhere in the Kingdom of Hejaz with Prince Faisal, the third son of the Sharif Hussein of Mecca and Medina."

"Why this Lawrence chappie?" asked Sir Percy.

"Because he has a feel for the Arab; between the two of us, I'm sure we can pull a rabbit out of the hat."

~

Kingdom of Hejaz

The prince looked at Lawrence choking in the corner of the room. The poor man's face was puce and Faisal was concerned the Englishman was about to vomit on the rug.

Every time Lawrence straightened and tried to compose himself, he suddenly doubled over and began to cough and retch again, apologizing between the coughing bouts. A servant moved towards him, but the prince waved the man away, knowing Lawrence would have to recover on his own if he was ever to face the shisha again.

Eventually, after sipping some rose water, red and watery eyed and still flushed, Lawrence was sufficiently composed to splutter, "I'm so very sorry, Highness."

"Not at all, Mr. Lawrence. But I did warn you, didn't I. Are you feeling better?"

Lawrence nodded. His throat still burned and his eyes were smarting, but he felt well enough to return to the divan from which he'd just ejected himself.

"Would you care to try again?" asked the Prince.

"No, sir, I most certainly would not."

"But if you had taken my advice in the first place you wouldn't have suffered so badly. Take another sip of rose water, and try one of the tobaccos soaked in the juice of an apple. Using a nargile for the first time can be difficult for the non-smoker, but using it with unflavored tobacco is asking for trouble . . . and trouble just found you, Mr. Lawrence."

"I would prefer to watch Your Majesty. I will indulge myself in other pleasures while I am a guest in your house."

"But Lawrence, the shisha is such a source of infinite pleasure for us. It originally came from India, you know, but it was a very primitive piece of equipment when it reached us. It took Arab ingenuity to turn it into the ultimate machine of pure pleasure. We received it from India in the form of a coconut shell and some water. But when it came to Persia, and then spread throughout the whole of the Arabic world, we refined the design and today it's a wonderful part of our customs. But raw tobacco, Mr. Lawrence? Very silly, when we have such exciting and soothing flavors as apple and cinnamon and pomegranate and rose oil."

The prince nodded to a servant, and another hookah was brought, its lower bowl filled with pure water, and the long stem of the pipe filled with a tobacco which had been subtly flavored with the juice of strawberries. Reluctantly, Lawrence put the smoking tube into his mouth, and tentatively drew on it. The smoke which filled his mouth was delicate, as though he tasted an unusually aromatic fruit salad. The prince smiled when Lawrence turned and nodded to him in gratitude.

They continued talking and smoking until they had finished their wads of tobacco. The servants removed the hookahs and both men settled back onto the divans.

"It's really very good of Allenby or whoever it was, to have sent you over to me," said the prince.

"Actually, sir, it was my request to be sent here. As you know, I'm particularly keen to use the authority your family has as guardians of Mecca and Medina to convince the other leaders to join us in overthrowing the Turks."

"You have quite some experience in our area of the world, don't you Mr. Lawrence?"

"I do sir. I've done mapping of Palestine and Aqaba, and I've been on a number of archaeological digs. And I speak your language quite well."

The prince nodded. "And your fascination with the Arabs, Mr. Lawrence?"

He thought before answering. "You enjoyed one of the world's most profound and fecund of histories, yet it was within a desert culture where little blooms. You once were a great people ruling half the world, almost conquering the southern half of Europe right up to the borders of Hungary and Vienna, but now you're nothing but an enslaved people, divided into a hundred minor principalities. Your people are warlike, yet you have written the most sublime love poetry. Your mathematicians and astronomers were as great as the Greeks, yet almost none of your people can read or write. Your people are commanded by sheiks and yet they owe allegiance to mullahs and ayatollahs. You write the most elegiac love poems to your women, yet you treat them as little more than sexual and kitchen slaves. You revere Mohammed as though he were a demi-god, yet unlike Christianity and Judaism, you have never sought to question the teachings of your Prophet, nor have you enjoyed a Renaissance which would have undermined the power of your religious leaders and given power back to the people. You've never coalesced into one great nation because you're tribal, and how can a great man rise to lead you when your people pay such close attention to your religious men. You have no history or experience of democracy, yet you are keen to participate as an equal nation in the affairs of the rest of the world. You're fanatical about your allegiance to your tribes, yet throughout your history, you have continually played with the idea of pan-Arabism as a way out of your pettiness. You are a fascinating complex of paradoxes which I'm struggling to comprehend."

Prince Faisal nodded, and reflected for some time on what Lawrence had just said.

"While you were just speaking, Lawrence, had I closed my eyes, I would have sworn that Miss Gertrude Bell was in the room, speaking to me."

Lawrence grinned. "I have been a good pupil."

"But will the student outdo the master? Or in this case, the mistress?"

Sheepishly the Englishman continued, "Miss Bell is currently working with the generals in Basrah. And in a way, I'm pleased she wasn't here, for if she, or any of my English colleagues had been listening, I'd probably be thrown into military prison for treason. I've just insulted you and your people, whereas I should have been a sycophant, paying you nothing but compliments. If I have insulted you, sir, I apologize."

"Are you saying that Miss Bell would have been a sycophant?" asked Faisal, a grin appearing on his face.

"Hardly, but she's a lot more diplomatic than I am. And I think I should have considered my words much more carefully. I often say what I think without considering the consequences."

"On the contrary, Lawrence; one of the reasons I readily accepted your attachment to me was because in you, I can always rely on the truth. I appreciated that the very first time we met in Egypt when you burst into my surreptitious meeting with Miss Gertrude Bell. You could have been a sycophant, but instead you risked Miss Bell's ire and that led to her telling me the truth about my father's situation. I have no time for those who tell me what I want to hear, rather than what I need to know.

"In that, I'm reminded of a story told of the court of Queen Elizabeth, daughter of your Henry VIII. When she had just become queen, she appointed Sir William Cecil to be the keeper of her nation under her. She appointed him because she trusted his advice absolutely, and she knew he would never tell her anything which might harm England, even at the risk of his own life when his advice might not please her. You, Mr. Lawrence, are my Cecil."

Lawrence smiled. "Cecil became Lord Burleigh, and made a fortune. I, unfortunately, will always remain on the meager salary of a minor office in the British Army."

The prince smiled at the Englishman, and snapped his fingers. "But perhaps I can provide you with some extracurricular benefits of our association, then, Mr. Lawrence."

At the cue, two lithe young women entered the room bowing low. They were dressed in the richest and most gossamer-like fabrics, their bodies clearly visible through the voile.

They sauntered towards the divans, their faces barely visible through their veils, their eyes cast to the ground. One sat at the feet of the prince, the other at the feet of Lawrence.

"My gift to you, Mr. Lawrence. True Arabic beauty. Strong limbed, willing, and lusty. I have had both of them recently, and can highly recommend either, or both if that is your wish. They are very experienced in making a man content."

"I—I"

"They aren't to your pleasing?"

"Yes . . . but I don't think that . . ."

"You don't like them?"

"Yes. But I'm a serving British officer, and I don't think I should be involved in this sort of thing."

"Don't be so stuffy, Lawrence. You're not on duty now."

"It's not right, sir. We English don't do this sort of thing."

"You're in Arabia now, Mr. Lawrence. When in Rome . . ."

"I'm sorry, Highness, but I fear I must leave and go to bed on my own." He stood, and bowed to the astounded prince.

As he was walking out of the door, the woman who had been at his feet looked up at the prince, and shook her head in bemusement.

"Is there something you haven't told me, Mr. Lawrence," Faisal called after him. "Perhaps women aren't to your liking? I can present you with some lovely boys, if you'd prefer? I want to accommodate your pleasures."

Lawrence silently walked out of the room. As he paced towards his apartments, he bit his lip in anger. If his earlier arrogance and impertinence hadn't ruined his relationship with the prince, then walking out on his gift of women would certainly have done so.

He might as well pack his bags and return to Cairo in the morning. At least he had an excuse for the failure of his mission.

~

The sun burned the landscape with such violence that the yellow of the desert fused with the white of the sky, making the distant horizon invisible. There was neither distance nor closeness, length nor breadth, height nor depth. Measurement became meaningless when the sky and the ground were one, and only the ebb and flow of shadows gave both significance and perspective to the passing of a day. Not in Aqaba nor Palestine nor Egypt had he known a landscape where the sun had leached color and forms and distances so completely.

The sun! How could an Englishman possibly begin to comprehend the supremacy of the sun which bleached the very rocks themselves, draining the sky and the ground and the animals which walked upon it of any recognizable feature. It was already halfway above the endless vista of the desert, and all around him seemed to be blended seamlessly into unity. There was no ground, but a continuous hemisphere of yellow which seamlessly transformed into a powdery white-blue sky. Nowhere ahead of him, nor behind, could he look and say, "now I'm arriving at my destination." It was all a blur, a heat wave, an illusion.

They were no more than three hour's camel ride from Ragibh, halfway between Mecca and Medina, and yet they could have been riding for weeks through the wilderness. Gertrude had told him about the Nefud and the other great deserts of the Arabian

Peninsula, and he thought he was used to deserts, but he'd experienced nothing like this.

He and the prince and their entourage were hundreds of miles from these other anvils of the Earth, these other hellish deserts, yet even in this place, relatively civilized compared to the very worst of Arabian deserts, Lawrence felt the sun as never before. It burned through the keffiyeh he wore, through his thick khaki uniform, through the socks and the boots. It burned into his bones and even felt as though it was boiling his blood. It was enervating yet somehow strangely comforting, like riding within a gigantic womb. It was as if all the conflicts of his life, all the problems of his past, his physical stature and lisp and limp, were all of such little importance, all so negligible, that he was suddenly just like every other man struggling to survive in this alien landscape.

He took his fob watch out of the top pocket of his uniform. The steel back felt hot in his hand as he unhinged the front. It was only mid-morning, yet it seemed as though they had been riding for the entire day. And then he noticed the prince was far ahead of him. Lawrence realized he was riding slower, more painfully than the others. His pride made him kick the camel's flanks and whip its backside so it flared its lips, growled, belched and suddenly bolted forward to join the other men, jolting him into renewed consciousness.

He rode up level with the prince, who looked at him in concern. "You don't have to prove you are a man of the desert, Mr. Lawrence. You are an Englishman, used to the green highways and byways of Surry and Middlesex. This is not your environment. If you're having difficulties in keeping up with men who were born in the sand, simply say and we'll slow down."

"Thank you, Highness," Lawrence said, his voice rasping and dry, "but I am not feeling too much of a strain. I'm quite sure I can keep pace with you and your men."

The prince rode onwards, Lawrence by his side. After ten or so minutes of silence, broken only by some of the camels growling in complaint, Prince Faisal said, "I'm interested in why you declined my offer of one of the women servants last night. Was it really because of your English reserve, or was there another reason. In the time I've known you, you have never appeared to have an eye for women, or men for that matter. Are you one of those very proper Englishmen who are so reserved they're incapable of enjoying life, or is there something about your, shall we say, personal life you wish to keep to yourself?"

"An Englishman is always reserved, Highness. And part of that reserve is never to talk about matters of the body in polite company. We are only just now recovering from perhaps the most restrictive of all ages the English have ever known, supervised by our glorious Queen Victoria. During her reign, sexuality was an unfit topic for thought, let alone discussion."

"You are joking, of course Mr. Lawrence. What about Oscar Wilde? The underside of London? The prostitutes, both male and female, children and adult? The lewd theaters and music halls? Come, Mr. Lawrence, proper English society might not have discussed it, but sexuality was rampant during the reign of the queen. And Victoria's son, your former king, the late King Edward, is known to have had mistresses in almost every great house in the country. The aristocracy kept their daughters under lock and key when he was in the area. We in Arabia might be a . . . what were the words you used recently? Oh yes, 'nothing but an enslaved people, divided into a hundred minor principalities', but we are honest and open about our bodies and our needs. Our women are happy to please their men."

"Then why cover them head to toe in clothes which hide their very real beauty?"

"We were told by the Prophet, peace and blessings be upon him, to prize modesty. The women in Arabia are the possessions of the men. We men must guard our possessions carefully so no other man covets them."

Lawrence become angry at the prince's words, but restrained himself.

"But you still haven't told me of your own pleasures. Why can't you just be honest, and assist me in your likes and dislikes, so I can assist you in fulfilling your desires. Is it women or men you prefer? Boys or girls? Camels, horses, goats . . . ?"

Captain Lawrence burst out laughing. "Sir, might we not discuss other subjects than my unworthy needs?"

The prince looked at him curiously. Softly, he asked, "Are you a virgin, Mr. Lawrence."

Like an Arabic woman before her husband, Lawrence cast his eyes towards the ground in embarrassment and deference. The Englishman's silence gave the prince his answer. Yet despite his oddity, he felt strangely drawn to this complex, attractive, enigmatic young Englishman.

EIGHT

Basrah, Mesopotamia, March, 1916

The rain was torrential, hanging like a shroud, falling as gray fingers from a dead sky. Major Thomas Lawrence left his ship to enter a land in which he'd only once in the past set foot, and his first thought was how oddly out of place such a deluge was for a desert country.

But then again, maybe it wasn't. This, after all, was the place where the original story of the deluge had been dreamed by an ancient people. It was where Noah, the rescuer and progenitor of life on Earth was the first to see God's symbol, the rainbow, as the cosmic link between heaven and Earth signifying mankind's cleansing and return to supremacy. This place was the origin of so much of humankind's creativity. Here was written the Epic of Gilgamesh. It was here that Gula, the Goddess of Medicine, first healed those who worshipped her. This was where Abram journeyed to find the one God who would eventually rename him as Abraham, the father of many. Here was where, for the first time in mankind's history, the epic battles between the gods who controlled the Earth, the seasons, the crops, and the weather fought against those gods who had control of the sun and the moon and the stars—where people first wrote the most exquisite words about how their lives were ruled by the whims of unseeable and unknowable deities which they represented by crude clay idols.

And it was here that Thomas Lawrence's favourite deity legend was born—that of Mithras, which was originally Persian, but which spread throughout the Middle East and eventually became one of the Roman's favourites. Mithras was the origin of the Christ in Christianity. According to the legend, Mithras was born hundreds of years before Jesus, and on Mithras' birthday,

December 25th, three wise men from Persia came to visit him, bringing him gifts of gold, myrrh and frankincense. He was born of a virgin, and during his life acquired twelve disciples who represented the twelve signs of the zodiac. Before he was executed on a cross, he celebrated a last supper with his disciples who were among the first to form a celibate priesthood around his worship. And the final nail in Christianity's coffin, as the one true religion, was Mithras' ascension into heaven during the same time as the Jewish Passover, a time when there is equal night and day.

When, he wondered, would the self-righteous Christian and Jewish and Muslim priests acknowledge that not only were their religions not the word of some non-existent God, but nothing more than inventions of frightened ancient minds who created myths proving their deities weren't deities at all, but explanations of natural phenomena which their pre-scientific minds couldn't explain.

He looked out from the deck of the ship which had just docked. The sight before him led his mind into a hundred different by-roads. He often pondered the myths and legends and the extraordinary diversity of the people in the Middle East as he thought of the distinctions between his own Christian religion and that of Islam.

Christianity was such an arrogant religion, Lawrence thought, as his feet settled on the solid ground which was the dock. He surveyed the melee around him . . . why did Christian priests think they had all the right answers when almost all of the stories in the Testament were merely appropriations and adaptations of what had been told and retold to countless generations during the millennia which led to the birth of Jesus? Why did Westerners treat the Arabs with such contempt, when so much of Western thought and myths and philosophies had derived from this desert people? He shook his head and relished the joy of being where he was.

But his joy lasted only for a short while. Soaked to the skin, exhausted from walking through the deluge, Lawrence had only been in Basrah for a couple of hours, but yearned for the heat and dryness of the desert. If ever he needed an ark to save him from this particular cosmic destruction, this downpour of biblical proportions, it was now. After his ship had landed, it had taken him two hours to walk from the dockside of Basrah to the headquarters of the Chief Political Officer for Mesopotamia, Sir Percy Cox. First of all, he had taken a taxi, but when he'd been sitting in it for half an hour and it hadn't even left the dock due to the congestion at the port's entrance, he paid the fare for the two hundred or so yards he'd traveled, picked up his kitbag, and decided to walk the remaining distance despite the drenching he knew he'd get.

The roads, once compacted earth and gravel baked by the sun during months of dry weather, were now as sticky as toffee in the deluge and he was in danger of falling flat on his face in the mud and slime, which seemed to creep up his shoes and into his leggings, making them squelch and making him feel miserable. And the rain weighed down the khaki of his uniform and made it feel as heavy and stiff as canvas.

Just ten days ago, he'd been sweltering in the deserts of Hejaz. There were times when the Englishman thought he'd fry in the merciless burning heat, but his constitution seemed to acclimatize quickly and it took him only a few days to become as one with the others with whom he was riding. He thought he was sufficiently experienced in desert conditions from his time in Egypt to be used to almost anything, but the Egyptian desert was a civilized and almost fruitful land compared to the deserts of the Hejaz.

No matter the hardships he'd suffered, it had all been very well worth it. He and Prince Faisal had reached more than a political accommodation, more than an understanding—they'd gained a deep friendship, an intimacy which only true male friends could begin to comprehend. He was now as close and intimate with Faisal as he'd been with his friends when he was up at Oxford. He and the prince had ridden together, eaten together, bathed together at the oasis of Ain el Hadid, slaughtered a lamb together and had each eaten one of the eyes, the greatest compliment a host could pay a visitor. They had discussed the most intimate aspects of their lives, their upbringing, their triumphs and disappointments. It was only when the prince tried to uncover the details of Lawrence's loves and preferences and experiences that a strain developed between them.

In the evening, the prince had always ended the day by visiting Lawrence's tent, where they had discussed philosophy and archaeology, and Lawrence had read to him from the poetical works of Browning and Shelley and Keats. And for his part, the prince had told Lawrence of the joys of being a ruler in a feudal land which wasn't particularly enamoured of the Western notions of democracy, where he and his father and brothers had the power of life and death in their hands and at a whim could banish some enemy to his certain death in the lands of ibn Sa'ud or ibn Rashid, or where they could chose to lie with any woman or man who took their fancy.

Were the women—or men—who were so chosen to be the lovers of the rulers, ever hurt or insulted by such *droits des seigneurs*? The prince was amazed that Lawrence could even think such an event could hurt or insult some inhabitant of the city. After all, there was no greater honor than being chosen to pleasure one of Hejaz's rulers.

It had been an educative experience for Lawrence, but it had come to an abrupt end. He and Prince Faisal had been riding to Medina to convince the local leaders to rise up against the Turks when suddenly a messenger, appearing out of the desert in a column of sand and dust and arriving with the warlike fury of an avenging angel, suddenly thrust a letter in Lawrence's hands. It contained instructions from Military Headquarters in Cairo, dated a few days beforehand, to make all haste for Jeddah, where he was to pick up a ship to sail to Basrah.

Waiting on the ship was a Lieutenant Colonel, originally stationed in Jerusalem, who'd been instructed by Cairo to deliver Lawrence's sealed orders. The colonel, who had recently been transferred from Shanghai to Egypt, found it discomforting that he had to *kowtow* to a junior officer, but everybody had told him Major Lawrence was a rum one, very odd, and that he had the ear of the top brass in Cairo and London. So the colonel determined to enjoy the sea trip and not to let Lawrence's rudeness in not disclosing the orders ruffle his feathers. When they arrived in Basrah, the colonel had looked in disgust at the Arabic town, turned up his nose at the stench from the marketplaces, and declared he preferred to remain aboard in his cabin and wait for the following day and his return to Suez.

And now Lawrence was in Basrah. He'd first been here in 1911 when he'd taken a walking tour through northern Mesopotamia. It was somehow comforting to be back in the land where true civilization had begun. There were those who were now saying that human life had begun in the jungles of Africa, where man had developed from apes and had emerged from the trees to inhabit the land as a competitor to lions and elephants. But this was where early man, truly civilized man, had first fashioned those putative forms and patterns which, when fully developed by European civilization, had enabled him to conquer the Earth.

Mesopotamia! Was it pouring with rain when Nebuchadnezzar had brought the Jews back as slaves half a millennium before Jesus, after despoiling their lands and sacking their temple in Jerusalem? Was it as torrential as this when the Tigris and the Euphrates had been tamed by ancient engineers and walls and channels and dams had been built to ensure irrigation throughout the year? And was it like this when a once-great and magnificent community of poets and philosophers and mathematicians had somehow slipped off their perch of industry and achievement and for over a millennium had become nothing more than illiterate desert brigands?

As he slithered and fell for the umpteenth time over a muddy rut into a deep water-filled pothole, Lawrence stopped wondering how he was going to clean his uniform in order to present himself to Sir Percy Cox, and started thinking about the nature of his mission. He had been given two jobs. The first was to secure the release of many thousands of British soldiers trapped in Kut al

Amara. He'd been authorised to give the Turkish commander up to a million gold sovereigns.

And his second task was to find a replacement in Mesopotamia for Gertrude Bell, and bring her back with him to Cairo so the two of them could work together on the maps and dispositions of the Arabian Peninsula and assist in encouraging the Arabs to revolt against the Turks. The revolt was becoming increasingly important to British interests, both because the Turks were proving to be a more formidable enemy than first anticipated, and because being able to field a million or more Arab fighters against Turkey would prevent Britain and the Allies from moving men away from the battlefields of Europe.

Within sight of the British Indian Army's headquarters in Basrah, Lawrence stiffened himself for the final lunge. He had only about fifty yards to go between the street corner on which he stood, and the entryway to the HQ. He started his run, but his first step landed him in a water-filled gutter which hid a monstrous crevasse that had opened up in the road, and he plunged headlong onto his belly, propelled forward like a penguin on ice and stopping only when he was in the middle of the road.

"Lawrence?" asked a voice which he could barcly hear above the tympany of the rain on the nearby tin rooftops.

Major Lawrence looked up and towards the shops on the side of the road. He saw the shape of a woman . . . an Englishwoman. He knew she was English because unlike the other men and women dressed in the clothes of Arabia, through the downpour he was just able to determine that this woman was dressed in a flowered hat, a long skirt, laced up boots and had the pinched waist of a Western lady.

"Lawrence, is that you?" the voice asked louder.

"Gertie?"

"For God's sake, dear boy, you look like a drowned rat. Here, get up, and take my arm. You look awful."

He stood, and looked at her. She, too, was soaked, but unlike Lawrence, who looked as though he'd just been swimming fully clothed in a mud bath, Gertrude still managed to look fresh and womanly.

She helped him up from the street and guided him underneath a waterlogged awning, where she promptly burst out laughing. "I don't think I've ever seen a more pathetic specimen of humanity than you," she told him. Then she threw her arms around him, and hugged him.

"Gertie," he said. "I'm terribly wet. You'll get yourself muddy."

"As if that matters, my love."

"Gertie," he said. "It's so awfully good to see you."

"And you too, poor boy, even though you look as though you've got half the mud of Basrah on your clothes. You can't possibly see Percy like that. I live five minutes from here . . . come over to my house, and I'll get you bathed and my servants will clean and press your uniform."

An hour later, he was seated sipping tea on the veranda in one of her silk bathrobes, looking out over the tops of the houses towards the port. The rain was still torrential, yet he felt comforted and warm being in her house, in her company. As she sipped her tea, she looked fondly at him. She wore an almost permanent smile at the pleasure of being with Lawrence again.

"I've missed you, Gertie. Missed you terribly. You were the only person I could ever talk to in Egypt. I learned so much from you, you know. And you were the only one who was kind. The others were beastly in the way they treated me."

"And they were often cruel and horrible to me, too. At least you're a man, and you could go to the Officer's Club and drink with the fellows. Me? I spent all day working, then I dined with a small group of friends who couldn't wait to leave me after port and cigars so they could all go to their club and stand around the piano and sing and drink. Imagine how it was for me, being a woman, all alone, with no military rank and no way of getting on the inside."

Lawrence mused, and said, "But surely I brought a spark of life to your miserable existence?"

"Of course you did. You were tremendously considerate. But was it because we were friends, or was it because I was teaching you so much about Arabia?"

"Gertie," he said shocked. "How can you even think that? Oh, you were a wonderful teacher, but we were pals. We're such good friends. I love you, you know that."

"And I love you, Thomas. But I'm afraid that the sort of love we feel for each other isn't exactly the satisfying sort of love that I need at the moment."

"Are things any better here for you?" he asked.

"Worse, if anything. At least in Egypt, I had you. In Basrah, I have Percy Cox, who's wonderful, as is Lady Cox, but they're a family, and although they invite me over very often, it's not the same as having my own close-knit circle. I do have some friends here, but the so-called experts from the Indian Expeditionary Force consider me to be a pariah. I'm seen as a spy for Viceroy Hardinge, a spy for London because of my connections and the letters I write to the foreign secretary who happens to be a friend, and I'm also seen as a friend of the Arabs. They only thing they haven't yet suspected me of is sleeping with the Turks."

"Gertie!" Lawrence shouted in horror, and suddenly burst out laughing. "I never knew you had a wicked streak in you."

"There's much you still don't know about me. Did you know I swear like a trooper when I'm annoyed, but never in public. Still if you listen to what's said about me in Basrah, you'd think I was the devil incarnate. Oh Thomas, I do so hate not having you and my friends from England here. I have some acquaintances, but no bosom friends. I spend much of my spare time, what little I have, outside Basrah, and wandering the deserts to meet with the Arab chieftains. And I've been doing some archaeology while I've been stationed here . . . good stuff which I'll tell you about shortly."

She devolved into sadness for a rare moment. "Why has this damnable war made life so fraught? You know, when I was first starting on my travels, I had my degree, one man who wanted to marry me, a position in society, everything. But now, it's all so bloody hard. I feel I'm approaching that point in my life where from now on, everything's going to be going downhill, and I really don't think I've lived a life at all."

He burst out laughing. "Are you mad? You do more in a year than most Englishmen do in the whole of their miserable lifetimes."

"But I've never married."

"Lots of women don't marry, Gertie. And lots of men, too."

"But I wanted to marry, Thomas. I wanted children and my own home and family. And today, despite all the vital war work I'm helping with, that's what I want more than anything. I know that sounds silly and frivolous, but at night, I'm so lonely. Oh, when I was young and exploring sights which no Western man had ever seen before, I didn't think about a family, but now, it's more important to me than just about anything."

"Is it a family you want, Gertie, or a husband, and all the husbandly things that entails?"

She looked at him askance. "Why shouldn't I want the comfort of a man? What's wrong with a woman enjoying the yearnings of her body? Here, in Arabia, they mutilate girls' genitals so they can't enjoy what their menfolk so freely enjoy. Is that fair? Is that right?"

"Of course not, but you're making it sound as though your whole life has been barren. Yet you've had wonderful lovers."

"And still do. I try to keep it discrete, but I've had a number of liaisons with gentlemen of, shall we say, a military bearing. Not those whose wives are here, of course, but there are still a few around who are quite able to go the distance."

Lawrence burst out laughing. "You're such a frightful slut, Gertie. I love you for it."

She knew she should be miffed by his description of her, but she also knew Lawrence too well to take offense. "And you, dear. What of you in Faisal's company. Did he introduce you to any bodily pleasures?"

"Lots. Every night there were different women. And boys...lots and lots of gorgeous boys. And for something new, we made delicious love to some sheep and goats and a very attractive camel."

"Still a virgin, then?"

Lawrence sipped his tea. "'fraid so."

"Thomas," she shouted. "When are you going to lose that terrible albatross around your neck?"

"Not until you give yourself to me totally, Gertie. Not until you slip off your clothes and wrap me in your arms, and say 'take me, Thomas, I'm yours.'"

"I keep telling you, dear, that young men are the answer to your needs. Accept it, and you'll live happily, but perhaps not in England. There are lots and lots of lovely young men in the Middle East who'd delight in being yours."

"I'm not like that, Gertie."

"Yes you are, Thomas. And you seem to be the only one who doesn't know it."

He finished his tea, and thought about her comments. From anybody else, they would have been such an insult he'd have risen, and stormed out of the room. But he knew Gertie loved him, and had his best interests at heart. As he did hers.

"But why didn't you marry, my dearest?" he asked. "You could have married a buffoon, had his children, called yourself Lady or Duchess, and then buggered off to the Far East or Arabia."

She shook her head. "You don't understand, do you, Lawrence? I'm a woman of great zeal. My life is lived with a passion and to my regret, I love with a passion. I can't do things half-heartedly."

"Like you love me with a passion?" he asked wryly.

She smiled. "With the passion of a mother."

"Then why do you keep saying no to me? I'm more than happy to explore the physical side of life with you, and you could teach me so much," he said.

"Thomas!" she shouted, and hit him on the arm.

"Well why not? You know I love you, and you certainly love me."

"Of course I love you, dear boy, but as a friend. Not in that way. I'm far too old for you, and conversely, and somewhat obviously, you're far too young for me."

"The Greeks understood the importance of love between an older and wiser person, and a young boy taken under the wing and taught the ways of life."

"That was the relationship between a catamite and his pathic, dear boy, and they were both males. Women weren't included in that particular association."

"Well, how about the other ancient Greek women? Not Sappho of course, but one of the Hetaerae, the women prostitutes used by parents to teach young boys the art of love making?"

She looked at him in shock. "I may be many things, Thomas, but I'm not one of the Hetaerae."

He laughed. "I wasn't going to pay. I just thought you could—"

"I'm not interested in a physical relationship with you," she said. "I love you for your helplessness, for your wonderful mind, for all your potential to do great things, and most especially for your mischief. You do and say things in public which I would love to say, but couldn't possibly, because were I to say them, I would be considered a harridan and expunged from genteel society. You're the catalyst which enables those baser instincts which I have to keep hidden to be brought out, and you do it most wonderfully, dearest. I shall always love you, Thomas, but as mother to son . . . or at least considerably older sister to very young and naughty brother."

He shrugged, reached over and kissed her on the cheek. As he put down his teacup, he stood and Gertrude's servant walked in, carrying his clean and dry uniform.

He retired behind a screen to put them on.

~

General Headquarters, Basrah

"I have to tell you, Major Lawrence, I'm personally disgusted by the very notion of an Englishman transmitting a bribe to anyone,

194

especially a Turk," said Sir Percy Cox. "I'm so sorry I had to involve an Englishman to conduct such a compact with the devil. And I want you to know, Lawrence, I'll have nothing whatsoever to do with this transaction. My name will not be attached to the orders, I will not recognise you at official functions when you're applauded and bemedalled for this exercise, nor will I enter into correspondence concerning this shameful incident. This is a moment of infamy in the annals of the conduct of British warfare, and it humiliates me even to know of it.

"We have brave men in France dying at the war front for principle, and yet London and Delhi have instructed me to sully these brave men's reputation by offering a bribe to—"

"Sir Percy," said Lawrence, interrupting, "with the very greatest of respect, it doesn't matter a hoot what you or I think of this issue. Only two things are of importance—firstly, the lives of tens of thousands of young men are at stake, and secondly London has given us our orders."

"I'm well aware of the stakes involved, Lawrence. I've done everything in my power to send reinforcements and relief to the poor blighters stuck in that hellhole. But if we descend to bribery, what next? Will we pay them not to fight us? Will we offer them money to quit Mesopotamia? What happens when Great Britain descends into the same depths of disrepute and dishonesty as our enemy? Eh?"

"Sir Percy, how much is a British soldier worth? To the war effort, I mean? Or to his parents and his wife and his sister? How much is it worth to find a way so that thousands and thousands of men aren't unnecessarily slaughtered? To know the answer, you just have to look at what's happening on the Western Front in France and Belgium, Sir Percy. Thousands of fine young men are being slaughtered just for a couple of yards of ground. Wouldn't you rather reach an accommodation with the Kaiser and pay him to go away? In that way, you'd save countless lives and England would get its young men back."

Sir Percy shook his head in amazement. "And what about king and country, Major Lawrence? What about the morality of fighting for a cause . . . a cause in which we all believe? The Kaiser is an adventurer who needs to be taught a lesson, not paid for his bullying and thuggery. The Ottomans are a corrupt and effete group of nepotistic criminals. Look at the way they've enslaved the Arabs for these past hundreds of years. We have a duty, Mr. Lawrence. A duty to fight and rid the world and ourselves of people like these, and make it a better place, a land for heroes. We don't have the right to descend to their level in the gutter and treat with them there. We have to be above all that, or else there's no point in our fighting."

Lawrence breathed deeply, and said "And when we've rid the world of the Ottomans, will the Arabs then be free, Sir Percy? Will Britain pack its bags and say to the sheiks and emirs and sharifs now we've cleared off the Ottomans, Arabia is yours?"

Sir Percy banged his desk and said, "Don't be so damned insubordinate, Lawrence."

"I'm sorry, sir, but with great respect, everybody knows we're here merely to replace the Turks, and I think it's a disgrace."

"I don't give a damn what you think, Lawrence. You're a serving British officer, and as such, you'll follow orders."

"Of course he will, Percy. Major Lawrence is tired from the journey and is saying things which should not be said," Gertrude said hastily.

Lawrence realized by her intervention that he'd gone too far, and had once more allowed his emotions to run away with him, something which had previously caused him problems with the bigwigs in Cairo and Alexandria. Everybody wanted to know what he knew, but nobody was interested in his opinions.

"Sir, I apologize if I've been insubordinate. But unless we come to terms with the fact that the Arab belongs in Arabia, and it'll only happen if the British respect his rights, then all hell will break loose. Maybe not now, but in ten, fifty, or a hundred years' time. Sir Percy, the Arabs are literally up in arms. Under Ottoman rule they were subservient—often willingly, often not, but Constantinople will always have the advantage over Great Britain in that they and the Arabs are all Muslims. If we Church of England British think we can impose our rule on the land of Islam, we're in for a shock. Now, if you'll forgive me, I need to spend some time with Miss Bell in assessing the best way to Kut al Amara, and the contacts I'll need to get to the Turkish commander."

Lawrence saluted, swivelled on his heels, and walked out of the utilitarian office, leaving Sir Percy staring in astonishment. Never had a subordinate been so arrogant, so insulting. But what could he do? Lawrence was here on orders from the War Office in London and Military Headquarters in Delhi. As the Senior Political Officer, all he could really do was to tell Lawrence how rude and uncivil he was. Gertrude looked at Percy Cox and shrugged her shoulders, both in apology and dismay at the way the interview had gone.

"He's very unsubtle and much too frank, my dear, but I'm afraid Major Lawrence is absolutely right," said Gertrude. She looked at Percy's face and saw a man who had yet to come to terms with the powerlessness recent war events had caused. "When this whole bloody disaster is over and what's left of our boys has returned to their homes, we'll be stuck with an almighty mess, and people like you and me will have to clear it up.

"And if you seriously think the Arabs will allow us simply to take the place of the Turks, you're sadly mistaken. Our only hope when all this is over is that a leader emerges, probably not a tribal leader, but one who'll coalesce all the tribes into one great Arab nation, and who'll join with Great Britain in a partnership. A man who'll have the foresight to know Arabia is pre-industrial, and will need a partnership to develop the extraordinary assets of this land, its agriculture, oil, and all its resources. Especially its women."

Cox looked at her, and asked quietly, "And who might such a man be? Where will he be found? All I've met these last months have been scoundrels and thieves."

"That's why a leader will have to come from outside the Arab family. Another Saladin."

"And is there such a man?" asked Percy Cox.

She remained silent, wondering what his reaction would be when she answered.

"I think there is. I think he was just here, talking with you."

Cox looked at her in shock. And then he burst out laughing. He laughed so hard, he collapsed back into his chair.

Gertrude silently turned and followed Thomas Lawrence to the mess hall, the sound of Percy's laughter echoing throughout the building.

~

Sir Percy was alone. Lawrence and Gertrude had disappeared, which gave him time to ponder over the young man's words. Gertie, brilliant as she was, spoke nonsense when she said the Arabs would follow such a fey and silly chap as Major Lawrence. The fact that he was English was the least of the reasons. Putting his nationality to one side, he had to admit Lawrence was quite brilliant and maybe he was right. Maybe Britain had no place in Arabia. But British industry and British ships and British factories needed oil, and all the indications were that there was oil aplenty beneath the sands of the desert. And nothing on Earth was going to prevent Percy from ensuring Britain got what it needed. After all, it would do no good laying in the ground in Arabia, the soft underbelly of a culture which could only use the oil's ubiquity for lighting primitive wick lamps. None of the Arabic counties in the Persian Gulf had any skills in development. They were just illiterate nomads. So it was to both Arabia's and Britain's advantage to uncover, and then to control the flow of oil, just so long as the Turks or the Germans or worse, the bloody French didn't get hold of it.

~

Outside Percy's office, Gertrude ran to catch up with Lawrence. When she did, she could see his face was a mask of fury.

Still striding, he said, "I know you're angry with me, Gertie, but he had no right to say that. How dare he put the lives of thousands and thousands of our boys at stake for some obsolete notion of honor or morality or heroism? God Almighty, this is a bloody awful war, with millions of young men dying because of the vainglory of people like Percy Cox and Allenby and Haig and Kitchener and all the others buggers. Well, I'm damned if I'm going to allow British soldiers to perish, just for the sake of the reputations of a couple of men with epaulettes on their shoulders who should have been put out to graze years ago. Who the hell does Cox think he is to—"

"He's the senior political officer in Mesopotamia, that's who, Thomas. He's a brilliant man, a wonderful diplomat and a man who thinks deeply and passionately about Great Britain and her place in the world. As such, he deserves your respect. You can't just turn and walk out on a political officer as senior as he, without being accused of insubordination. I know you're on a mission, but Percy is still the civilian commander of this area, and as such, you have to respect his authority. And I promise you he isn't just standing on principle for the fun of it. He's agonised over this issue ever since Townshend got himself and his army trapped in Kut. Percy's organised columns of relief, ships, everything to send reinforcement and supplies to our lads, but they've all been defeated or had to turn back because of overwhelming forces."

Lawrence stopped walking, and faced her. The corridor wasn't the best place for them to speak, but he was in such a fury he couldn't restrain himself. "If everything's failed, why does he object to paying to have them rescued?"

"Because when all else has failed for a man like Percy Cox, my dear, the only thing left to him is honor. Percy is terrified that if the British dishonor themselves over a matter such as this, it'll just encourage the Turks and the Germans to think we're weak and effete and have no moral fibre. That'll spur them on. More of our men will be ransomed and it'll turn into a damnable free-for-all."

They stood there, looking at each other for a long moment, before Lawrence shrugged, and said, "Oh well, regardless of what he or I think, I have my orders. Let's you and me go back to your home, have a cup of coffee, and work out the Arab disposition."

The rain was still torrential, but they stepped bravely out of the headquarters and tried to find shelter. They ran through the downpour and couldn't help but laugh at each other as they both slipped and slid in the mud, one assisting the other every couple of steps. Eventually, looking utterly sodden and dejected, they arrived at Gertrude's house.

For the second time that day, Major Lawrence's uniform was stripped off him by Gertrude's servants, and he bathed in jasmine scented water, dressing himself again in one of her silk dressing-gowns. It was far too long for him, and he was in danger of tripping as he walked. He hoisted it up like some vaudeville actress in order to descend the stairs to her living area. When he got there, he poured himself a scotch and water, and stood looking out over the veranda at her garden. Even though it was waterlogged and the plants drooped with the weight of the rain, it was a truly beautiful garden. He knew Gertrude had laid it out when she first arrived. There were beds of palms, roses, hydrangeas, and pathways lined with lime, pomegranate, orange and lemon trees. All were in bloom and pendulous with fruit, though each sagged heavy, over-burdened by the deluge.

He heard her walk into the room, turned and greeted her with a smile. But there was no smile on her face.

"Thomas, I've been thinking since we left Percy's office. You know, a wrong word from him and your prospects of advancement are nil."

"I don't want advancement in the army, darling. I want fun. I want this bloody war to be over, and to get back to archaeology or something. And yes, I know I'm here because of what I know, but what the grand Sir Percy Pooh Bah doesn't know is that everything I know, dearest, has been taught to me by you," Lawrence said, knowing he was in for a scolding. "From the first time we met, I've been your willing student. You've taught me so much about the Arab's history, language, custom, tradition . . . everything."

She tutted in annoyance and refused to give in to his boyish charms. "Look, now isn't the time to play games. You're here to save the lives of thousands of men. Arguing with Percy was silly and reckless and arrogant. You need his support. And mine. Frankly, it's me who should be going to negotiate with the Turks, not you. I know the Arab sheiks they're supporting with money from Constantinople, I know the country our lads are trapped in, and I know the pressure points to apply to get the Arabs to turn against the Turks. Yet because I'm a woman, the powers in London and Delhi think I'm incapable of negotiating with men. What they don't realize is that before this war I was negotiating and advising and spying for the British government, and—"

"You're jealous," he interrupted.

"No, I'm not!" she said archly, but then she responded more slowly, "Well, yes, frankly I am. Look, I don't know what I am. It's only because the generals here thought they needed a man that I sent for you. They know before this damned war I was the first Western woman to have crossed the Arabian deserts. I negotiated myself out of prison in Hayil. I've dealt with the leaders of the Arabic world, one on one, as equals. Yet it didn't make a blind bit of difference to them, and just because I wear a skirt, I'm disqualified from political and military office, from having any say in what should be done with Arabia, in everything."

Lawrence went over and put his arm around her. She hugged him, and whispered into his ear, "You know, sometimes I feel cursed by my sex."

And he whispered back, "Yes, I know the feeling."

They looked at each other, and burst out laughing.

Settling down with a glass of scotch, she said quietly, "Do you think it's going to happen? The Arab uprising? Do you think they'll finally understand they have to come together as one people, and not a disparate group of little tribes?"

"Faisal thinks so. He thinks he and his father will rise up in Hejaz, and because of their control over Mecca and Medina the rest of Arabia will follow."

"Hah!" she said loudly. "And what about ibn Sa'ud and ibn Rashid? Do you think they'll meekly sit back and let things happen? I fear for Arabia with men like ibn Sa'ud on the war path, no matter which side of the fence he's sitting on at the moment."

Lawrence nodded. "Yes, ibn Sa'ud is a problem, more so than ibn Rashid. There's no question ibn Sa'ud has his eyes firmly set on capturing the Kingdom of Hejaz, for all sorts of reasons—to put the holy cities under his control, for territorial expansion, to gain access to Suez, to become the guardian of Islam—that's why his eyes are firmly set on Hejaz. But I've given assurances to Faisal we'll protect him in the eventuality."

"Come on Thomas. Don't be naïve. If ibn Sa'ud agrees to join us and give us a million men against the Turks, in exchange for us not interfering when he attacks the Hejaz, do you think Allenby or Haig or anyone else will turn him down just for what they consider to be a slither of useless land? Right now our lads are dying by the truckload, and we'll do anything, agree to anything, to restore our pride and dignity after Gallipoli."

He remained silent for some time. Gertrude knew there was something he wanted to tell her, but like a rabbit caught in lamplight, one false move and she'd lose the initiative.

Barely audibly, he said, "Can you keep a very dark secret?"

She said nothing.

"Gertie, what I'm going to tell you is top secret. You mustn't breathe a word. Some months ago, Faisal went on a secret mission to Damascus to negotiate with other Arabic leaders. Only a handful of top brass from Cairo knew anything about it. I was the liaison. He went there to negotiate terms with nationalist groups and sheiks and . . ."

"I know. He went to drum up support for the Arabic revolt. He got agreement from almost everybody, except those who are being paid a fortune by the Turks. Sheik Ibrahim ad-Dawlah and Sheik Mohammed ibn Farhan of the Shammar people turned him down flat, and so did a number of others, but he's got a consensus of the nationalists. Is that the great secret?"

He looked at her in astonishment. "How . . . ?"

"Don't be silly, dear. I'm a spy for Britain. Nothing happens in Mesopotamia without me knowing about it. You didn't think you'd keep that secret for long, did you?"

"Do the Turks know?" he asked.

"Probably. But the issue for the Turks isn't their knowing that there's some sort of revolt in the wind. What they need to know desperately is who's got the deepest pockets. The Arabs will trade their mothers for a gold coin. If we top what the Turk is giving them, they'll fight with undying loyalty for us. But of course, all the Turk has to do is to up the ante and then they'll change sides with the wind. Which is why I asked whether you think there's going to be an uprising."

He looked at her closely. There was anger in her eyes.

"Is something wrong?" he asked.

She shook her head, and sipped her drink

"Gertie . . . ?"

Putting the drink on the table, she breathed deeply, pondering whether to say anything. Then, as if unburdening herself, "Thomas dear, ever since I was a girl, I've been passionately pursuing a dream that somehow, despite my being female, I could help make Arabia into a great nation. Alright, so it's a silly conceit, and I know the odds are stacked against me as a woman, but Arabia has to become one if it's to achieve the greatness which is its destiny. This war, hideous and wasteful as it is, provides the catalyst for such a movement. This is the time for Arabia; don't you see that?"

For once, Lawrence knew he had to remain silent.

"Since the Young Turks led Constantinople into such a potentially disastrous situation, the opportunity for Arabic unification has never been greater . . . not in the past thousand years. Yet . . ."

She lapsed into silence, staring into her drink.

"Yet . . . ?" asked Lawrence.

Gertrude looked up at him. He knew that look well enough. It was when she had to deliver him bad news.

"Yet the generals who are running this war decided they should send you, a sweet but naïve lad, and Faisal, the third, and hence the inconsequential, son of the Grand Sharif of Mecca. How do you think the other Arab leaders felt when two somewhat naïve young men walked into a conference and presented plans for Arab unification?"

"So what should have been done?" asked Lawrence.

"The Sharif himself should have gone. He was the only one who could have pulled this off, the only person in the whole of Arabia who, as a descendant of the Prophet and the Guardian of Mecca and Medina, had the gravitas, authority, and prestige to stand in front of such an assembly, and command respect. And . . ."

She lapsed into silence.

"And . . . ?" said Lawrence

"Never mind."

"And I shouldn't have been chosen to go, but instead you should have stood by the Sharif's side. Right?"

Gertrude just shrugged.

"Do you think I didn't know that? C'mon, Gertie, this wasn't a decision I took on my own, y'know. I was following General Command's orders. Do you think I didn't feel your absence? The moment we got there, and I saw the look on the other Arab's faces, I knew we were doomed. Don't blame me, or Faisal. Sure, it was his initiative, and he asked that you accompany him to the meeting, but the top brass decided a woman couldn't possibly stand in a council of Arab men and win the day. I'm truly sorry."

She lit a cigarette, and hissed, "Those damned idiots. Have they no idea what I've been doing over the past God-knows how many years?"

Surprised by her vehemence, Lawrence said softly, "The old morons who are running this show on England's behalf, darling, can only stare at a glorious candle, and see dripping wax. I look at you and I see a brilliant light. The Arabs might be a medieval and patronising bunch of chauvinistic jingoists, but the Brass who lead us are a lot worse. But don't despair, darling. If we join forces, you and I, surely with your brains and my beauty we can prevail.

Is it fair a woman of your extraordinary genius should have to play second fiddle to a silly boy like me? Of course not, but if we want to achieve our dream of unifying the Arabs and with the new and strong unified nation being England's best friend, then surely it's best we work together, you and I."

She smiled at him, and kissed him on the cheek. "I have to be a realist, my love, and admit the powers that be in England will never allow me that sort of elevation. They won't see my brains or my skills or my knowledge, they'll just see my skirts and corsets and they'll shy away. There are only a handful of men in England, men of consequence, who see me for my abilities, and not my sex. Which means . . ."

Lawrence looked at her closely, "Which means . . . ?"

"That I'll be right behind you. I'll be whispering in your ear. I'll be your *Eminence Grise*. But it's you who will have to take the lead. You who'll have to bring all the forces at our disposal together and force these medieval and patristic buggers into one huge and almighty army. I can't do it, because of my bloody sex. But you, Thomas, you have to become Lawrence of Arabia."

He giggled. "Darling, they'll never follow me. I'm too queer."

"They'll follow you, once you've got a significant military victory under your skin. A devastating raid, perhaps, or some dramatic skirmish leading Faisal's men against the Turks. Then I'll spread the word among the tribal leaders that another Saladin has arisen, and they'll flock to you."

"You're more Saladin than me. Couldn't you do it?" he asked.

"Not a chance, my love. Oh bugger it, Thomas. I've spent a lifetime fighting against this ridiculous idea that men have about women and the role they can play. I'd just hoped and prayed that at this stage, in this place and at this time, a person's sex would be less important than a person's abilities."

"Gertie, dearest, if anybody can make it happen, it's you. So let's start. Let's join forces, and show these silly old farts just what it is you're made of. You asked earlier whether I thought the Arabs would rise up against the Turks. Yes, I think there will be an uprising. I agree most of the chieftains are only after what they can make out of this war, but not Faisal! I know you think he's only a third son, but let me assure you he's different. He's fighting because he truly believes in the Arab destiny and he thinks he's the one touched by the Prophet to unite the Arabic people. That's why he's so concerned about the future fate of Mecca and Medina and the Kingdom of the Hejaz after this war is over."

"Then use him. Use his men. But believe me when I say the other Arab tribes won't follow him. But they will follow his Saladin."

She sipped her scotch and mused. "Anyway, I've always had a profound distrust of messianic figures. Is Faisal really that different from all the others? You know him much better than I."

"Oh yes," said Lawrence. "He's a very different kind of Arab. He's deeply introspective, quite philosophical, very well educated . . . and he has the capacity to be a real statesman. Not a messiah, perhaps, but certainly a leading statesman of the Arab's cause."

"Does he have the capacity to be a real king?" she asked. "He could never unite all the Arabs, but could he be king of a new great nation?"

"When his father dies, if his brother Abdullah is made ruler of some other Hashemite kingdom, then I suppose he'll become the King of the Hejaz."

"I wasn't thinking of the Hejaz. I was thinking of a kingdom somewhat closer to home," she said.

He turned to look at her. She had a wistful expression, her face almost inscrutable. "Gertie? What's going on in that Machiavellian mind of yours?"

"Oh nothing. Now, let's have some supper, and we can get down to working on the maps. You've got some negotiating to do, and some lives to rescue."

~

As the night wore on they sat beneath the awning of her veranda holding hands. The simple act of friendship seemed quite natural and ordinary, as though they were blood relations rather than friends.

They should have been talking about the siege of Kut and how to negotiate with the Turks in order to relieve the town, but instead, every time Gertrude would get out the map and begin her instructions, Lawrence would somehow manage to steer the conversation around to day-to-day topics of life in Basrah— who was romantic with whom, which lady was forced to return unexpectedly to Britain because she was looking too longingly at some local chieftain in the marketplace, and who had made a fool of whom at some general's tea party.

At first, she'd told him tersely that she neither knew, nor did she indulge in the trivia of the private lives of army officer's wives; but his persistence, and her enjoyment of his mischievous love of scandal, broke down her resistance, and she became a gossip, eagerly describing embarrassing incidents which she'd witnessed and recounting conversations she'd inadvertently overheard. And when he was satisfied with that aspect of life in Basrah, he somehow managed swing the conversation around to them.

"You know, Gertie, when I say I love you, I really mean it. I was only saying to Prince Faisal how special you were. He thinks so too. Since he met you in Egypt, he's been a bit awestruck by you."

"Don't be foolish. Stop saying such tosh," she said, and smacked him on the leg.

"It isn't tosh. It's true. He said it to me when we were at an oasis in Hejaz. He was almost asleep, and he was musing on the war and how he and his father could get ibn Rashid and ibn Sa'ud to go against the Turks, and he said we really should consult with you, because you were the only person . . . he didn't say woman, he said person . . . who might know how to do it. From him, that was an almighty compliment. And then he said how amazing you were, and that he was in awe of you when he first met you."

"Thomas? He said this when he was almost asleep? Were you and he . . . ?" she asked.

He put his finger to his lips, and said, "I only have to give you my name, rank, and serial number."

"You devil," she shouted. "You haven't . . ."

"That's for me to know, dearest, and for you to find out."

~

The unrelenting rain clattered against the roof, the windows, the ground, and the broad leaves of the trees in the garden. It was as though an orchestra of snare drums and cymbals was playing just outside her window. It had recently become louder as the menacing black cloud moved from the gulf onto the land. Lawrence had to strain to hear what she was saying.

The map of lower Mesopotamia and Persia was spread out on her dining room table. In the southern end was the Persian Gulf and Basrah, joined to Qurna by the Shatt al Arab waterway. Gertrude had marked the last known location of the marsh Arabs' that season, as well as the directions of the nomadic tribes which criss-crossed the area.

"This place," she said pointing to the town at the confluence of the Tigris and the Euphrates, "is the last part of Mesopotamia where there's any sort of fertility until you get north of Baghdad, except between the two rivers of course. It's like a green dividing line between the desert and the sown," she said.

Lawrence smiled, appreciating her use of the title of one of her most famous books.

"Now, Thomas, the problems started after the Battle of Ctesiphon. Townshend was forced to retreat because he'd been ordered further north and his supply lines were stretched to breaking point, and that was when the initiative passed to the Turks. Until then, we'd had it all our own way, but once the Turks smelled victory all hell broke loose. The success of our drive north of Basrah made up for our disaster at Gallipoli, but then we got bogged down because our supply lines were overstretched, and suddenly it looked to the Turks and their Arab supporters as though our fighting men weren't made of much.

"The 6th Poona Division retreated to Kut al Amara in December last year. Whitehall ordered Townshend to retreat further, but the orders came too late and he was stuck in that filthy and overcrowded hellhole. Unfortunately, the damn town is situated in a loop in the Tigris, and because of its geography, he became trapped and he's still there, losing men every day to snipers and artillery and disease. He can't get out by land, and the waterway is blocked.

"He was promised rapid relief, and so thinking help was on its way, he kept his men on full daily ration. But within days, he was surrounded by ten thousand fresh Turkish fighting men. There were huge losses on both sides as the Turks tried to storm the town, and Townshend defended bravely. Now his men are starving, exhausted, sick and diseased and in a terrible state. They've been under siege now for a hundred days."

"But didn't we send men up north to relieve him?" asked Lawrence. "Why didn't we just send the whole bloody army north and break through the Turkish lines?"

"Up till now, we've tried many times, by land and water, and we've even dropped supplies from an aircraft. But we can't get through. There are virtually no roads, and we're attacked every step of the way by masses of Turks who have flooded south from Baghdad, anticipating another Gallipoli. We've suffered hideous losses of life in trying."

"How bad?" he asked.

"About twenty-three thousand men have died trying to save those poor boys," she said softly.

"WHAT!" Lawrence shouted. "Twenty-three thousand . . . I don't believe you!"

"It's true, I'm afraid. Which is why we're willing to pay the Turks to go away. We can't afford any more losses."

"Twenty-three thousand?" he said, shaking his head in horror.

"And that doesn't include the men under Townshend's command. We have to do something to prevent any more useless waste of life. Townshend managed to get word to the Turkish commander, Nur-Ud-Din, as well as the local German liaison and commander, Baron von der Goltz. He's offered them a million gold sovereigns. He's also agreed the troops will be sent home to England when they're released and won't be used to fight the Turks again.

"I've managed to persuade our generals here that you from the Intelligence Service, and Colonel Herbert and Colonel Beach of the Mesopotamian Command should negotiate the terms of the bribe and the surrender. They've fortunately agreed, and you can be on your way immediately . . . well, once this damn rain stops."

~

It was two weeks before Gertrude heard the first rumours. They were whispered into her ear by Arab travelers. She knew Lawrence wouldn't be able to get word back, but the desert had a thousand ears and long before he returned to Basrah, Gertrude knew precisely what had happened. At first, she refused to believe the news, but when it was confirmed by increasing numbers of caravans traveling to the southern port, she realized to her abject horror it must be true.

She immediately reported the appalling news to Sir Percy, who merely shook his head in sadness, and buried his face in his hands.

Major Lawrence's sudden appearance out of the desert surprised her. She had come back to her home from the political residency, had already dined in the commissariat, and was taking an aperitif in her bedroom, when she heard a knocking on her front door. Listening carefully, she heard a servant downstairs speaking urgently to a man in Arabic. Then she heard steps on the stairs and by the time she'd turned, Thomas Lawrence was standing at the lintel of her boudoir.

"It's a blunderland, this place," he said, his calm exterior masking the fury in his voice. "A bloody blunderland. They'll all be dead in a couple of weeks, you know. Thirteen thousand British and Indian troops, all taken prisoner and sent on a forced march out of Kut. They're starving, sick, in dreadful shape, desperate, and the Turkish bastards have forced them to march God knows where. I saw them, Gertie. A column of them. They were struggling to stay on their feet, and the bloody Turks were beating them and shooting them through the head when they fell. Savages! I hate this bloody war and this killing, I really do!" he shouted, close to tears. "When my two brothers were killed in the fighting in France last year I thought I'd go mad, but now I see everybody dying around me and I wonder if anybody will be left alive. We're nothing more than fodder for the cannons and the Gatling guns. That's all . . . just fodder . . ."

"Oh my dear boy," she said, rising to comfort him. She put her arms around him and felt how thin and slight his body was. He felt like little more than a schoolboy.

"Townshend begged for food for his men, but the Turks wouldn't give any. Instead our lads are dying from starvation and typhus and malaria and God knows what else, and the Turks are just looking on. And smiling. The bastards!"

"But the million gold sovereigns . . . ?" She already knew, but realised he must take control of the telling.

"Ha!" he shouted. "The Turks made a fool of us. We had no idea our lads had already surrendered. Herbert and Beach were hiding with me in a trench, trying to work out how to convince the Turkish commander to speak with us. He flatly refused to meet with us, and threatened us with death, even though we'd come under a flag of truce. Anyway, we tried again, and got our white flag out, and climbed over the trench and walked as bravely as we could a couple of hundred yards to the Turkish side. We were blindfolded and then taken to their commander. It was he who told us Townshend had already surrendered. We tried to use the money to beg for an exchange of prisoners, but even that was too late, because some of the British sick had already been exchanged for some Turkish prisoners of war. We had a meal, and turned and came back. It was like bloody Wimbledon, Gertie. Advantage to the Turks. Game, set and match."

She tried to let go of him, to lead him to a seat, but he just stood at the doorway in her arms, trembling.

"I tell you, Gertie, it was a fiasco. A blood nightmare fiasco, and while the Turks were joking about how we were too late, and everyone was laughing, our poor bastards were marching to their deaths."

She continued to hug him, and as he became drained of the pent-up emotions, she felt his body loosen up somewhat. "You did your best, my love. You did your best."

"Tell that to the mothers and fathers of boys who are nothing more than skeletons, and who face the rest of eternity in some sandy desert thousands of miles from hearth and home. Oh Christ, Gertie, I hate this bloody war. I hate the bloody generals. I hate everybody."

She stroked his hair, and whispered in his ear. They lay on her bed together, and she stroked his face and neck and played with his yellow hair until he fell asleep in her arms.

NINE

Basrah, Mesopotamia, October 1916

"My God, woman, I had no idea you'd been so ill. I knew you had typhoid, but I never thought it would . . . I mean, I never thought you were . . ." He continued to stare at her as Gertrude walked unsteadily from the door to his desk. She looked emaciated, almost cadaverous, her cheeks sunken, her skin pallid and her hair unusually dull and lifeless, but despite her demeanour, her eyes had retained their gleam even though her hair had thinned dramatically and was streaked with gray.

Still mortified by her appearance, Percy continued, "I sent flowers and always sought after your health, but I never realized it was as bad as that. I've been traveling so much, or I would have visited you. Didn't my wife . . . ? Gertrude, I'm so very sorry."

"Wasn't just typhoid, Percy, but I also had malaria and jaundice. Damn nearly carried me off to my maker. But I'm back on my feet, so please don't concern yourself. You couldn't have done anything even if you sat by my bedside for a month. And Lady Cox was absolutely marvellous. She visited me often and really bucked up my spirits, but I was bedridden for the whole time, which is why I'm so gaunt and tired now, and you have no idea how jaundice simply drains you. Lying in bed, I often felt fit as a fiddle, but the moment I got up, I felt as though I was drunk as a lord and I had to lie down again. All my life I've been right as rain, strappingly able-bodied, and just when I'm so badly needed here, I fall victim to these horrible diseases."

She was dressed in a violet felt winter scarf, a black satin dress, on top of which she'd put on a blue silk shirt, and even a cardigan, yet it was mid-morning and still 90 degrees outside. Sir Percy knew she had to return to her sick bed, and told her so.

"I'm fine, Percy. Stop fussing. I'd much rather be here than at home. At least here I can be of some use. But I must admit the last two or three months haven't been fun. The weather has been so damnably hot, and I was quite out to the rest of the world. I was in such a fever all I could do was let the servants and the doctors look after me. I slept on the roof during July and August, because the cold night-time desert air was so refreshing."

She seemed to fall into the armchair opposite him. The huge desk separated them. It was piled full of papers. He continued to look at her in consternation, not knowing how to convince her she was still sick. "You really shouldn't be here, Gertrude. You should be at home, resting."

"Another day at home, and I'll start eating the wallpaper. I can't stand not working, Percy. And there's so much to do. Now that Sharif Hussein ibn Ali has begun his uprising in the Hejaz, I have to keep tabs on it and ensure the other Arabs follow his lead. I've read the reports about the battles against the Turks outside of Mecca, and now they're pushing the enemy back up north to Medina. Lawrence is doing a wonderful job blowing up the trains and things like that."

She began to cough. Her frame, which now seemed too small for the clothes she was wearing, appeared to shake. Percy half stood from his chair, poured her a glass of water, and handed it over to her.

"Gertie, I really think—"

But she cut across him. "Isn't it absolutely wonderful the Sharif has finally found the backbone to fight the Turks. I tell you, Percy, because he's a descendant of the Prophet and the guardian of the holy cities, the moral and political imprimatur which this will give to the uprising of all Arabia is huge. It could be the turning point we've all been praying for in this damn war. Everyone in Arabia looks towards Mecca and Medina, and now that Sharif Hussein has vowed to overthrow the Sultan of Constantinople and kick the Ottomans out of Arabia, it'll be much easier to persuade the other Arab leaders to follow suit. And thank heavens it was his

214

son Faisal who's taken the running on this. He's a future king when these nations' boundaries are redrawn, Percy, you mark my words."

He tried to interrupt her again, but she seemed so keen to talk to somebody other than her servants or some kindly visitor, he found it difficult to cut into the conversation. Eventually, he had to speak over her.

"Gertie, you're becoming quite a celebrity in Britain. London has written to say how marvellously pleased they are with your reports. The Foreign Office says they're the most important documents coming out of Arabia, and that they're absolutely vital to our war effort. They've asked me to tell you they're recommending you for special commendation in the House of Commons, with votes of thanks from the Prime minister and the foreign secretary themselves."

He was flushed with pride in her achievements, and waited for her response. But all she said was, "Oh good. That's very nice. But right now, I have to concern myself with what's going on here. What I really want is for Major Lawrence to be more involved in this Hejaz business than blowing up trains. I need him there to ensure things go Britain's way, which means I have to give him more instructions about what to do, other targets, where to dispose of his troops, how to persuade smaller tribes to join him.

"And from what I've been told, ibn Rashid and ibn Sa'ud could be a problem, because they're still playing their silly games, and not saying whether or not they'll support us. If they side with the Turks, then our Arab uprising could come to a grinding half. We have to persuade ibn Sa'ud to back us. I'm not so worried about Rashid because he's a spent force, but Sa'ud is crucial to our plans." Again, she began to cough and looked as though she was about to faint. She sipped more of the water.

"Gertie . . ." Sir Percy began to say, looking at her in pity, as she seemed to be swallowed up by the large chair in which she sat, "Doesn't it mean anything that you've been mentioned in dispatches? In the House of Commons? And with you not even holding any military rank. It's an enormous honor. Nobody can remember when it's happened before to a civilian. It brings credit to us all. But I fear you're too unwell to realize. Look, my dear, there's plenty of people who can look after things here while you regain your health."

"Nonsense, Percy. You know that's just not true. Nobody here knows the Arabs like I know them, and now more than ever you need my connections. If the High Command accepts my advice and Lawrence is supported in leading this revolt, he'll need all the information at my disposal. Initially I want him to destroy the Turkish attempts of reinforcement by knocking off the trains carrying their troops. But what I really want is for him to conquer Aqaba. That'll really put the wind up them, once we control the gulf."

Percy tried to interrupt when she began to cough, but she took a sip of rose water, and continued, "You see, despite the sharif joining us, there's every chance things could go wrong. All we need is for even a minor reversal of fortunes against the Turks, and then the rest of the Arabs will be in a quandary. Right now many of them will be inclined to join Prince Faisal and attack the Turks, but in almost every tent or town or city, there are voices whispering into ears that they should play it safe and do nothing, and there are also voices which think Britain is going to lose this war, and they should side with the Turks to ensure the loss. That's why taking Aqaba is so important.

"Without the Arabs, we're in trouble, and you know it. I need to continue to negotiate with the leaders of the tribes. And I also have to communicate with Lawrence before he goes and does something silly and somehow manages to insult and alienate important people. Now, more than ever, he has to remember he's not marching to his own tune, but is responsible to others. He's so impetuous, that boy, wonderful but impetuous. I'm terrified of what he'll do if he suddenly finds himself at the head of an army of a million men at arms."

Sir Percy looked at her in astonishment. "You don't think he'd . . . you're not saying he'd—"

216

"Of course not! He's an Englishman, through and through. But give a child a gun, and more than likely, he'll shoot somebody—give Lawrence unconstrained access to an army and God help the world. He's got the capacity to act like a warlord, even though he doesn't think like one."

Sir Percy said, "But from the reports I'm getting, Major Lawrence seems to be behaving very responsibly. He's commissioned and designed some stamps for the Hejaz postal system which make the country feel more independent. He's even helped them design their own Arab revolt flag—horizontal stripes of black, green and white with a red triangle in the hoist. Marvellous, it looks, too. And it appears Lawrence anointed Prince Faisal as the man to lead the Arab revolt. That was against my better judgement, because I thought it should be the older son, Abdullah. But Lawrence was insistent that it should be Faisal."

"Good. The right man for the job provided the other tribal leaders know it's Lawrence pulling Faisal's strings. I need them to see Lawrence as the brains and the brawn of this attack against the Turks."

"You don't think . . . what you said about Lawrence being the man to lead the Arab nation into some sort of renaissance . . . a renaissance which would give rise to another Saladin . . . but surely you're not thinking Faisal . . ."

"More so than ever, dear," she said, again breaking down in a fit of coughing

He waited for her to recover, and said softly, "Quite a dark horse, that Faisal. Right from the very beginning, Lawrence backed him to mount the Arab revolt against the Turks. I'd have put my money on the older brother, but it appears both you and Lawrence have better judgement. So hopefully, they're going to give the Turks a merry dance."

She stood, and straightened her back, massaging her hips. "Sorry, but all those weeks in bed have given me lumbago or arthritis or something. Would it disturb you greatly if I walked around while we talked?"

"Of course not. Perhaps a stroll in the garden?"

She followed him outside into the fresh air. The headquarters was surrounded by a high sandstone wall with facings of white marble, within which was what Gertrude had often described as a perfume factory of fruits and flowers.

She grasped Percy's arm, and they ambled around the stone pathways.

Softly, she said, "I'm so pleased the revolt in the Hejaz is starting off well. But how do you feel about what our own troops are doing? The news from Palestine isn't all that good, I hear, and our lads are still trying to break through the Turkish lines and reach Baghdad."

"I'm afraid it gets worse. Between you and me, not everybody is overjoyed the sharif has begun his revolt."

"Hardinge, our noble viceroy in India?"

Sir Percy nodded.

"I hope he's not going to use any influence with London to put an end to it. This has nothing to do with the sub-continent. He should keep his nose out of it. This uprising is courtesy of Cairo and our boys in the Egyptian Intelligence Service."

"That's as might be, Gertie, but Hardinge is terrified of tens of millions of fanatical Indian Muslims rising up in revolt because a Christian army has tried to overthrow the Muslim Sultan of Turkey whom they seem to revere."

She huffed, and said, "But that's so short-sighted. Doesn't he realize if Britain works with the Arabs and has influence in this part of the world, he'll always be able to use the Suez Canal as his supply route, whereas if the Turks are victorious, they'll block the Canal to British shipping for certain. We'll have to go round South Africa, and that'll add six weeks and God knows how much to the cost of supplying India and vice versa. And if we play our cards right against the French, we might even have control of Palestine, and as we've already got Egypt that means the eastern Mediterranean will be friendly and always available to the Empire. Can't he understand that?"

"All he can understand is an uprising on his own doorstep, when he's already sent God-knows how many divisions to the Middle East. His strength is down, and he's scared we could lose India."

"What? Is he mad?"

"I'm afraid not. There a strong nationalist movement there and it's gaining strength rapidly, but especially amongst the Hindus. There's this chap called Gandhi. Mohandas Gandhi. He caused trouble for Smuts over in South Africa, and now he looks set to cause trouble for Hardinge in India. And we trained the bugger as a barrister in the Inner Temple in London, which makes it all the more galling. What Hardinge doesn't need is trouble from the Muslims at the same time trouble is brewing from the Hindus."

"If I know anything about India, my dear, there'll be more trouble between the Hindus and the Muslims than there will be between them and us. They hate each other with a vengeance, and each wants their own faith to be the dominant national religion. Terrible."

They continued to walk, both she and Percy deep in thought. The walking and the smells from his garden put her into the most euphoric mood she'd been in since falling sick two months earlier. But she sensed Percy was holding something back from her.

"Come on, Percy, what is it?"

His silence confirmed she was correct.

"Percy . . . ?"

"I have to admit I'm particularly glad you're back, because we've got a bit of a situation right at the moment, and I really don't know how to handle it. You see, this revolt against the Turks by the sharif has somewhat gone to his head. I'm afraid he's crowned himself king."

"So? He's the sharif. That means he's sort of King of the Hejaz, and . . ."

"No! He's called himself the King of the Arabs . . . of all Arabia. He's taken the title of caliph. It's a tricky situation, because the other emirs and sheiks have rejected him outright."

219

"Oh dear!" she said. "That was a very imprudent thing for Hussein to do. Lawrence and I have been discussing whether he was suitable as the leader of all the Arabs, and we decided against it. The other leaders will only follow a man who proves himself to be worthy of following, not one who appoints himself without proof. I hope in my absence, Lawrence didn't put that idea into the sharif's head. And what of ibn Rashid?" She could barely mention his name without shuddering. Yet political expediency forced her to make an accommodation despite the fact that he'd been her jailer.

"Ibn Rashid's the biggest problem. We almost had him on our side, and now that Hussein has declared he's the leader of the Arabs, ibn Rashid and ibn Sa'ud don't want to know us. Despite the revolt and the minor tribes joining in on our side, I'm afraid Arab unity is further away than ever. It's a very tricky situation, Gertie, and we need all hands on deck to solve it."

She nodded. "Well, time for mending bridges, then."

~

Bir Abbas, Kingdom of the Hejaz

Thomas Lawrence strode between one gun emplacement and the next, checking that there was sufficient ammunition, and that the machine guns were ready to be fired the moment the Turks appeared over the horizon. But the real reason he was checking was to ensure the warriors were keeping their eyes open and remaining alert in the heat of the desert, and not being distracted by idle chatter or silly games. They were an ill-disciplined army at the very best of times. He'd attempted to discipline them, to teach them order, but the more he commanded, the more they ridiculed him behind his back. Every time he was in danger of losing them, Faisal would step in, and with a few words of command, they would square front, face up and behave like soldiers. It was discouraging. He'd imagined they would be like the wildcats which were led by Salah al-Din against Richard Coeur de Lion. That was the last time the Arabs had been united—the common threat of the Crusades—and Lawrence was coming to terms with the fact that he was no Saladin.

Behind him walked Prince Faisal. Though both were dressed in the flowing white robes of important men of the kingdom, they were easy to tell apart. The prince was a good six inches taller than Lawrence, with dark leathery skin under the black beard which hid half of his face. Lawrence was only five feet, four inches tall due to a childhood attack of the mumps. But the main difference was Lawrence's straw-yellow hair and blue eyes which made him look like he was the desert and the skies. Yet despite the outward difference in appearance, the men treated each other as brothers.

As one thought, the other espoused the words. As one looked into the horizon, the other knew what pictures he was seeing, and what ideas were going through his mind.

"I hope they get here soon, sir," said Lawrence. "The worst thing for an army which is primed for a fight is to have the fight delayed. They become sloppy and careless and then disaster can strike."

The prince nodded. "Our intelligence tells us the latest reinforcements are heading for Mecca. Unless they go via Hong Kong or Singapore or the Antarctic this is the most direct route."

Lawrence smiled. So few Arabs had an understanding of the world beyond the boundaries of the desert. They stood on a tuft-covered hillock and surveyed the distant horizon for signs of the dust a Turkish company would make if it were on the march.

"Have you ever thought of traveling to the Far East?" Lawrence asked.

"One day, *inshallah*, I would like to visit Hong Kong and China and many other parts of the world. I have greatly enjoyed the travels I have undertaken so far. I like seeing other places, other realms."

Lawrence nodded, still surveying the horizon with his binoculars.

"And you, my friend," said the prince. "What travels have you undertaken outside of your journeys through the Holy Land and Arabia? As the son of a Lord, you must be welcomed wherever you go."

"Sir, although my father is a baronet, which is a fairly minor member of the Anglo-Irish aristocracy, my mother was the governess, and I was born out of wedlock. Because of the scandal of my father's relationship with my mother, the family had to move from Ireland to Wales before we settled in Oxford."

"Really," said the Prince. "I'm surprised. You seem to have a very close relationship with your family."

"I do. And I suppose I'm the embodiment of my family's motto, which is *virtue thrives under oppression*, which just about sums up my life. Oppression, that is, not necessarily virtue."

"Oh come, Lawrence. You haven't suffered oppression. You have no understanding of what oppression is. Wait until you're a servant of another race, wait until you're imprisoned at the whim of some overlord, wait until your land and everything you've worked for all your life are suddenly taken away from you at the whim of someone thousands of miles away whom you've never met, leaving you with nothing. These, my friend, are the marks of oppression."

Putting down the binoculars, Lawrence turned to the prince, smiling. "I have been oppressed, sir. Look at me! I'm shorter than most, I have a silly girlish giggly laugh, and I'm far cleverer than almost everybody I work with. I'm detested in the Arab Bureau in Cairo and in General Headquarters. They think I'm very odd, and can't wait to see the back of me, and even the men I'm supposed to be commanding here look at you for permission whenever I give an order."

"That will change, Lawrence, when the men see your decisions bring the benefit of good results. I've seen you lead men. You have a gift. These are my men," he said, sweeping his arm over the hundreds of fighters laying in the sand, their rifles at the ready for the oncoming train, "and they follow my commands, but it is different when you are standing beside me. I order them, and they look towards you for approval. Truly, you are a leader."

Lawrence remained silent, and after a few moments, said, "I wish my colleagues in the British Army felt that way, sir. I'm held in low regard, I'm afraid."

222

"But in the headquarters, surely you have good friends. What about Miss Bell? She's your friend, isn't she?"

"She's my dearest friend, sir. She doesn't judge me. She enjoys my mind, my company, and she admires my love of the Arab people. I wish there were more like her."

The prince thought for a few moments. "Tell me, what is it about the Arab people which attracts those such as you and Miss Bell? Is it the mystery of the desert? The way we look in our funny clothes, riding camels? What is it, Lawrence, which drives you and Miss Bell?"

Lawrence turned and started to walk away from the hillock and back down to where the men were squatting for their surprise assault against the Turks. The prince followed him. "I don't think I can explain it simply, sir. There's certainly an element of mystery and exoticism in Arabia. It's a world which is totally unknown to the vast majority of Englishmen."

"But so are the jungles of Africa and South America. Yet they don't seem to hold out the same fascination as Arabia."

"Some are fascinated. But what you say is right—the desert seems to have some magical pull on the Englishman. Perhaps it's because underneath the beautiful canopy of an English forest is mud and dirt, whereas the desert is simply pure. Drill down through the sand, and all you find is more sand, until eventually you find the bedrock of the very Earth itself. Nothing can hide from you in the desert, and you can't hide from anything. It's just you and the elements."

The Prince nodded, thinking about the allusion. Lawrence continued, "Or perhaps it's the vastness of the landscape, where you can look into eternity. Poor England is tiny compared to Arabia, and we don't seem to be able to settle our eyes on any far horizon. Or perhaps it's the people of the desert—dark, swarthy, mysterious, dangerous, unknowable." He remained silent for a few moments, cogitating, before saying, "but for me, I think it's the purity of the desert when so much of the Earth is so hideous."

"Pure?" said Faisal, bursting out in laughter. "Pure? Our deserts are vast and relentless. Full of hazards which will kill an Englishmen piteously and without giving him a chance."

"Then if it's not the purity, sir, maybe it's because this land is painted with the world's history," said Lawrence.

"Ah, now that could very well be true, Mr. Lawrence. Your fascination could be with our history? We were present at the very beginning of civilization. When Abraham set out from the banks of the Euphrates and began the journey which put man and Allah together for the very first time, it put an end to the darkness of primitivism, and enabled mankind to see clearly the truth of the world, that there is only one God, and that God is Allah."

Lawrence nodded. "While I respect your religious beliefs, sir, I fear my fascination with your history is more to do with its archaeology than its religion. And I believe this is true for the vast majority of Christians and Westerners. Islam is an unknown quantity to the Western mind. We're only just coming to terms with Christianity. Only God knows how long it'll take for us to come to terms with Allah."

The prince smiled at Lawrence's remark. As they walked back towards the encampment, they were greeted by the hundreds of men at the machine gun emplacements. Some of them said, "Blessings be unto you and upon your family, Aurens," finding difficulty in their tongue with the 'L' at the beginning of his name.

They looked impressive, even though a more than cursory look would show that against an implacable enemy, performing real soldiering instead of ambush and guerrilla tactics, they'd be crushed. But the army of the Hejaz had certainly managed to claim some victories against the Turks in Mecca and had driven forward as a line pushing them back towards Medina, but these were little more than minor skirmishes, and the Arab uprising hadn't yet happened. Perhaps because, against Lawrence's advice, the sharif had arrogantly nominated himself as caliph of all Arabia, or perhaps because those such as ibn Rashid and ibn

Sa'ud were watching the way the wind blew, the rest of Arabia seemed to be biding its time.

"Tell me about Miss Bell. She is a fascinating woman. Have you and she been together as man and wife?"

"She wouldn't have me, sir. She says I'm too young and impetuous. Anyway, her true love died many years ago, and she's consumed with love for his memory."

The prince and Lawrence continued to walk around the camp. Almost as an afterthought, Faisal said, "A woman such as Miss Bell needs a man. There is no question of that. She has done well to succeed in a man's world, but she cannot continue to remain alone. When my work is done here, I will consider making her one of my wives."

Lawrence looked at the prince in astonishment. He wanted to warn him, but couldn't think of any way to say it.

~

Basrah, Mesopotamia, December, 1916

Gertrude sat. Then she stood and paced the reception room. Then sat again, finally deciding to choose another chair so she had a better view of the door and the corridor it opened onto.

Her colleague St. John Philby hissed, "Oh for God's sake, Gertie, sit down and keep still. Anyone would think you'd never met an Arab leader before."

"Idiot!" she whispered. "This isn't an Arab leader. This is ibn Sa'ud. The one and only! Here. In our headquarters. This visit could turn the entire war around."

"It's all been seen to by our lords and master, Gertie, so this is just a formality. The potential for our winning this war has already improved since ibn Sa'ud signed the document of understanding in Kuwait, and since we made him Knight Commander of the Indian Empire." said Colonel James.

"And since we agreed to pay him five thousand quid a month, just to smile at us," said Philby.

Suddenly a car screeched to a halt, and the pipes and drums of the Poonah Regiment began to play *God Save the King*. Gertrude stood and was joined by all the other men in the room. They all stared at the door, which remained stubbornly closed. The army men remained at attention, despite the fact that all the activity was going on outside in the parade ground, but Gertrude and Philby and others who were Arabists relaxed until they heard noises and footsteps in the corridor.

The door opened, and a huge Arab in a royal blue *galabiyah* and wearing a red and white checkered *keffiyeh*, showing he belonged to the people of whom ibn Sa'ud was supreme leader, entered and shouted, "All rise for His Most Serene Highness, Abd al-ʿAziz ibn ʿAbd ar-Rahman ibn Faysal ibn Turki ibn ʿAbd Allah ibn Muhammad Al Sa'ud."

The British remained standing. Gertrude held her breath awaiting the entry of the thirty-six-year-old ruler of half of Arabia. She'd seen drawings and photographs of him, and was intensely interested as to whether or not in life he'd look like his father whom, decades ago as a young girl, she'd managed to insult in a Romanian orchard.

And when he made his entrance, she continued to hold her breath. It was like meeting ibn Sa'ud's father once again, as though her adolescence had suddenly been catapulted into her presence. The son was six feet, three inches tall, wearing his people's traditional red and white checkered *keffiyeh* and flowing white robes, his flesh like dark leather and his black pointed beard and aquiline nose making him look like a magnificent bird of prey. He towered both physically and emotionally over the entire room.

Sir Percy, who was tall, seemed dwarfed beside him as the two strode into the room. He was introduced firstly to the senior ranking men of the army, and then to the most senior men of the Political Office, and by the time he got to Gertrude, she had begun to breathe again.

As they arrived where she was standing, Sir Percy said, "Your Eminence, may I introduce Miss Gertrude Bell."

Smiling as sweetly as she knew how, Gertrude said in classical Arabic, "Abdul Aziz, it is an honor for this unworthy woman to meet your illustrious self in the hope that one day I might sit at your feet. Your reputation as a man of men proceeds you."

Ibn Sa'ud looked at her in surprise, and said to her in a classical tongue which none of the Englishmen in the room understood, "These other of your colleagues speak the language of the streets, whereas your Arabic is the voice of scholars."

"How may a mere woman who is also a scholar dare speak with a man of greatness whose arm is a sword and whose tongue is a dagger, other than in the most perfect and beautiful of languages?"

"Your name again?" he asked admiringly.

"Gertrude Bell, Abdul Aziz. An unworthy subject of His Majesty George, the Fifth King of England who holds that great name."

Sir Percy grasped his arm gently and guided him to the next man in line. But even while he was being introduced, ibn Sa'ud couldn't resist glancing back at Gertrude, who knew she'd made an impression. It was most unusual for a woman to be allowed to greet such an Arabic leader among a party of men, but a woman without a veil was unheard of. And she and Percy had agreed she should greet the sheik as a representative of the British Crown while ibn Sa'ud was within a British building in Basrah.

As the party left the room, ibn Sa'ud seemed to delay for a moment. He stood filling the doorway, and turned to everybody, saying, "Thank you for your courtesy, gentlemen. Miss Bell, perhaps with the permission of Sir Percy, you could join me as I review your British technological superiority."

She looked at Percy, who nodded imperceptibly. She began to walk forward to join the notables, only to hear St. John Philby whisper to her, "Give him your body for England, but don't let him bugger up your mind."

She turned and whispered back, "I think he already has."

She walked a respectful distance behind, and thought of the number of times their paths had crossed, yet she'd never met him and now that she was walking in his footsteps, she regretted it deeply.

She knew much about him, of course. She knew he had sixty-five wives and he was probably the most daring and adventurous man in all of Arabia. He was the natural leader, rather than Faisal, the man who could unite all the Arabs. But unlike Faisal, ibn Sa'ud was a man who thought in a narrow sphere, and simply couldn't be trusted, either by the British, or by the other Arab tribal leaders. Whatever he did, she knew he'd do only for himself.

She would love to spend some time with him alone, not just because he was so important to British and Indian interests, but because he could fill in so many of the details about Arabia which were hazy in her mind, such as the way in which he'd recaptured his kingdom from the Rashids. Maybe one day, she'd discover the true story.

Outside the headquarters, those troops who had been relieved in the assault northwards towards Baghdad were on parade ready for ibn Sa'ud's inspection. He walked up and down the rows of troops, towering above most of them. Every now and then, he would stop and ask one about his adventures in Kut or some other battle. Gertrude would translate seamlessly and flawlessly and the interchange lasted only a matter of moments before the sheik walked onwards.

At the end of the inspection, Sir Percy asked ibn Sa'ud whether he would accept the salute and the presentation of arms. Gertrude explained discretely what that implied and whispering into his ear what was expected of him. She followed him up to the inspection podium. To the tune of another march from the band, the troops paraded past and ibn Sa'ud did his best to salute. After the last man had left the parade ground, General Maude, the new British Army Commander, presented ibn Sa'ud with a jewelled ceremonial sword.

Gertrude didn't know whether to retreat back to her office now that the formalities were over, but at a subtle nod from ibn Sa'ud, Percy asked her if she would like to continue to accompany their guest, and she found herself sitting between the sheik and Sir Percy, with General Maude in the front, as they drove to the recently-built railway terminus. Here, ibn Sa'ud saw the pride of British industry, as well as having his hand placed under a new X-ray machine. Fascinated, he spent long moments wiggling his hand and watching the skeletal bones move clearly beneath his skin. He invited Gertrude to join her hand with his in the machine, adding to his amusement.

After more parades and a demonstration of British firepower and the use of high explosives in the nearby desert, the sheik was driven to his hotel where he asked to be excused from the dinner in his honor that night in the Officer's Mess, saying he was exhausted from so much British hospitality, and would prefer to spend a quiet evening alone.

Everyone bade him good night, and Gertrude excused herself, going home. She hadn't been indoors for more than fifteen minutes, and was preparing herself a scotch and soda, when there was a heavy-fisted knock at the door.

She waited in her lounge-room, listening to her servant open the door. She recognised the voice of the sheik's servant and immediately went out to greet him.

"Is His Highness well?" she asked.

"Perfectly. He commands your attendance in his rooms. I am here to take you."

Her mind traveled back to Egypt and a similar interchange between the servant of Prince Faisal and herself. But this time, she would not make the same fuss. This time, British interests were paramount, and her positioning as a confidant of ibn Sa'ud could potentially save thousands of lives.

Grabbing her coat, she followed the servant outside, where a car was waiting. Within a few minutes, she was seated in the suite of rooms occupied by Sheik ibn Sa'ud, enjoying his hospitality of apple tea and cinnamon cake.

"I thought you might not come. Is it not improper for a man to entertain an Englishwoman alone in a room?"

"In our case, sir, it is neither improper nor unwise. You are a very important person to the British government. I am a servant of that government, and my sex is of no consequence. It is only right and proper that I should be at your service."

He nodded. With some difficulty, he said, "You are the first Western woman I have ever seen. Are all Western women like you?"

"Are all Arabs like you?" she asked.

He began to smile, but suddenly burst out laughing. "Of course you are an exception. You are a woman in the world of men. To be such, you must be very different. In what way are you different, Gertrude Bell?"

"Your father knows in what way I am different, sir."

He looked at her with his piercing eyes. "You know my father?"

"When he came to Romania many years ago. I was a young girl in the embassy. We had many discussions. He is truly a man of men."

"Did my father take you?"

She tried to hide her smile. "No, Majesty. He didn't. He was respectful of me as the niece of the ambassador."

"He spoke of a woman. A young girl who had impressed him. But he also told me to beware of women like you. He said you have tongues which can cut a man's flesh. Is this true?"

"My tongue is sharp, Excellency, but I use it cut through anything which impedes my journey."

Ibn Sa'ud looked at her closely. His father had described a girl's face to him, a tall red-headed girl with striking looks and eyes which were the color of precious gems. Could this middle-aged graying woman be the same? How cruel were the years.

"You have grown old, Chatrude Pell."

"Just as we all grow old, Excellency, and in the years to come, regret that while our manhood today stands firm before our wives, in the future we soften and bend with time."

"This will not happen to my manhood, woman. I am a rock for my people."

"Even rocks erode with time, sir, and become small pebbles."

They looked at each other, neither giving ground, until ibn Sa'ud smiled, and again burst out laughing. He had never had such a conversation with anybody in his kingdom, let alone a woman. "Truly you are an English woman, because any Arab who said that to me would lose his head." He moved towards the sofa, and sat down. "And my father did not take you. It surprises me, as he knew many women and had many wives."

"He respected me."

Ibn Sa'ud frowned. "But if he respected you, then he would have had you. In my country, a king can take any woman. It is an honor. And now I, his son, will truly tread beyond his footsteps, for tonight, you shall know the true meaning of Arab manhood. Tonight, I shall have you."

"No, Excellency, you will not have me. For then you would only look on me as a woman, ibn Sa'ud, and not but as a representative of the British crown. As a British official, I am worth far more of your time than were you to take me for your pleasure."

And when she saw his face, she realized he'd been having fun with her. Just as his father had made fun of her half a lifetime ago. She laughed, and said, "You mustn't play these games with me, Abdul Aziz. As a diplomat, I take things very seriously."

Ibn Sa'ud nodded, and said, "I like you, Gertrude Bell. You will one day learn to laugh. Is this why you're different? Can you offer me more than you gave my father?"

"I have learning, sir, which is at your disposal. And I've sat at the feet of great men whom I can bring to your service. I know your lands and your peoples. I have been an explorer in Arabia, travelling throughout your lands—"

Suddenly his face lit up with understanding. "Now I remember! Hayil! Many years ago. An English woman was imprisoned by that son of pig who was sired by a whore, ibn Rashid. It was said she was traveling to pay me homage."

"That woman was me, Highness."

"Yes. Now I know. They say many things about you. They call you the Daughter of the Desert. They say you are an honorary man. You have learned our language and lived in our tents."

"Sir, you didn't ask me to come here simply to find out more about me. In what way might I assist you?"

Ibn Sa'ud nodded. "My family ruled all of Arabia for one hundred years, but when I was nothing more than a baby, my family was driven from its home by our former servants, the evil and merciless Rashids. For this the Sa'uds will hate and revile them into all eternity."

"You were exiled to Kuwait, weren't you, sir," she said, wanting him to know she had studied him and his life.

"Correct, but in your year of 1901, when I was only twenty-one, I left Kuwait with forty soldiers on camels and with a vow on my lips to reclaim my family's land and honor, or to die in the attempt.

"In January of your year 1902, we crept into our old capital of Riyadh. We were concerned that we would be discovered, or some of our old retainers would make a fuss on seeing us, so we hid like thieves until the early morning, when the governor came out of doors to say his prayers. I slit his throat from ear to ear and we seized the castle. Suddenly all our families and tribes and kinfolk rallied to our cause by our bravery, and for two years, we raided and fought and took back everything which the Rashids had taken from us, until once again, half of Arabia was ours."

"When ibn Rashid received help from the Turks, how badly were you affected? Could you fight them and the Rashids without the help of others?" she asked, mesmerised by his narrative.

"It cost us dearly. We had bravery and camels, they were cowards with machine guns and howitzers. We suffered defeats at their hands, but for five years we drove them and drove them, fighting them at every opportunity, taunting them, hurting them, until eventually we came between them and their supply routes, and we starved them to death. Now, God be praised, like my forefather ibn Sa'ud, I have returned my entire people to the path of righteousness. Today, they worship Allah in the manner taught to us by Muhammad ibn 'Abd al-Wahhab, of blessed memory. Through his guidance, I have been able to create a tribe of religious warriors which I call the *Ikhwan*, and through these soldiers of God, we are in control again, and the Turks are on the run."

Gertrude had heard of the band of brethren called the *Ikhwan*, the most feared soldiers on the entire Arabian Peninsula. These were men who had stopped the tribes from continuing their centuries-old nomadic ways, and forced them to live around oases and wells, so the land was settled and populated. She also knew of the sect which were called the Wahhabists, fundamentalist and narrow and against any form of modernity.

She decided to remain silent. She had been summoned, not to listen to his history, but for a purpose which was yet to unfold. It could be hours before he came to the point, as was the Arabic custom, but she had to listen patiently, and not usurp his position in the narrative.

"Tell me, Gertrude Bell. You are a woman who listens as well as speaks. I have been given five thousand pounds a month by your British colleagues. Is this sufficient for a man of my importance?"

"Sir," she responded, "this is not a question I can answer. My advice was not sought by the British government."

"But how much would you have paid me to be loyal to Britain? If you had been in command?"

"Five thousand pounds is a very large amount of money, sir, and adequate for any needs you might have."

He nodded, and drank his glass of apple tea. She poured herself another glass, wondering when the purpose of her summons would become clear. He moved over to the window to look out over the city of Basrah. She stared at his body and his huge shoulders. It was said he needed many wives to satisfy his cravings and ensure he was never alone for any night of the year. The women which he had undoubtedly brought with him to see to his physical requirements were almost certainly hidden away and locked in one of the bedrooms, waiting for him to finish his business and take his choice. Gertrude could just imagine the jealousy and cattiness in the bedroom as younger women vied with each other to convince Abdul Aziz' first wife, their mother hen, that they should be the ones allowed the privilege of bedding the sheik.

His back turned, he asked, "And Sharif Hussein of Hejaz? How much are you paying him?"

Knowing he already knew, she immediately retorted, "A far lesser amount than yourself." Telling lies would destroy any future trust he might place in her.

He turned. There was a look of fury on his face, which at first frightened her, until she suddenly remembered she was his guest, and was completely protected.

"You know that camel-loving piece of dog's flesh has claimed he is the true king of Arabia. He calls himself Caliph. Just because he claims descent from the Prophet and because he is the guardian of Mecca and Medina, he thinks he can rule over me, Sheik abd Al-'aziz Al Sa'ud.

"He has said this, Gertrude Bell. It will be my honor to cut off his manhood and throw it down the deepest well. He will be a eunuch and forever a laughingstock in the company of men. I will cause him to suffer hideous boils for the rest of his life and when he eats, may his right hand die and wither. This is what I shall do to him for daring to think himself greater than me."

"Many years ago, sir, I talked to your father about the need for another Saladin to rise up and unite the Arab people, and he agreed. Yet you object to Sharif Hussein having that role."

It was a dangerous statement, but an opening gambit on what could be an exciting prospect.

"By what right does Hussein claim the mantle of Saladin?"

"By his right as a descendant of the Prophet, peace and blessings upon him. And by his right as sharif of the Holy Cities."

"And who gave him this right? Did he earn this right by conquest? How many men did he kill, how many battles did he fight? None, woman. He was suckled by his mother as he sat on the throne. He has done nothing to make others of us follow him."

"Then who should the Arabs follow, Excellency?" asked Gertrude, trying to keep her voice impassive.

"Me!" he bellowed. "Abd al-'Aziz ibn 'Abd ar-Rahman ibn Faysal ibn Turki 'Abd Allah ibn Muhammad Al Sa'ud. I am the man of men! I will lead the Arab people to their destiny. I will destroy this sharif and all others who stand in my way."

"But Sir," she said quickly, "your brother Arabs will follow your leadership if you remember the true enemy of your people are the Turks."

"Ha! How little you know, you woman of learning. The Turks are diseased and dying. As soon as they are driven from my country by us and you British, I shall turn my attention to that flea in Mecca, and I shall crush him between my thumb and my finger. And then I shall destroy his four sons and all those cursed breed who call themselves Hashemite."

"But how can you unite the Arab people by destroying them? This will build hatred and lead to further repression. Leadership, Excellency, is gained by setting a good example so people wish to follow you."

He looked at her as though she was mad. "Leadership, woman, is gained by those whose arm is the strongest and whose sword is the sharpest. Men follow a leader out of fear of what will happen to them if they fail to follow. Before a battle, I always assemble my men and ask them who is the most cowardly among them. Those whose name the majority shout out is pushed out of the ranks, and without speaking, I walk over to the terrified man, draw my sword, and cut off his head with one swipe. From that moment onwards, every man in battle fights like a lion.

"When I am paid by you British to use my armies, and when we have destroyed the Turks and sent them scurrying back to Constantinople like frightened dogs, I shall march to the Kingdom of Hejaz, parade the sharif and his brood in front of all his people, and one by one cut off their heads, women and children included. Then we'll see if the people of the Hejaz are brave enough to resist me."

He smiled and looked at her. Gertrude looked back at him, but lowered her eyes, deciding not to comment further. Oh dear, was all she could think.

TEN

Baghdad, 1917

She had been anticipating the knock on the door ever since she was told he was in the city. Although only in his mid-20's, people were already speaking of him as a pioneer in the art of making radio broadcasts as well as magazine photography. The stories he had written about the European front since Woodrow Wilson had gained Congress' consent to sign the Articles of War on April 6th, had excited the interest and rallied the patriotism of the entire continent of the United States, and when it was known he was coming to the Middle East, the British War Cabinet had given orders that he was to be treated with great consideration.

Of course, Gertrude realized, there could only be one reason why Lowell Thomas was in Baghdad, and that was to report on the Arab Revolt which was now developing a life and a mind of its own. Even Allenby, whom she believed would soon be racing Lawrence and Faisal to Damascus in Syria, was talking of the uprising by the Howeitat and other tribes as being fundamental to ultimate British success.

Certain ambitious officers in Europe, she knew, had acquiesced to all of Lowell Thomas' requirements for special journalistic consideration, as though he was a headmaster visiting the upper prep. But she had no intention of repeating such fawning and obsequious behaviour. Why should she? After all, she was well enough known in Great Britain, he was only an American, and she was a senior British diplomat. He was merely a reporter of events, while she was a prime mover in the war against the Turks. She would make him wait at least two knocks.

"Come in," she shouted eventually.

The door slowly opened. In walked a tall young man, fresh-faced and eager, wearing a blindingly white suit, white fedora, and black shirt. His tie was a kaleidoscope of color and patterns which made her wince.

"Miss Bell?" said the young man.

"Mr. Thomas. I've been expecting you," she said, rising to shake his hand. He had a firm grip, and had presumably been a college football player. Wasn't that what all young Americans used to be before they grew up, she thought.

"You know who I am?"

"I'm Great Britain's local busybody here in Mesopotamia. I have my finger in every pie."

"Then you know I'm a journalist, and that—"

"That you've recently been in Europe telling the Americans what their lads are doing. Yes, Mr. Thomas, I know who you are and presumably why you're here."

He looked at her in surprise. He'd only informed his magazine in New York by cable of his intention the other month. They sat and smiled at each other. She offered him water from a pitcher. It was flavoured with aniseed and as he sipped it he mentioned its unusual and captivating taste.

"My own invention. I'm so fed up with the taste of apple tea and cinnamon and rose water. I wanted something which was different."

"That's what they all say about you—that you're different," he said. He had a muscular voice, its cadences clear, its measure precise. She liked that in a man.

"In what way am I different, I wonder," she asked rhetorically. "I suppose being a woman political officer is somewhat uncommon, but I've been in this role for so long I no longer see myself as anything but one of the team."

He smiled at her modesty. Since leaving Europe, landing at Basrah and traveling the hundreds of miles through the marshlands and deserts to Allied headquarters in Baghdad, he'd heard of little else but the brilliance and importance of the legendary Gertrude Bell. Arabs as well as British army men spoke of her in the most glowing terms. Yet nobody spoke of her on the battlefields and the headquarters in Europe, and her name was unknown in America.

"You're quite something, from what everybody says about you. As you know, Gertrude, I'm here to cover stories on the war for back home. Europe's all written out and it's crawling with reporters, and so I wanted to be the first to bring what's happening in Arabia to the world's attention."

"Really? And why do you think our little war out here would be of the slightest interest to anyone in Europe or in America? Hundreds of thousands of young men are dying every month on the battlefields of Belgium and France. This is hardly more than a side-show."

"On the contrary, if Turkey wins and defeats the Brits, and Germany wins over Europe, this land will be the first they make for. Everybody's talking about the vast quantities of oil here, which is the future of industry and automobiles. Whoever controls Arabia controls the future of the world. That's what they're saying, and I guess that's what it's all about. That's why Great Britain wants a stake in the ground, and so does everybody else. No, Gertrude, this place has it all for a reporter. The magic of the desert, the mystery of the tribes, the romance of the sheiks and the harems and everything else. And of course, there's this Englishman who rides a camel and wears Arabic clothing and is leading the Arab armies. Now *that's* a story!"

She smiled. "Mr. Lawrence?"

"Yes, that's the guy—Major Lawrence. They say he's the one out of the box. I mean, a white man riding across the desert on a camel. Is that unique, or what?"

"It's far from unique, Mr. Thomas. Hundreds of Australian troops ride camels in the Middle East. Being the ship of the desert, it's the preferred choice of transportation."

Undaunted, he continued. "Okay, so maybe others have done it before, but nobody knows about this guy Lawrence in the States. I want to capture the essence of the man . . . the romantic . . . the adventurer . . . a white man who throws off the mantle of civilization and respectability and goes native. Major Lawrence of Arabia."

Gertrude looked at him in amusement. "I'm sure he'd love that," she said.

"And I want to do a feature on you, too. A story and pictures for the magazine. I want to tell the world all about Gertrude Bell, and what you've been up to. A woman who's succeeded in a man's world—that sort of thing."

"Don't be ridiculous. I wouldn't dream of it. I have no intention of becoming like a circus curio."

Offended, Lowell said, "It isn't like that. I'll do a really nice story about you, with pictures taken beside some of the old ruins south of here. They say you're a famous archaeologist and an explorer. I'll make you even more famous in the States, so after the war, you can—"

"Absolutely not, Mr. Lowell. It's completely out of the question. You will not take my photograph, nor will you write about me for your magazine. I'm a very private person, and you'll respect my privacy. Anyway, the work I'm doing is top secret. Under no circumstances will you report any of it. Is that clear?"

He shrugged his shoulders. He'd met people like Gertrude a dozen times before, and eventually they all changed their mind, incapable of missing the opportunity for fame which his magazine features would bring. "Fine. So tell me all about this guy, Lawrence. I need to find him. Any idea where he is now?" he asked ingenuously.

She scrutinized him thoughtfully. She was concerned a blaze of publicity might compromise Lawrence's ability to maintain the respect of the tribal leaders. "Is it so important you meet with Mr. Lawrence? Surely the Arabic leaders such as Prince Faisal and Sharif Hussein ibn Ali or even Abd al-'Aziz ibn Sa'ud himself are more important than some middle-ranking British officer who's little more than a military advisor. If you want, I'll try to arrange interviews with you. I'll even act as your translator.

239

"You seem, if I might say so, to be somewhat askew in your understanding of this offensive," she told him. "While Mr. Lawrence has been of great value to the cause of fighting the Turks, you must remember he is under instructions from Britain, and that—"

"He's under instructions from you, if everything I've been told about you is true, Gertrude."

She burst out laughing. "What an extraordinary thing to say."

"Extraordinary or not, I'm a reporter. I ask questions. My job is to get to know information. And from Cairo to Jerusalem, Basrah to Baghdad, everybody keeps whispering your name into my ear. They say you're the brains behind the Arabic uprising. They say you write notes to Lawrence telling him what to do next. If that's the case, then you're the real story. And they say you're conspiring to bring all the Arab tribes under one flag when this war is over. If that's true, then that's a big story. But as you won't let me do it, I guess I'll have to settle for Lawrence."

"Nonsense! Piffle! I don't know what you've heard, or who you've been talking to, but I'm just a diplomat promoting British interests in this war. I'm a minor cog in the wheels. The Arab Bureau in Egypt and we here in Mesopotamia are working in conjunction with the leadership of the Arabic people in fighting centuries of Ottoman oppression. This isn't a one-man show, Mr. Thomas. Or a one-woman show, either. It's a co-ordinated, sophisticated program to overthrow the Turks, to right the wrongs of history, to give the Arabic people back their country, and to—"

This time, it was Lowell Thomas' turn to burst out laughing. "Come on, Gertie, pull the other one. It's got bells on it. You're here for one reason, and one reason only, and we all know it. You're here to carve up Arabia when Turkey is pushed back north out of Asia. The Brits, the French, and the Italians all want their slice of the action. Even the Russians are keen, from what I've heard. The new Russian government is all over the place right now, and doesn't know whether it's coming or going. They say they'll soon be more trouble for the Russkie government trying to hold the country together, and these guys Lenin and Trotsky are raising support for another revolution. You think they'll sit on their backsides when the Black Sea is up for grabs. Come on!"

She remained silent.

"Well, do you deny you're the brains behind this Arab revolt?" he asked.

"I most certainly do. And I find your tone and your manner impertinent, offensive, and completely inaccurate. I think it's time you left my office. You can expect no further help from me."

"I'm sorry if I've offended you. It wasn't my intention at all. I'm a reporter and I get results by asking questions people often don't want asked. So I'm sorry if you're upset. But ever since I left Europe, I've heard nothing other than the way in which all the allies are fighting for the Arabic cause, and quite frankly, after the way the Brits have treated the Egyptians since they took over the country thirty years ago, it seems as if you Europeans look on the Arabs as little more than extensions of your Empire, slaves to your cause, yours to do with as you want."

"Mr. Thomas," Gertrude said in anger. "You came into my office in good standing, requesting information. You have no right to make these remarks. Have you forgotten who I am? I'm a senior political officer of His Majesty's government. How dare you make these assertions? I've nothing but the highest respect and regard for Arabic history and culture. These implications are monstrous."

"Look, Gertrude. I didn't come in here for a quarrel, but from everything I've heard about you, you're the full dollar and you cut straight to the chase, which is why I didn't beat around the bush. I thought you'd give me a straight bat, not some English doubletalk. I guess I was wrong about things, and I'm sorry. But you should listen to what people are saying on the streets. In Jerusalem, in Suez, all over Arabia, people are talking about Britain and France replacing the Ottomans and being little better for the Arabic people. The Arabs support the uprising because they hate the Turks, but are very dubious about their future. Sure, everyone wants the Turks to go home to Constantinople, but everybody's wondering what happens after that. Is Britain just going to pack its bags, and quit the area? I don't think so."

"Great Britain has strategic interests in this area, and will protect them. But Great Britain is also committed to the Arab revolt and to Arabic nationalism, and it's a policy which has been stated over and over again in public."

Again, Lowell Thomas burst out laughing. She thought she needed to remove him from the building in case there were any Arabic leaders who might overhear what he was saying in his stentorian voice.

She stood from her desk, hoping her movements didn't indicate to the American that this was becoming an increasingly dangerous conversation. She was used to dealing with British journalists, but she'd never experienced an American reporter before, and the differences were startling. Unlike the British reporters, especially for the quality newspapers, this American was direct, aggressive, and intrusive.

"Perhaps if we were to go out for a walk in the gardens, it might cheer us up and cool down our tempers," she said, leading him through the double glass doors of her office.

Somewhat humbled, he said softly, "I guess I've gotten off on the wrong foot, haven't I?"

"You certainly have."

"Can I get back onto the right footing?"

"That depends on where you tread," she said.

They remained silent, walking through the perfumery which was the gardens. He appeared not to notice the glory of the trees or the spice bushes, but was deep in thought.

"Are you sure you won't reconsider, and let me do a feature story on you. If you don't like the idea of a magazine story, I could do you on wireless. You're such a remarkable woman. I've heard all about you—mountaineer, linguist, explorer, archaeologist, diplomat—you've done more in your life than ten other people put together. I'm sure millions of readers would be thrilled to read of your example."

"Ah, Mr. Thomas, but would I be thrilled to know they're reading about me. That's the point, isn't it? Before the war, I regularly wrote for *The Times*, and published books. But now, as a diplomat, I require anonymity and complete freedom from the public gaze to do my job here. How on Earth could I gain trust and respect from the Arabic chieftains if my name and the nature of our discussions were trumpeted all over the front page of your magazine?"

"Then why haven't you objected more strongly to the idea of me going to see this Lawrence guy? I mean, what's sauce for the goose surely is sauce for the gander?"

"I did at first, but right now, I think it could be a good idea. He's not a diplomat, after all, he's leading an army, and a bit of notoriety wouldn't do any harm. It suits my purposes to be like Richelieu and Mazarin, a secretive *eminence rouge* between the Arabs and the British, whereas it probably would suit Mr. Lawrence's needs very well for you to portray him across the world as Lawrence of Arabia. Yes, I'm sure he'd be tickled pink at the thought."

"Okay," he said, full of enthusiasm. "Okay, then tell me how I can find him. It's a big desert out there."

She looked at him with a bemused smile. "My dear Mr. Thomas, what on Earth gives you the impression that I have the faintest idea where he is."

"Oh, come on, Gertrude. Everybody knows you're in touch with him and supply him with all his information. Everyone says so. You tell him where to go, who to talk to, what the Arabs are doing and thinking . . . everything."

She shook her head. "My, but you do have an unusual picture of my importance."

~

Towards Damascus in Syria, 1918

He was a boy again, doing the dare-devil things which boys did, the heart-thumping, throat-drying, knife-edged manic thrills of an adult-free adventure. He was the leader of the biggest gang any schoolboy had ever commanded. Now he had his own army to order at will. Now his physical disabilities meant nothing compared to his successes at derailing a train or massacring a squad of petrified Turkish conscripts, spilling blood into the desert sand. And the real beauty was that the desert soaked up the blood and within days it had returned to its purity and absolved him of his crimes.

For a year, he had been slowing the Turkish advance by crippling the Hejaz Railway, stopping the trains in their tracks which ran from Damascus to Medina, killing Turkish soldiers and preventing reinforcements and supplies from reaching the beleaguered remnants of their army.

And now his glory and his shame were being trumpeted around the world on the front pages of newspapers and magazines, thanks to this American journalist. At first, he'd been thrilled to see himself on the front of a magazine cover, staring enigmatically into the infinite distance, dressed in the flowing white robes of an Arabic chieftain, his *keffiyeh* wafting in the gentle desert breeze. And he'd laughed out loud at how such a picture would be received in the mess halls of Cairo and Whitehall and by his classmates who were today bankers or stockbrokers or selling insurance or motor cars or permanently socializing and doing nothing adventurous with their lives.

But then he'd wondered whether Lawrence the Warrior and Lawrence the Hero and Lawrence of Arabia would become Lawrence the Murderer when it was known how many prisoners were murdered in cold blood because there wasn't enough food or water for the enemy and his army in the desert. This wasn't the gentlemanly warfare between cricket and rubgy teams performed according to ancient rules on the playing fields of Eton and Harrow; this was maiming and mutilation; this was fear and retribution; this was life and death.

A shadow passed across his face, infiltrating its presence onto his musing. "I believe the expression you English use is *a penny for your thoughts*."

Lawrence opened his eyes, and looked up to see Prince Faisal standing between him and the sun.

"Most noble and excellent majesty, man of men, ruler of the world, guide and mentor to the friends of Islam, greetings," said Lawrence with a mischievous grin on his face. He was pleased to have had his disturbing thoughts interrupted.

"And greetings to an Englishman who is redeeming Arabic pride and making this third-born prince into a king of leaders."

"*Inshallah*" quipped Lawrence.

"Do you ever think that day will come?" asked the prince. "I have two brothers older than me, and my father, though old and sick, is energised by this revolt, and has no thoughts of retiring from the guardianship of the Holy Cities."

"Sir," Lawrence began to say, standing up and shaking the sand of the desert off his khaki uniform, which he had taken to wearing as he moved closer to civilization. "We are on the outskirts of Damascus. The way this war has gone, I think opportunities will arise for greatness for the Arabic people. Once Turkey is pushed back across the Bosphorus and out of Asia and Arabia, it'll leave vacuums to be filled, and we all know that nature abhors a vacuum. There will be vast areas left without rule, and men of vision and with charisma will fill those areas with wisdom and leadership. You are the man whom the Arabs will revere as having led the uprising; you are the man they will turn to as their natural leader."

"Really, Lawrence? Will I even be revered by Abd al-Aziz and the Sa'ud family? I think not."

"While ever this war is on, Majesty, the Sa'uds are earning a king's ransom for fighting on our side. When the war is over, we British will protect the eastern flank of the Hejaz from any adventure he might launch against Mecca and Medina."

"And does Gertrude Bell agree with you?"

"Gertie and I are of one mind on this issue. We recognize the Hussein family and the men of the Kingdom of the Hejaz led the uprising against the Turks, and contributed magnificently to our success in the mighty Arab army we've built. We British don't forget such support. Abd al-Aziz has certainly contributed many fighting men, but the cost every month is staggering. Again, sir, we won't forget such avarice. Don't concern yourself about the safety of yourself and your family, or indeed your kingdom, when this war is over. The Kingdom of the Hejaz will last for a thousand years."

"From your mouth to the ears of Allah, Lawrence. And hopefully your generals and diplomats will also have been listening."

The prince smiled. They began to walk together to the top of the hill in order to spy out the horizon and search for that telltale smudge of smoke which foretold of a Turkish reinforcements train.

"Your words, Lawrence, are music to the ears of one such as me. But when the music has stopped playing, then all that is left is the aching memory. This vacuum you speak of will appear if Turkey is defeated. And while that looks as if it might be the will of Allah, why do you assume Arabs will fill this vacuum?"

"Sir?"

"France has many interests in this area, Britain needs to ensure its passage to India through the Suez Canal, and when the reserves are proven your country will need the oil which is beneath the sands of Basrah and Abadan. Or Germany might win the war in Europe and spread its influence from Berlin to Baghdad and beyond to the Persian Gulf, push the Turks and Arabs out of the way, and control the oilfields."

"All these things assume, Prince Faisal, that our interests in this area do not accord with yours. How many times do I have to tell you Britain has no interest in replacing Turkey as an overlord, but—"

"Mr. Sykes and Monsieur Picot do not agree with you," the prince said quietly.

"I beg your pardon," Lawrence asked.

"Sykes and Picot, Mr. Lawrence. Sir Mark Sykes from London, and Monsieur François Georges-Picot from Paris have spent these last many months pouring over maps and deciding how the Middle East shall be divided up after Turkey is forced out of Arabia. You didn't know this?" the prince asked in mock astonishment.

"Nonsense," Lawrence whispered. "I know of Sir Mark, and he wouldn't do this. I don't know the other gentleman. What's he been up to?"

The prince didn't answer directly, but continued. "And I assume you also don't know that Russia and Italy are eager to get their teeth into our land, unable to restrain themselves from participating in the carving up of our Arabia and all its oils and fertility."

"Sir, I swear to you this is all new to me."

"I believe you, Mr. Lawrence. Like me you've been in the desert for a long time, but unlike me you're reliant on information which comes to you from your British colleagues, whereas I have friends in many places. Decisions are made above our heads, and we only learn of them later. This is the tragedy of men such as you and me. These decisions are made by vultures flying high in the sky looking for pickings on the ground. Men such as us are forced to deal with whatever they might leave behind."

"Like I say, I know Mark Sykes. He's a diplomat and an MP. He served with the British Army against the Boers. I know he's done a lot of traveling in Arabia, but . . ."

"More than traveling, Lawrence. I'm reliably informed by our Arab friends in London that Sykes and Picot have put together a scheme for spheres of influence in Arabia after the war. They've even involved the Russian government because of the Turkish assaults in the Black Sea. My friends in London found out about the plan from a very drunk and very unwise diplomat, and they are naturally upset. It seems Russia will be given Armenia and some of the Kurdish territories, and France is to be given Syria including the Syrian coastlands of the Mediterranean, as well as Beirut and the lands between Cilicia and the Upper Tigris, and Great Britain will be given southern Mesopotamia and the lands of the Tigris and the Euphrates, including Baghdad and Basrah and Khanaqin. Great Britain will also wield its influence over the Palestine ports of Haifa and Akko. However, the holy Christian places of Palestine shall be given to some international body to protect them. Interestingly, they do not feel that the holy places of Islam, Mecca and Medina, are worth considering at this stage."

Lawrence felt as though his legs were turning to water. It had always been a possibility, but he never thought it would happen, not after the assurances he'd been given by Gertrude and Sir Percy and others. He couldn't believe what he was being told. Yes, the betrayal of the Arab Revolt was something often mooted in the Officer's Mess at Cairo, but it was nothing more than talk by ignorant army men who didn't understand and who detested the Arabs, describing them as surly, dirty and ignorant. But now, suddenly, and courtesy of the diplomats and politicians, it had become a reality.

"This cannot be, Highness. You're wrong! Your friends are wrong! I have been instructed to liaise with you in this revolt because we in Britain are committed to a partnership with the Arab world. Surely you must realize this is what Gertrude Bell has been spruiking throughout the corridors of Whitehall? Arabic nationalism is the way forward, not Arabia being a part of the British Empire. And an equal partnership with you after the defeat of Turkey. A partnership, Faisal, between equals. The whole basis of asking you to rise up on our behalf was to assure you the Arabs would control Arabia after we'd won the war. Yes, we would be here, but it was always meant to be your land. Sir, I can't believe that—Allenby gave his word—the British Government—Miss Bell assured me—"

"It's true, I'm afraid, Major Lawrence. There is no mistake. Believe me," said the prince.

Lawrence remained silent for some time as the two walked slowly towards the rising sun. "I don't know what to say, Prince Faisal," he said.

"Oh, but that's not the end of the story, my friend. Some time ago, your foreign secretary, Mr. Balfour, with the complete agreement of Mr. Lloyd George, wrote a letter to Baron Rothschild, who is the leader of Britain's Jewish community, in which he gave assurances of your government's support for a national homeland for the

Jewish people in Palestine. Yet we were never consulted. I find that somewhat strange, Mr. Lawrence, especially as it probably includes Jerusalem, one of the holiest sites of Islam."

"But we can't have Palestine flooded by Jews. The Arabs will never—"

"I disagree. Jews are among the ancient inhabitants of this land, and need to return to fulfil their destiny. All I demand is that they respect our holy places. For centuries, Jews and Arabs have lived in peace, worshipping the same God. They are a worldly people who have been separated from their Temple for two thousand years. Yet despite having no land of their own, look at their achievements. They are modern and industrious and knowledgeable. And most important, they are international. They have contacts in every corner of the world. They will bring commerce to our lands, as well as trade, factories and offices and international connections. They, far more than the British, will be of great value to us in the development and modernisation of Arabia when the turkey is carved up."

He laughed at his own joke, but Lawrence was in no mood of humour. He was thinking deeply, and asked, "I'm stunned by this news. How do you know these things? How did you know about this letter from Lord Balfour, this agreement between Sykes and-and-whatever the Frenchman's name is?"

"Picot. A French minister. How do I know? My Arabic friends in London are close to senior diplomats in your Foreign and Empire Service who advise your government. These men are favourably disposed to the current Russian government, trying to keep it in power and to defeat the ambitions of Mr. Lenin and Mr. Trotsky and the other revolutionaries who want to spread the ideas of Karl Marx to their people. My friends are very angry that Britain has broken its word to the Arabic peoples, and will almost certainly interfere in Russian politics. But all these things are not of concern to me at the moment.

"You see, Lawrence, the point isn't how I know, it's what I should do with this information. If I were to tell my father and brothers and the other Arab leaders what I have been told, especially now we are so close to victory over the Turks, they would howl treason. We are following Britain's desires like faithful friends, putting our trust in your word. We Arabs are often accused of stabbing our friends in the back. Now it appears we Arabs have been on the pointed end of your diplomatic dagger. Your government assured us that when the Arabs rose up and joined in fighting the Turks, then after the war we would be no more than friends and trading partners . . . that Arabs would control Arabic nationalism and Arabic destiny and all of Arabia. Imagine what will happen now, after all we have done for you, if I tell my brothers and the other leaders of other tribes that the British have been treacherous, and that this treachery has been going on behind our backs while they smile at us and shake our hands like equals."

"Why don't you?" asked Lawrence, his temper flaring. "Why don't you tell them, and to hell with the British? It's all so bloody disgusting and political and rotten. It's not only you who's been stabbed in the back, Faisal, but me. Allenby is courting me on the one hand, using us to protect his eastern flank while he fights from Gaza to Damascus, and on the other hand, he's doing rancid deals with the French to prevent the Arabs from finally becoming a nation. Gertrude Bell is sending me screeds of advice on how to fight this war, and she's probably in on the conspiracy.

"We have an historic opportunity here to make your people into a great nation, and now the bloody politicians and diplomats are wriggling around like snakes. Well, it's all too bad. Why not tell your brother leaders that Great Britain is setting a trap for you?"

"What?" Faisal said softly, "And have my brothers sheath their swords and disappear back into the desert? Have them leave us and risk the British being defeated? But that would consign us once again to the domination of the Turks? And worse, to their merciless revenge, because they know that we sided with you." the prince said quietly. "No, Lawrence. We are committed now to winning this war, so I do not think it appropriate to cause problems for you British. You see, we can't afford to lose. And if we do help you win this war, then I will count on you to help us win the peace. Now that, my friend, will be a real challenge."

There was a shout from a lookout. Both Lawrence and the prince glanced over to a hill, and saw a smudge of black smoke in the pristine sky.

~

Baghdad, 1918

Gertrude sat down in shock. She looked over the desk to Percy Cox, whose face was white with fury. Only her demeanor as a lady prevented her from screaming out her anger in a string of invectives at the hapless man who thought he'd be delivering a simple and welcome message.

It was Sir Percy who eventually broke the leaden atmosphere in the room, when he said, "How dare you? How dare you connive and scheme and then come in here so smugly and try to convince Miss Bell and me of this obscenity."

A look of shock on the man's face replaced the self-satisfied smile and air of importance with which he'd entered the office. Humphrey McHugh was secretary to Sir Samuel Wordsworth, Plenipotentiary of the British government. While the prime minister had given Sir Samuel the job of traveling to the capitals of France, Italy, Russia, Egypt, and India on behalf of his government in order to inform those who were deemed sufficiently important of the conditions of the Sykes-Picot Agreement, it had been left to the lowly Mr. McHugh to travel to Arabia and inform the Arab Office in Baghdad of the terms under which Arabia would be sliced up after the war.

As secretary to a plenipotentiary, he had expected to be received in accordance with the standing of his master, which is why he was so shocked at the reception he was getting from Sir Percy and Miss Bell to the news of the Agreement.

"I beg your pardon," he said, his voice raised at the surprise of the vehemence."

"Silence, you ridiculous little man. You heard what Sir Percy said," Gertie hissed, having regained her tongue. "The idiots for whom you work, without consulting us as experts on the situation, have undone years of painstaking work, and have likely lost us the war."

"Are you aware of who I am?" asked McHugh. "Are you aware I am secretary to Sir Samuel—"

"I don't give a damn if you're secretary to the king himself. What you've just told us is devastating," shouted Sir Percy, banging his fist on his desk. "And you walk in here with a mellifluous smile all over your grovelling suburban face, expecting us to congratulate you, when you and those you represent have sold out British interests and will make us a laughingstock throughout the Arabic world. Miss Bell is absolutely correct. This obscene decision will likely cost us the war," he fumed.

Mr. McHugh took the glass of water on Sir Percy's desk and drank it. He began to perspire, and not from the heat of the day. "I'm not certain whether you properly understood. This agreement will assure Britain and France of—"

"It'll assure us of nothing," shouted Sir Percy, shaking his fist at the hapless bureaucrat. Gertrude, surprised, had never seen him in such anger. "Nothing except increasing our chances of the Arabs walking out on us, putting an end to the revolt, and resulting in us losing the Middle East. And if that doesn't happen, it'll assure us of losing any influence we might have had over this area, the loss of untold British soldiers who'll be shot by Arabs once this news gets out, and quite likely the loss of potential oil revenues, the passage to India, and God knows what else. This is a bloody disaster," Sir Percy said, his voice rising an octave.

"We've all been deceived by this. What's going to become of Mesopotamia? I've been working under the impression that this place would be annexed under the protection of the British government in India, and that ibn Sa'ud would be made king. I've virtually promised him that, with the full knowledge of the government and the cabinet. We were at a stand-off with our people in the Arab Bureau in Cairo who want to make Sharif Hussein king, and now you tell me that Baghdad will be under some minor local ruler, Mosul in the north will go to the French, and Great Britain will control Basrah. I demand an explanation. This is a disaster . . . a bloody disaster . . ." He was suddenly lost for words.

Recovering his composure, McHugh said, "Well, Sir Percy, you're the only one who thinks it's a disaster. Everybody else is very pleased with the way things will be in the future—"

"Be silent, you pompous nonentity," said Gertrude. McHugh stopped speaking. "You know nothing of the situation here. Sir Percy isn't the only one who understands what a disaster this Sykes-Picot thing will become. I think so too," said Gertrude, her voice beginning to break with emotion. "And in case you think your lords and masters in England know more than we do, be quiet and listen, because it's more than likely that Sir Percy's is the only opinion which matters. Who else thinks this is a good idea, Mr. McHugh? The entire British Cabinet? The French and the Russians? Has anybody thought to ask the Arabs what they think of it? We've spent years persuading the Arabs they'll be better off with us as friends and associates under our protection. Finally, they're beginning to come around to the idea. The Arab Revolt is just taking off, and now you and Mark Sykes dump this in our laps, without even bothering to ask the people on the ground. Thanks to you, my voice will have no credibility any longer with the Arab leadership. I'll be a laughingstock."

She stood, her eyes beginning to brim with tears, and shouted, "It's all too much. It's destroyed all my work over the past years. Really, it's just not fair." She ran out of the room.

~

He found her a half an hour later. She was sitting on a deckchair on the flat roof of the Baghdad headquarters.

Silently, he pulled another deckchair over to where she was sitting, and together they silently surveyed the sun setting over the western desert. Softly, she said, "You know Percy, I was last in Baghdad in 1914. I came here as an utter failure. Oh, to the outside world, I was a champion, a heroine, but in my own mind I was a dismal failure. I was totally spent from my journeys around Arabia and was looking forward to returning to England. But how to tell my father and mother and my friends that I'd failed to find any archaeological sites of any value, or that I'd failed totally in my proposed meeting with ibn Sa'ud, or that I'd been imprisoned and nearly died at the hands of ibn Rashid? And then I was called in by the foreign secretary himself to assist the Empire in her war with the Turks, and suddenly I had a way to redeem my own standing in my own eyes.

"But it's not just me, Percy. Look what we've achieved, my dear. Between us, we've helped turn the Arabs around and raised the revolt, we've almost beaten the Turks out of Arabia, and now we've entered Baghdad as conquerors and we're on the cusp of retaking Damascus. After that, the Turks will really have to pull up stumps and return home to Constantinople. And just when we're looking at the laurels of victory, the jaws of defeat suddenly open up and threaten to snap our legs off."

He nodded, and began to say something, but Gertrude was in a reflexive mood, and he sensed she just wanted to talk. "I love this city, Percy. Twelve hundred years ago, Harun al Rashid, the fifth Abbasid Caliph, along with scholars in his court, wrote of Scheherazade, and the way in which her husband the king had threatened to kill her after her wedding, yet she kept herself alive by amusing him for a thousand and one nights with her stories about Aladdin and Ali Baba and his forty thieves.

"Under the Abbasids this was the largest and richest city in the world with more than a million people of every religion and every nationality flocking here to learn and to teach and to grow rich. A thousand years ago, Percy, the bookshops and literary coffeehouses did a roaring trade at a time when almost no Englishman could read or write. The geniuses of ancient Greece were translated and mathematics and astronomy reached unimaginable heights. Were it not for the Arabs and the Jews in this very city, we in the West would know nothing of Homer and Socrates, of Plato and Aristotle."

She turned to him, her eyes again brimming with tears. "We could have been an honorable part of this, Percy. Another worthy chapter in its history. Yet all the while, all the time we've been honest and upright in our dealings, Mark bloody Sykes and this bloody damn Frenchman have been making fools of us. They've undone all our work, my dear. We can pack our bags and go home for all the good we're going to be able to do from now on."

She looked across at him. She held him in such high regard. What would he do now? Would he resign and end his distinguished career? Or would he be a true servant of the British Crown and soldier on, regardless of the stupidity of his political masters?

Percy remained silent for what seemed an eternity, and then took out a letter, which he handed to her. It was addressed to him as Senior Political Officer, the most important man in all of Mesopotamia, alongside of the Chief Military Commanding Officer.

She opened the envelope and read the letter. It was from the foreign secretary. It told Sir Percy that because of her outstanding and meritorious dispatches and the exemplary work she had done in identifying Arabs who could become loyal to the British cause, and because of her singular skills in uniting all the disparate Arab tribes into one fighting nation on behalf of Great Britain, Gertrude Bell was to be elevated to the rank of Oriental Secretary, chief intelligence expert and adviser on Arab affairs to the British Government, effective immediately.

"You're the most senior woman political official in the entire British Empire, my dear, the most important woman ever to work as a diplomat for the crown" said Sir Percy. "Isn't it unbelievably ironic, Gertie, that the ridiculous little man downstairs brought us this wonderful news glorifying your lifetime's achievements, along with the devastating information that all our work has been ruined. Well, I suppose that's life."

He reached over extending his hand, and formally congratulated her. "This is a very important day for you, Gertrude. To become the top woman British civil servant, the most senior lady in the whole of Great Britain in a political role, is a true reflection of your capabilities. This will be recorded in the annals of both the House of Commons and the Lords. And God knows you deserve it."

She smiled at him, and said softly, "Odd, Percy. All my life, I've been striving for recognition of my value to Great Britain, and fighting the entrenched male establishment, not because I'm a woman, but because of what I've achieved. But right at this very moment, I find it hard to recognise my own country."

~

Damascus, 1918

Lowell Thomas stood on the hilltop overlooking the ancient city of Damascus, staring through his binoculars at the minarets and cupolas, the palaces and the parks.

He sensed the diminutive Englishman beside him, smelling of atar of roses, his *galabiyah* flapping in the late evening breeze which blew in from the distant Mediterranean Sea.

"This is a bloody disaster, Lawrence. A bloody disaster." He lowered the binoculars and turned to face the man with whom he'd spent the best part of three months.

"Disaster? But we've taken Damascus. Look." Lawrence said.

"We've taken Damascus? No, sir, they've taken Damascus," he said pointing to the lines of the Australian Light Horse Division pouring through the gates.

"You told me you'd be there to greet Allenby. You told me the photograph of you standing on the steps of the palace with Allenby walking up to shake your hand would be worth a fortune. You said it would make history. Well, where's Allenby and where's my picture? All I can see is bloody Australians on horseback."

The two men looked at the scene in the distance. The Turkish Fourth Army had fled the previous evening in fear of the advance of Allenby and his troops. Lawrence and Faisal had rushed at breakneck speed to overtake them, but nobody counted on the inexhaustible and unrelenting Australians, and their seemingly tireless horses, desert warriors from the other side of the world, as much at home in the Simpson and Nullarbor deserts of their vast and dry continent, as they were in the Nefud and other deserts of the Middle East. Expecting a fight, they had rallied outside the gates for an assault, but when the gates were opened and they were welcomed inside the city, they formed up, and parade-marched as conquerors in Allenby's name.

"What if I was to get into a Rolls Royce, and drive in through the gates wearing my Arabic national costume? Surely that'd make a good picture, wouldn't it?"

"But the bloody Australians have already liberated the city."

"The bloody Australians, as you so ungallantly call them, have done more than liberate Damascus, Mr. Lowell. They've also liberated Beersheba, Jerusalem, Megiddo, and just about every other town and city between here and Egypt. Allenby says they're the greatest cavalry in the history of warfare. So don't undermine their achievements."

"It's not their achievements my readers back home want to know about, Colonel Lawrence. It's yours. I've made you into Lawrence of Arabia. You carry all the sand of the desert on your back. I cabled my bosses last week to say I'd be sending photographs over to them with you liberating Damascus. That's what you promised. Now I'm going to be a laughingstock."

"Why don't we say a few men slipped into the city last night, knowing the Turks had evacuated, and it was really me and my army who liberated the citizenry?"

"A few men? Are you crazy? There's four thousand horsemen riding through the gates right now."

Colonel Lawrence turned around, hearing footsteps approaching them.

"Highness," he said, welcoming Faisal.

Lowell stepped aside to allow the prince to stand between himself and the Englishman. Without acknowledging the two of them, Faisal looked at the city of Damascus with a beaming smile. "This, gentlemen, has been my greatest dream. Ever since we began our journey from Mecca to drive the Turks from our lands, it was always my goal to liberate Damascus. The capture of Deraa and Aqaba were great triumphs, but nothing shall compare to Damascus being in Arabic hands once more. And none of this could have been accomplished without the genius of Mr. Lawrence. You are a true leader of men, Colonel Lawrence. And now that you are our voice, Mr. Thomas, the world knows about the renaissance of the Arabic peoples. Once again, we will be united and a force to be reckoned with."

Both men remained respectfully silent.

"Tomorrow, I shall enter the gates and I shall claim the city for the Arabic peoples."

"And what if General Allenby claims it for the British?" asked Lowell Thomas.

"He will not do that."

"The Sykes-Picot agreement?" he said again.

Faisal shrugged his shoulders. "There are some things, Mr. Thomas, which are a political reality. We Arabs could not have defeated the Turks on our own. We have to reward our friends for their assistance."

"Reward, Your Majesty? You call it a reward when you give away your lands?"

Faisal sighed. "The issue at hand right now, Mr. Thomas, is getting into Damascus and being part of the liberation of the greatest Arab city in all the world."

"Greater than Mecca?" he asked.

Lawrence interrupted. "Mecca is the city of the triumph of the Prophet, Damascus is the history of the Arabic Peoples. It's their past, their present and their future."

Faisal nodded and said softly, "Yes, their present . . . but only the Prophet knows what will be the future."

Lawrence shuffled his feet in the sand of the dune overlooking the distant city. "Sir, there's something I've been asked to do by my lords and masters, which I was going to do when as we entered

Damascus, but it appears the Australians have pre-empted my little bit of theatricality. I was informed last night by dispatch from Cairo that Allenby is to offer you the crown."

The prince and Thomas looked at Lawrence in surprise. The British Colonel pointed to the distant city, and said, "Damascus is to be your seat, Highness. You are shortly to be informed by the King of England that you are to be ennobled as His Majesty, King Faisal the First of Syria. Allenby wrote and asked me to sound you out on the issue. He's asked me to see whether Your Majesty will accept the throne of the Kingdom of Syria. May I be the very first to congratulate you."

Instead of shaking his hand, Lawrence kneeled, and kissed Faisal's hand, to the astonishment of Thomas, who was too stunned to set up his camera and tripod, and record the scene for posterity.

As he stood, Lawrence said, "Your Royal Highness, it is my honor to present you with the news that you have been waiting for all these years. You will no longer be a prince, sir, but are to be a king in your own right."

Faisal could barely understand the enormity of what had just happened to him. He whispered, "I am overwhelmed, Colonel Lawrence." The new king looked at the ancient capital city of his new domain, and breathed in the fragrant air of Damascus, his crowning glory.

"This is ... it's ... I don't know what to say. I never thought I'd ever become king and ruler of a nation, but Damascus ... Syria ... it's ..."

He lapsed into an awkward silence, until Lawrence said, "There's another bit of good news as well, Your Majesty. "Remember that parcel of letters I received just this morning?"

The king nodded.

"Well," said Lawrence, "it appears you aren't the only one who has been recognised by King George's government in Great Britain. Our friend, Miss Gertrude Bell, has been made into a Commander of the British Empire. A CBE. That's quite something, isn't it, your Highness?"

ELEVEN

Baghdad, 1919

It was all over. The war to end all wars had finally come to an end, and silence descended on the sinking mud of Europe and the sinking sands of the Middle East. The blood of millions of men drained into the land and was soon washed away by the rain, or bleached by the sun. Gone forever were the voices from the maw of Hell itself, the deafening roar of cannon, the staccato rattle of machine gun, the howling frantic screams of the wounded and the whispered fearful prayers of the dying gasping their last breath.

Gone too were the frenzied commands of officers trying to cajole already dead men to make one last effort for king and country by climbing up and over the barbed wire trench to engage the enemy. And gone was the perfume of the battlefield, the languid drifting fog of gun smoke, cordite, and poisonous gasses, of sulfur and chlorine and mustard gas and the stench of rotting flesh.

From the moment of the declaration of the armistice, families began to breathe free again, knowing their surviving menfolk at home wouldn't be called upon to don a uniform in order to defend a long-dead cause and be transported to a battlefield whose name they couldn't pronounce for a reason they didn't understood. Wives and mothers and sisters who had dreaded every door-knock in case it presaged the arrival of the black-banded telegram began to hold their breath and pray silently that their loved ones would emerge out of the haze of war and return home to the warmth of the hearth and the love of their homes.

In the center of London, a patriotic crowd accreted to the railings of Buckingham Palace to await the arrival of the king and queen on the balcony overlooking the main quadrangle. Shy and diffident, unlike his portly father Edward who loved to disport himself in the public eye, George and his wife Mary and their many children walked onto the flag-shrouded balcony and waved to the hundreds of thousands who were standing there. It was the ultimate recognition of an end of the past, a semiotic broadcast to the nation of Great Britain that all was normal again.

But even though there was a mood of euphoria, it was muted by the stark reality which was beginning to dawn on the people of England, that a large part of the generation of young men who should have led Britain into the future, was now dead. There was an implied understanding in the crowd that thanks to the adventurous German Kaiser and the evil Hun and their bed-mates, the Turks, something within England had changed forever.

Even the king had changed. He had entered the war with the surname of Saxe-Coburg-Gotha, but the hatred of everything German had forced him to re-Christen himself as Windsor. And his ties to his German relations, or his Russian cousin the Tsar—to whom he'd refused sanctuary in 1917 after the Bolsheviks took power—were permanently at an end. England, for all its victory, was diminished by the war and isolated from the kings and queens of Europe. As King George sighed and turned to re-enter Buckingham Palace, he wondered whether life for the Royal family of Britain would ever be the same again.

The war had changed so much of Europe and the Middle East. As England and France struggled to come to terms with their lost generation and began to wonder how they would recover, so too did the Germanic and the Ottoman people, who felt less hope in their futures as pawns to the victorious powers. Their empires had been soundly thrashed and their leaders and populations waited in trepidation for their punishment.

Everyone, not only those whose menfolk would never return, was yet to fully understand the real cost of the war, for while despair at the loss of humanity was the reaction, hope had yet to become the word of the day. Hope and glory. Today, victorious generals were waxing the tips of their moustaches and preparing to climb over a mountain of corpses in order to receive yet another medal for valour or some honor for service from their monarchs. Diplomats were starting to take out maps with boundaries which no longer had any relevance and initiating the process of drawing red lines through decimated counties, between towns and across neighbourhoods. Bruised, battered, and diseased soldiers were crawling and crowding onto trains and boats and into lorries and buses to be returned home with a few coins in their pockets and the grateful thanks of some famous commander who had been thousands of miles from where the fighting occurred. Mothers and wives and sweethearts were waiting anxiously at docksides to retrieve their loved-ones from hospital ships or transports, praying the next convoy would return to them the whole man, and not a physical and emotional ruin, and neighbours were talking about their need to console neighbours whose empty homes would no longer resonate to the sound of men's voices.

While most attention in Europe was centred on victory parades and monarchs taking bows and salutes before their grateful peoples, the remnants of those who once commanded the Ottoman Empire in the Middle East painfully withdrew their disarrayed men and material and contracted to the rump which was left to them, a toehold in Europe and the Turkish remains on the continent of Asia. Today, Turkey was being called the sick man of Europe. It had abandoned its empire and left the Arabs to care for themselves as its government prepared to meet the fury of its own young officer class and the vengeance of its people.

But in Arabia, the rejoicing at the overthrow of the Ottoman overlords was becoming muted by a reality which was dawning in the minds of peasant and emir alike—what would happen now?

In early November, 1918, the British and French had published a declaration which every Arabic radio station, every newspaper, and every poster on a village wall detailed prominently. It proclaimed the final liberation of the populations living under the Turkish yoke, and that now the Turkish enemy had been beaten, national governments would be established, chosen by the people themselves. The declaration made promises to the people of Arabia that England and France would assist them in creating new governments and would grant them recognition as soon as they were established. Even President Woodrow Wilson of America promised the right of self-determination. When he had published the fourteen-point plan he proposed to Congress ten months earlier it had hardly made news in Arabia, but now that the war was at an end it was trumpeted as a vision of a future world in which nations could determine their own fates for their own people and would no longer be subject to the dictates of some distant power.

But now that the armistice had been declared, now that the guns were silent, people began to wonder what their nations would look like in the future. Who would rule them, Arab, English, French, Italian, or Russian? What sort of freedom had they won? What laws would they have to obey? Would they be Syrians or Mesopotamians, would they call themselves Iraqi's, after the 7th Century settlement in the area, or would they still be members of ancient tribes, free to wander the traditional routes of their lands, or live in peace and security in their age-old capitals?

These were the questions which were vexing Gertrude Bell's mind as she read the early Arab responses to the Anglo-French Declaration of self-determination from Cairo, Damascus, Amman, Jerusalem, Aleppo, and Baghdad.

"It's all too sudden, too soon," she said to her friend, General George MacMunn, over dinner at his Baghdad home. The others around the table listened carefully to what she was saying. Gertrude was the guest of honor and people had gathered to hear her opinion. If anybody could see the way through the diplomatic fog left after the end of the fighting, it was Gertrude.

"But something has to be delivered to the Arab. After all, he fought with us."

"For God's sake, George, the whole world's just suffered ten million fighting men killed, about five million civilians dead, and twenty million wounded. Entire empires are no more, kings and queens and emperors and tsars have been blown off the face of the Earth, and the people of whole nations are floundering in uncertainty. We can't rush into some form of utopian government and have untested administrations which devolve into anarchy in a matter of months. What needs to be done now isn't self-determination, but the fatherly oversight of a slow transition into joint-rule, and when the instruments of government are firmly established, when women are liberated and a thousand tribes blended into one nation, then, and only then can the locals take over. We can't rush these people into democracy," she said firmly. "A government built on the philosophy of democracy can't exist in a vacuum. It has to have a written constitution delivering a free judiciary administering proscribed laws and regulations, an untrammelled and fiercely independent media which can criticize the government without the editor being beheaded, the Doctrine of the Separation of Powers, and most important of all, a separation between Mosque and State. Just telling these people they can vote for whomsoever they want will lead to all sorts of chaos.

"Britain and France have the responsibility to ensure this area doesn't descend into tribal anarchy. We've lost so many of our good men in the desert we deserve by right to remain here, to share in the benefits of the oil and food and wealth that this place is capable of producing."

She remained quiet for a moment. George MacMunn wondered whether to intervene, but decided not to as it was well known that interrupting Gertrude Bell when she was in reflective or philosophical mode was dangerous.

As though he were merely a wall and she was using him to draw her ideas upon, she said, "You know, at the beginning of this war, in fact since I was a young girl, I've had the idea of melding all the little petty Arab tribes into one great nation, with us as the partner in the region. And I thought this war might provide the catalyst. But I think time and events might have gone beyond me. I was hoping a certain man would rise up and lead the Arabs into nationhood, but it seems fame and fortune has seduced him away from the path I hoped he'd follow."

She sipped her glass of malmsey and lit another cigarette. She was now smoking three packets a day, the result of a dreadful wartime diet and the tensions of conflict. The women at the table were used to Gertrude's idiosyncrasies, and long ago had accepted her habit of smoking, drinking and talking at the same time.

"Surely these decisions are made at a level far higher than ours," the general said. "How often have you and I discussed what has to be done in Arabia, only to find that Mr. Balfour or Sir Mark Sykes or that dreadful little Frenchman Picot have failed to take into account any advice we might have given them, and have gone off and done things which are certain to lead to dreadful results?"

Gertrude snorted. "I'm well aware of the mess politicians are capable of making when they're only interested in their own ends. But this damnable declaration to create democracy has thrown the whole of Arabia into a tizz. You can't suddenly tell a people who have been oppressed for the best part of a millennium that their own future as a nation is suddenly in their hands, and then almost casually ask them what they'd like to do with it. It'll lead to internecine bloodshed. It's what I predicted decades ago. Leave the Arabs in charge of their own destiny, and all hell is going to break loose. Here in Mesopotamia alone there are at least a dozen contenders who'll want to lead whatever's left of the nation, and you know as well as I do, George, how many conflicting undercurrents there are in the rest of Arabic society.

"Not a hundred miles from where we're sitting, you have the seeds of a future disaster. We've got educated Sunni in the towns and illiterate Shi'ite in the countryside to contend with. We've got Christians in Mosul who are concerned about their freedom to worship under an Arab regime, we have nomadic tribes who covet the lands and rights of other nomads, and don't forget there's a huge Jewish community in Baghdad which is terrified of Arabic rule and the very real prospect of restrictions on synagogues and their right to worship. In fact, they're so scared of an Arab ruling them they've all petitioned for British citizenship. That'll put the cat among the pigeons in the War Office."

MacMunn began to interrupt, but Gertrude was in full flight, and wouldn't yield to anyone. She barely drew breath, her friends around the table noticed that since the end of the war, she'd become, somehow, more concerned, more manic in her desire to tie up loose ends.

"And as if all that's not problem enough," she continued, "you've got those Arabs who want a partnership with the British and those who want to side with the French, you've got the same promises made by Britain to the Arabs and the French. Allenby told Colonel Lawrence to make promises about territory when he was leading the Arab revolt, and those will soon come home to roost. An independent Arabic constitutional government has been established in Syria under the kingship of one of Abdullah's sons, Faisal, which will really irritate the French and which puts the whole Sykes-Picot Agreement back in the melting pot . . . I tell you, George, it's a bloody disaster, and the mess will soon have to be sorted out, or we'll have another war on our hands."

General MacMunn was concerned her conversation would worry the other ladies at the table, and suggested they retire to the withdrawing room while the men, other army officers and members of the Baghdad British diplomatic staff, smoked their cigars and drank their ports and whiskeys. Gertrude waited until the women had withdrawn, before continuing, "I'm sorry, George, I should have had more sensitivity towards the ladies. I keep forgetting they're wives and daughters, and not members of the political office."

St. John Philby, sitting at the end of the table, quipped, "I was wondering whether you'd stay with the men, or leave with the ladies."

Gertrude smiled. "Like Queen Elizabeth when she ascended the throne in 1558," said Gertrude, "I have the body of a woman, but the heart and mind of a man."

George MacMunn asked her to continue. He'd invited the army and political officers and their wives to the dinner party because he wanted everybody to be singing from the same hymn sheet, as he put it, now that the damn war was over. Gertrude had been privy to much correspondence and many dispatches from

Whitehall, and so was able to fill in details about the situation the British would be facing now that the hostilities were over.

She continued, "As you know, I recently had a holiday in Persia, and I regret to say we have problems there which could very well spill over into Mesopotamia. The Persian government almost decided to fight on the side of the Germans at one stage, but fortunately they decided not to. But now we've got Bolsheviks from Russia all over the border between Persia and Mesopotamia, and we've got disaffected Turks making trouble for us up there, and that imperils our route to India. And the oilfields are also far from safe. I tell you, it's a bloody mess, and no mistake. That's why poor Percy Cox was sent to Persia but he's needed here more urgently than he's needed there. This is the place where we need a shrewd and sophisticated mind like Percy's."

An orderly knocked on the door and asked for permission to wheel in another trolley full of liquors and spirits. The room fell into silence as he placed the carafes and decanters on the table. When he left, Gertrude continued, "All of these issues could have been resolved if Percy hadn't been told to go sort out Persia. He has to be recalled to Mesopotamia, and he has to be named British High Commissioner, because everyone admires and respects him, and he needs to be given five years to advise an Arab government here on transition. But this bloody declaration about self-determination has thrown a large and unhelpful spanner into the works. It's all too bad, really. There has to be time for things to settle down before we can even contemplate handing over rule to the Arabs. If we pull out now, they'll be at each other's throats, and they'll be massacres on a scale which will make the war we've just fought look like a picnic."

General MacMunn nodded slowly, finished his whisky, and said, "I'm afraid we're beneficiaries of the Chinese curse. We're living in interesting times."

~

The peace was more frantic for Gertrude than the war. During the conflict with the Ottoman Turks, she had been hellishly busy, working out logistics, placements, treaties, and advice to the War

Office, working eighteen hours and more every day while eating bad wartime food and grabbing whatever she could from the Mess canteen. She'd spent much of her time cajoling tribal leaders and emirs into siding with the British, reassuring them that once the war was over, she would ensure a leader arose whom they would follow and revive the days of the Caliphate.

And now the peace was here, she was given increasing responsibility to deal with the manifold problems besetting the land which once was Mesopotamia, but which more and more people, especially natives, were now beginning to call The Iraq, though why the land between the rivers should be named after an obscure 7th century settlement of little or no consequence was beyond her. Maybe it was all about wiping the slate clean, getting rid of the Greek name and the European influence, and making everything Arabic, especially the name of the country.

Gertrude spent whole days with vast numbers of women who came to see her to seek advice . . . women who were Muslim, Jewish or Christian. Now that the war was over and the Ottoman overlords had retreated back to Constantinople, there was a surge of optimism that the oppressive hand of men, of mullahs and ayatollahs and those who policed shariah law so vehemently, might be loosened. Women who were shrouded in niqabs so their faces could only be seen by their husbands suddenly appeared in the streets wearing a simple hijab. Women who walked two steps behind their husband and sons were suddenly demanding the right to their own piece of roadway. And strangest of all were the women who left their houses with their husband's permission, not to do the shopping, but to walk around in full view of everybody and breathe in the heady air of freedom.

All the women who came to see her wanted to be freed from the constraints of their upbringing and tradition, and Gertrude arranged with a visiting pedagogical expert sent out by the government from England to create an entire syllabus for the education of Iraqi girls. The more women with whom she spoke, the more she was coming to the conclusion that Arabia could only become a single and united nation if women were included in its running. Not, perhaps, in a governmental or bureaucratic function, but freed from their households and the domination of their male relatives to enter the workforce, and labor side by side with men. Great Britain had adjusted rapidly to women working in factories, driving ambulances and trains and doing the jobs which their menfolk fighting on the battlefronts had once done. Was it too much to hope that Arabic men would cast off the sexual chauvinism which had denied half the Arab population their rights, and invest in their women, the greatest assets of their nations? Unfortunately, knowing the thousands of Arabs she'd dealt with over the years, she seriously doubted Arabia was ready for the sort of cultural transition and sexual revolution which was taking place in the West. But if the dream of a united Arab nation was slipping away from her because of the *realpolitik* of bureaucrats and politicians in London and Paris, then perhaps part of her lifelong goal could still be realized—to create an Arabia in which women held equal status to men.

Increasingly her work was to create the borders for the new nation over which the British, for the time being, had taken control. The Foreign Office had just announced a new state, but hadn't fixed the borders. She had been asked by Whitehall to study the maps of Persia, Turkey, Syria, Kuwait, and Mesopotamia and advise them on where the new nation should be located.

She found herself continually shaking her head. What she'd been asked to define would be a nightmare to control, no matter who was ultimately put in charge. Because of the fertility of the land between the rivers and other factors which were written as coded and veiled hints—as though she didn't know everything about the country—the British Foreign Office wanted the new nation to include Mosul in the north, Baghdad in the middle, and Basrah in the south. But Mosul was Kurdish, and the Kurds hated the Sunni Arabs with a vengeance. Not only that, but because Mosul was the ancient Nineveh, the city of Jonah, it was also sacred to the Jews, and there was a significant Jewish community,

269

a synagogue, and much more Hebraic culture. Baghdad and the center of the new land was Sunni, and the Sunni Muslims hated the southern Shi'ites so much they had engaged on massacring them over the ages, and Basrah was the center of the Shi'ite Muslims and the Marsh Arabs in the Shatt al Arab waterway at the confluence of the Tigris and the Euphrates, and they would slit a Sunni's throat rather than talk to him.

To put the three utterly disparate portions of Mesopotamia together within the one border was madness. It would create an uncontrollable entity. But as she sat for long hours going through every possible permutation and examining the reality of the situation, it quickly dawned on Gertrude that it was worse than her British masters could possibly have imagined. Mesopotamia had always been a fabulously rich country and a major grain and fruit producer. But that was on top of the surface. That was where the water flowed, the wind blew, and the sun shone. But deep in the bowels of the Earth, like a stream of rich black blood which seemed to power the muscles of the nation, was what appeared to be a vast and limitless reserve of oil. And that, once it was proven, would create tectonic divisions between tribes and peoples and religions. It was a nightmare, and only a Prophet like Moses or Mohammed had the capacity to put such a disparate collection of tribes together and make them into a nation.

Yet those were her orders. She knew every inch of the lands she was supposed to cobble together, and more than the lands, she knew the people, which was why she'd been asked to undertake the task.

Engrossed in her work, surrounded by red and blue pens and marking lines on maps, she was interrupted by General MacMunn, who knocked tentatively on her office door, and coughed. Without looking up to see who was there, Gertrude smiled, and said, "Come in George."

She knew it was him, because the rest of her colleagues and superiors weren't so polite as to knock, they barged in regardless of what she was doing, and demanded answers to their questions.

"Have you got a moment, m'dear?" he asked tentatively.

"I have no moments whatsoever to spare, George. I'm playing God, inventing a country which it's impossible to invent. But for you, George, I'll play God yet again and I'll invent some time. What can I do for you?"

Diffidently, he said, "You're a writer. You've written books and things. Published them with respectable publishers, had them on sale in bookshops and all that stuff."

She put down her pens, and poured him a whisky. "And . . . ?"

"And, well, look, this is a bit difficult, but . . ."

She knew where the conversation was going, and took pity on him. "Allenby is writing his memoirs. Haig is too, and you think you should write an account of your wartime experiences."

"Good God, how did you know?" he asked, accepting the whisky and grinning sheepishly.

"Because I'm playing God, and I'm omniscient. Because, George dearest, there is nothing in this world I don't know. And because your wife whispered into my ear yesterday over lunch, 'try to persuade him not to write his memoirs.'"

"Madeleine said that to you?"

Gertrude nodded. "It's not that she doesn't want you to be recognised for your wonderful achievements in Palestine and here in Mesopotamia. It's just that she's seen virtually nothing of you for the past four years, and she wants you to herself. She's terrified you'll lock yourself away in a closet scribbling away at your exploits and she'll spend another four years alone."

MacMunn, a portly man with a florid face and a bushy moustache, asked simply, "And do you agree with her?"

Gertrude thought for a moment before responding. "Partly. But I don't see why you can't write your thoughts down when you come home from a picnic in the Home Counties, or a day at the races. I suppose I'm lucky, because writing comes naturally to me. I write voluminous reports on the situation here which I send to Whitehall, I write a daily diary for myself, I write daily to my mother and father and friends in England. For me to write a memoir wouldn't be such a monumental task as it might be for some general who only knows how to sign orders and requisition slips."

"Why don't you write your memoirs?" he asked. "After all, my dear, you've done more than just about anybody in this entire theater to hasten the end of the war. Look at the people you've met, the deals you've struck, the places you've seen which no other white person has been privileged to gaze upon."

"I wouldn't dream of it," she said firmly. "That dreadful Mr. Lowell Thomas, the American reporter, tried to get me to be the subject of an article he wanted to write for Life magazine. I said no flatly. I want my privacy and I don't want people to know what I'm doing, or with whom I'm doing it."

"So he gave all the publicity to that damn Lawrence," snorted MacMunn.

"Colonel Lawrence deserved it," she said. "Look what he achieved. He rallied the Arabs into a wonderful fighting force, he took Aqaba and got to Damascus and he prevented the Turks from being supplied so they became much less effective."

"Tosh!" hissed MacMunn. "Everybody here knows it was you who supplied him with all the intelligence and information he needed to do his job. All those conversations you had with the Arab leaders and sheiks and emirs, persuading and enticing them to get their men to join with Lawrence's army. Lawrence only acted as a figurehead and blew up a few trains. If it hadn't been for you and your relationship with the Arabs, there wouldn't have been a revolt. You were the brains, he was just the brawn."

"Not that I agree with you, but if it were the case, then it's best left unsaid. Let Lawrence bask in the limelight. Let him become a celebrity. I've never sought fame and glory."

"But if anybody deserves fame and glory, it's you. It's incumbent on you to let the world know what really happened. I think anybody instrumental in the cause of the damnable war, on any front, deserves to put his or her point of view. That's why I want to write my memoirs. All I want is to publish a little book

272

which sets the record straight about the war we British fought in Palestine and here, and to explain my role in it. Is that too much to ask?"

"For you, no. For me, yes. I'm a very private person, George, and I want to stay that way."

He shook his head and stood to leave. "Look, I'll tell you what I'll do," she said. "I'll contact my publisher in England, and tell him I've managed to persuade one of the great war heroes, General MacMunn, to write his account of the war in the Middle East. If he writes to you and commissions the manuscript, maybe that'll change Madeleine's mind."

He sat down again with a thump. "Good God, are you willing to do that?"

"Of course, my dear, as soon as I get this damnable Act of God behind me, and I've invented a country which almost certainly shouldn't be invented."

MacMunn looked at the map. "Still having problems with the borders?"

"Not so much problems, because I know virtually every dry creek bed and mountain pass. No, it's trying to complete a jigsaw puzzle with pieces which aren't made to fit together. Of course I can draw lines around this or that and call whatever is inside Iraq, but when the people I've encircled begin to understand what they've got themselves into, there'll be hell to pay. I tell you, George, it'll take a ruler with the skill of Solomon to run this country."

"And look what happened to Solomon's Israel after he died. The country split in two and the northern half was captured by the Mesopotamians. Chaos," mused MacMunn.

Gertrude nodded. "Come on," she said, putting down her pens with determination. "Let go for a drink."

~

Of the many different people who came in to see Gertrude while she was attempting to determine the borders of the new Iraq, the most fascinating was one she called Haji Naji, both because the name amused her, and because Emir Ibrahim Abd Binalb bin Naji had been on the Hajj to Mecca and was entitled to style himself as a man who had completed the injunction to all Muslims.

One of the reasons she so liked the occasional visit from Haji Naji was because he grew the most sumptuous oranges and limes, and always gave her a case whenever he visited her. Now that the war was over, his visits were more frequent.

Haji Naji was an old man, one who was feared by his enemies, but beloved by his clan. He had twenty-seven children, twelve of them boys and men whom he loved and respected, the remaining fifteen girls and women whom he regretted having as being the unworthy offspring of a great leader.

Haji Naji often visited Gertrude in her office in the Residency with its vaulted ceilings and oaken floors, cool in the summer and often cold in the winter. When he did, she always made time to see him, regardless of the other work or appointments she might have in her diary. For more than anybody in Mesopotamia, Haji Naji was the source of all knowledge, a man of strong opinions and elegant thinking.

She was already deeply embedded in plotting the future borders close to Syria in the west, when he had walked into her office unannounced, and said, "Khatun of the City, thy face is fair and thy back is straight, and thou art an honorable woman who should have been born a man."

She looked up, and beamed a smile as the old man, stick in his hand, walked slowly and painfully over to the chair. "And thou, Haji of revered standing, beloved of God and the apple of thy family, art a man of infinite wisdom whose mind is as bottomless as the ancient seas. Sit, master, and share thy thoughts with this unworthy woman."

Gertrude grinned mischievously, and came round the desk to kiss his hand. She loved the traditional and ancient greetings which Haji Naji insisted upon as a prelude to re-entering the twentieth century.

She kissed his other hand, a sign of great respect, and poured him a glass of barley water, which he drank greedily.

"Haji Naji, are you here to pass the time of day, or is there a purpose to your visit?"

"Why would any visit to the revered Khatun be merely to pass the time of day?"

She loved being called by her nickname, Khatun, which was Arabic flattery for a gentlewoman or a lady of fine quality. "Then what is the purpose for which you grace my offices, Haji Naji?" she asked.

"Because, Khatun, you have the very finest barley water in the whole of Baghdad. That, alone, is reason enough to visit you," he said.

She knew it would take at least another fifteen minutes of flattery and evasion before he came to the purpose of his visit. Eventually, after spending ten minutes vacillating, searching for a way in, she managed to find the key question to ask him which opened up the conversation to the purpose of his visit.

"And what does Haji Naji hear from other kingdoms of the Arabs."

He smiled, and nodded thoughtfully. "The news, Khatun, is disturbing. You are aware, of course, of the great resentment which was caused by Sharif Hussein calling himself King of the Hejaz. He sets himself up as caliph. His claim to be a direct descendent of the Prophet is also something with displeases many. But while the war was being fought, we Arabs paid little attention to the man's aggrandizement. Now that the war is over, however, there are eyes which are looking towards the west and there are lips saying that a great wrong must be righted."

Knowing she should restrain herself and not interrupt, she felt impelled to say, "But Haji Naji, the Sharif's sons, Ali, Abdullah, Faisal, and Zeid were among the bravest of all Arab warriors in fighting against the Turkish overlords."

"As were many sons of many fathers, Khatun. But this isn't the issue. We Arabs acknowledge the Hashemite dynasty as one of the oldest Muslim families. We also acknowledge their line was founded by Hashim, he of the Name, the grandfather of the Prophet Muhammad, peace and blessings be upon him. But for Hussein of the Hashemites to call himself king of the Holy Cities, and to say he leads the Muslim community by also elevating himself to be the caliph is too much for some people, who also see themselves as leaders now that the war with the Turks is over."

Her heart beat faster. This was major intelligence she was being given, subject matter which could influence developments in the Middle East. But because of the convolutions of the Arab mind, she had to unpeel the meaning carefully.

"Tell me, Haji Naji, the eyes of which you speak . . . from which direction do they look . . . towards the dawning sun, or towards the setting sun?"

"As the sun rises, Khatun, the eyes which seek the future look towards the shadows of morning, and in the evening as the sun is setting and the shadows lengthening, Khatun, these eyes cannot look towards the object of their ambition for fear of being blinded by Allah's majesty."

Gertrude nodded. So ibn Sa'ud in the east of Arabia was casting his eyes westwards ready to break out from his base in Riyadh towards Mecca and Medina in the Kingdom of the Hejaz with the intention of conquering it. She knew of his ambitions. He'd told her himself. But Haji Naji's visit must have been impelled by ibn Sa'ud's desire to bring forward his offensive.

"And tell me, mighty warrior, for how long will these eyes be looking from the east before they can end the day bathing in the waters of the gulf, or worshipping in the Great Mosque of Mecca?"

The old man shrugged, and said softly, "Insh'allah."

Gertrude poured him another barley water, and skirted around the subject for a few more minutes. It was possible he knew when ibn Sa'ud would launch his assault, but it was just as possible he knew no more than he'd told her. The Byzantine ways of extracting information from Arabs always fascinated her, but she had to be incredibly cautious not to overplay her relationship or she'd damage her standing in his eyes as an honorary man, and then she'd get nothing more out of him. So she decided to approach the subject from another tack.

"Tell me, great leader, do you profess the beliefs of the great Muhammad ibn Abd al—Wahhab?" she asked innocuously.

Contemptuously, he said, "Of course not, Khatun. Do I look as though I am a Wahhabist like the Sa'ud's? Do you think one as me would practice the beliefs of the Muwahhidun?"

"What does such a believer look like?" she asked, knowing the answer, but seeking to engage him in a subject which she knew would irritate him and perhaps force him to lower his defenses.

"Such a believer looks like he lived in the desert over a thousand years ago. Such a believer wouldn't know of the benefits of motorcars and airplanes and tanks and rifles. Such a believer wouldn't know of the power of the British Empire and the American steel and iron industries, the railroads and telephones. Such a believer, Khatun, would wish to live in mud huts and turn his head backwards in time, rather than forwards towards the future."

"Could you explain to this humble woman why the Wahhabists look to the time of the Great Prophet and not to the promise of the future?" she asked.

"You, Khatun, and outsiders, call them Wahhabists. They call themselves Muwahhidun, or those who strive for unity with the Prophet and His times. They look backwards, woman, because they despise the present and the ways of those of us who have advanced beyond the Caliphate. They see worship of Allah only by the worship of the time of Muhammad, and believe modern life holds only godlessness. They want to halt the future of the Arab people, and take us back to the time when we were safe in the desert. They would have all men wearing long beards and all women covered from head to toe. They would have no smoking or enjoyment. Our Mosques would be built as four walls, and we would not be allowed to have minarets, and we would be forced to pray every minute of every hour of every day. I tell you, Khatun, some may wish to live like this, but for me and those who follow me, it will never be thus. I look towards England and America for the future of Arabia. To be a Muslim means more than praying towards Mecca, it means fulfilling God's promise, and not just promising God."

She smiled. "And ibn Sa'ud? If he took over the Holy Cities of Mecca and Medina, he would try to introduce the beliefs of Wahhabism to all of Arabia?"

"Without a doubt. And beyond Arabia to all lands where Islam is the belief of the people—to India and the Far East and elsewhere. Ibn Sa'ud has made a pact with them. For the past seven years, he has established agricultural settlements around oases in order to re-settle those lands which once were his, and which he has taken over by conquest. Once he has order and security in his domain, he will continue his expansion. Then he will ride to the borders of the Hejaz, and wage war against Sharif Hussein. And if he wins, the whole of Arabia will be Sa'ud's. From there, he will expand his kingdom, and then God help us all."

She could now ask a direct question. "When?"

"When God wills it! But we are only talking of a handful of years. Now that the war is over, he is talking about moving his army to assault those of the Hejaz. It is time, Khatun, for England to throw its arms around Sharif Hussein and his sons, and to give them peace and security. Faisal did much for the British, and he has been rewarded with a kingdom in Damascus. But Sharif Hussein gave his consent for the Arabs to support the British and now it is time for the British to support him in his hour of need. Tell that to your prime minister."

Tired, the old man stood, and again she kissed his hand. "Peace and blessings be upon you and your family, Haji Naji," she said softly.

He smiled as he looked at her. "What a waste of a life, Khatun. If only you had been born a man, you could have risen to greatness."

TWELVE

Paris 1919

It was ever meant to be thus!

This was the life to which she'd been born, and after years of living in tents and second rate government accommodations in cities with almost no modern amenities, this was the life to which she had now returned. A life of extraordinary luxury after years of making-do, a life of elegance after decades of traveling on top of camels and being deprived of those little extravagances which English men and women took for granted every day.

Her life of denial and rigour now became one in which the men wore silk toppers and white ties and tails as though they were a second skin, and their women simply blended into the environment in organza swathes of indecently colored fabrics mimicking the hues of parrots flying in the canopy of some South American jungle. It became a life in which the convolutions and guarded meanings, codes and double-entendres of speaking to an Arab tribal leader, became the much more straightforward language of diplomacy, where nothing was directly stated, but everything covert was understood.

Even the very perfumed air of the Élysée Palace seemed to be a participant in the Peace Conference—at once thick with conspiracy and double-dealings, yet erotically fragrant with the hair washes and pomades and colognes in which the most important men in the world presented themselves as they emerged from their early-morning clusters and confabulations and caucuses.

But it wasn't only men who were meeting to carve up the world! One woman stood above the crowd, tall and proud, to be numbered amongst their ranks! A British woman, an expert, an enigma, a cause for comment and speculation, here to advise Lloyd George and Winston Churchill about Mesopotamia and the confluence of British and Arab interests. Only one woman of importance as a participant, along with the hundreds of men who had assembled at the invitation of the diminutive premier of France, Tiger Clemenceau, to—what was the phrase he had used?—'decide upon the disposition of what remains of the world now that the snakes have been sent slithering back to their pits and the whipped dogs are cowering in fear of their punishment.'

There were many things to discuss in a freezing cold and snowy Paris in the early months after the end of the war. One thing upon which Clemenceau had demanded was that each of the five treaties which would eventually emerge from the conference, being held to deal with the defeated powers, had to carry the name of a Parisian suburb, so that posterity would remember for all time the suffering of the French people. This had brought sneers from the British and the Americans, and a loud aside from David Lloyd George for the entire table to hear, when he whispered to his principle advisor in a thick Welsh accent, "odd that, because I don't remember France really being involved in this war. I thought it was British boys who had suffered most, and British blood which was watering French soil."

Nonetheless, in order not to alienate the irascible French premier, the allies had agreed the treaties would be designated with French names . . . Versailles for the treaty concerning Germany, St. Germain for Austria, Trianon for Hungary, Neuilly-sur-Seine for Bulgaria, and Sèvres for Turkey.

Gertrude glanced around the room. It was still early in the day, yet the atmosphere was already charged with intent as foreign secretaries, counsellors and advisors and walked into and out of the antechamber and the conference room, carrying their portmanteaux under their arms, and in their hands holding cups of coffee or glasses of aperitif, talking and huddling and discussing the items which their political masters were due to raise when the rulers of the world recommenced their deliberations. Although sometimes abrasive, the atmosphere was one of victors dividing up the spoils of conquest, and everybody seemed to wear a perpetual smile.

It was only her second time in the precincts of the conference hall of the palace. She had been requested to attend the conference by Percy Cox and the redoubtable A.T. Wilson, Percy's one-time deputy with whom she had had an abrasive relationship, yet who recognised her unique qualifications for assisting Great Britain in Paris, even though she was a woman.

Since Percy had left Mesopotamia for Persia and Wilson had taken over in his stead, Gertrude had supported and respected him, but increasingly, her support had not been reciprocated, and her respect had not been returned. At times, he had been more than off-hand and curt . . . in staff meetings he had often been deliberately rude. She hoped their time together in Paris could establish a better working relationship. But what concerned her was that he was pushing Britain's interests at all costs, regardless of the consequences for the Arabs and Gertrude knew this would lead to disaster. His insensitivity also encompassed a conversation she and he had held some time ago, concerning the need for Arabic unification.

"Don't be ridiculous, women," he'd snapped long before they'd left for Paris. "Divided we'll rule them—allow them to form a union and Britain will be squeezed out."

She'd begun to explain why he was wrong, but he'd refused to listen and had walked out of her office without the courtesy of a goodbye.

During the weeks she had been in Paris, Gertrude had visited many people from all over the world in their hotels to lobby them over the future of the Middle East. She had dined with them at Fouquet's and Le Pré Catalan and Le Trianon, she had walked with them through the parks and along the banks of the Seine, and she had shopped with their wives and attended theater parties with delegates from America, Japan, Italy, Greece, and Australia. The Australian delegation—more British than the British—were particularly excited to be present and participating because this was the country's first time as an independent nation representing its own interests in an international forum. And the delegation felt that after their fledgling nation's army had fought with such extraordinary distinction in the Middle East, as well as its unconscionable losses at Gallipoli, they had merited a seat at the table and the respect of the gathering. By directly negotiating on behalf of their young government, the Australian delegates were relishing the legitimacy their presence would give them in the eyes of the rest of the world.

Most of the deliberations of the conference concerned the disposition of Europe after the war. The fate of the former territories of Germany and Austria-Hungary were up for grabs, and because of the numbing losses of young men's lives on the battlefields of the Somme and the Marne and Ypres, numbers which Gertrude was incapable of absorbing, the dismemberment of the German and Austro-Hungarian territories of the belligerents took precedence over all other theaters of war.

Mesopotamia, Persia, and the former Ottoman Turkish lands were barely discussed in the early weeks of the conference, but were always in the background. Indeed, the word *oil* seemed to resonate constantly from wall to wall, salon to salon, like some dark mantra which held the secret of eternal life.

Britain had struggled in the latter part of the war because her battleships were oil-powered, and she had no natural oil of her own, France wanted to maintain its territorial hold in the Middle East because of its own need for oil, as did Italy and Russia. Only America and Persia were self-sufficient in oil and, as though to prove its potential for the future, John D. Rockefeller, the founder of the Standard Oil Company in America, had become, almost overnight, the world's richest man.

But in the question of oil lay the source of the intractable problems facing Gertrude, for Britain wanted mastery of the entire area, Great Britain wanted both Persia's oil and also to remain firmly in place in Arabia because it held out similar promises of huge reserves. Yet British officials had made promises to King Faisal and King Abdullah and ibn Sa'ud and others about independence for their lands after the war, and Britain had made diametrically opposite promises to the French, to the Russians, and to other allies in return for their co-operation in the war effort. The Arab Office in Cairo had made promises to the sheiks and emirs about collaborating with them in the best way to gain their independence after the war. Colonel Lawrence had given assurances in the British government's name that Arabia would be sovereign in return for its Arab revolt against the Turks. Britain's Indian government clearly stated its intention to continue ruling the area and expanding its influence out of the borders of the sub-continent as far as the banks of the Suez Canal. Italy had expectations, as did France and Russia.

The environment Gertrude entered was a seething mass of distortions, contradictions, lies, evasions, prejudices, denials, and demands that promises be upheld. It was a poisonous place, and because she was the British expert, she was expected to clean up the mess which had been made without her knowledge or approval by British politicians, diplomats, civil servants, and military men.

Sitting in the chandeliered hall of the Élysée Palace, looking at the men whose faces she knew from the pages of *The Times* or the *Tatler*, Gertrude felt as though this was where capricious destiny had determined she would be. The idea of convincing the world's leaders of the necessity and value of uniting all Arab tribes and peoples into one nation with a single voice was still her goal, even if the political realities of the place would cause her insuperable difficulties. And to make matters even more complicated, she'd have to use all her subtlety, all the guile which she'd learned in observing how Arabs negotiated, to ensure that she wasn't marginalized because she was a woman.

Her thoughts were interrupted by the stentorian voice of Winston Churchill, who always sounded to Gertrude as though he was inebriated.

"Ah! The redoubtable Gertrude Bell, peerless I see, as the only woman here. How very charming you look this morning, my dear."

"Good morning, Winston," she replied quickly, "I was lost in my daily musings."

"I'm glad somebody here is a-musing," he said conspiratorially. "I've heard nothing but cant and humbug since I've got here. But it's not just humbug, Gertie, it's also Machiavellian. Very Byzantine. In your dealings, m'dear, don't underestimate the danger of the cantankerous cauldrons of malevolence which these witches of Endor have been stirring. I've just been speaking to Smuts and the South African delegation, and those dunderheads want to forgive Germany and offer the hand of reconciliation."

Gertrude stood and towered above him. "But—"

"Precisely, my dear. When are the guilty to receive the full measure of their punishment, I ask you? The good Lord might have said that vengeance shall be His, but whilst-so-ever I draw breath on His Earth, I shall make those Hun scoundrels suffer miserably for the devastation they've wreaked upon the entire civilized world."

"Winston," she said, "The South Africans are the very least of my problem at the moment. I'm glad we've met, because I was going to seek an appointment with you this afternoon, if you had any time. Frankly my dear, I'm in a bit of a pickle. The more I perform my allotted tasks, the more I realize I just don't know what to do. There's no way I can reconcile the promises that have been made to the Arabs and the all-too similar expectations which have been raised with the French. I fear I'm going to leave here an utter failure. I hit a brick wall every time I speak with another delegation. Everybody has been made promises, and the promises are all vastly different. Who do we chose, and how do we deal with the accusations of reneging on our agreements? I don't know how to tell Mr. Lloyd George."

"I'll tell David. That's my job. But your job, Gertrude, is to be the oil on England's troubled waters, to assist us in reaching an honorable compromise that is acceptable to all parties."

He stood close to her and whispered confidentially, "It doesn't surprise me that you're finding things a bit tricky, after the promises Mr. Lawrence made to all and sundry when he was leading that Arab revolt. And now that he's here in Paris, the accursed Mr. Lawrence isn't helping your cause overly much, it seems to me. Poncing around like some nancy boy! He's an embarrassment to England and all she represents. People here are asking questions about where Great Britain stands when one of its senior ranking officers waltzes around the conference hall like some catamite of a Grand Arabic Vizier."

"Winston!" she hissed, hitting him on the arm with her purse. "You know very well Mr. Lawrence is a dear friend of mine. He can't help his mannerisms."

"Maybe he can't help them, my dear, but he can certainly hide them. He can dress like a Colonel. And he should also determine on which side of the border to place his arse. I have no problem with him assisting King Faisal, but he's acting like the king's agent and accomplice instead of being a senior officer in the British Army. The problem is those robes he wears. For God's sake, Gertrude, advise him on his dress sense will you. It's right and proper for an Arab to wear Arabic robes at a formal conference, but not an Englishman."

"He's an honorary sheik of the Howeitat. He's entitled to wear the robes."

"Not at the Paris Peace Conference, he isn't!" shouted Churchill. "He's entitled to wear the uniform of a Colonel, and nothing more!"

The hubbub of noise around them suddenly quietened and eyes turned in their direction. Gertrude grabbed Churchill by the arm, swung him around, and walked him out of the conference hall.

Calmer in the more frenetic atmosphere of the antechamber, Churchill said, "I know you and he are pals, my dear, and I didn't mean to upset you, but I'm afraid he's causing us a degree of humiliation, and that's the last thing we need when we're dealing with a stubborn old bugger like Clemenceau. But there's more at stake at the moment than Mr. Lawrence and his pantomime king. More, even, than Mesopotamia and the promises made to a handful of desert dwellers, despite the oil question. As I told you, there's a move afoot by certain of the Great Powers to forgive the Kaiser and his Hunnish people any need to repay the debt they owe the rest of the world for their adventure into war. We and the French are pushing for reparations, so that for decades to come, the Germanic peoples will be burdened by the cost of their aggression and will think twice about such an act of bastardry in the future. But others think differently. They think that demanding compensation will lead Germany into penury which will give rise to a monster that cannot be controlled. That might be so, but we've already controlled one Germanic monster and we'll decapitate any other monster before he can raise his ugly head. Will reparations lead us down a dark tunnel into an uncertain future? Only the Almighty knows."

Gertrude was stunned. "But Winston, not reparations? You can't surely be thinking of forcing the German people to pay compensation. It'll ruin their economy which is already on its knees. God knows what'll happen if—"

"There's a precedent. Germany extracted huge reparations from France after the Franco-Prussian War in the 1870's, as well as taking the territories of Alsace and Lorraine. Let's see how the Hun likes it when he has to empty his pockets to pay for what he and Kaiser Bill have done."

Across the enormous antechamber, Gertrude spied a sudden flurry of activity. Two men had just arrived in the precincts, both wearing traditional Arabic headdress and robes. One was tall, bearded, leather-skinned and leonine, the one beside him was shorter by more than a head, blond-haired and fair skinned with luminous blue eyes. Both men walked into the room, their dress and self-confidence making them the centre of attention and gossip.

Lawrence saw Gertrude and waved. She smiled back, and looked on in horror as Lawrence guided Faisal, the recently crowned King of Syria, across the length of the hall to where she and Churchill were standing. Despite her attempt to send a covert signal to Lawrence to back away and save Churchill from

286

an awkward situation, the young Englishman continued to guide the king towards the two of them.

"Damn!" said Churchill. "The little bugger is coming our way."

Gertrude looked at him, and wondered whether he meant the term literally or accusatively. "Winston, don't underestimate Colonel Lawrence. I still hold out great hopes for him."

"Don't be silly dear," said Churchill. "Men like Lawrence have one great moment in their lives, and the rest of their life is devoted to enhancing its memory. Lawrence's was leading the Arabs and now he's a spent force, like yesterday's *Times*."

"I wouldn't be so sure," she said hastily as the king and Lawrence advanced towards them. "He might be fey and feminine, but thousands of Arabs rallied around him. He could become a leader of the Arab world, if he plays his cards right."

Churchill glanced at her. "I'm afraid, Gertie, that Lawrence is a joker in a deck of knaves. He doesn't stand a chance of leading anybody, especially the Arabs, now that the war is over."

Both Gertrude and Churchill bowed in deference to the king when they arrived. "Majesty," said Churchill. He looked at the king's diminutive companion. "Lawrence," he said gruffly, before turning back to the king. "I hope Your Majesty found yesterday's deliberations interesting. Let's hope today, or tomorrow, the subject of Mesopotamia comes up, so that we can begin deliberations on what's to be done."

"The deliberations over the Middle East, Mr. Churchill, will begin when the Great Powers sitting at the table have carved up the main course of Germany and Austria, and turn their eyes southwards to their deliciously oily dessert."

"Let's hope they don't come to the dessert course with dyspepsia," said Lawrence.

"Majesty," said Churchill, ignoring Lawrence's remark. "The Great Powers at this victors' conference revere those who supported us in our battle against the forces of evil. You, Majesty, when you were in the Hejaz, were instrumental in raising the Arabic peoples against their Turkish overlords and slave-masters, and so helped the entire world gain a stunning conclusion. We, the Great Powers, will not forget the part you and your people have played."

"You ignore the role Colonel Lawrence played," said the king.

"Not at all, sir. Colonel Lawrence was magnificent in his role as a British Army officer. And he seems to be starring whenever I purchase a copy of a newspaper. But had it not been for the courage of the Arabs in throwing off the shackles of your Ottoman overlords, Colonel Lawrence and those like him, would have been a footnote in history."

"I'm grateful, Mr. Churchill, for your words. However, words are like grains of sand in the desert. They look solid from a distance, but slip through your fingers when you examine them. What we need is for you to maintain the assurance you gave us when you asked us to rise up against the Turks. You told us we would have our independence. It is a debt of honor. I am here to collect on that debt," said Faisal.

Gertrude froze. It was she who had been having these conversations with so many people over the past weeks. Deliberately, she hadn't brought any member of her government into the fray for fear of compromising them. But now, by ill-luck, Churchill was confronted with the reality of what she had had to suffer.

"Sir, many promises are given, many received, during wartime. What's important isn't that which was promised, but how to make the best of the worst. Catastrophic events oftentimes overtake promises, and leave good intentions floundering in the wake of an advancing army, or bogged down in the mire of war. How many young men, whose bodies today are rotting in the stinking marshes of Belgium or France made promises to their sweethearts that they would return and marry them? How many husbands said to their wives that they would be home by Christmas, safe and sound, yet whose dead eyes stare at the strange constellations of an alien sky? How many sweethearts and wives, mourning their dead, will hold in contempt their beloveds for swearing empty promises made with fervor and in sincerity, yet now tragically broken?

"No, Your Majesty, look not to the promises which were made with good intent in the cauldron of conflict, but think rather that a resolution must now be made in terms of what's best for you, the Arabic people, and for the entire Middle East. We British people have lost countless multitudes of our finest young men—an entire generation—in this dastardly war. Had any of us known the cruel price to be paid, we would have walked down any road to avoid such a heavy burden. Our industry has been devastated by the loss of our manpower. We must modernize it, just as I've modernized the navy. We British must encompass the new methods of production which are making America into such a powerhouse of capital and business. But to do that, sir, we must have a partnership with the Arabs and their oil. A partnership, King Faisal! A partnership in which you prosper as much as we."

"And does your partnership begin with the agreement Mr. Balfour made with the Jews over their resettlement in Palestine behind the backs of the Arabs? I am in favour of the Jewish presence, but it has caused, and undoubtedly will continue to cause, much hatred and anger in the Arab world. Is it a partnership when such things are done in secret?" asked the king.

"Majesty," said Churchill, "the Jews have given to Western society, and soon to Arabic society, a system of ethics which, even if it were entirely separated from the supernatural, would be incomparably the most precious possession of mankind, worth in fact the fruits of all wisdom and learning put together. Never underestimate the value of the Jews to Arabia. Given the chance, they will transform you from a medieval people to a modern people, able to sit as equals at the tables of scientists and writers and scholars. Your people have a proud history of scholarship and intellect, one which lasted five hundred years. You had courts which welcomed scientists, scholars, poets and philosophers, black men and white men, Muslims, Christians, and Jews. All peacefully sitting side by side as brothers discovering the laws of nature and looking deeply into mankind's soul. But that all came to an end in the thirteenth century and you haven't advanced a single footstep since. The Jews will return that status to you, given the simple chance to live in your midst."

The king began to interrupt, but Churchill was in full flight. "But you talk to me of the promise of partnership. Yes, promises were made to you by us and the French and others. But they were made with the good intent of friends and fellow combatants in a time of great and universal uncertainty. Shall we hang our promises like petards on an ancient battlement when they were made in moments of *extremis*? Is a man to be held liable for the pledges he whispers into the ear of his mistress when he is in the throes of making love? Surely, sir, unlike Janus, we can only afford to look forward, as we don't have the luxury of looking in both directions. We can and must look forward, sir, to a prosperous future, and not backward to demarcations made by drawing lines in the sand, lines which the desert winds have now blown into the ether of man's forgetfulness. Now, if Your Majesty will excuse me, I have a speech to prepare."

Churchill bowed again, kissed Gertrude's hand, and patently ignored Lawrence. He turned and walked away leaving the three in his wake.

"Insufferable windbag," hissed Lawrence. "Why does he always sound as if he's performing on stage at the Old Vic?"

After a moment's silence, Faisal said quietly so he couldn't be overheard, "That man will either end up living in the prime minister's residence, or spend his life in some British prison. Listening to him, I can't tell which."

"Is there a difference?" asked Lawrence.

Gertrude held her breath, uncertain how the king would react. He looked at her, and asked quietly, "Miss Bell, do you find it sometimes difficult to follow the reasoning of a man such as Mr. Churchill?"

"He has a mind like a sewer rat," hissed Lawrence.

Gertrude shot him an unkind look. "Majesty, Mr. Churchill is a rising star in the English political firmament. He strives to

290

impress, and sometimes sounds a bit pompous, but he's a man of great moral standing, and—"

"Gallipoli?" asked the king. "Surely Mr. Churchill's arrogance can be blamed for the disaster at the beginning of the war. But enough talk of disasters. Might I suggest we meet in the privacy of my apartments for dinner. The strains on you at the moment must be overwhelming. What you and I need is some private entertainment, an oasis of calm in this maelstrom of confusion and compromise. What do you say, Miss Bell? Dinner tonight?"

She flushed. Was he asking her out for an assignation?

"That sounds jolly," said Lawrence.

The king turned towards him. "But surely, Colonel Lawrence, you have other arrangements to which you have to attend?"

"Oh! Yes! Of course. How could I have forgotten?" he said.

"Eight o'clock, then, Miss Bell."

The king and Lawrence retreated into the inner sanctum. Gertrude stood there, rooted to the spot, wondering what on Earth had just happened. She turned when she felt a presence beside her.

"I didn't know you were familiar with Faisal," said Winston Churchill, having returned to find out the reaction to his comments.

"It appears, Winston, that by the end of this evening, I'm destined to be much more familiar with him than I believed possible."

Churchill looked at her in surprise. "He wants you for his harem?"

"I wouldn't go so far as to say that."

"But he wants you for a private rendezvous?"

"So it appears. But I'm nearly two decades older than he is. He couldn't possibly want me for my body, could he?"

"Why not? You're still a handsome woman, Gertie. How old are you?"

"I'm just over fifty, Winston, and it's very impolite to ask a woman her age."

"But that's the whole point, m'dear. Some women grow increasingly attractive as they grow into their prime. You, Gertrude, are fortunate in that the desert sun, the healthy outdoors, and your marvellous fortune in being rich and able to wear the very finest of clothes, have made you into a real head-turner. You are an object of desire."

"Perhaps for men in their sixties, or elderly retired generals nursing their whisky and soda, but surely not for somebody like Faisal, who would have been pleasured throughout his life by the most beautiful dusky-skinned maidens. What on Earth could interest one such as he have in an old lady like me?"

Churchill burst out laughing. "A liaison with the famous Gertrude Bell. It's all about status, m'dear" said Churchill, and turned on his heel to walk away. As a Parthian shot, he shouted to the assemblage, "His, not yours."

~

The king was dressed in a three-piece Saville Row suit of dark-brown cloth. It accentuated his height, and his standing. As his servant showed Gertrude into the room, Faisal stood and greeted her. She held out her hand, and he took it gently, and kissed it.

"It's very generous of Your Majesty to have invited me," Gertrude said. She was already a bit light-headed from two gin and tonics which she'd drunk to give herself courage.

They sat together on the sofa facing the window, which looked out over the riotous traffic of the Champs Elysees.

"This reminds me of a time, Miss Bell, when we were also together in another hotel room, this one far away. Do you recall it?"

She smiled. "Indeed I do, sir. It was in Egypt, I was dressed in a bathrobe, and you looked particularly debonair. I saw you as a young prince trying to fathom the British mind and which way you should take your country."

"And now I'm a young king, still trying to fathom the British mind."

They sipped glasses of Chateau d'Yquem and nibbled on canapés while she waited for him to expose his reasons for asking her here.

"Tell me, Miss Bell, what do you think of my relationship with Mr. Lawrence?"

"He's a very fine young man, and I'm sure he'll advise you well, sir," she told him.

"But how can he walk the path of Arabia and the path of Great Britain at the same time?"

"It isn't easy for him, and he's certainly being criticized by very senior people in this conference . . ."

"Mr. Churchill?"

"And others. They think he's changed sides. They think his loyalties are only to you. I know that's not the case. He'll fight for justice for you and your people, King Faisal, but not as a traitor to Britain."

The king nodded. He put his hand on the back of the sofa, close to touching her shoulder. Softly, he said, "But you also have a problem, don't you, Miss Bell. Your love of Arabia and its people must cause you agonies when you're negotiating their territory away from them."

Should she tell him? Should she confide in him her great ambition, first instilled in her when she was a young woman in Romania? The flame which had burned in her ever since it had been lit by ibn Sa'ud when she was little more than a girl in an orchard in the foothills of the Carpathian Mountains. But today she was the most senior woman diplomat which Great Britain had ever produced, a woman at a peace conference representing both her country, and the interests of nations which had been hideously brutalized by barbarians. No, she thought, this wasn't the time to tell Faisal her innermost hopes and wishes.

She breathed deeply, and began coughing. She'd been smoking far too many cigarettes and she really did have to cut down, and the alcohol exacerbated her problems with the remnants of the cigarette smoke still in her throat. "Sir," she said, "My loyalties are to Great Britain. But that doesn't mean I will allow the powers who are deciding these things just to ignore the interests of the Arabs. If the Arabs are deeply unhappy with the outcome, then in five or ten years, we'll be at war again, and this was supposed to be the war which ended all wars."

They continued to sip on their drinks. Then she turned to him, and asked him, "Is that the reason you've asked me here, King Faisal? Was it to find out where my and Mr. Lawrence's loyalties lie?"

He smiled, and shook his head. "Of course not. I knew already. I just wanted to listen to your explanation. No, the other reason I've asked you here is because of my growing respect and affection for you. Mr. Lawrence was continually talking about your grace and beauty and brilliance while we fought the wars in Arabia. I just wanted to see for myself whether he was being poetic, or whether his flattery was based on fact."

"And?"

"Fact! I think we shall become very good friends, Gertrude."

"I hope so, Majesty."

"And what do you view as the measure of true friendship, Gertrude?"

She thought for a moment, and then said softly, "Loyalty. Truth. Understanding."

They remained silent, sitting watching the night lights of Paris. "It must have been very hard being a woman, alone, in a man's world."

"You can never imagine, Faisal, just how hard it has been," she said, nursing her glass of wine.

"Oh, I think I can imagine it. I have observed Mr. Lawrence in our Arab society. It's been very hard for him, being a woman in a man's world."

She turned in surprise, and looked into his eyes. They were twinkling in mischief. She burst out laughing. So did he.

~

The interchange with Winston Churchill was still very fresh in their minds even a week later, and Gertrude determined to lift everybody's mood by keeping Lawrence and King Faisal active. So they spent much of their time traveling between the Élysée Palace, the American delegation in the Hotel de Crillon, the

British delegates in the Hotel Astoria, and the French diplomats in their many offices on the banks of the Seine, talking, cajoling and making their presence felt.

As the three were entering the Élysée one morning, they ran into a tall, moustachioed man with a pointed beard, prematurely balding for someone in his mid-forties, dressed in an immaculate gray three-piece suit. He immediately spied the king, and bowed.

"Your Highness, it's good to see you again."

"My dear Dr. Weizmann, how very nice to see you this morning. Do you know Miss Gertrude Bell, the most senior lady in the employment of the British government?"

As the king introduced Chaim Weizmann to Gertrude, he explained he had met with Dr. Weizmann, the head of the Zionist delegation to the conference, in January in London when they had discussed the principle of a Jewish homeland in Palestine and had agreed to support the principles of the Balfour Declaration.

Gertrude was shocked when the king explained the nature of the understanding he'd come to with the Zionist leader. They moved to an unoccupied part of the antechamber, where Gertrude explained to the King, "Sir, without wishing to embarrass Dr. Weizmann, I feel that your signing this declaration was very unwise. You know how much your Arab brothers will resent a Jewish presence in the Middle East. The principle of the establishment of a Jewish homeland in Palestine has already been agreed to by Mr. Balfour and the British government, and its ramifications will be among the issues to be discussed here in the near future; but for you to put your signature to a piece of paper supporting the British position of a Jewish presence will compromise your standing in Arabia."

Weizmann interrupted, "Miss Bell, there has been a Jewish presence in the Holy Land since the beginning of recorded history. All His Highness has done is to recognize the inevitable. The responsible Arabic leaders welcome the renewal of a Jewish presence in our shared ancestral lands, because we bring with us liberal ideals, an understanding of democracy, an international network of contacts in business and finance, industry and commerce, and trade and diplomacy. We, more than any others, are a universally educated people of the world, whose ancestral lands have become malarial swamps under the negligence of absentee Ottoman landlords. When our own lands are regenerated, our Jewish men and women will bring great benefits to the region.

"And more than that, Miss Bell . . . the return of the Jews to Palestine and the end of the diaspora will enable history to complete its circle and will right the wrongs perpetrated by the Romans in 70AD. For century after century the Jews have lived side by side with the Arabic and Islamic peoples in Damascus, in Baghdad, in Constantinople and in many other cities of the Arabian and Muslim world; we have contributed to the wealth of Arabia, of Europe and of the East, both materially and intellectually. Yet because of our religion, we are excoriated wherever we try to put down our roots. Never forget that the decline of two of the greatest European powers, Spain and Portugal, began when they expelled their Jewish communities.

"Enough is enough, Miss Bell. Since the time of the Crusades in the eleventh century, the Jews have been persecuted and have suffered from murderous pogroms throughout all of Europe. It's right and proper that the Jews should return to their ancestral home, and not be strangers in strange lands any longer," he said.

"Dr. Weizmann, I have nothing but the greatest sympathy for the plight of the Jewish people. But England and France have just fought the most devastating war in all of our recorded history, compared with which, Jewish suffering pales into insignificance. You must also remember the Arabic people were instrumental in assisting the Great Powers in fighting this war and defeating the Turks. Our indebtedness to them must come before any moral claims which the Jewish people might make for a Jewish nation in the region. My fear is that such a claim will merely cause—"

"Miss Bell," said King Faisal, interrupting. "Perhaps you should listen to a letter I have just sent to Professor Felix Frankfurter, the head of the American Zionist movement . . ."

He nodded to Lawrence, who opened his briefcase, and extracted a vellum letter, a copy of the one he'd sent to the United States. He handed it to the king, who cleared his throat, and read the contents in a voice which only those in his immediate circle could hear.

Dear Mr. Frankfurter,

We feel that the Arabs and Jews are cousins in race, having suffered similar oppressions at the hands of powers stronger than themselves, and by a happy coincidence have been able to take the first step towards the attainment of their national ideals together. We Arabs, especially the educated among us, look with the deepest sympathy on the Zionist movement. Our deputation here in Paris is fully acquainted with the proposals submitted yesterday by the Zionist Organization to the Peace Conference and we regard them as moderate and proper. We will do our best, in so far as we are concerned, to help them through. We will wish the Jews a most hearty welcome home.

Dr. Weizmann has been a great helper of our cause, and I hope the Arabs may soon be in a position to make the Jews welcome in return for their kindness. We are working together for a reformed and revived Near East, and our two movements complete one another. The Jewish movement is national and not imperialist, our movement is national and not imperialist, and there is room in Syria for us both. Indeed, I think neither can be a real success without the other.

People less informed and less responsible than our leaders and yours, ignoring the need for co-operation of the Arabs and Zionists, have been trying to exploit the local difficulties that must necessarily arise in Palestine in the early stages of our movement. Some of them have, I am afraid, misrepresented your aims to the Arab peasantry and our aims to the Jewish peasantry with the result that interested parties have been able to make capital out of what they call our differences.

BELL OF THE DESERT

I look forward, and my people with me look forward, to a future in which we will help you and you will help us, so the countries in which we are mutually interested may once again take their places in the community of civilized people of the world.
Believe me,
Yours sincerely, Faisal.

"And so you see, Miss Bell," the king continued. "The situation is well in hand for the Arabs to welcome back to Palestine their brethren, the Jews, and for all of us to benefit."

"Sir," said Gertrude, "I don't know where this will lead, but I do know the minds of Arabic leaders, the Islamic Arabic leaders, very well indeed. I know their likes and dislikes, their hopes and aspirations for the future, and I tell you, Majesty, there will be great distress and fury if millions of Jews leave Europe and descend on Palestine."

"I think you are wrong, Miss Bell," said Dr. Weizmann. "Some will resent us, certainly, and I'm sure there will be many uncomfortable adjustments, but when leaders of the Arabic tribes see the very tangible benefits a Jewish presence will bring to the area, I know our lives will be lived together in fulfilment. There has been Jewish migration into Palestine for going on forty years, and our presence is visible. We've drained swamplands and turned them into orchards and fields, we've created factories and settlements which are open to Arab and Jew alike. Whether the Arabs in Palestine or Syria or Egypt like it or not, if you journey through the areas where Jews have settled in the Middle East and you'll see crops and fruit and vines and flowers now growing where once there was a festering miasma, or a waterless desert. You'll see schools teaching boys and girls, and men and women industrially working side by side for national prosperity. You'll witness wonderful buildings growing on land which once housed camels, goats, and the occasional Bedouin. And no people wants to share its knowledge and skills more acutely than we Jews with our brother and sister Muslims. We are, after all, both born of our father Abraham. I am the son of Isaac, whilst Faisal is the son of Ishmael."

"If you remember your Book of Genesis, Dr. Weizmann, Ishmael was the son of Hagar, a servant of Abraham. I don't think the Arabs will be willing to be servants to the Jews," said Gertrude.

"Indeed not, for together Arab and Jew will be building Zion as equals, developing the land for the Arabs who live there, and for the Jews who will emigrate. We will be making it into a fertile home instead of a malarial swamp. We will cultivate and make fertile land which is today of use only to mosquitoes, snakes and vermin." He smiled, not knowing whether to continue. But the look of scepticism on her face encouraged Weizmann onwards. "But it's not just the Arabs who will welcome a renewal of the Jewish presence in Palestine, Miss Bell. There is very strong Christian support for the creation of a Jewish state. It found its public voice in England in the middle of the last century. When he was foreign secretary, Lord Palmerston strongly recommended that the Ottoman government encourage a Jewish return to their lands. It was Lord Shaftesbury in the middle of the 1850's who coined the phrase, 'a land without a people for a people without a land'.

"If you're familiar with Daniel Deronda, the novel by George Eliot, she espoused a very strong Zionist philosophy for the entire world to read. Just thirty years ago in America, over 400 prominent Americans, including the Chief Justice of the Supreme Court and the Speaker of the House, along with industrialists such as Morgan, and Rockefeller, signed a petition for the creation of a Jewish nation in Palestine.

"You might think Zionism is a new idea, Miss Bell, but let me assure you it has very old, and very deep roots in Western thinking. You might want to close the stable door, Miss Bell, but I'm afraid the horse has not only bolted, but is halfway around the paddock. Now, if you will excuse me, I have much work to do."

Weizmann nodded to Gertrude, shook hands with Lawrence and the king, and walked into the body of the antechamber to meet with his delegation.

Furious, Gertrude asked, "Did you know anything about the king's letter, Thomas?"

"Of course I did," Lawrence responded. "The king has asked me to act as his translator, amanuensis, and companion. I know everything that's going on."

"Then how could you have allowed the king to make such a declaration. You really should have consulted me first. Are you aware of how badly His Majesty has compromised himself with this correspondence?"

"Don't be angry with Mr. Lawrence, Gertrude," said Faisal. "We are in the midst of re-shaping the world. Old alliances may be broken forever, but new ones will be forged. It's not only Dr. Weizmann who thinks so, but also your Mr. Churchill who reminded me only last week, 'we must only look forward, and not in both directions.' "

"Majesty, might I have a quick and private word with Lawrence," she asked, grasping the man's arm and pulling him away. When there was distance between them and King Faisal, she whispered angrily, "How could you have done this, Thomas? Do you realize what you've allowed Faisal to do?"

Stunned by her vehemence, he said, "All Faisal is doing, Gertie, is to—"

"That letter, and his support, will have destroyed any hope that Faisal might become a unifying force in Arabia. Good fortune and the expediency of war made him King of Syria but his only way of surviving the coming assaults of the Sa'uds against the Kingdom of the Hejaz was to show himself as an Arab leader. But now that Faisal has done this, Abd al-Aziz will simply scream the word traitor and all Arabia will rally behind him in his conquest of the Hejaz. And knowing that brute, he'll probably take the throne of Syria as well. Oh Thomas, what have you done?"

"Nothing, Gertie. I promise. You've massively over-dramatizing the situation. There'll be a couple of thousand Jews who'll come to Palestine, settle there, and work happily with the Arabs. It's a storm in a teacup. You don't think American or British or French

Jews will want to leave their comfortable homes and settle in the desert, do you?"

"And the millions of Russian or Polish Jews who have been living squalid lives and with anti-Semitism for hundreds of years? They'll flock there. Oh you bloody idiot. Well, let's get back to Faisal, and see if we can retrieve the situation."

~

When they returned to stand beside the king, he asked, "Is all well between you?"

Gertrude shook her head in consternation. The problems of the area were almost insurmountable with just the Western powers and the Arabs involved, but now that the Jews had staked their claim and somehow got some Arab leaders to back their demand to return to their land of Palestine, the situation had become even worse. It was like trying to grasp a knot of writhing snakes. "Majesty, the problems which the emergence of an independent Arabia faces are huge. France is your true enemy, and the only way to beat Clemenceau and George Picot and those who advise him is to convince him, and the rest of the allies, of your legitimacy as King of Syria. Fail to do that, and you and all the others will be prey to hostile forces which have their eyes on your oil."

The king nodded. Lawrence listened in deference to Gertrude's wisdom, unwill to cross her again. Normally it would have been he who advised the king, but whenever he was close to Gertrude, he wisely remained quiet and observant, something which King Faisal found bemusing. Lawrence had a growing reputation throughout the world as an adventurer and was being promoted as the Englishman who had won the war against the Turks. Faisal had asked Lawrence to join him in Paris specifically because the Englishman added a cachet of mystery and excitement to the diplomacy of the Arabs, especially now that the journalist Lowell Thomas had made him famous world-wide as Lawrence of Arabia. Yet for some reason, Lawrence deferred to Gertrude whenever they were together. Faisal acknowledged her intellect and her superb knowledge and understanding of his homeland, but despite that, he had to keep reminding himself that she was only a woman.

Yet he'd spent a number of evenings alone with her, without Lawrence being present, and they'd been some of the sweetest times he could remember. She was charming, deferential, knowledgeable, and very sophisticated. And she was also a romantic. Twice, on leaving him and returning in his carriage to her hotel, she had kissed him at the door to his hotel apartments. The first time it had been a sisterly kiss, the second time her lips had lingered just a little bit too long. He'd been tempted to move his lips to hers, but she must have sensed that something was going through his mind, and so smiled and withdrew.

One day, though, he would decide the time was right, and he would make her his. She was, after all, a single lady in need of a husband, and it was his duty as a man to accommodate her needs. Though how his wife, Hazaima, would accept Gertrude Bell, he wasn't at all sure.

~

A week later, Gertrude received a hand-delivered letter to her hotel suite. It was early in the morning, and she had been lying in bed since waking an hour earlier, trying to rouse her spirits from the after-effects of the party the previous night. She knew her maid had deposited breakfast on the table outside of her bedroom door, but couldn't stomach the thought of brioche and baguette and *petit pain au chocolate* washed down with the thin and feminine coffee which the French loved, especially as her taste for coffee now was the strong mud which the Turks and Arabs drank.

She answered the respectful tap on her door, and her maid tentatively entered the darkened room, excusing herself, but telling Gertrude it was now past ten o'clock, and the messenger had instructed her to hand over the letter immediately as it was very urgent.

Gertrude tore open the envelope, and read the contents. She recognised the cursive Arabic script of King Faisal's hand. *"My dear Miss Bell,*

This afternoon at 2:00pm, I am informed that I am to address the French, British, American, and Italian delegations in the offices of M. Picot at the Foreign Ministry. Mr. Lawrence will be my translator. I would be very grateful if you could meet me half an hour beforehand, so that we could discuss the approach you believe I should take.

Your Friend, Faisal

~

"Run my bath," she instructed her maid, a smile appearing on her face.

~

Three hours later, wearing a simple gray dress and pink jacket beneath her heavy black velour overcoat, crowned by a somewhat extravagant hat composed of ostrich feathers enmeshed in black voile, Gertrude Bell waited outside the French Foreign Ministry building, and gravely shook hands with King Faisal and Thomas Lawrence when they emerged from their carriage. As they walked the dozen meters to the nearby café, Gertrude said, "Sir, I fear I must remind you I am here as a friend of Faisal, and not as a counsel for the Arabs. My position in Paris is to represent the interests of Great Britain, and anything which I might say to you in this private meeting is the expression of my personal opinion, and not that of my government."

The king nodded and remained silent until they were seated in the restaurant, and had ordered their coffees. The café was particularly hot and steamy, even though the people outside in the street were enjoying the freshness of the spring weather.

"As a friend of Faisal," he said softly in Arabic so he couldn't be overheard by the other patrons, even though Lawrence and she were the only ones who could understand the language, "What is your view of how we should approach this meeting with the victorious powers?"

"As a friend of Faisal, I would urge you to make the strongest case possible for being anointed King of Syria by the French. You hold the title of King of Syria as a gift from Great Britain, but under the Sykes-Picot Agreement we have also promised Syria to France. It is imperative you remain king in the eyes of the French, even though they will insist that you do so under their control. That is a battle which you must fight at another time, but your legitimacy as king must be maintained if control of Syria is passed from one country to another. Failure to gain French support today will cause your legitimacy to be questioned by the victorious powers, and that will be catastrophic for the cause of Arab nationalism."

Lawrence nodded. "That's what I've been telling Faisal for the past two months. But His Majesty seems oddly unwilling to engage with the French, and negotiate. Despite my entreaties, Faisal has avoided any confrontation. I said to him that—"

"And Faisal was quite right in not doing so," interrupted Gertrude. "Since the end of hostilities, the Great Powers have been in the process of the settlement of post-war Europe. Even though oil was on everybody's lips, the opportunity simply hasn't existed before now to discuss Arabia. For Faisal to have come to Paris and thumped the table would have pre-empted everything. He would have been seen as quixotic, as impractical, and worse, as an unreasonable adventurer. The Great Powers here have only been thinking of the battlefields of Europe, of the loss of untold millions of British and French and Italian young men. They're not thinking of the future, but of revenge and punishment and how best to bleed Germany dry so they can recoup some of their losses.

"But everybody knows that once their bloodlust is over, they'll have to start dealing with the Middle East and the demise of the Ottoman Empire. By remaining majestic, by appearing as a calm and reasonable monarch in the corridors and chambers, Faisal has remained above the fray. Nobody knows what Faisal thinks, or how he is going to negotiate. The French would have loved a good excuse for turning aside from Faisal and telling the world that his matters were far too trivial for them to deal with now. But right at this very moment, none of the Great Powers has any idea what stance Faisal will take in negotiating the question of Arabic nationalism, and His Majesty remains an enigma. This call to address the Great Powers will be his first opportunity to present his case to people who have no idea what he will be asking for."

Faisal smiled, and reached over to hold her hand. She was older than him by twenty years. It was an odd gesture, like that of a son to his mother. But she responded warmly, and squeezed his hand in return. They looked at each other, both in admiration and shared warmth. Thomas Lawrence wasn't certain what was going on. Could the king and Gertie . . . no, it wasn't possible. She was far too old for him . . .

Eventually, she let go of his hand, and said softly, "Faisal, if you negotiate and walk out of here as King of Syria, then the whole of Arabia can be yours. You could be the figurehead which leads the Arabs in unification, in nationalism. And if Lawrence stands behind you, you'll be invincible. Your success here will enable you to put a stop to the aspirations of certain other leaders. But be warned, the French have no love of you or your objectives, and seek only their own advantage."

He nodded, and wanted to hold her hand again; but propriety forbade him. Gertrude continued, "I shall be praying for you when you confront your makers". Faisal didn't smile, although Lawrence giggled. The pun didn't translate into Arabic.

~

Faisal had chosen gold robes and a gold-braided headdress. Lawrence emulated the headdress, but chose instead to wear white robes in deference to the king's standing. They walked over parquet floors, through massive oak double-doors, beneath blazing chandeliers, and past vast tables covered with maps and dispositions and flags. They were preceded by the Maître de la Bureau, wearing a formal black dinner suit, tails and white gloves. As the King approached a double door, somehow and miraculously it opened to admit them to yet another inner chamber, until they found themselves in a huge room with a view over the rue de Faubourg Saint- Honoré, a blazing log fire at one end spitting embers, and a table at which were seated the delegates from France, Italy, America and Great Britain.

The maître showed Faisal and Lawrence to the seats which had been placed before the table, as though they were schoolboys being called into the offices of the headmaster.

Faisal sat in the front seat, Lawrence at the seat behind his. The king smiled at the leaders of the world, men whose faces he knew so well, yet to whom he had only spoken on the few official occasions such as dinners or receptions. America's president Woodrow Wilson, an intellectual patrician, spare and elegant, was desperate to create a league of all the nations of the world to ensure open and public debate stopped war ever erupting again on the face of the Earth. Beside him, and his diametric opposite, sat David Lloyd George, a provincial Welsh lawyer whose incendiary oratory had captured the hearts and minds of the British people, a brilliant and crafty man who had emasculated the House of Lords, and given real power back to the ordinary people. Next to him sat the premier of Italy, Vittorio Orlando, another lawyer and intellectual, but one whose emotions were too often expressed as outrage against Woodrow Wilson who opposed many of Italy's territorial demands. And finally Faisal smiled at the French Prime Minister, Georges Clemenceau, the oldest man there by twenty years. Called the Tiger because of his passion as a speaker, Clemenceau was loved by the right-wing of the country, but hated by the workers and socialists, against whom he had fought all his life. And he was equally detested by Woodrow Wilson and David Lloyd George for his uncompromising stance against the defeated powers, wanting to punish them severely.

Clemenceau's stance had led Lloyd George to shout at him during one of their discussions, "Treat Germany like this, and Germany will become Bolshevik, and where will that leave Europe?"

Clemenceau screamed back, "Don't treat Germany like this, and France will become Bolshevik, which is a much more terrifying proposition."

But today there appeared to be harmony in the room, as Lawrence translated Faisal's words, paying greetings and prayers and thanks to the assembly on behalf of the Arabic peoples and the nations who professed Islam.

And then Faisal began to speak. Rather than wait for questions or an invitation to address the gathering, Faisal looked at each man, fixing him with his gleaming eyes, and spoke in mellifluent Arabic, his voice deep, sonorous, and unfathomable, carrying with it the wisdom of Mohammed conjoined with the eloquence of Omar Khayyam.

The four leaders of the world were transfixed as Faisal's voice washed over them. Those around the room stopped their discrete whispering, and listened to the eternal beauty of his voice speaking in a tongue which they couldn't understand, yet which spoke to all of their hearts. Only when Faisal turned, and imperially nodded to the man sitting beside him did Lawrence offer a translation of his words.

Faisal spoke initially about the beauty of his land, about the eternity of its sands and its rocks which had nurtured the earliest aspirations of humankind when men rose up and became sentient beings capable of recording their own history; he spoke about the development of language, about the creation of writing, about the origin of the great myths which had given mankind its imagination. He spoke about Arabs being the inventors of numbers and alphabets and dividing the day into twenty four equal parts. He told them about the way in which Arabic cities such as Damascus and Baghdad had been the capitals of the intellect of the world, where eastern and western scientists and philosophers and writers and artists had met and nurtured each other's ideas, sparking the renaissance which had led to the explosion of European culture.

Then Faisal continued, "With this beginning, you might wonder why it is we Arabic people today lag so far behind the Great Powers of the West, why it is we are considered a primitive people."

The four leaders all began to argue as soon as Lawrence had translated Faisal's words, but the king put up his hand to silence them. "The answer, I regret, is in our geography. Being at the crossroads between Africa and India, Europe and Asia, our lands were looked upon with avarice by conquerors throughout time, from the Egyptians to the Romans, from the Mongols to the Crusaders, from the French to the British to the Russians to the Italians; and soon, no doubt, to the Americans," he said pointedly. At the mention of his country, Woodrow Wilson looked up frowning. As soon as his words had been translated, two of the four prime ministers looked down in discomfort towards the table. Clemenceau stared at him in bemusement. Only Woodrow Wilson beamed a smile of appreciation.

"In our past, we were a people who were tribal rather than national, and we were ill equipped to fight the vast forces which were arrayed against us. If only a Saladin had arisen more than once in a millennium!"

It broke the mood in the room, and the four men laughed, as Faisal continued, "As a tribal people, we roamed across the vastness of the deserts, only occasionally putting down roots sufficiently long to establish great cities. But now that we have thrown off the shackles of the Ottomans, we are determined, gentlemen, that we must become a great nation, and take our place at the table of nations. We must establish strong and eternal identities for our people as Syrians and Iraqis and Arabians and Egyptians. We must have secure borders within which our peoples can develop and benefit from modern education, within which they can learn the skills of the modern world and put behind them forever their nomadic ways. We must be a nation and no longer a collection of tribes, gentlemen. And that is what I am here to discuss."

He cleared his throat, and sat back in the chair to await the response from the four leaders and was surprised that several people at the back of the room applauded.

It was Lloyd George who spoke first. Flushed with the oratory and with the mesmerising resonance of what he had heard, he said, "Your Majesty, be assured that Great Britain stands side by side with the aims and ambitions of the Arabic people. Europe has been decimated by the barbarity of the Germanic peoples, but Europe will rise again like a phoenix from the ashes. And America is a young, but strong and willing ally in supporting its older European cousin's hope of moving towards a bright and confident future. There is a place for the Arab people at the table, King Faisal, and your place, Majesty, is assured while ever Britain stands."

"And what of the Sykes-Picot Agreement?" shouted Clemenceau. "What of the arrangement which our diplomats worked so hard to come to? We mourn the sudden and tragic death of Sir Mark Sykes the other day in Paris, but are you, Mr. Lloyd George, prepared to abuse his memory by abrogating a binding treaty? The Sykes-Picot Agreement spelt out in clear and unambiguous terms the disposal of the lands of Arabia after the war. There is no going back. There is no concession which can be made to Faisal and his people. Syria is French, Lebanon is French, Palestine is British . . ."

Lloyd George began to argue, but Clemenceau held up his hand for silence. "Let me remind you of one of the salient points of that historic agreement, Mr. Prime Minister. 'France and Britain shall be allowed to establish such direct or indirect administration or control as they desire . . .'

"Let me further remind you of promises made to the French government during the war. Promises which I shall hold you to," said Clemenceau.

"And may I remind you, Mr. Prime Minister of France, and Mr. Prime Minister of Great Britain," said Faisal sternly, moving the focus of attention to himself, "that the Arabic peoples, whose land you are currently dividing up, were never consulted about this agreement. You have given away property which was not yours. And don't also forget, gentlemen, that without the Arabic people, you would not have won the war in the Middle East. Nobody, not a prime minister nor a diplomat, asked any Arab to be a party to the discussions between Sir Mark Sykes and M. Picot. I also seek to remind you that had not the Arabic people risen up in vast numbers against the Turkish overlord and fought to the death, you would not be having a discussion about the disposal of my lands. I will have a voice in any discussion which concerns the future of Arabia, M. Clemenceau. The agony, the history, and the righteous demands of the Arabic people will be heard."

The room descended into silence, but there was no need for Lawrence to translate, because to everybody's surprise, Faisal had just responded in fluent French. Even Clemenceau, red-faced and preparing for a shouting match, was stunned and sat back in his chair, surveying the young monarch.

"There is much about Arabia which you gentlemen have yet to understand," said Faisal in fluent English.

THIRTEEN

Hotel de Crillon, Place de la Concord, Paris 1919

The King of Syria sat in his damask dressing gown, a column of smoke rising in coils from the burning cigarette at the end of his long filigree holder. He surveyed the other man sitting on the couch opposite, also quietly smoking and reflecting, lost in some distant dream about other lands, other times.

There was only a three-year gap in their ages, yet Faisal felt much more than three years older than Lawrence. He felt more like a father to a brilliant but unruly son, a man who needed to temper the exuberance and extremes of his younger charge, yet who was also aware and concerned about the damage which could be done by dampening the very qualities which made Lawrence so different, so special.

It was the end of a difficult week, fraught with tension and argument, and the Great Powers, their advisors, supporters, diplomats, and acolytes had decided to take a well-deserved break. They had gone to different chateaux in the countryside to fish, to hunt, to read and relax. Faisal and Lawrence had decided to remain in Paris, and use the rich and pleasurable resources of the city to relax. They felt they had done all that could be done, and now it was up to fate and the Great Powers to determine what would happen.

The two of them had enjoyed an extraordinary couple of months since meeting up in Great Britain prior to traveling to France for the Paris Peace Conference. During their time in London, which was ostentatiously bright and colorful and frenzied after four grave years of war and was beginning to come to terms with the loss of countless men, the king and Lawrence felt they deserved to celebrate their personal victory over the Turks, and engaged in a riotous round of parties, socializing, and meetings with politicians and journalists, Arabic émigrés and diplomats, sometimes with as many as four or five appointments in a single day. London had been eagerly anticipating the beginning of the Paris Peace Conference, and both Faisal and Lawrence were minor celebrities, the talk of the town, and eager hostesses worked hard to ensure their presence at parties.

During some evenings, the king and Lawrence would find a gaming house or a place of questionable morality, or a theater or vaudeville playhouse or a nightclub where they would unwind and enjoy the pleasures which were always on offer. There was a newfound sense of freedom in London, which evaporated like a sea mist as they set sail for France. The White Cliffs of Dover disappeared behind them and a sense of great responsibility loomed as their steamer crossed the English Channel. The task they had set themselves became frighteningly clear.

Paris was outwardly as gay as London, the citizens showing the whole world that they were victors in the Great War and were entitled to let their hair down. But there was no sense of frivolity in the places where the Great Powers were meeting. These places were weighed down by an altogether more serious atmosphere, and because the king and Lawrence were overtly discernible in their robes, they were always on show and had restrained themselves from anything which might rank as light-heartedness. In Paris, they quickly became objects of curiosity and strangeness and, as in London, they were the toast of Parisian hostesses who were thrilled to have two such famous and exotic men as the centrepiece of their *soirees*.

Of course, he knew he was an object of fascination among the dark-suited men of serious mien and somber countenance. His Arabic clothes and mysterious demeanor ensured him of celebrity status, even though in terms of the pecking order he was one of the least important dignitaries there. And in certain circles, his exoticness made him and Lawrence the butt of facetious comments. He'd been told Clemenceau had recently described them as Don Quixote and Sancho Panza, tilting at the windmills of fantasy by imagining the Arabic people had done something to make them worthy of nationhood, but since Faisal had addressed the powers he knew he had David Lloyd George on his side, as well as the American President Woodrow Wilson. And he had privately promised he would rally the Arabs to support this new League of Nations which Wilson was so keen on initiating.

But it hadn't been a smooth ride. On the day some three weeks earlier when he had addressed the meeting of Great Powers, Faisal had been confirmed in his belief that Clemenceau and the Italian Prime Minister Vittorio Orlando were still vehemently opposed to giving up their stake in the ground of Arabia. "Greater Syria is French", Clemenceau had shouted at him. "It is today, it will be tomorrow, and when Jesus Christ returns to Earth, he will be met by men wishing him *bon jour.*"

This had caused Faisal to lose his temper for the first time, shouting back at Clemenceau, "I, and my Arab army, rode with Allenby at the head of a huge column of British and Australian soldiers into Palestine and Syria. Indian soldiers died by the thousands to free my people from the Turks. Yet somehow, Monsieur Prime Minister, I didn't notice any French troops had risked their lives for any of our territory. Tell me, M. Clemenceau, are you prepared to risk the fury of fifty million Arabs and the certainty of another war for land in order to claim land which you didn't fight for?"

Faisal had seen Lloyd George blanch at the prospect of a war with the Arabs, and the Briton had been forced to calm the meeting down, but Clemenceau, wearing his morning suit and gray gloves, sitting like a descendant of the Bourbon dynasty with his back to the roaring fire, imperiously slammed his hand onto the baize tablecloth, and hissed, "Continue with the next agenda item of this meeting. This discussion is ended."

The incident had lasted no more than a few minutes, yet for the past three weeks it had been the major topic of discussion at the conferences and huddles of diplomats. Would the Arabs go to war against Britain and France should the Great Powers insist on retaining their sovereignty in the area? What about the oil? If there were a war with the Western powers, would the Arabs sell it to Russia or Japan? How would the Balfour Declaration, which promised a homeland for the Jews, affect the balance of power in the area? Did the Arabs have the willpower for another war, this time not against the Turks, but against the British and the French? And did the British and the French, devastated by the loss of millions of their finest young men, have the stomach for another war so soon?

These were the sorts of titanic questions which floated around Faisal's mind as he relaxed in his hotel suite, smoking on his cigarette, musing over the events of the day, comfortable in Lawrence's presence. The two men were now so close they could sit in complete silence in each other's company, lost in their own thoughts, and it was as though they were having a spirited conversation.

Lawrence! Now there was a dilemma in the body of an enigma, thought the king. How did one explain Mr. Lawrence? When they were in London, especially in the fleshpots, Faisal had partaken of what was on offer, but Lawrence had always drawn back, unable to commit himself, unwilling to lose himself to his bodily needs.

Something had happened to Lawrence in the desert, something which the Englishman wouldn't discuss, yet which had had a profound influence on him. He'd been captured for a short while by the Turks in Deraa three years earlier, and they must have tortured him. But whatever happened, Lawrence wouldn't unburden himself, even to Faisal. Something in his personality had changed. He was still jovial, facetious, and mischievous, but he had returned from the desert seeming older, as though a darkness had stolen the light of his youth. Some event, some incident had caused him to metamorphose from a boy to a man. Perhaps it was too much killing, too much death, or the effects of a Turkish prison. But one day, no doubt, Lawrence would tell him. When he was ready. *Insh'allah.*

Faisal had discovered more about Lawrence from those who knew him than he had been told by the man himself. He'd been reticent in offering anything more than cursory information about his past. Faisal knew he was illegitimate by birth, but that his natural father had not abandoned his mother, and they had moved in and co-habited together to the shame of the family. He knew from Gertrude Bell that Lawrence was a good student at Oxford, having studied medieval pottery, or some such subject. And he knew his limp had been the result of a childhood accident. But that was just about all he knew of the young man's private life.

Gertrude wouldn't discuss Lawrence's sexual proclivities, even though it was the subject of unspoken humor between them. However, the man's comfort with mature women and with young—even very young—men told Faisal all he needed to know.

He knew Lawrence had always been a strange young man, brilliant and mercurial, but since the end of the war, and since his growing notoriety, he'd become more outwardly showy, yet more inwardly introspective, as though mind and body were rapidly drifting apart.

"Where are your thoughts taking you, my friend?" asked Faisal.

As though in a trance, and without even looking down from the ceiling, Lawrence said softly, "The Nejd."

Faisal frowned. "You dream about the most inhospitable desert on the face of the Earth?"

"Yes, I do," Lawrence said, looking down from the ceiling to where the king was seated. "It's odd, isn't it, Faisal? The Nejd is such a fierce desert, with leathery-skinned nomads the only people who can wander through and live in it, with goats and sheep whose hide is tough enough to withstand the burning sun, and with camels which stink, yet can go for days without drinking. It's a land without water, without life, without hope. Yet within that desert grows one of the most exquisite and valuable plants in the world, more valuable than gold and diamonds, and smelling more beautiful than a thousand virgins in a harem."

Faisal smiled and nodded. "Lubban."

"Yes," said Lawrence. "What the Jews call Levona, after the oil of Lebanon, and what we call Frankinsence, because it was the incense which the Frankish crusaders brought back from their assault on your nation. You see, Faisal, that's the whole mystery, the whole point of why I love the desert so very much. Because just as you crawl through the utter futility of it all, just as you struggle to stay alive with all the elements trying to kill you through heat or thirst or hunger, you suddenly come across the ugliest bush, the most gnarled tree you've ever seen . . . but when a branch is broken by a passing animal, the tree bleeds a resin which hardens in the hottest sun on Earth, and which, when burnt, gives off an aroma which makes a man into a god. Once you've smelled the perfume of frankincense, any other perfume smells gaudy and cheap.

"I first smelled it at a wedding I attended in Mesopotamia. It was given by the local chieftain, and his daughter was marrying one of the young men of the tribe. Frankincense was burned in the tent to perfume the air. I remember breathing deeply as I entered the tent, but from then on things became a blur, except for the smell of the frankincense. And I've never forgotten the aroma. It's like opium for the senses, mysterious, vision-filled and eternal. Yet the most glorious scent in the whole world comes from an ugly piece of resin which exudes from an unsightly scar on a repulsive tree in a dreadful desert. And that, my dearest friend, is why I love the desert—because of all the contrasts which I find so utterly fascinating."

Faisal began to speak, but Lawrence wasn't in the mood to listen, only to reflect. "And the people. Hard and insular and dark and as leathery as a camel's skin, yet beneath that exterior they are the softest and gentlest and most generous I've ever known. Some are brave in external appearance, yet inwardly the bravest warrior can be the most immeasurable coward—vicious evil brutes. They'll follow anybody who has the patina of authority, yet everyone sees himself as a desert chieftain, a fearless leader of men. And the women . . ." Faisal looked at Lawrence in surprise. "Hidden in veils and scarves so no man can look at them, ugly mounds of artifice like Lot's wife, yet voluptuous and sensuous and lithe and

316

overwhelmingly sexual because of their mystique, the object and the result of every man's desire."

Faisal looked closely at his friend. He really didn't need to be in the room. Lawrence's conversation was of himself and within himself. After a few further moments of introspection, Lawrence turned and stared at Faisal. "Tell me, have you ever read a book called Heart of Darkness by a man called Joseph Conrad?"

The king shook his head.

"It's a wonderful book about an Englishman who goes native in Africa. The book is about the contrast of civilization and primitiveness, of light and dark, of appearance and reality. Although it's about the deepest jungles of Africa, it's as though Conrad was writing about my experiences in Arabia, about the life I led in the desert. You know, six years ago, I began work on a book about my time in Arabia, but I want to update what I've written since I was leading the Arab revolt. I've decided to call it *The Seven Pillars of Wisdom.*"

Faisal frowned, and said, "My friend, there are five pillars of wisdom that one must live by if one is to lead the life of a Muslim—the declaration of faith that there is no God but Allah, to pray five times a day, charity, the pilgrimage to Mecca, and the observation of Ramadan."

"I'm not referring to the life of a Muslim, Faisal. The title comes from the Christian Bible's Book of Proverbs in which wisdom is seen as a good woman enlightening mankind. 'Wisdom has built a house and has hewn out her seven pillars. Give instruction to the wise man, and he will be wiser; teach a just man, and he will increase in learning.'"

"You will confuse the entire Muslim world if you publish a book with that title," the king said softly.

"It's not written for the Muslim world, Highness, it's for the Christian world of the west, to enable them to open their eyes to the wonders of Arabia and the small and insignificant part which I played in the great drama."

As he was speaking, a noise came from the outer suite. The sound of voices and the tread of feet, though muted by the carpets, could be heard in distant rooms. Both men looked towards the door. It was opened by Faisal's huge bodyguard, who said simply, "The woman, Bell."

~

Gertrude walked in. Beneath her thick Angora coat, she was dressed in a knee-length black skirt, and a scarlet blouse, her gray hair hidden by an ostrich-feather hat.

"What on Earth are you two doing in your dressing gowns? I thought we were going out to dinner."

"We were," said Lawrence, "but we're both feeling bruised and languid and spent, and so we rather hoped we could simply order from room service and have an early night. If that's alright with you."

She smiled. It was precisely what she wanted. She had been dining out virtually every night for the past two months, entertaining this delegation or being entertained by those diplomats. She had gained some weight, though her increase in smoking had dampened her appetite so apart from breakfast, she only really ate one meal during the day and even at these sumptuous banquets she only ever ate a first and a main course, and then she left half of the plate of food.

The thought of a night in, with good and amusing company, spent in informal talk, and not having to consider every word she spoke, was appealing.

"Good!" she said, taking off her coat and tossing it to the bodyguard. "Let's order because suddenly I'm starving."

Thirty minutes later, they were drinking onion soup made with Amontillado sherry accompanied by a bottle of Veuve Clicquot champagne, eaten with the freshest baguettes she'd ever tasted. As though by some miracle, waiters appeared as they finished the last mouthful of soup, and cleared their plates. They then brought in trays full of *Cailles en Caisses*, each quail served in an individual

318

ramekin and dusted with shavings of truffle. They talked and ate, and as Gertrude finished the last of her wine, once more the doors of the suite opened at the precise moment of climax and the waiters entered with trays of *filet de boeuf en croute.* This they served with a mouth-wateringly full-bodied fifteen-year-old Saint-Emilion Grand Cru.

Their conversation had meandered from the appalling weather to the fashions worn by the women accompanying the delegates, from the state of Europe months after the end of the war to end all wars to the way in which the Great Powers were manipulating the world for their own ends.

As they attacked their dessert, a deliciously light-headed *chocolat mousse au champagne,* Lawrence asked Faisal, "This book—?"

"What book?" interrupted Gertrude as she ate another mouthful of the dark aromatic chocolate.

"Thomas is writing a book about wisdom," said Faisal.

"And what do you know about wisdom, my dear boy?" asked Gertrude. "I'll happily accept that you have knowledge, but do you have wisdom?"

"It isn't about wisdom. It's called the Seven Pillars of Wisdom. I've been writing it for years. It's about my time in Arabia, and I'm bringing it up to date with the true story of the Arab uprising."

"Oh Thomas, my lovely boy, you can't write about wisdom. You'll be laughed out of Great Britain. Everybody knows you know a lot, but they also know you're not the wisest of men."

Hurt by her words, Lawrence said, "But King Faisal called me his genius only yesterday."

"What an overused word. Jonathan Swift said that when a true genius appears in the world, he will be known by all the dunces in confederacy against him. Dear boy, the people in this conference are the very opposite of dunces. There have been comments about your dress and your manner. I'm afraid, Thomas, that you're going to have to behave like a Colonel if you want to look wise as His Majesty's advisor."

"Are you not impressed that Lawrence will be writing his book about his time in Arabia, Gertrude?" asked the King.

"Have you asked Lowell Thomas whether that's a good or a bad move?" she asked Lawrence pointedly.

"Lowell Thomas doesn't own me or any part of me," he said, the words sounding angrier than he'd intended.

"Maybe not, but from what he's writing about you, you'd think the entire Arab uprising was brought to us by Lawrence of Arabia Enterprises. He's turning you into the equivalent of one of those cinema idols, Thomas. Your picture's on the front of the magazines, speaking engagements being arranged, magic lantern shows are mooted in England and the United States. My friends in the American delegation even tell me your exploits are becoming so famous in their country that somebody called George Melford is going around to all and sundry raising money to make a film called *The Sheik*, in which some desert dweller in Mesopotamia or Arabia or somewhere, living his life in a tent, decides to abduct an English woman of high birth. She, naturally, being a silly female, falls madly in love and goes native. I sincerely hope there are no references to me in this film," she snorted, "or I shall sue the producers.

"Frankly, my dear," she continued, "Lowell Thomas might not own the man, but he's certainly in charge of the image. Is that why you're writing this book . . . to offer balance to the real events of history?"

Lawrence remained silent for a moment, wondering how to respond. "I want to tell the world what really happened. Whatever you think, Gertie, it was a momentous time in the history of a hideous war, and the implications of what I did out there will have repercussions for the rest of the world for years, maybe even centuries, to come."

"What you did, Thomas? Weren't there a couple of hundred thousand Arabs involved in the fighting as well? Wasn't King Faisal a part of the grand scheme? And wasn't it me, dear boy, who was supplying you with the information and background you needed on Turkish troop movements which enabled you to be in the right place at the right time to play around with your gunpowder? You really will have to be very careful with your pronouns when you're on your lecture tour."

Stung, Lawrence flushed red. "I didn't mean to infer—"

"Perhaps not, but it certainly sounded as though the entire war had rested on your shoulders. One day, Thomas, you'll acknowledge the role that money played in your campaign. Had it not been for Allenby handing out £200,000 to the Arabic tribes to persuade them to join you, largely on my advice I might add, you'd have been dynamiting those Turkish trains on your own."

The two men looked at her in surprise at her vehemence. This was unusually straight talk to which they weren't accustomed. She'd obviously been drinking before she arrived at their hotel room, and the wine she'd drunk during dinner was loosening her tongue.

"And another thing, Thomas. I think it was marvellous that you led the Arab army and did all that derring-do stuff to the Turks, but what's happened since? What have you done since then? I had such great hopes for you, my love. I wanted you to rise up and for the Arabs to follow you, like Saladin, but you disappeared. You left the battlefield just when you should have been there to receive the loyalty of all and sundry, just when you should have made a great speech and everybody would have followed you into the sunset and you could have become a leader of a great nation, but you didn't, did you Thomas? You left Arabia to follow the image which this Lowell Thomas person was creating for you, so instead of you being the reality, you became the reflection. Well, it's too bad . . ."

She lapsed into silence, and realized both men were looking at her in shock. She sipped her wine, and looked at the floor.

Faisal looked from one to the other, from mother to son. "Is there an undercurrent here which needs mediating?" he asked. "I've spent the last several weeks in dialogue and mediation, and I'm getting rather good at it."

Lawrence burst out laughing. "We're more in need of ministration than mediation. Gertie and I are a bit like an aging mongoose and a fangless cobra, dancing around each other with a lot of menace and a great deal of hissing, but incapable of hurting each other. Still, what she said about my role in the war is quite right, but she wanted me to become a leader, and I'm just not made of that stuff. That bloody journalist Lowell Thomas is making much of the concept of Lawrence of Arabia in his reports, and Gertie's absolutely right. Today, I'm in danger of becoming the image rather than the substance.

"It's been worrying me ever since we were in Damascus together. I'm rather hoping *The Seven Pillars* will tell the other side of the story." He took a deep breath, and continued, "But therein lays a major problem for me. You see, if I tell the public what really happened, then it's an adventure story and exciting, but not vastly different from any one of a dozen other exploits of the war which right now a dozen generals are busy scribbling down as their memoirs in the hope that history will remember them kindly. As a mere colonel, I don't really rank all that highly in publishing circles. But as Lawrence of Arabia, I'm top draw stuff. So you see, if I extrapolate the Lawrence of Arabia theme, then it'll give the public something mighty to read, and will do the Arab cause a lot of good."

As though by some sort of thought process, the moment they finished their deserts a waiter from the hotel knocked politely on the door and effortlessly wheeled away the table of spent crockery and cutlery, leaving them with their bottles of wine and glasses. As he left the room, another table was wheeled in by more waiters, this one with pots of coffee and petit fours, decanters of brandy and dessert wines, and a tray of four perfumed flavors of Turkish delight covered in a dusting of caster sugar.

Faisal looked at the tray of sweets, and frowned. "Years of fighting the Turks, and I can't seem to get rid of them."

His remark relieved the tension in the air. Gertrude waited until the waiters had disappeared with deferential bows, and as the doors

322

closed, she said, "Thomas, my dear. You must tell the truth. Nothing more and nothing less. You fought a magnificent campaign, one that will go down in the annals of history. If you exaggerate your achievements, you'll undermine what you've really done. Rely on the truth, and the public will appreciate you even more. Tell them what happened."

He nodded. "Everything?"

"Everything!"

He paused, and sipped his coffee. The pregnant pause made Gertrude and Faisal look closely at him. A change had transmuted his face. The mischievous and boyish youth had become the hardened man of experience.

"Everything," he whispered.

Gertrude looked at the king. He gave an imperceptible nod.

Softly, slowly, she said, "Some things are better said to close and trusted friends than kept in your bosom."

"Even things which I haven't confided to you or to Faisal? Even things which I've not even confided to myself?"

She looked at him with kinder eyes. "You're talking about Deraa?"

Lawrence dropped his gaze to the table, and nodded slowly. He poured himself and the others a brandy. Softly, he said, "Perhaps there are things which might be better to leave unsaid."

"But if you don't say them, then they'll grow and grow until they hurt you terribly," said Faisal. "We have a tradition in our lands that allows poets and singers to express the emotions which we sometimes find too difficult to espouse. You, my friend, are that poet."

"What did happen, Thomas?" Gertrude asked. "I mean, we've all imagined. Our minds have encompassed the possibilities. Was it as bad as we thought?"

He sipped the brandy, and stared upwards to the ceiling. Then he took a large swig, and with a sudden finality drank what remained in his glass. "Yes, it was as bad, and worse than you could imagine. When I was captured, I was attractive to the Turkish commander, the Bey. I was blue-eyed and blond-haired. I was girlish in my looks, and slight in my build. Just like a boy. I spoke to him in gutter Arabic so he wouldn't realize I was in disguise. He raped me repeatedly, tore my anus until I bled, and then raped me again. And when I was a horrible mess, he had me beaten and whipped and tortured and cast down into a filthy dungeon full of water and rats and excrement. But I was freed along with all the others, and I determined never to speak of what had happened to me."

Gertrude realized she was gripping her brandy balloon so tightly it was in danger of being crushed. "Oh my dearest boy," she whispered, and reached across to hold his hand. Faisal reached over and held his other hand.

Lawrence shrugged. "How could I have told you of my shame?"

"But there's no shame, my lovely boy. No need to feel anything but anger and fury towards those who did this evil thing to you. Thomas, with my help, you will recover."

Faisal nodded, and said, "I had assumed something of the sort had occurred. From the time you were captured to the time you went to see Allenby in Cairo to request you be relieved of your command, I assumed something momentous had happened to you. Fortunately for us, he refused your request. But I say this to you, my dear friend, and what I say must be accepted by you, no matter how callous it might sound.

"Many women and girls are raped in times of war. But it's not often realized that many men are raped, too. Not just by homosexuals, but by ordinary soldiers on instructions from their commanders. It is a part of the process of humiliation which one army exacts upon another. This has been the case since ancient times. Raping a soldier means stealing his honor and his strength. A victor will rape and emasculate a vanquished enemy in the belief that by penetrating him forcefully, he will rob him of his virility, and make him impotent as a fighting man.

"It always has been, and it always will be so. Be thankful you were not in uniform, or known to be of the officer class, for then the Turks would have been even more vicious with you. I have known of many men from different tribes who committed suicide after being captured and raped, rather than return to their families and suffer the shame. This was a punishment which was well known from the time of the Romans, and has been practised by the Persians, the Ottomans, and our own Arabic tribes.

"I know you have suffered grievously, my friend Lawrence, but you must see your suffering in the context of the suffering of all soldiers in times of war, and not as some special punishment reserved for you and you alone."

Lawrence poured himself another brandy. "Faisal, that's as may be, but you have no idea of the after-effects I've suffered. Those nightclubs you took me into in London. I couldn't bear to be so close to people. Do you know, since my capture, I'm scared to touch people? I'm terrified of being touched, as well. When someone I barely know does more than shake my hand, I erupt into a cold sweat. I can't stand intimacy . . ."

Gertrude shifted over, and sat close to him. "Can't you stand intimacy from your closest friend?" she asked.

He shrugged.

She put her arm around his shoulder, and pulled him towards her. "Can't you stand the woman who loves you so dearly, being close to you?"

He sank into her body, and the tension which had built up seemed to unravel. She stroked his fair hair, and kissed him on the brow. Faisal looked on and smiled. Gertrude looked at the king, and motioned him towards her.

And they sat there for an eternity, the three of them. Locked in an embrace, each holding the other tightly. Three people who loved each other. Three people who found solace in each other while the outside world tried to undermine them. Three who were so utterly different in almost every respect, yet who were as close as any family possibly could be.

Gertrude kept kissing Thomas, Faisal embraced his dearest friend, and in a moment of closeness and intimacy, Faisal kissed

Gertrude, a mark of love and reverence and friendship and respect.

And when the eternity had ended, they separated, smiling at each other, the warmth and strength had been shared one with the other. They sat quietly for a moment, the two men contemplating their brandy balloons, Gertrude sipping her liqueur.

"Before we leave this difficult subject, my friend Thomas, tell me why you blame your imprisonment and the brutality you suffered upon what has always been a part of your character. As long as I've known you, you never were comfortable with intimacy. Remember when we first met, and I offered you a choice of beautiful boys or girls, and you rejected my offers. I couldn't understand why you had such difficulty doing what we Arabs take so much for granted."

"Because as an Englishman, I had a certain standard of behaviour."

Faisal laughed. "Oh come, surely being in Arabia, not England, you could have lived like the Arabians lived? If you didn't want to do it in England, nobody would have known what you were doing in my country."

"I would have known," he said. "And you make me sound like some eternally dry old stick. At Oxford, I was seriously attracted to a lovely young woman called Janet Laurie, but from the moment I graduated, I was removed from young European women, because I chose to go on archaeological digs. Almost straight after Oxford, I spent years in the desert in Mesopotamia, and there was no chance of meeting young English woman. Unlike people of your race, Faisal, Englishmen don't copulate like rabbits. We wait until marriage."

Gertrude coughed to remind the two men she was present in the room, and that the conversation had taken an awkward turn.

"And are you, too, a proper English gentlewoman who doesn't discuss topics such as this in polite company," asked Faisal. He was being facetious and playful, wanting to divert the conversation from Lawrence's traumas onto a lighter topic.

"Sir," said Gertrude. "As a proper Englishwoman, I never discuss matters of the heart in public, and rarely in private. But as an Oxford educated woman, as a diplomat, as a senior servant of the crown, as a delegate to the Peace Conference, I feel entitled to discuss any suitable subject with any gentleman, under any circumstances."

"Bravo," said Lawrence, clapping. Gertrude and Faisal burst out laughing. Now that his revelation was on the table, Lawrence was feeling more light-hearted, even happy.

"And thank you, my friend, for raising the mood," Lawrence said to the king. "We mustn't let what happened in the war color our peace."

They drank a toast to peace, using brandy instead of champagne. It was a very fine brandy, but it burnt Gertrude's throat. Her father liked brandy, but she always preferred sweeter wines and liquors. She poured herself another Amontillado to take away the bitter taste of the brandy.

"You must be very proud to be the King of Syria," said Gertrude. "It's what you were born for, what you've prepared all your life to achieve."

Faisal shook his head, and smiled wryly. "You'd think so, wouldn't you, the way I've been walking around here so imperiously? I've played the king while dear Lawrence has played the knave. But you could hardly say I was born to it. Indeed, I very nearly wasn't born at all."

Gertrude frowned.

"I was a very sickly youth. My father was the guardian of Mecca and a descendant of the Prophet, but my mother was a peasant from my father's village. Their wedding was vehemently opposed by my father's family, but he insisted. They were cousins, you see, and people were afraid for the continuity of the line. But they fell in love, and married, and I am one of four healthy brothers, though from the very beginning, you'd have sworn that there would only be three survivors. I was born in a tent and the midwives didn't give me any chance for life. Apparently, I was a limp child who just lay there and barely had the energy to cry. But survive I did, and I was taken to Constantinople for my schooling. Compared to the other boys in the Ottoman Palace where I grew up, I was a weakling. I barely ate, and was more attracted to poetry than being a warrior. But my father insisted that I learn the manly arts, and while I was there, I learned to ride horses and camels and soon developed the skills of the desert dwellers. From the Ottomans I learned the art of negotiation, from the desert I learned the arts of war, and from the scholars I learned the genius of our Arabic culture. And now, God and the French willing, I'm the King of Syria with my seat in Damascus, the greatest Arabic capital of them all."

"I'm sure the French will support your position," said Gertrude.

"You think so? What about the agreements between them and the British?" he asked.

"Lloyd George has made it pretty clear he will have his way. Now that Sir Mark has so unfortunately passed on," said Gertrude, "The Sykes-Picot Pact doesn't seem to be carrying so much weight."

"But the other agreements?"

"Your Majesty," she said, "there have been so many agreements and undertakings, the water is so muddy, they'll probably all be thrown out of the window and we'll just have to start again. Look at the conflicts between the Sykes-Picot Agreement which gave Syria to the French, the discussions between McMahon and your father, Sheik Hussein which gave an undertaking for an Arab Kingdom and the restoration of the Caliphate incorporating Arabia, Syria, Lebanon, and Iraq, the Balfour Declaration which gives a homeland in Palestine to the Jews, the promises made through Lawrence by Allenby and the natural right of the Arabic people to self-determination. It's a terrible mess which will have to be cleared up by other arrangements."

"The situation is fraught in Syria, but what do you think will happen with Mesopotamia?" asked Lawrence. "Your brother Abdullah has been offered the Kingdom of Iraq. But what kingdom? Gertie, have you finished drawing up the boundaries?"

"In a way, but it's terribly difficult, because of balancing the needs and expectations of the Kurds in the north, the Sunni in Baghdad and in the central regions, and the Shi'ites in the south. Then, of course, there's the oil question. Britain must have access to Basrah, but now there's talk of oil having been found in Mosul, and that could be huge. And we've got to spend a fortune restoring the fertility of the land between the Tigris and the Euphrates so it's cultivatable again. It's all very difficult," she said, a note of despair entering her voice.

Faisal shook his head. "Do you think it will happen? All this talk about Arabic kingdoms! Isn't it all pie in the sky? The British were very free with their promises during the war, because they wanted the Arabs on their side to help them overthrow the Turks, but the feeling I've been getting at this Peace Conference is we're a backward and underdeveloped people, and aren't worthy of real nationhood. Oh, you'll appoint us as kings and emirs as though we were all characters in Mr. Gilbert and Mr. Sullivan's Mikado, but the real objective is to leave the control of the Middle East and its oil to the British and the French, and have the rest of the world run by this new League of Nations which President Woodrow Wilson is so keen on. Aren't I right, Gertrude?"

Without waiting for an answer, he continued, "So should I sign some pact which offers me some titular monarchy and for me to be a puppet of the French or the British, or should I refuse to sign anything, and walk out in disgust, taking my pride and my oil with me?"

Gertrude began to answer, but shook her head sadly and shrugged her shoulders.

~

It was already the secret hours of the morning, yet she didn't feel like getting up and going to bed. She was in the company of the king, and even though he wasn't a real king like England's Edward or George, he was a king in name and a king of Arabia, and that made it terrible exciting . . . and naughty. For she was sitting in his presence, her clothes somewhat askew, her shoes off, in her stocking feet, and slouching in a chair with her feet on the coffee table.

Normally, at this hour of the night, she would have excused herself from the dining table, thanked her hosts for their excellent company, retired to her room and written up her report of the evening's conversation for dispatch to Britain's foreign secretary. Then, under the normal circumstances which governed her greenhouse existence in Paris, she would have fallen into bed at three or four in the morning, slept until ten or eleven, then prepared for the afternoon round of meetings.

But tonight, or more properly this morning, she would prepare no reports, she would not think through the ramifications of the conversation, and nor would she ponder on what to do next. Tonight she was floating on air, a young woman again, as light as a feather. Tonight, she had been toasted and admired by two extraordinary men, both of whom professed their unbounded approbation for every aspect of her nature. She had been embraced by the King of Syria, kissed as though she were his lover, hugged by the famous Lawrence of Arabia and treated like a woman, and not like an honorary man. She felt in part a mother, in part a wife, and in part a lover. She hadn't been held or kissed or even touched intimately in years, and she'd forgotten the joy of familiarity, of being held in a man's arms, of the erotic ecstasy of closeness when a man held his body against hers. Tonight, she had felt like a woman, and not like a civil servant, a diplomat, or a political officer of the crown. And it felt marvellous.

She knew she must return to her room, but she was held in position by the ache of desire. It was as though she was in a bubble, and any movement would make it burst and reality would once again force itself upon her. Gertrude was sitting on a settee in King Faisal's suite in the Hotel de Crillon, legs up, drinking her—how many was it?—eighth or ninth glass of Amontillado sherry. She couldn't feel her toes or her fingers, she knew she was giggling, she was aware she'd made very improper remarks about her awful and aggressive new boss A.T. Wilson and the verbosity of Winston

Churchill and the mendacity of Tiger Clemenceau. But she knew her words, and the utterly improper and very rude remarks of both of the men in her company, were like the morning mist and would disappear into the ether with the rising of the sun.

During the evening, the king had taken off his tie and undone the buttons of his shirt, and come to sit next to her on the settee. Lawrence had removed his Arabic headdress and his multi-colored gown and was now sitting on the other side of her, dressed only in a silk shirt and linen slacks. It was a replica of the intimacy they'd experienced earlier in the evening, but this time, the alcohol and the relaxation had replaced their need to minister to Lawrence's wounds.

"I thought you didn't like people touching you, or you touching people," Gertrude said, removing his head from her shoulder and his hand from her bodice.

"I'm drunk," Lawrence grumbled. "I can't feel a thing."

"Well, I'm the thing you're currently feeling, dear boy, and it's not altogether right and proper."

The king laughed. "Right and proper! How very English. Should I call my servant to escort you back to your chambers so that no word of scandal shall attach itself to you, Gertrude Bell? Let no man say the honor of the great woman Political Officer of Great Britain was diminished in my presence."

"Faisal, I am totally at ease in your company, and I know you'll go to great lengths to respect my person. I may be silly, but I'm not drunk."

She frowned at something which didn't sound quite right, thought about what she'd just said, and corrected herself. "I mean, I may be drunk, but I'm not silly." She giggled, and the others giggled with her.

"Ah," said Lawrence, "but will I?"

"Will you what?" she asked.

"Will I respect your person, or will I take advantage of the barriers which have been broken by your inebriation, and will I carry you off to my bedroom and have my way with you?"

"Thomas, you're being a very naughty boy," she scolded him.

"But what if I have my way with you?" asked the king.

She thought deeply, and responded. "That, sire, is an entirely different matter. Thomas is only Lawrence of Arabia, prancing around on a camel to impress the Americans, whereas you are a king, and I am your subject. And I will subject myself, willingly, to any command of my Majesty. If it is your desire, and you carry me away on your white charger to have your way with me, then like a true servant of the crown, I shall simply allow it to happen."

She listened to her words, and knew she should be mortified by what she'd just said. But she giggled again.

"I'm cut to the quick, Gertie. I thought I was going to be the man in your life."

"Ah, Thomas, but there's got to be life in the man, hasn't there."

They all burst out laughing. In concern at the sudden explosion of noise, the king's servant burst into the room, and when he saw the three people hysterical on the sofa, he closed the door quickly to resume his position.

When they'd calmed down, the king said, "Thomas, you know very well that your interests lie more in my direction than in Gertrude's."

"Gertrude is a wonderful, beautiful, brilliant woman, but right now, my friend, you'd leave her side and our company in a minute if an attractive boy walked into the room."

"Do you think so?" Lawrence asked. "I mean, I know there are whispers and rumours in the Officer's Mess and in the corridors here in Paris about my sexual proclivities, but I don't honestly fancy boys. Or girls. Or men. Or women. I don't fancy anything much these days. I truly think I've become asexual. Hermaphrodite. Androgynous. The only thing I fancy these days is the good company of a wonderful brother in you, Faisal, and a wonderful friend in you, Gertie."

"What you need, dear boy," she said, barely able to restrain her laughter, "is a *midinette*. One of these lovely young women who works in a shop during the day, and sells her body at night.

Somebody to take you in hand, so to speak." Her restraint disappeared, and she again burst into gales of laughter.

"Miss Bell," said Faisal sternly. "Are you trying to seduce my friend Lawrence into immoral ways?"

"Absolutely," she said. "He needs some solid immorality to make him whole again. He needs a good man or a good woman to switch back on the flame which burns within all of us. His flame, unfortunately, has become little more than a dull ember."

"And yours?" asked the king.

She didn't respond for some time. Even though drunk, he had touched a raw nerve, something she didn't necessarily want exposed.

"I am a very passionate woman, Faisal," she said, rubbing her finger around the lip of her glass and making it sing. "When I was young, many centuries ago, I was the belle of the ball. And I had lovers, Faisal . . . lovers whom you would envy for their manhood, their strength."

The two men looked at her in astonishment.

She lifted her face to the ceiling, and suddenly shouted, "Why did I always fall in love with the wrong bloody men?"

Her voice filled the room and slowly died away.

"You're in love with me, and I'm not wrong," said Lawrence.

"I'm in love with many things, Thomas . . . dogs, cats, children, books, you . . . but none can satisfy that most basic desire of a woman. And women are entitled to have desires, and to satisfy them."

"But what you have suggested for Lawrence is also available to any woman who has the means. Even to you, Gertrude," said Faisal. "There are men in Paris who will take money to satisfy the needs of a woman . . . especially a passionate woman like you. It can be done with great confidentiality, and nobody will be the wiser. It can be done in your chambers . . . these hotels are very used to men and women coming and going and no questions are asked, no word of scandal passes anybody's lips."

"Your Majesty!" she shouted. "How dare you implicate me in an unlady-like adventure?" She reached forward to the table to pour herself another glass of sherry, but her glass missed the table, and fell onto the carpeted floor. "I think I've had enough. I'm in danger of losing my reputation. I shall leave, and see you two reprobates in the morning."

"But," said Faisal, "you promised to come to my room. You said you'd obey any commands the king made."

She smiled, and kissed him on the lips. "Unfortunately, dear, I was talking about King George."

She stood on teetering legs, steadied herself against the outstretched arm of King Faisal, and straightened her dress. Faisal and Lawrence also stood, and she threw her arms around the king.

"A humble commoner kisses the newest and most wonderful king in all the world." she said, and kissed him on the cheeks.

She turned to Lawrence, "And a passionate woman, full of the lust of life, embraces a man of questionable morality without becoming compromised." And she put her arms around him, though he was much shorter than she, reached down, and kissed him on the head.

As she walked unsteadily out the door, Faisal said softly to Lawrence, "What a waste of womanhood. She should have made somebody a wonderful wife and produced many fine sturdy children."

"Ah, but then Britain would have missed out on the only person who can truly make a difference in the Middle East."

FOURTEEN

Palestine, October 1919

Her stay in Egypt had been hot and dusty and distressing, the antithesis of her time in Paris. Talk of rebellion against British rule was everywhere, and there were times when Gertrude felt in very real danger of her life just because she was English. The British had created another Raj for themselves in Egypt, with opulent golf courses, luxurious hotels, obscenely decadent spa baths and sporting clubs which the hunting, shooting, and fishing brigade in England would have envied. It was Surry under a blazing sun.

But there was something unreal, unworldly, about the English community in Cairo. Despite a huge force of soldiers, there was an undiluted assumption of temporariness about the place. And the resentment towards the British occupation was palpable amongst all but the ruling class of Egyptians, who were becoming incredibly wealthy and ostentatious. Because Egypt was a British protectorate, the Egyptians had been forced to donate men, munitions, supplies, food, and four million pounds to fight the Turks. Even though there was universal resentment towards the Turks because of the centuries of debased Ottoman rule, the British were seen as little more than a replacement, an alternative imperial master race, another transient moment in Egypt's five thousand year history.

When, at the end of the war, the Anglo-French Declaration of Arab liberation was announced, the local Egyptian leaders had marched into the office of the High Commissioner, and demanded the right to rule themselves. Their request had been transmitted to London, but the mandarins of Whitehall refused to countenance the suggestion.

This had caused an outrage among the mullahs and clerics and reactionaries and revolutionary Caireens, and the sounds of rifle fire had become a perpetual backdrop in the streets of the capital city. English soldiers were being picked out by snipers, the deaths causing fury in London. Trains carrying British soldiers southeast from Cairo to defend the Suez waterway, and to different parts of the country, were ambushed and officers and men were pulled off by marauding tribes of Egyptians, beaten and clubbed to death, their bodies left by the tracks to rot in the sun.

And it wasn't just the military who were the target of the fury of the Egyptian people. Caireens who had actively co-operated and enriched themselves through the British presence were dragged from their houses at night, and their bodies were hanged from lampposts in the streets as a warning to any other merchant thinking of dealing with the imperialists.

In retaliation, and to round up and punish the ringleaders, armed raids were undertaken by squads of troopers into the homes and houses of terrorists. Men were arrested on suspicion of associating with someone who might be a radical, or because they were in possession of a firearm, or because they had been reported by somebody for saying something anti-British . . . it was an altogether terrible situation, and Gertrude was pleased when her inspection of the Arabic mood in Egypt was finished and she was able to sail away on her journey to Haifa in Palestine. And the growing mood of nationalism in the area began to change her opinion of the presence of the British in Arabia. Gertrude had always believed the Arabs deserved self-rule, but that a long transition period in partnership would be necessary to bring them into the twentieth century. Then, she hoped, a leader would emerge to unite all of the Arab nations. Her idea for an orderly evolution had been for the Arabs to be in command, but for the British to be in control . . . that there should be a British High Commissioner and his staff enacting London's decrees, but the visible organs of authority should be in Arab hands. In that way, the people would learn government firsthand, and all should be well in a decade or two.

But Gertrude had seen of the mood of the Arabic delegations in Paris when Faisal had walked out and refused to acknowledge the final communiqué, now she had witnessed for herself the tenor of the nationalistic feeling on the streets in Egypt, and it was obvious the Arabs were in no mood to accept some over-lordship by the British or, God help them, the French.

And if the situation was fraught in Egypt, how much worse would it be in Mesopotamia. The vast landmass of Egypt was a nation which was modern by Arabic standards and which had in place the necessary instrumentalities for self-government. But Mesopotamia had no such structure necessary to govern, and was far from being a land composed of one people, united in their aspirations. The landmass of Mesopotamia was composed of numerous conflicting tribes, the Sunni and Shi'ite branches of Islam, Jews, Christians, and Kurds, making government by an experienced power such as Britain difficult at the best of times, but making self-government virtually impossible. Who, after all, was the self? Who would demand majority say in such a government?

She decided, with the permission of the prime minister and the foreign minister, to go on a fact-finding tour of the Arab world, so she could write a report and give advice to the British government. She had reported her conversations to A.T. Wilson, explaining she wouldn't be returning immediately to Mesopotamia, and her trip and the subsequent report were to be welcomed as necessary intelligence by the government.

Wilson had fumed when she told him. He at first refused her permission to go, but when she informed him she didn't need his permission, and nor did he have the right to contradict a direct instruction from the prime minister, he had stormed out of the room. Gertrude knew when she returned to Baghdad she would have a great deal of fence-mending to do.

Her mood of despondency at the situation in Cairo improved as her ship sailed through the night and arrived at the port of Haifa in the early hours of the morning. It was a breathtaking setting with the sun rising behind the large hill which overshadowed the port. As the gloom of night gave way to the brilliant crystal clarity of the morning, she saw the hillside was dotted with white houses and red roofs, their windows painted blue to mimic the sea because the Devil couldn't swim and so, thinking there was water in the house, he wouldn't fly in through the window. Halfway up the hill, she saw the recently constructed Shrine of the Bab, leader of the Baha'i faith. Immediately below that was the German colony, established at the time of the Crusades by the Templars. Dotted around the hillside of Haifa were synagogues, churches, and mosques. It was only by seeing Palestine from the distance of the sea that the melting pot of people, religions, cultures, and beliefs could be comprehended.

Even from a mile out to sea she could hear the sounds of the dock, a dozen different languages, the noise of machinery and hoists lifting cargo, the monotonous grind of wheels on tracks, and the ever-present churning sound which the engines of ocean-going vessels made as they entered and left their berths.

To her surprise, she was met on the dockside by a young man from the office of the commander of the British regimental forces, a young man called Captain Haldane. Tall, fair-haired with hazel colored eyes, he wore with obvious pride and self-importance the uniform and epaulettes of a captain of an artillery regiment. The lad couldn't have been a day over twenty-two, and was obviously relishing the responsibility he'd been given in escorting a British person, who may or may not be important—his colonel hadn't given any details. He saluted stiffly as Gertrude stepped off the gangplank, and introduced himself.

As they walked out of the disembarkation lounge towards the waiting cars, Gertrude asked him, "Did you see action during the war, Mr. Haldane?"

"Yes, ma'am. In Flanders. But not front-line action, I'm afraid. I was a junior staff officer, and was in Regimental HQ."

"Then you're a very lucky man, Mr. Haldane," said Gertrude. "Look, I can't keep on calling you Mr. Haldane. What's your Christian name?" she asked.

"Timothy, ma'am", he said as they stepped into his motor vehicle.

"My name is Gertrude. If you're going to be my escort and advisor in Palestine, I think it's right and proper we should be on first name terms. So for heaven's sake, Timothy, don't call me ma'am. That's reserved for the wives of kings, barons, or archbishops. I, thank goodness, am none of these."

The young man smiled wryly.

"Are you here on holiday, Gertrude?" he asked.

"Not exactly," she replied.

Timothy ensured the second car, carrying her maid, also had all of her voluminous luggage safely stowed in its boot and on top of the roof. When everything was ready, he instructed the driver of the second car where to go in case they were separated, and then ordered his driver to take them to the Hotel Imperial on the Street of the Prophet. "It's very high on the hill, which is a problem if you want to walk to the markets down here, but the views from up there are spectacular, and because it's so high up you get a wonderful afternoon sea breeze which cools down the rooms and makes sleeping at night rather more comfortable. The hotel has beautiful rooms, and also has a swimming pool which you'll enjoy."

"And how would a young man who should be sleeping in his barracks know about the comfort of a hotel room in the evening?" she asked.

He flushed beetroot red.

"Oh come now, Timothy, there's no need to feel embarrassed. Just don't let the colonel catch you." Then, as an after-thought, she added, "Unless, of course, you were dallying with the colonel's wife?"

He turned to her in shock, and she burst out laughing at the expression on his face. The relief of being out of Egypt was palpable.

~

When she had bathed and refreshed herself and had some breakfast, she took the rickety cage lift to the ground floor, where Captain Haldane was waiting for her in the foyer. He complimented her on her clothes, and suggested they go for a drive along the seashore, as far as Acre.

"There's a marvellous castle there, loads of ruins. Do you know anything of the history of Palestine? It's really interesting, especially down south in the capital, Jerusalem."

He obviously hadn't been briefed by his Colonel on who she was, so Gertrude smiled in bemusement. "I know a little something about history," she said softly.

He held open the back door of the car and told the chauffeur to drive north. "You know, Palestine is an extraordinary place. You should really get around and visit the country. I've been to Jerusalem and quite a few other places. Very old, and extremely interesting."

"Yes," she said, "I have been here before, you know."

"Really?"

"Once or twice."

"I'm so sorry. My colonel just told me to ensure you didn't get into trouble because of the rum times around here. He just said there's an English woman arriving from Cairo, and that I was to look after her. I'm afraid that's all I know about you, Miss Bell. What were you doing in Palestine?"

"Oh, a bit of this, and a bit of that. Tell me, what's happening in Palestine today? What's the talk on the streets? Is it all about the British and the French, and how they're going to divide up the countries?"

"That," he said, "and this new thing about the Jews. They've been coming to Palestine for twenty or so years, but since this war, they're beginning to come to the country in droves. Ever since this Balfour thing, they've been emigrating from all over Eastern Europe, from Poland and southern Russia and the Baltic. You should see them when they arrive. Filthy men and women and their ragamuffin children. Barely a suitcase between them. And all they do is fall down on their knees when they set foot on dry land and kiss the ground. Honestly. You'd think they'd just arrived in Paradise. But the look of them! They're really down and out. For the past six months, they've been arriving here with thick woollen coats and scarves in the sweltering heat and some of them don't even have suitcases, they just carry bundles of things wrapped in wax paper or some foreign newspaper and tied up with string. When they've kissed the ground like some wog in a mosque, they stand on the wharves like children on their first day of school, just waiting for someone to come along and help them."

"And does somebody come along?" she asked.

"Oh yes. The Jews are very well organized. There's a very wealthy Jew called Rothschild, and he's spent a fortune making sure they've got somewhere to go and clothes and stuff. He's bought lots and lots of land from the Arabs and the Turks so the Jews can settle here. They all seemed to get absorbed into the small farms. They're really very enterprising. I've only been here for a couple of months, and even in that space of time I've seen them transform the landscape. And they can't even speak a word of English. Very enterprising, these Jews. Tell me, have you heard of this chappie called Rothschild. I've heard of him . . . I suppose he's part of the banking family."

Gertrude thought back seven years, before the Great War, when she was in London, and had attended a dinner party given by the chancellor of the exchequer at No. 11, Downing Street. She was the guest of the foreign secretary, and at the dinner party, the English, German, and French branches of the Rothschild family had been in attendance, probably for the last time together, bemoaning the fact that Europe was heading for a catastrophe.

"Yes," she said casually, "I've heard of him."

Gertrude was beginning to become a bit tired of the callow and ingenuous Timothy Haldane. At first, it had been amusing to be so anonymous in his youthful eyes. Everywhere she went her reputation seemed to precede her, and people treated her either with grave suspicion, or with embarrassing deference. When she first met him on the dockside, she was thrilled he didn't know her, he didn't treat her like some minor visiting royalty, and she enjoyed the experience of being treated like an ordinary English lady traveling the world after the war. But now she found Timothy to be somewhat silly and superficial, like all the young men she'd been introduced to when she was coming out, all marriageable candidates, yet none of whom held the slightest bit of interest for her.

"I've got a good idea," she said enthusiastically. "Why don't we go to Jerusalem, so you can introduce me to Haj Mohammed Amin al-Husseini."

The young man looked surprised. "I think you mean Kamil al Husseini, who's the Mufti of Jerusalem."

"No," Gertrude insisted. "I'll meet the mufti at some stage in the near future. Right now, I want to meet Amin al-Husseini—same family, different person. You see, he's much more interesting. I've heard he's a bit of a young firebrand, and is setting himself up to become the next mufti when the current one shuffles off this mortal coil. Meeting Amin is a priority of mine, and it should be fun."

Timothy looked at her in astonishment. "But . . . good God . . . Husseini? I'd be much happier if you met the current mufti, who's a much more reasonable fellow. But not Amin. I really don't think I could introduce you to him."

"And why not?" she asked, her tone somewhat imperious.

"Do you know what kind of person he is?"

"Why don't you tell me," she asked in a much less harsh voice.

"Well from what I gather, he's a nasty piece of work. I know he's pro-British, indeed a keen supporter of our rule here, but I'm not given to trusting him. He's running with a pretty nasty group of people, inciting all sorts of problems. He hates the Jews with a vengeance, and is whipping up trouble for them, talking about killing them and murder and pushing them into the sea and all that sort of stuff, an attitude which I must say I find quite surprising from a man of God."

She turned to him, and asked, "What makes you think he's a man of God?"

"Well, he's studied Islam, and he's preaching in the Mosques, and . . ."

"Dear boy," she said, "I've studied Christianity, and I too could set up a platform and preach in the marketplace, but that wouldn't make me a woman of God. Amin al-Husseini is a hideous anti-British, anti-Jewish bigot who's going to cause the High Commissioner of Palestine, when one is appointed, the most awful trouble. Just because he's got some qualifications in religious law from an Egyptian University, and just because he's been on pilgrimage to Mecca, doesn't make his heart or his mind holy. Quite the reverse, in fact. And as for him being pro-British, he's the most anti-British person in Palestine. He fought for the Turks until a year before the war ended, and then when he realized they were going to lose, he defected from the army, crawled back to Jerusalem, and without feeling the slightest bit of shame, told everybody he'd swapped sides."

Timothy Haldane looked at her in astonishment. "How on Earth did you know all that?" he asked.

"It's my job to know all that. It's also my job to meet with people like Husseini, and advise the British Foreign Office about what he's likely to do in the future. He's dangerous now, and I predict he'll be a constant source of trouble for our administration, for the Jews, the Christians, and just about everybody else in the future.

"Now, young man, if you'll kindly instruct your driver to turn south and take me to Jerusalem, I'd rather like to call in on Haj Amin al-Husseini, and see what he's like for myself."

Timothy did as he was told, and sat quietly beside the gray-haired lady as the car negotiated the narrow streets from the top of the hill overlooking Haifa to the coastal road which ran between the north and the new city of Tel Aviv, formed in 1909 when the Jewish quarter of Jaffa became so overcrowded with immigrants new buildings had to be erected with the creation of a nearby suburb. Gertrude took out some briefing notes from her portfolio, and began to read them.

After a few more minutes of silence, Timothy interrupted her, and asked, "I know this might sound impertinent . . . well, silly

really, but are you important? I mean, and I don't want to seem
as if I'm being rude or anything, but the colonel usually escorts
important people. I assumed because he'd asked me to look after
you, you were, well, I don't quite know how to say this, but . . ."

"Unimportant? I suppose importance is a relative thing. I don't
know your colonel, but I assume he views women as little more
than adornments to men, and therefore not particularly worth
bothering with."

She turned back to the notes which the Foreign Office had
prepared for her and which were waiting for her when her ship
docked in Haifa.

Almost in a whisper, the increasingly concerned Timothy
Haldane asked, "Are you in the government?"

"No,"

"Are you in the Foreign Office? I notice you're reading—"

"Oh for Heaven's sake, Timothy, what is this? A parlour game
with lots of questions? Your intelligence service should have told
you about me. I'm a senior political officer in Mesopotamia.
I'm advising the British government on the mood of the Arabs
throughout the whole of this area so they can decide future policy.
That's why the prime minister particularly asked me to come here
to Palestine. And I've been here many times before you were born,
living in the tents of Arabic and Druze tribal leaders."

And suddenly his eyes widened in shock. "My God, you're the
woman who . . . Lawrence of Arabia . . . that woman from the Paris
Peace Conference. You're—"

"Gertrude Bell. Yes, Timothy, I know who I am, and I'd like to
catch up on my reading. Keep an eye on the driver and don't let
us get lost."

~

His house was large by Jerusalem standards. It was made of the
cream-colored stone which made the city burn white in the
morning and transmute into burnished gold as the sun descended
into the Mediterranean. The house was set on one of the hills

overlooking the old walled city, and in its grounds were olive trees and a small number of grape vines hung from trellises. In the gardens, beneath the trellises and in the house were large numbers of people, standing around in groups, talking and listening. And waiting.

Looking through the car window as it drew up to the front door, Timothy said urgently, "I think he's having some sort of gathering. We're not expected, so maybe we should come back tomorrow."

"No! That's what happens with the houses of all religious leaders. From morning till night, they're packed with well-wishers and supplicants and quacks and schemers. It's common practice, believe me. We'll just walk in, say we want to see the Haj, and he'll see us."

She put her hand on the doorknob, but Timothy restrained her. She knew he was terribly ill at ease, but didn't know why. "Look Miss Bell, Gertrude, I'm not sure this is the best idea."

"Timothy, please let me be the judge of that. I've considerable experience in dealing with people like Haj Husseini."

"But I really don't think my colonel would like us to be seeing him without the permission of HQ. My colonel always requires us to ask his permission on political and religious matters, and the colonel hasn't given us permission to visit this gentleman."

She turned to stare at him, and laughed. "Your colonel's permission? Dear boy, I have the permission of the prime minister of England, Mr. Lloyd George, to investigate the feelings of the Arabs in Palestine. That means I can visit anyone I like. I also report directly to the foreign secretary. I really don't need your colonel's permission to do anything."

He breathed deeply. "But I'm not ready for this. I'm only a junior officer. Mr. Husseini is a very important man, and a long way above my level. His uncle is the mayor of Jerusalem. My colonel should be visiting him, not me."

She smiled, and put her gloved hand on his. "Timothy, just follow me, do everything I do, salute to show you're British and you're not intimidated, and don't say a single word. Nod if you want to, but remain absolutely silent during the whole interview. Is that clear?"

He nodded. She got out of the car, straightened her dress, and marched confidently down the path and into the house. Timothy rushed to follow in her wake.

Inside the house, they were looked at with suspicion by Husseini's servants as an aisle opened through the throng to allow them access to the inner rooms. In fluent Arabic, much to Timothy's surprise, she said to a servant, "Inform His Excellency Haj Mohammed Amin al-Husseini that Miss Gertrude Bell representing the prime minister of Great Britain is here and seeks an audience with him."

They were shown into a large room, at the end of which was seated the man who's aspirations were to become the mufti of Jerusalem and spiritual and political leader of the Arabic world. Haj al-Husseini was a thin young man with an angular face and a growth of goatee beard on his chin. His clean-shaven cheeks were ruddy and leathery. Sitting cross-legged on a pile of cushions, he was wearing the black robes of a cleric but, Gertrude noticed with surprise, the white turban of a mufti, a rank to which he was not yet entitled, and an indication of the man's hubris.

Gertrude bowed low, so did Timothy, who straightened up immediately, and saluted. Gertrude continued her abasement until Husseini said, "Rise Miss Bell. Please, come and sit before me. And your young man may also approach."

Gertrude told Timothy to follow her and sit behind her.

"To what do I owe the pleasure of this visit? Your reputation precedes you. You are known throughout Palestine and the lands of Arabia and Mesopotamia. But I didn't know you were in Jerusalem, or I would have invited you to dine with me."

"Excellency," she said, "I only arrived in Palestine this morning, and my first visit has been to pay you my respects."

He beamed a smile, but behind his obvious pride and delight, she perceived the eyes of a rodent.

"You visit me before you visit the mufti? Is this courtesy or disrespect for Islam?" he asked.

"It is political expediency. His Holiness the Mufti is a man of august bearing and great stature. He dislikes the French, which pleases me, and he believes Palestine is and should continue to be Syria and has aligned himself with my friend and counsellor, Faisal, which also pleases me. But Excellency, I concern myself today with one who would be leader of Palestine. It is your views I seek on what should be done in this land of Abraham, Isaac, and Jacob."

"And Mohammed, Miss Bell? Where is the Prophet in this trinity of yours? Never forget that Islam has given the world the last and greatest of all the prophets of God, Mohammed, and that the Prophet, peace and blessings be upon him, has received all the truth from God that is ever to be revealed, and that Mohammed rested overnight here in Jerusalem with his horse Borak before he ascended into heaven and sat at the feet of Allah."

His followers murmured in assent, and repeated the reverence of the Prophet. Timothy, too nervous to look around and not understanding a word of what was happening, began to wonder if they'd get out of there alive.

She frowned. "But Excellency, my reading of the Koran finds no mention, even once, of the holy city of Jerusalem. And surely it is questionable as to whether Mohammed, peace and blessings be upon him, ever set foot in Jerusalem? My knowledge of the Koran, again, tells me his nocturnal journey was nothing more than a vision during which the Prophet visited a remote mosque. This is said in sura 17, verse 1. Yet how could the Prophet visit a mosque when the great religion of Islam had not yet spread beyond him and his immediate followers in Mecca and Medina? Your predecessors in the time of the Caliphate believed that by the words *remote*, the Prophet was referring to a vision of Kairuoan in Tunisia, or of Damascus in Syria. Never was Jerusalem mentioned."

She deliberately didn't look at him, but kept her eyes focussed on the ground at his feet. To look him directly in the eyes would be too much of a challenge at this stage of their conversation. She had said enough. Now it was time for her to remain silent, and for him to respond.

He nodded. "You are both right, and wrong," he said slowly, his voice rising so the followers could hear. "Tradition has it that by the remote mosque, the Prophet, peace and blessings be upon him, was referring to Jerusalem. It is for this reason I will put a covering of purest gold on the dome of the Mosque of Omar, and also restore to magnificence the mosque of al-Aqsa when I am in command of this nation."

"And will you seek the help of your brothers, the Jews, in purchasing the gold? They have excellent contacts in the markets and bourses of Europe."

"I will seek the help of nobody, Miss Bell, especially the Jews. Their home is in Europe. Their houses are the slums of Warsaw and Moscow and Budapest and Riga, in the ghettos which have been constructed and walled so Christians will not be tainted by having to look at them. And we're not the first to wish to exclude the Jews. Don't forget the founder of Protestantism, Martin Luther, sought to have all Jews in Europe killed."

"Only when they rejected his teachings," she interrupted.

"And we will accept them as brothers when they convert to Islam. But while ever they remain Jews, Miss Bell, while ever they reject Mohammed, and your Jesus, then their home is not and never will be in Jerusalem and Jaffa and Haifa. This is our land, Miss Bell. It doesn't belong to the British or the Jews or the Christians. We have inhabited this land since the beginning of recorded history."

"Your land, Excellency? But most of the coastal plain of this land was a barren malarial swampland until the Jews invited your people in to assist them in the orange groves and the farms which they created. This was the land of nomads and a handful of villages until the Jews began to build their agriculture and their industries and their towns and cities."

In anger, Amin al-Husseini shouted, "We are the owners, and we are being invaded by Jews from across the sea . . ."

"But your own Prophet, Excellency, talked of your common links with the People of the Book."

"Our Prophet, Miss Bell, tried to win the Jews over to the truth of the Koran, but they rejected him, and so it is our mission to expunge the Jews from Arabic lands. How can we tolerate a cancer growing amongst us? For Palestine and the whole of Arabia to be truly Islamic, it must contain only Muslims—not Jews, not Christians, not Kurds, not Druze, not infidels, and not those of loose morals and ways which will cause us to stray from the path of righteousness."

"But the Jews have been separated from their homeland for two thousand years . . ."

"I am not a Zionist, Miss Bell," he said harshly. "Palestine is Arab. It always was, and it always will be. Even your own Mr. Edwin Montagu, a Jew and a member of Mr. Lloyd George's government, agrees."

Husseini reached down, and picked up a letter. He told her, "Mr. Montague wrote a memorandum to his cabinet colleagues after the Balfour Declaration was published. It was translated into Arabic and sent to me by my friends in London. I'll read you what he said.

"'Zionism has always seemed to me to be a mischievous political creed, untenable by any patriotic citizen of the United Kingdom. If a Jewish Englishman sets his eyes on the Mount of Olives and longs for the day when he will shake British soil from his shoes and go back to agricultural pursuits in Palestine, he has always seemed to me to have acknowledged aims inconsistent with British citizenship and to have admitted that he is unfit for a share in public life in Great Britain, or to be treated as an Englishman.'"

He put down the document, and Gertrude, mentally cursing the Balfour Declaration and Montagu's memorandum in response, said, "Mr. Montagu speaks as a patriotic and powerfully assimilated Englishman who is accorded all the privileges which a democracy like England has to offer. But the same can't be said for the millions of downtrodden Jews who, for a thousand years, have been subjected to hideous persecution at the hands of the Russians and the Poles and the other governments of Eastern Europe. These pathetic wretches aren't members of the British establishment— they're a demoralized, subjugated, and oppressed minority living in a murderous atmosphere of hatred. They look towards Palestine as their own land to which they can return and which they can share with their brother Muslims."

"Then, Miss Bell, they will find a welcome in this land which will be a million times worse than any persecution they faced in their ghettos. Let them leave Russia and Poland if they want, but let them go to America or Africa or Patagonia. Let them not come here if they want to live, because they will be pushed into the Mediterranean by the iron fist and righteous zeal of Islam."

As his tirade ended, his followers applauded and shouted encouragement. Timothy Haldane was shocked by the sudden increase of noise and tension in the room, and became even more concerned for their safety, looking around the room for an escape plan. His hand slipped towards the sidearm in his belt. He didn't know what was being said, but he knew Gertrude was getting the worst of it, and they were alone and nobody knew they were there.

"But Excellency," she said when the hubbub had quietened down. "Surely it is against the tenets of Islam to separate a worshipper from his place of worship. For there are places of great significance in Palestine for all people, and especially to the worship of the Jewish and Christian faiths. This was recognized by that greatest of all Islamic warriors, Saladin. It was he who allowed the Jews and the Christians their worship, despite the havoc wreaked by the Crusaders. It was he who allowed all religions their right to their holy places. Jerusalem is the home of the three great religions which worship the one true God. For the Jews, there is the Temple of Solomon with its Western Wall. And for Christians, there is the Church of the Holy Sepulchre and many other churches of the faith. And for Islam, there are the two mosques on the Holy Mount. There is room for all. Can Islam be happy to separate the faithful from their worship?"

"Indeed it can, if that worship excludes the truth of the Koran. But Miss Bell, you didn't come here to discuss Islam with me, did you? For what purpose did you seek this interview?"

"To see what type of leader you will make, Excellency, so I can report back to my prime minister and advise him on the future of this land."

"And why should I concern myself with the views of your prime minister, when the tenure of the British will be so short they will not even be noticed. Like the Crusaders, you will be driven from this land."

"And are you Saladin?"

"If that is God's will."

"But Saladin wasn't an Arab, Excellency, he was a Kurd. And isn't it also the Kurds you want to expel from Palestine?"

For the first time, Husseini frowned, feeling that he was losing the conversation. He looked anxiously at his followers, listening carefully to the extraordinary spectacle of a woman dealing with their leader.

He was now worried this woman had scored an important debating point. "Miss Bell, please give my compliments to your prime minister, Mr. Lloyd George. I think our conversation is at an end."

He picked up a document, and began to read it. But Gertrude didn't move. Surprised, he looked up. She was staring at him directly, challenging him, her mouth a thin grimace.

"You wish to say more?" he asked.

"I wish to say this, Haj Husseini. Many British soldiers fought and died in this land to release you from the yoke of the Turks. In a few months, a high commissioner will be appointed by the British government. He will rule this land. He will be supported by a host of British soldiers, not the mere handful which you see today in the streets of Palestine, but reinforcements which will be as grains of sand in the desert. This could become a great nation for Arabs and Jews and Christians alike. There is space, provided there is good will. But be assured, Excellency, any hostility towards the British, or the Jews under their protection, or the Christians, or the Kurds, will bring forth a mighty response, and many of your followers will die. Is that your desire, Haj Husseini? To turn Palestine into a graveyard?"

"Insh'allah, Miss Bell. But be you also assured, that if the British reinforcements come to Palestine with their rifles and artillery, then I shall declare *jihad*, and every man, woman and child will consider it their holy duty to kill a soldier. Can your army, no matter how many grains of sand it numbers, fight an army which numbers all the stars in heaven? I think not. Please convey that message to your superiors."

Gertrude sighed, and rose from the stool. She shook her head at Timothy, and felt desperately sad for the Jews who were flocking to the Holy Land with hope in their hearts for a secure future.

~

Damascus, October, 1919

He held out his arms and embraced her, to the surprise of the entire court and especially his younger brother Zeid. Normally, those who entered his court bowed and abased themselves, but this tall, middle-aged English woman had walked ramrod straight towards Faisal's throne and stood there beaming a smile. And Faisal, ignoring the protocols he had introduced when he became King of Syria a year earlier, had left his throne, walked down the three steps of the plinth, and hugged her as though she was his closest male friend.

The court, composed of his friends from the Kingdom of Hejaz, khaki-clad army officers, as well as black Abyssinian eunuch slaves sent as a gift from his father, had not seen anything like this level of familiarity with a woman.

"My dearest Gertrude Bell. How delightful and unexpected a pleasure this is. Why didn't you tell me you were coming to Syria? I would have organised a banquet in your honor."

"The British Foreign Office informed our people here, but there was nobody to greet me when I arrived, and I had to find a hotel room on my own. That's why, Highness, you didn't know of my coming. I shall have words with Great Britain's *Charge d'Affair* in Syria."

The king took her hand, and led her away from the audience chamber into an ante-room, where they sat at a long table. They were joined by Prince Zeid, Jafar Pasha and Nuri al-Sa'id, the king's closest advisors. She knew of Jafar's and Nuri's standing in the king's eyes, and was interested that they were both of Mesopotamian origin. She also knew they were both zealous nationalists who resented both the British and the French, but also that they were men of the highest intelligence and both realized there had to be a transition period of many years before the process of self-government could take place without disaster resulting.

As they sat, a servant immediately brought in glasses of apple tea and licorice water. Faisal introduced Gertrude to the three men, and explained their close relationship. In his remarks, he tended to overstate her wisdom and her importance to foreign policy, telling his advisors were it not for Gertrude, Britain would undoubtedly have lost the war in the Middle East.

She wanted to object to his flattery, but before she could do so, he turned to her and asked, "What do you hear of my friend Lawrence?"

"After we left Paris, he returned to England to work on his manuscript, *The Seven Pillars of Wisdom*. As far as I know, Your Highness, he's only just beginning the process of re-writing it. He fears he's going to be interrupted in his literary endeavours because of circumstances beyond his control. He sent me some correspondence a few weeks ago, telling me Mr. Lowell Thomas is, to quote the American journalist, 'playing him up big time' in the United States, and there is a lecture tour mooted of New York, Washington, and Chicago. God help us all if it goes to Lawrence's head, which I'm sure it will. Knowing the dear boy, he'll blow the whole thing out of proportion, and then he'll have to justify his actions to history."

"And why are you here, Gertrude? I would hope you're here on a personal visit to your friend Faisal to continue the joyous nights we spent together in Paris, but knowing you, you're here as a secret agent and a spy, covertly gathering information for the British government, or some such dastardly act. Are you here to report to the government on how well Syria is doing as the world's first totally independent Arab nation in a thousand years?"

She laughed. "As I'm sure you already know, Majesty, I've been asked to visit all the countries of the Middle East in which Great Britain has an interest in order to report back on the mood of the Arab street. The question of self-rule is uppermost in the minds of His Majesty's government."

"Then your visit to Syria is wasted, I'm afraid, my dear. For tomorrow, I am off to England myself in order to report that after a year of independence, we're running well, if not altogether efficiently. I also need to gather British support for my kingdom. The French are particularly unhappy about our independence, and believe they have an inalienable right to Syria and all the land to the north of Palestine. It is my hope to persuade Lloyd George to force them to look elsewhere for a colony."

She nodded. "And how are the French behaving? Are they rattling their sabers?"

"They're very angry that the Americans, King and Crane have come down firmly in favor of a mandate over this land which should be operated by this new League of Nations their President Wilson is setting up. M. Clemenceau is beside himself with fury. They see this as their land, and are unhappy about sharing the rule with me. But no matter how many French soldiers there are, or how many reinforcements will be sent from Paris, there are many more Syrians than French, and they cannot hope to colonise an unwilling people."

She shook her head in sadness. "A few days ago, sire, I interviewed a man who will be a future spiritual leader of the Palestinian people when the present mufti dies. He said the same thing. He is preaching an *intifada* to his people."

354

"You speak of Haj Amin al-Husseini. Yes, he is an ambitious young man."

"Ambition which will inevitably lead to danger and distress for his people if he continues with his present militancy," Gertrude said.

"Or danger and distress for the British?" said Nuri al-Sa'id.

Gertrude turned and looked closely at him. "Indeed, Excellency, it could be a disaster for all concerned. This war has caused millions and millions of deaths. Many countries have lost an entire generation, the flower of their youth. Surely we've learned enough about the futility of war to understand nothing is gained by fighting. Surely it's time to compromise, to appreciate each other's point of view, to accommodate the needs of the needy and eschew the greed of the greedy."

"And who are the greedy, Miss Bell?" asked Prince Zeid. "The French who hardly fought in this theater of war, and yet who are shouting out that this is their country by rights because of some agreement made by two men called Sykes and Picot who didn't bother to ask the inhabitants of the land for their opinion? Or the British who want to administer Mesopotamia and Persia and everywhere else because we Arabs are rich in oil and you need oil to drive your cars and ships and machinery? Are we greedy, Miss Bell, for wanting ownership of land which we've lived on since the time of Adam and Eve?"

She began to answer, but he cut across her, "And who are the needy? The Jews who live in Europe and who now are immigrating to lands in which Jews haven't set foot since the time of the Romans? Yes, they're needy, but why should they benefit at the expense of the Arab?"

"Prince Zeid, your brother, King Faisal, reached an agreement with Dr. Weizmann, the head of the Zionist movement, in which he clearly expressed his approval of a Jewish migration to develop the land of Palestine. He had the foresight to understand the need for sharing the country. I think we could all learn from his wisdom," said Gertrude.

"Is that another reason you've come here?" asked King Faisal. "To speak on behalf of the Jews?"

She shook her head. "No, I'm here on behalf of my government to try to find a pathway through the morass of promises and undertakings and expectations. But I can see both sides of the problem when it comes to Jewish immigration into Palestine. I have great sympathy for their plight, as I have great sympathy for the expectations of the Palestinian peoples. And that, sir, is why I'm asking whether you will intercede with Haj Husseini. I believe he'll listen to you. You are the most respected Arab leader of an Arab nation. You have great status in the eyes of your people. If you intercede on the part of the Jews with Husseini, he might soften his stance."

Faisal looked at her in surprise. Before he could say anything, she said softly, "Majesty, when I was a young girl, I harboured a dream that I could assist all the Arab tribes into uniting to become a single nation called Arabia. But to unite, they have to coalesce under one leader, as the Arabs united under Saladin in ancient times. Many said it was a girlish dream, that the Arabs will always remain a disunited tribal people. But I believed then, as I believe now, that it is possible. After such a terrible war, with such hideous losses, I don't believe the Arabs will look towards a tribal leader. A man such as Abd al-Aziz ibn Sa'ud. Men such as he cannot see beyond their tribes and their own needs. But I believe the Arabs will unite under a fearless warrior—one who was victorious in leading his army against the Turks—a man of wisdom and one who rules wisely and leads his people for their benefit. You are such a leader, Excellency. Under your guidance I believe Arabia, under the benign insight of Islam, can become one of this new world's great nations and take its place as a united nation of many different peoples with different approaches to the same God."

Faisal shook his head sadly, reached over and held her hand. "My poor Gertrude. The differences between the Arab peoples are as nothing compared to the differences between the Europeans.

356

France is currently planning to topple me from my throne, against the demands of England and America. My dear, I'm flattered by your confidence in me, but I am a puppet controlled by those who pull my strings."

"Perhaps if you were to go to Jerusalem, and negotiate with Haj Amin al-Husseini, the British and the French would view your rule here differently. Then—"

"But Gertrude, surely Palestine is a British problem."

FIFTEEN

Baghdad, November, 1919

The question uppermost in her mind was whether to sign the report Gertrude Bell, or Gertrude Lowthian Bell CBE. The latter, which included her imperial honor, and which trumped any that her boss had been granted, would send the senior political man in Mesopotamia into an apoplectic rage. It was mischievous of her and she'd love to see A. T. Wilson in a state of fury. But whilst the latter would possibly cause her to be considered ostentatious in London, the former was more politic. Then, of course, she could simply call herself G.L. Bell, but that was equally problematic, for some might fail to recognise the report had been written by a woman. In the end, she settled for simply adding the initials GLB to the last page, which would pacify Wilson, mollify London, and act as an enigma for the bright young things in the Foreign Office to work out.

The report had taken her weeks to write from a thousand pages of notes which she'd been carefully keeping since she'd left Paris months earlier. Nor was it a simple question of transcribing the notes, for what the government in London needed was interpretation, analysis, and objectivity. They were receiving facts from their intelligence services and high commissions throughout the region, but only someone of vast experience like Gertrude was capable of reading between the lines and construing meaning from seemingly random events.

Her concerns about the growth of Arab nationalism on the streets were justified by the events which were beginning to become the norm rather than the exception. British political officials were being held by armed groups, not for ransom, but to extract promises of freedom or to relinquish land and territory. Tribes which had once fought the Turks were now turning their gun sights on the British forces, and towns which had once flown the British flag were becoming hotbeds of dissent and resistance.

Gertrude was deeply worried for the future of Britain in Arabia, and also for the Arabic nations themselves. The emotional desire for Arabic homelands to be free of imperial Europe was impelling the march towards self-government and nationhood at a pace which would eventually lead to disaster. She knew the Arab people weren't ready for self-government. There were no Arabic-run organs of government in place, no civil service bodies which they could easily take over without years of training, and worst of all, there was no experience of governance among the leaders. A free press, free judicial system, a police force distanced from government, universal education for both boys and girls, equality between the sexes, a fair taxation system, a way of promotion which didn't involve nepotism or bribery . . . all these were unknown in Arabia. The doctrine of the separation of powers was an idea which had never entered an Arab's head.

So any pre-emptive move towards nationhood, let alone pan-Arabism, would result in anarchy, in internecine battles, in death and bloodshed. Eventually the strongest, the most violent, and not necessarily the best, would become ruler, and with the potential of a fortune of oil which lay beneath the sands, that could spell disaster for everyone. Her dreams of a united Arabia were slipping further and further away. Even she now saw them as utopian.

But neither could Britain, or France or Russia or Italy or any of the Great Powers, hope to replicate the sort of hold which the Ottoman Empire had over the Arabic nations before the war. Gertrude knew, and had written, that Britain must accept the idea of partnerships with the Arabs in order for both to benefit. And she stressed that Zionism and the Palestine question must be worked upon as a matter of great priority, or the area would erupt into a new battlefront. She informed the government in her report that King Faisal, who ruled Syria between Damascus and Aleppo, was doing better than expected, despite the obstacles which had been placed in his path by the French, and must be considered as a future leader of all the Arab peoples.

She sealed her report, toasted her monumental effort with a glass of champagne drunk alone late at night in her office, and sent it by urgent diplomatic courier to Lord Balfour, David Lloyd George and a handful of others in the British government. And she pointedly refused to give a copy, or even inform A. T. Wilson, her boss and Percy Cox's replacement, of the contents of her report. Something mischievous within her wanted to irritate the nasty and officious little man who had been given the job which clearly would have been hers, had she not been a woman. He was the embodiment of all that was wrong with Britain's imperial system of patronage and its chauvinistic attitude towards ability. All her life, she'd fought and struggled against the oppression of those who saw her as a woman, not as a diplomat or an explorer or a linguist or one of the most skilled political brains in the nation. And people like Arnold Talbot Wilson, an army man of little education and minimal ability, who treated those around him with contempt and condescension, was the epitome of what she was fighting against. His superciliousness towards his staff, and his arrogance towards Arabs, Jews, Kurds and others, caused him to be known in headquarters as "the despot from mess-pot"

In the ensuing three weeks between sending off her report and receiving the response, Gertrude did a round of socializing by visiting important people in Mesopotamia. She also met many of the dozens of young English women who were allowed into the country to marry their soldier sweethearts, now that the hostilities were over.

But in the middle of December, during a particularly thunderous downpour, Gertrude arrived at her office, and found a note from A. T. Wilson. She and Wilson hadn't formed anywhere near the same relationship she had enjoyed with Percy Cox. Indeed, their exchanges swung between cold formality and restrained hostility. During the last years of the war, Wilson had become Cox's deputy in Mesopotamia. From the very beginning, he had taken an intense dislike to her. He didn't believe there was any place for women in government service, except as amanuenses, and objected strongly to her using her contacts at the high levels of the British government. He was an odd man, trying to prove he was utterly brilliant academically despite his lack of a university education, sprinkling his reports to India and London with quotations from the greatest of English writers and Greek and Roman philosophers. But he shut her out of the loop in the transmission of his information, making her work as though one of her eyes was permanently closed. She'd sent off the report to Whitehall without showing him, to let him know what it felt like to be left out of the loop.

Percy Cox was so different to Wilson. Percy was the archetype of the gentleman mentor, but he'd gone to Persia as British Minister, taking charge of the entire country, and had been overruled by Whitehall when the mandarins didn't take his advice to elevate Gertrude into the job, but instead was forced to leave Wilson in charge of Mesopotamia. She knew he was opening and reading her incoming mail, as well as criticising her to all and sundry, and she knew he'd tried on a number of occasions to have her recalled to London as an incompetent, but his demands had fallen on deaf ears.

She picked up the note, politely asking her to visit him in his office at her convenience. She knew what it was about, and she was as prepared as she could be. Gertrude steeled herself for the onslaught, walked the corridors from her office upstairs to his suite, and knocked on his door.

"Ah, Miss Bell. I'm so pleased you've found the time to visit me. Thank you for coming."

She smiled, and walked over to a chair. She saw a copy of her report on his desk, the one which she'd sent to Balfour. She was surprised it had been returned so quickly.

Wilson stood from his desk, and walked to the window. He faced the garden, his back to her, and said, "I've asked you here because of this unfortunate report you've sent to London, a report which should, by rights, have come through me. I wonder if you'd be so good as to explain your actions."

Gertrude remained silent. As did Wilson. After an embarrassing lapse of time, he turned, and asked, "Did you hear what I said?"

"Of course. But I thought you were talking to the window, or someone in the garden. When a gentleman addresses me, I expect to be able to see his face."

Tight-lipped, Wilson returned to his desk, and sat down facing her. "Miss Bell, do you have any idea of the damage which your report could do if it got into the wrong hands?"

"Are you saying the prime minister and the foreign secretary have the wrong hands?"

"You're suggesting Britain gives up its interests in Mesopotamia. That it leaves the area in the hands of Arabs and nomads and tribesmen. That we support the elevation of a suitable candidate with money and facilities to become the leader of a pan-Arab nation which you seem to think would partner Great Britain in the development of this new mega-nation's riches. Have you lost your senses? Are you completely mad?"

"I'm not in the slightest bit mad, Captain Wilson. Indeed, I don't think I've ever said anything saner in all my life. To expect the Arabs, in their present mood, to accept suzerainty by a foreign power—"

"Foreign power?" he shouted. "Foreign power! We are that foreign power, Miss Bell. May I remind you the British fought for this land! We beat the Turks. Thousands of our men died for this wasteland, and you expect us just to give it away. Well, Miss Bell, let me state quite clearly we have no intention of retreating when we have such a wealth of assets at our disposal. To even suggest such a move would, in my opinion, rank as high treason."

"Then we will be driven from this land by force, Captain Wilson. I've seen the mood of the Arab in the streets. I've been to the capital cities and the large towns, and I've seen for myself the frame of mind of the people. We're sitting atop a volcano, and unless we can reach some form of accommodation, it'll blow us all to kingdom come."

He shook his head in disbelief. "You really have taken leave of your senses. For five hundred years, the Ottoman has been in charge, for better or for worse. And in all those centuries, while Britons were being shaped by minds such as Shakespeare and Milton and Blake, while we were industrializing and modernizing and inventing new sciences with which to explore the inner workings of the Earth and the movement of the stars, the Arab was sitting under a date tree letting someone else do his thinking. What on Earth, my good woman, makes you think he's suddenly going to change into a noble savage and rise up in righteous anger to cast off the shackles of imperialism? Eh? He's lazy, indolent, duplicitous, and utterly untrustworthy. And he'll cower like a dog when he stares down the barrel of a Lee Enfield."

"My God!" she snapped, "You sound just like the wife of an army cook."

He stared at her, not understanding the remark. Gertrude stood up and turned from him. She had intended to remain calm through the inevitable tirade, but it was all too much. Trying not to make her voice shake with fury, she said, "Firstly, Captain Wilson, you will alter the tone in which you speak with me. And kindly do not refer to me as your good woman. I hold the honor of being a commander of the British Empire and whether you like me or not, you will respect me for an honor in which I was invested by His Majesty. Secondly, I am the most senior female political officer in the empire, not some typist you can bully by screaming and shouting. Thirdly, I was commissioned directly by the prime minister through the foreign secretary to write my report which I have sent to them directly. If they have sought to include you in their correspondence, then kindly take issue with them, and not with me. And finally, might I remind you that while you've been wining and dining in the mess here, I have been onto the street in most Arabic capitals during the past months, so I assure you that I know far more about the mind and intent of the Arab than do you!

"But that's the real problem, isn't it Captain Wilson. Your fury is less with what I said, than because I sent the report to Whitehall, and not through you. Do you wonder why? Because you would have sought to influence me, you and the other members of the general staff here. You believe Great Britain can maintain her interests indefinitely by dint of force. Well, my travels and my enquiries have proven to me without a shadow of a doubt that yours is an untenable position. It will not work, Mr. Wilson, and you will have the blood of many people on your hands if you advise the government otherwise. Had you been with me as I travelled around Arabia listening and observing, Mr. Wilson, instead of sitting in your office drinking cups of tea, I might have more respect for your opinion."

She began to walk out of his office, when he said, "Miss Bell, I haven't dismissed you yet."

She turned and glowered at him, "No, but you've been trying to do precisely that ever since Percy Cox went to Persia. Do you think I don't feel the insult of being ignored in the mess, that I don't know about your correspondences with London concerning how to rid yourself of me, and that I'm not hurt by your snide remarks to the other officers about my relationship with the Arabs? I'm not given to tears, Captain Wilson, and you will never see them in my eyes, no matter how much you try to drive me to them. But I am not somebody you can denigrate without suffering the very grave risk that I will give as good as I get."

He looked shocked. "I'm not trying to make you cry. I just have very grave reservations about your competence. This report," he said, slapping it with his hand. "It's monstrous. Are you quite aware of how large Britain's commercial interests are in Mesopotamia? Half of everything this country imports comes from Great Britain. Not just coal and iron, but clothes, wool, cotton . . . everything. And do you realize Britain imports nearly half of the goods this country produces? Figs, olive oil, dates, grain. But that's nothing compared to what's being discovered beneath the sand. Our people estimate there's enough oil here to supply the British Navy and our new air force, and our entire industry, with enough oil for a thousand years. Look at America. They're producing nearly 400 million barrels of oil a year, and England's got none. Not a blessed drop. And now, suddenly, by the grace of God, we could develop wealth beyond anybody's wildest imagination. And by the grace of Gertrude Bell, the British government is being encouraged to give it all away!"

He sat down, feeling spent, looking suddenly gaunt and gray. She was too angry and hurt by his remarks to offer him any consolation.

"I'm not convinced you fully realize the impact of this report and the damage which it could do to British interests. Oil will turn the wheels of industry during the next few centuries. Oil, Miss Bell, of which England has none . . . not coal of which England has much. Persia has a large supply of oil and is under our control. Our boffins believe there's oil in vast quantities in Mosul in the north, as well as under our very feet in the Tigris and the Euphrates area. If we build a railroad and a pipeline to the Mediterranean, then England's position as the pre-eminent naval power in the world will be unquestioned. It will lessen our utter dependence on the Suez Canal, the most vulnerable point in our passageway to the East. This will protect India, the jewel in the monarch's crown.

"Don't you see what you've done, Miss Bell. By your damnable report, you've put at risk all of that. If anyone in the British government acts upon your report, it could be the whole undoing of everything we've built over the past two hundred years."

She breathed deeply, and said softly to him, "Self-rule for Iraq, for Mesopotamia, is the only route possible to take this nation forward. A partnership in the development of the oil, in purchasing the produce of the country, will work. But the assets of this country must be owned by the Arabs, or the bloodbath I've spoken of in my report will surely happen. Whatever happens to Suez and India in the future is something which will happen anyway, oil or no oil, Iraq or no Iraq."

She turned back to the door. "I'm sorry we've had this disagreement, Captain Wilson, and I have no doubt you'll send a report to the government asking them to ignore everything I've written. That is your right as our senior man in Iraq. But one of us will certainly live to regret the consequences of his or her action . . . and I pray to God it's not me."

She turned to leave his office, but before she walked through the door, Wilson raised his voice again, and told her, "While you and Lawrence were away in Paris, Miss Bell, your reputation grew in Baghdad. Do you know what the Arabs are now calling you? You're now Umm al Mu'minin, the Mother of the Faithful."

She stopped again, and turned to him in shock. He sat at his desk, looking older than when she'd walked in a few minutes earlier. He wore a condescending smile. "Do you know the last person who bore that name, Miss Bell? It was Aisha, the wife of the Prophet Mohammed. Which makes me wonder on which side of the fence you're sitting. Theirs, or ours?"

She allowed him his pyrrhic victory and returned to her office, where she burst into tears.

~

The Palace of Westminster, London, England, April, 1920

The Speaker of the House called for order. The members on the treasury benches were sitting quietly, smirking at the opposition on the other side of the House of Commons. And the members of the opposition were shaking their order papers vigorously, shouting in anger at the government's attempt to stonewall on such an important issue. Winston Churchill had enlivened the debate, but it was now time for the Speaker to choose somebody from the Labor Party.

"Order! Order! Honorable members will remain seated, and will come to order. I call on the Honorable, the leader of the Labor Party, Mr. William Anderson."

Anderson, a tall, thin Scot, stood in his seat. His side of the House settled down, anticipating verbal pyrotechnics.

"Mr. Speaker, tonight we have heard, delivered to this Parliament from the mouth of the man entrusted by His Majesty with the governance of the nation, what can only be described as an excuse for an explanation from an excuse for a prime minister . . ."

His side of the House burst into laughter. The Speaker cautioned him for using un-parliamentary language, and called the House again to order.

Anderson continued, "Well may the prime minister deal with potential, but we on this side of the House deal in realities. And the reality I'm talking about, Mr. Speaker is the reality of £40 million a year. £40 million, Mr. Speaker, enough to keep His Majesty's government in pheasant and smoked salmon for a good many months . . ."

He was interrupted by a roar of laughter and a barrage of *here here's*. He continued, "Certainly there appears to be copious quantities of oil beneath the sands of Mesopotamia, but at what cost to the British taxpayer will it be delivered onto our British shores to grease the cogs of our industry? And what benefit will be this cost to the ordinary working man who is the backbone of this country, sleeves rolled up in the mill or choking to death down a coal mine, paying six pence a week in taxation so some Lancashire cotton mill owner or some Sheffield steel millionaire can make more money through enabling his machinery to run more cheaply and more efficiently?"

Again, his speech was punctuated by *here here's*. He turned to his colleagues to signal his approval, and noticed with some satisfaction the prime minister, Mr. Lloyd George was looking increasingly uncomfortable. Anderson held a folder in his hand, a blood-red folder of the type used by the Foreign Office for its ministerial briefings, and Mr. Lloyd George was looking with keen interest at the folder, no doubt wondering precisely what mischievous information, leaked to the opposition by some disgruntled civil servant, it contained. And glancing across at the press gallery, Anderson was equally pleased to notice several reporters had put down their newspapers, and were beginning to take interest in the debate. He wasn't concerned with the gentleman from *The Times*, but with the reporters from the *Daily Sketch* and the *Daily Express*, who wrote for the constituency which elected him and his colleagues. Next day's papers would make interesting reading.

"Mr. Speaker," he continued, opening his folder and extracting a piece of paper. "The Honorable members might not be aware of the precise commitment which the House has made to stationing troops in foreign lands. I would have thought once the war was over, it was time to bring our lads back. Yes, Mr. Speaker, we have to defend our empire, for that is in our national interests, but there has to be a balance between the money we spend on maintaining our overseas colonies, and the value of those colonies to the working class man.

"Stationing so many men abroad is costing this nation a fortune. It has already cost us untold misery in the millions of wonderful and brave young men we've lost on foreign fields, but today, Mr. Speaker, we have seventeen thousand British and forty-four thousand Indian troops in Mesopotamia."

This time he was interrupted by shouts of *shame*. He continued, "And if we add these sixty thousand expensive young men, plus their commanders and all the claret they can drink to the twenty-three thousand troops we've got stationed in Palestine, we're looking at nearly £40 million a year to keep our garrisons in place.

"Mr. Speaker, no man in this Parliament could deny the value of Mesopotamia to the future of Great Britain. They are inextricably linked. But surely, with Britain sitting on a thousand years of coal reserves, and with oil not yet proven as a fuel to equal the majesty of our own black gold, and with the very real prospect of damaging the livelihoods of our own coal miners, we should be far more circumspect in our funding to keep these warring factions of Arabs apart."

He closed the folder, and sat down to the cheers and approbation of his side. Those behind him slapped him on the back, and from the look on Mr. Lloyd George's face, he knew he'd done some damage. The question was, would the prime minister release the attack dogs in the form of William Ormsby-Gore and Winston Churchill, who could demolish logic with a brilliantly turned phrase, or would he rise to the occasion himself.

With some satisfaction, Anderson noticed the Prime minister indicated to the Speaker he wished to refute the argument himself. As the old Welshman stood, the House came to order.

"Mr. Speaker, I wonder what the Honorable member would say if we were to wander together through the wheat fields of Leicestershire or Nottinghamshire on a sunny day, and gaze across at an acre here, or an acre there of nodding grain about to be harvested. I wonder if he'd say to me that England could be so much greater, could feed herself better, if we had more land."

Anderson found himself frowning, wondering where the old fox was going with his argument.

"And the Honorable leader of the Labor Party would be right. England has some of the best farmers and the best farming land in the world. But not enough of it. We are hampered by our size. We are a great nation in a small land mass. It is my intention, therefore, Mr. Speaker, to give the House this assurance . . . that completely aside from the dates and figs and other wondrous bounty we can import from our friends in Mesopotamia, I intend to make fourteen thousand acres of land, land which was ravaged and devastated by the war with the Turks, rich and cultivable again, and that land, between the Tigris and the Euphrates, watered by the melting snow of the Taurus Mountains where these magnificent rivers rise in Turkey, nurtured by that golden orb of the sun which shines its munificence on the land, and grow such quantities of wheat it will become the greatest granary in the entire world producing inexpensive grains for bread to feed the families of Great Britain."

His remarks were greeted by government back benchers standing and cheering and waving their order papers at the opposition. But the prime minister wasn't finished.

"The Honorable leader of the Labour Party has asked whether the oil which will shortly be pumped from the depths of the desert will just benefit the wealthy mill owners and landed gentry. Yes, Mr. Speaker, it will. It will benefit the very rich. And it will also benefit the very poor. It will benefit everybody who buys a newspaper, who rides to work on an omnibus, who buys shoes made in a factory, who buys bread and butter and cheese. It will lower the costs of production and make our growing industries the most efficient in the world. It will clean the atmosphere from the terrible smogs and fogs caused by the burning of coal. It will power the motor cars which today are the province of the rich, but which will, within a handful of years, be cheap enough for everyone to drive. I predict a day, Mr. Speaker, when inexpensive fuel will not only drive our ships and make us masters of the High Seas, but will fuel such miracles of transportation that villages will no longer be remote, so families can leave their homes and drive into the pleasantness of the countryside to rest and relax after an exhausting week's work. I predict all these things, Mr. Speaker, because of the very real prospect of oil rising from the bowels of the earth beneath Mesopotamia, bubbling to the surface, and finding its way to our shores for the benefit of the British taxpayer."

The House erupted into cheers and cries of joy, but Lloyd George continued to stand waiting for silence. When the House had quietened down, he continued, "There is talk, Mr. Speaker, of Great Britain withdrawing its forces from that rich and wonderful desert land, talk that we should abandon the country because some of our soldiers are being killed by the Arab tribesmen. But what would happen if we withdrew? After the enormous expenditure which we have incurred in freeing that benighted nation from the withering despotism of the Turks, to hand it back to anarchy and confusion, and to take no responsibility for its development would be an act of folly and quite indefensible. Yet this is what the opposition wants us to do."

Again, the House erupted, except for the glum opposition, who merely sat there. Lloyd George resumed his seat, and was pleased to note the gentleman from *The Times* was still writing copious notes.

~

Baghdad, A Week Later

As she approached the headquarters of the British High Commission in Baghdad, she noticed A.T. Wilson's office lights were ablaze even though it was just after six o'clock in the morning. It was the very early hours of the morning which she most enjoyed, because there were no visitors, no interruptions, no urgent messages, and she could do at least a couple of hours work before everybody else's day began.

So as she walked through the gates of the commission, she was surprised to see not only his lights ablaze, but Captain Wilson walking about in his room. She was afraid something might be awry, but if it was, let him come and ask for her assistance. She wouldn't volunteer her help in the almost certain knowledge it would be rejected in the early stages of whatever the crisis was.

When she arrived at her desk, she saw a copy of *The Times* open onto the reports of parliamentary proceedings. And even as she read the first, second and third headlines of the story, she knew that was the reason Wilson had come in so early—to gloat.

Gertrude sat down and read the report of the parliamentary debate carefully. She glanced at the date on top of the newspaper, and realized the debate had occurred four days previously. Yet not a word had been cabled or transmitted. The cascading headlines in the newspaper told the story . . .

Mr. Lloyd George Commits to British Control Over Iraq

Labour Claims Unwarranted Expense in Keeping Troops in Middle East

Iraq Will Be World's Greatest Granary

Oil to Drive British Machinery

371

The report clearly inferred Mr. Lloyd George had decided to ignore Gertrude's report, and instead follow Wilson's, and the Baghdad High Commission's, and presumably the Foreign Office's advice.

She was devastated. She had assumed her carefully reasoned arguments would win over the calmer and more mature heads in London, and over-ride the jingoism of voices which put British interests as paramount over common sense. Why did they all think she was advocating a complete withdrawal of British interests from the Middle East, when she wasn't! All she was hoping was that Britain could avoid terrible conflicts in the future if it supported a supra-national leader and entered into a mutual partnership with Arabia. The results for England in the short-run wouldn't be as rich, but longer term, they would be secure, and England would prosper far more.

She re-read Lloyd George's words, and felt like crying. All her work, all her efforts had been in vain. What was the use? Why didn't she just give up, return to England, write her memoirs like everybody else, and live the life of a wealthy, spoiled woman, spending her declining years eating rich food in Claridge's and going to the theater. She would write for *The Times* or some magazine, and become the darling of the London set.

Footsteps approached her office over the polished wooden floor. She knew it was Wilson. She put down the newspaper, and determined now was the right time to announce her retirement from being a political officer. She would tell him, then write to dear Sir Percy Cox in Persia, and then she would sell her house, pack up her things and be back in London within three months. She felt like crying, like throwing things at the nasty little man who would soon be gloating in her office, but she would leave Iraq on her own terms, as a lady and as one of the most powerful women the British Empire had ever produced.

Captain A.T. Wilson appeared in the doorway. He was immaculately dressed in a three-piece gray woollen suit, a crisp white shirt and a brown school tie.

"Might I have a word, Miss Bell," he asked.

Without being given leave, he entered her office, and sat down in the chair before her desk. She was stunned by his appearance. He seemed to have aged ten years overnight.

"It appears we've both been somewhat ignored by our political lords and masters."

She looked at him in surprise. He nodded at the newspaper.

"The prime minister has decided not to accept the advice you gave the foreign minister in your report, but by a similar token, I have been informed the recommendations of myself and my political staff are also to be ignored. I seem to have been passed over."

She felt herself frowning and shaking her head. "I'm sorry, I have no idea what you're talking about," she said.

He sighed. "I might not be making much sense. I've been up all night with half the political officers, and I'm very tired. We all are. You see, London has just informed us the prime minister is going to a conference in San Remo—it's on the Italian Riviera—with George Clemenceau to finalize their arrangements for the lands which were formerly under Ottoman occupation."

Gertrude looked at him in consternation. The Paris Peace Conference had not ended with any conclusions for the Middle East, Faisal had walked out in disgust, and she knew another conference would have to be held to sort things out, but she had no idea it would be so soon.

"And what is likely to happen in San Remo?" she asked Wilson.

He cleared his throat. "We have advised, and the Foreign Office concurs, that Mesopotamia—Iraq—should remain British. The prime minister even said so himself in Parliament just a few days ago," he said, nodding to *The Times*.

Before she could speak, he continued, "But it seems his statement was little more than a negotiating ploy for the French. It appears Lloyd George and Clemenceau have already agreed of the division of these lands. Arabia will remain as it is, an independent peninsula under the control of ibn Sa'ud, although we will be there to guide him and hopefully influence him not to be belligerent towards his neighbours. The French have won their right to Syria, which will include Lebanon and will be mandated through the League of Nations to France. Mesopotamia and Palestine will be mandated to Great Britain."

"Then you've won!" said Gertrude.

"No, on the contrary. I and my office here have lost out badly. Indeed, Miss Bell, it appears you've won more than the rest of us. But it really isn't a question of win or lose, is it? It's a question of what's best for Britain. It appears Britain and France will accept mandates from this new League of Nations body in Geneva until the Arabs are capable of governing themselves and standing on their own two feet. And Great Britain will hasten that process as expeditiously as possible."

Gertrude felt her jaw drop. To have stared into the jaws of her own political and professional annihilation one minute, and then suddenly to have become the architect of good and sensible foreign policy the next, was almost more than she could stand.

"But Captain Wilson," she said, pointing to the newspaper on her desk. "In *The Times*, it says that—"

"All for public consumption, I'm afraid. To keep the opposition quiet. The reality is we're going to form a partnership with whoever we nominate to rule Mesopotamia, and get out sooner rather than later."

Wilson cleared his throat, and continued, "In exchange for the territory of Mosul, which he gives to us, Clemenceau has agreed to share in the exploration and production of the oil in Iraq."

Unable to look her in the eyes, he looked down at her desk. "Because my advice has been ignored, I have tended my resignation from my present position to the British government, and suggested Percy Cox returns from Persia. He's better at this sort of thing than I am. I'm afraid all I can see is British humiliation and ruin if we follow the path which Lloyd George is set upon."

She looked at him in anticipation and judging what was going through her mind, he hastened to add, "But they've refused the request for my resignation or my transfer. They want me here, running things. It appears I'm to become the Whitehall puppet of Iraq."

For once, Gertrude wanted to extend the hand of friendship to him in his humiliation. He was beginning to look like a broken man. But instead, she said, "You're making it sound as if it's the beginning of the end. But it's not, it's just the end of the beginning. We're not going to pull out of Iraq. If we did just pull out, it would be the end of our empire and the land will devolve into chaos. If Iraq goes, then Persia will soon follow, and then inevitably India. That's not what's going to happen. What Lloyd George is obviously doing is setting us up in a relationship so we develop the Arab's ability to rule themselves, and if and when we manage that transition to everybody's benefit, then the Iraqis will continue to trade with us, because our relationships will be so strong."

He sighed and shrugged his shoulders. "Which is precisely what you suggested in your report, Miss Bell. The charade in the House of Commons was for the British people, and for the Arabs. Perhaps sharing is what will happen, but I doubt it. Knowing the Arabs as well as I do, I'm afraid they'll spit in our faces. The only way to treat them isn't with some form of partnership between equals, but to show them our strength and determination, so they'd be too afraid to rise up. A strong force of men and material is what's needed, and a strong policy regarding any move towards self-determination.

"But that's a battle I've lost, and I pray to God you're correct in your assessment, because if you're not, then only the Almighty will help us all. In the meantime, I shall put out a statement when the San Remo Conference is over. The communiqué will read something along the lines of the move bringing about a healthy body politic and that Britain will act as a wise and far-seeing guardian. I'll say steps will be taken to prepare the way for the creation of an independent Arab State of The Iraq."

He stood. "I suppose I should offer you my congratulations, Miss Bell. Your will has prevailed."

He turned, and walked from her office. She could have said something in repayment for her months of humiliation at his hands, but chose instead to refrain. It was the lady-like thing to do.

SIXTEEN

Baghdad, May 1920

Recovering from a nasty bout of bronchitis, Gertrude found it difficult to breathe in the high commissioner's residency, and sat by one of the windows, the only woman in the room. For the occasion she had dressed in a somber jacket and long skirt, a ruffed shirt and a large hat with her very favorite mixture of ostrich and peacock feathers. Gertrude did her best to muffle her coughs so as not to disturb the unofficial ceremony which was taking place.

The new commander of British forces, the man replacing General George MacMunn, stood resplendent in his dress uniform, a white jacket replete with epaulettes, medals, and the ribbons of campaigns. For the occasion he had chosen to wear black leggings which were so shiny his Indian servant must have spent the entire previous night just polishing them.

General Sir Aylmer Haldane looked very much the part of the commander of the Raj—pompous, overbearing, florid from being overfed and drinking too much mess claret, and . . . well, she disliked herself for thinking it, but . . . stupid. He would have made an ideal character study for the impertinent but wonderfully perceptive Mr. Gilbert and Mr. Sullivan.

As he met more and more people, the general huffed and puffed. It was obvious from his demeanor he didn't like meeting so many of the political officers, and probably felt more comfortable among military men.

Captain Wilson, whose resignation had been refused by the British Government, had naturally left Gertrude's introduction until after the last of the most junior male political officers had shaken hands with the new commander of British forces. When he finally deigned to acknowledge her presence, he said, "And this, General Haldane, is our only lady on staff, Miss Bell." No rank, no accomplishments, no acknowledgement of her status as a commander of the British Empire . . . just Miss Bell.

The general hadn't even bothered to shake hands or acknowledge her. He'd merely grunted acknowledgement, and turned. But she hadn't minded. She just wanted to finish with this nonsense and get back to her work.

She was already missing dear George MacMunn. Although one of the most important and impressive generals in the British army, George wasn't in the least pompous and had always sought her out for advice. She had been able to advise him on an adequate military response to the nationalism of the Arabs, and to use the policy of containment rather than aggressive punishment when nationalistic fervor made some of the hotheads get out of hand in the smaller villages and towns. But one look at General Haldane, and Gertrude knew another avenue in the hierarchy of the high commission was closing off to her.

Since the British government decided to ask the League of Nations to grant a mandate in order for them to govern Iraq, the prospect of national freedom had turned the Arab mood into a frenzy. Any delay had caused discontent on the streets, and now there was tension everywhere. After hundreds of years of living under the yoke, the Arabs wanted their freedom, and would allow nothing to stand in their way.

Trouble had erupted amongst the tribes, on the border between Syria and Iraq, and especially in the north around Mosul. Even the Turks had got back into the act and had the audacity to claim that Kurdish Mosul in the north of the country was their territory, and that they hadn't retreated from it, but it should rightfully be under their control and not part of the landmass which Gertrude had put together as the new country of Iraq.

In the regions and provinces, in the towns and the villages, there was fighting in the streets between rival factions, and between Arab and British. Christians and Jews were being assaulted and killed, Sunni fought against Shi'ite who fought against everybody.

British soldiers were being murdered, political and diplomatic and civilian staff were being held for ransom and their bodies were being thrown out of cars a week after the demand had been refused, and the execrable Captain Arnold T. Wilson blamed her for the growing disaster. He maintained that had the government listened to him and his Baghdad political office, none of this would have happened. But promising freedom had put ideas into the Arabic heads, and now Britain was reaping the rewards of what he was calling Gertrude's folly. The putative truce between them had lasted all of a couple of days.

In some ways, she grudgingly had to admit to a degree of sympathy for Wilson. He saw things falling apart as a result of a British policy with which he profoundly disagreed, and now intolerable pressure was on him to sort the situation out. He'd tried to resign a second time, and again have Percy Cox brought back from Persia, all to no avail. In dealing with the uprising, he'd begun by reasoning with the different factions, but when this had patently failed, he'd resorted to force to quell the situation. Now, he was being told to work with this General Haldane, a man who looked like a buffoon and who appeared more comfortable drinking whiskey and soda in a deckchair during a cricket match in the Home Counties, than leading men onto the field of battle.

Wilson called for order, and people shuffled to their chairs. "Gentlemen. And lady," he said pointedly nodding to Gertrude, who treated his remark with disdain. "We are here to welcome the new commander of British forces in the high command, General Haldane. The general comes to us in troubled times. Just the other week, an unruly mob of Arabs gathered in one of the mosques here in Baghdad, and the mullah began to foment trouble. Having our man in place in the mosque, he was able to get word to us, and we were rightly worried about a riot. Two armoured cars were sent out to show our presence. A rock fight, and then a gun battle began and a number of Arabs were killed. I have ordered that Mosques are not to be used for political purposes, and I intend to arrest any Islamic cleric who causes dissent among the people, and who acts as a rabble-rouser. There are to be no nationalist speeches from pulpits, no meetings on street corners or in market places. This uprising to try to force the British government's hand must be put down. If it means closing the shops and cutting them off from their food and their supplies, from their income and wealth, then so be it.

"Unfortunately, General," he said, turning to Haldane. "We're anticipating severe trouble in the lower Euphrates area within a matter of weeks. We're also assuming there will be serious trouble in Karbala, in Basrah, in Mosul, and in other places. I think we all know what the cause of this upsurge in Iraqi nationalism is."

He looked at Gertrude, who merely turned to stare out of the window. "General, perhaps you'd like to say a few words . . ." Wilson said, turning to Haldane.

Looking uncomfortable, General Haldane said, "There's only one way to treat the enemy, be he Indian or Arab or Blackamore, and that's to firmly let him know who's the boss. Any leniency, any show of sympathy for him or his cause, will send the wrong message and cause the problem to get much worse.

"Now, I'm fully equipped with armoured vehicles and munitions and airplanes. The Arab is equipped with a few rifles, camels, and nothing much more. I don't want to criticise General MacMunn, because he's a good man, but I'm amazed he's allowed us to get into this situation. Certainly the Arabs outnumber us, but we have the best army in the world, and the equipment and the skills to put down any tribal unrest. We've done it in India, we've done it in Africa, and I assure you we'll do it in Arabia."

The political officers stood and cheered. Gertrude shook her head in horror.

~

Tel Mahmood, Northern Iraq, Early June 1920

The village was just beginning to awake from its night sleep, as it had awoken every morning for the past eight thousand years. Except for the occasional motorcar which passed by on the distant road, virtually nothing had changed in all that time. As had happened since time began, it was the goats which were the first to break the silence of the night. They began their bleating as the women of the households rose to prepare the day for their menfolk.

And the goats continued their bleating as the tired shepherds emerged from their huts, walked across the rock-strewn ground, and began to herd them together out of the fields for milking. Mothers and daughters, who had roused themselves from their warm straw beds, had spent the past hour mixing the flour and the water for the flat bread which their husbands and sons would eat for breakfast and take to the fields for lunch, and were beginning the preparation for the evening meal, or were washing the clothes or cleaning the house.

The making of the bread, which they undertook twice a day, was a practised routine. First they would light the straw, which would light the twigs, which would light the sticks, which would light the logs, which would heat the oven and cook the bread. And the bread always had to be hot and fresh, so it had to be done in the early morning and again in the late afternoon to be ready for the meal when the menfolk returned after their work. The women also had to go out and churn the goat's milk which had been fermenting to make the thickened yogurt, which when mixed with honey was their men's favorite way of ending the day, and of beginning the next day by vanquishing the hunger of the night.

But although this day began as every other day, it would be a day which the villagers would remember for the rest of their lives. Because the routine which the village had followed for millennia was suddenly and unexpectedly broken by the sound of gunfire. Not at first realizing what was happening, women came out of their mud-houses and looked up at the sky, wondering whether it was an unusual electrical summer storm. But surrounding the village and dispersed throughout the hills, the women saw nearly one hundred black-robed and fiercely armed men of the Shammar people, the most powerful of the Sunni tribes which owned the desert between the Tigris and the Euphrates in the northern part of Iraq. The people of the village looked at them in horror, for they had a reputation for unspeakable violence and heartlessness to their enemies. But why were they here? The people of Tel Mahmood had no quarrel with the Shammar.

As the horsemen descended from the surrounding hills towards the village, they fired their rifles into the air. The women screamed in fear, and rushed into their houses to protect their children and babies. Men who were in the fields came running back in the hope of saving the lives of their loved ones.

But there was no assault on the village, no further rifle fire, no screaming and war-like blood-curdling din which preceded an attack. When the women realized they were not the target of the Shammar, they stood where they were, and shouted ululations into the air.

Within half an hour, the men and women of the village had gathered, and were standing in the central area. Had there been an assault, the men of Tel Mahmood knew they couldn't match the brutality and strength of the Shammar, and hadn't collected their weapons from their huts, hoping this act of obeisance would save them.

One of the Shammar, the leader, rode his horse into the center of the village, and ordered all the houses to be emptied and for everyone to gather to hear his words. Still nervous, the women and children huddled together. The women and older girls had thought they were about to be raped, despite the seemingly peaceful demeanor of the warriors. The women prayed that if they were raped, their husbands and fathers wouldn't reject them and force them to wander into the desert because of the shame they had brought to the family's honour.

The leader of the Shammar, Jamil al-Midfai again raised his rifle, and fired a single shot into the air. Some of the younger children screamed in shock.

"Listen to my words, people of Tel Mahmood. Your land is about to be taken away from you, your women and children sold into slavery, and you are about to become owned by some foreign power."

The men listened in shock. The women gripped their husbands' clothes for protection.

"A false king whose name is Abdullah, the son of a man who abuses the very name of God Himself, is on his way to Iraq right now, and will call himself your ruler. He is not your ruler, people of Tel Mahmood. He is a false ruler, and is no better than the British and the Turks who once ruled over you. This man, this would-be king, this Abdullah, is nothing more than a scoundrel, a wastrel, a rapist, a murderer, and a thief. He is a child-molester and is cursed by God Himself. He has spat on the Koran and vowed to kill any person who prays in a mosque. He is vile and evil and will rape your daughters if given the chance. This man Abdullah is a puppet of the British, and they will use him to rob and cheat you.

"I order you to rise up against Abdullah, to rise up against the British, to kill their soldiers and their servants. I order you, on pain of death, to pick up your rifles, and to fight for your freedom. Any Englishman or woman you see, any British soldier or tax collector, any official from England, any political person, must be killed on sight. Hide behind a sand dune, behind a rock, and put a bullet into his heart or his head. The more Englishmen you kill, the greater your chance of freedom. If you don't kill Englishmen, I will send my men back to Tel Mahmood and order them to kill you."

And with a shout of "God is Great," he wheeled his horse around, and the horsemen rode to the next village.

Not a man or woman moved until the last of the riders had disappeared over the hills, and until the dust had cleared from the air. Eventually, the headman of the village, Abdul ibn Nasi, spat in the direction they'd taken. A woman spat immediately after him, and then many people spat.

They looked at each other, and talked in hushed words about the threat that had just been made. Abdul advised it was better to kill a few English people and risk the vengeance of the British, than not to kill anybody and suffer the certainty of murder by the Shammar.

~

British Residency, Baghdad, Iraq, a Week Later

It was the first time she'd eaten in the residency's mess in a month. She preferred to dine in her home or in her office, and avoid the stares and the sneers and the deliberately snide remarks she received when she went in there. The caustic remarks and isolation which had been bad a month ago was now incomparably worse. She was on the point of packing it all in, and returning to England, but kept deferring the decision because she couldn't leave Iraq in its parlous state, for then she would be blamed for everything which was going wrong. At least while she was on the spot, she could do something to mollify the tense situation. She had stopped herself from leaving when she was told of the appointment of Abdullah as a future ruler of The Iraq. Abdullah, of all people, Faisal's elder brother as the emir of Iraq. It was absurd. He too had fought for a time alongside Lawrence and done much to defeat the Turks, but he was no ruler and couldn't possibly unite the disparate forces which her carefully drawn borders hoped to hold together in Iraq. His appointment was an absurdity, but nobody was listening to her. Still, she continued to write her objective reports, in the hope that one day, scholars would look back and realize that hers was the only sane voice in the arena.

For Gertrude, life was doubly bad. Nobody would eat with her at her table, or even talk to her any longer. Her fellow political officers were merely following the lead of A.T. Wilson, who, as the tension in Iraq increased, had for the past month been abusing her in public, accusing her in staff meetings of disloyalty, of stupidity, and incompetence.

Only occasionally had she responded, uttering a scathing rebuttal here and contemptuous aside there. But she knew the reason for Wilson's detestation of her was he couldn't control the situation in the country, and he believed she was responsible for his political demise. He was using more and more force against the Arabs, and as was their wont, the Arabs of Iraq were responding in the only way they knew how. Violence bred retribution which bred more violence. The prospects of negotiation were diminishing with every bullet ridden body, Arab or British.

She, for her part, was frantically talking to her Arabic friends, the chieftains and leaders and men of influence, trying to calm the situation and bring order to bear in the chaos, but she was afraid the genie was out of the bottle, and she had no idea how to put it back.

So when General Haldane had invited her for lunch in the residency mess, she had earnestly hoped he was going to declare his hand and seek her assistance. He had been in his position for only a matter of weeks, long enough to assess his men's disposition throughout the country, and certainly long enough to determine a course of military action. If George MacMunn had still been here, he would have refused to follow the requests of Wilson, and instead would have directed military activity towards some form of containment of the situation. He would have worked with her to identify the leaders of the revolts in the different parts, to contain them and therefore cut off the heads so the body of the Arab cohorts would have nobody to follow. George certainly wouldn't have used massive military might against the civilian population, because, as it was doing, it would just lead to more and more assaults against the British. Gertrude prayed Haldane was going to ask her how best to deal with the Arabs and with Captain Wilson.

At the beginning of the lunch he had been pleasant enough, inquiring about her place of birth, her interests, her activities in the English social set, her contacts in Whitehall and Westminster, and much more. But eventually, when the stewards were clearing away the main course, Haldane came to the point.

"I'm a military man, Miss Bell, and I don't like to shilly-shally around the point. I like to identify the problem, and then solve it.

Now I know you're on the outer here, and not many people like you, but I judge people not by what's said about them, but by how they follow orders. Well, I've got a plan which I think could do us both a lot of good. You see, the fact is, m'dear, there's something I want you to do for me and the good of the country."

She straightened her desert spoon and fork, and prepared herself for the real purpose of their meeting. "You should know, General, I'm prepared to do anything to assist you, provided your proposed course of action is reasoned and responsible."

"Of course, Miss Bell. Well, to be quite frank with you, I have a problem which requires a non-military solution. It's a bit tricky to be honest, and not something I've encountered in any field of battle I've ever been on. You see, I've never had wives and daughters living in such close proximity to a battle zone, not even in India. And the women are nervous. What I'd like you to do for me is to organize things for the officers' wives and daughters. You're a woman, and I'm sure you're good at that sort of thing. I'm increasingly concerned with their morale—a grumpy wife makes a grumpy officer—and with the current problems, we need to keep the ladies happy, and if you're seen by the big wigs trying to make things better, well, I'm sure they'll think better of you. Now, what about organizing outings on the river, or trips to some of these archaeological sites you're so good at? That should perk up their spirits, and allow the men to concentrate on the troubles."

She looked at him in amazement, and was about to respond in no uncertain terms, when an orderly came in, and delivered a message, proffered on a silver salver.

The general tore open the envelope, and read the contents. "Damn!" he exclaimed. "Buggers up north, tribesmen or something, have killed six Englishmen, two clerks, their drivers, and a tax officer. Sorry, m'dear, but duty calls. I have to see Wilson and find out what his orders are. Organize those things for the ladies, will you?" he said.

He stood, nodded goodbye, and retreated from the table. She was too stunned to scream at him.

~

Tel Mahmood, Northern Iraq, Mid-June, 1920

The women had just finished putting bread into the ovens, when they heard the noise of vehicles coming over the ridge. The sound fractured the quiet of the morning. The sudden mechanized tension in the air was picked up by the goats of the village, which began bleating frantically.

The horses began whinnying and men and women started to come out of their houses to look at the source of the noise. The road from Baghdad to Mosul, which was less than a mile away, was normally empty at this time of morning, but suddenly it was full of angry dust, rising up in clouds into the clear blue sky.

Frowning, the women stood to watch, trying to discern what the noises and the clouds of dust could be. Nothing like it had been heard since the Turks rushed north to escape the might of the British. Nothing like it since the end of the war two years earlier. But the men who came out to look at what was happening knew.

And then it dawned on the women. It was the war, coming to their village again. The women began to scream, turned, and run into their houses to gather up their children and escape to the caves in the hills surrounding their village. Unlike the arrival of the Shammar weeks earlier, the arrival of the cars and trucks with guns on them spelled instant death at the hands of a foreigner. They had to get away.

Slowly, the roaring noise clarified into the sounds of two dozen motor car engines. And out of the dust, machine gun motorcycles and cars and army vehicles emerged and rumbled down the road towards the village.

The officer commanding, a relatively young lieutenant on only his fourth mission shouted an order to his column to disperse right and left to prevent the villagers from escaping. Through his binoculars, he saw the rest of his patrol was approaching the village from the opposite hills to block any escape.

In desperation, some of the villagers ran into the path of the oncoming vehicles and were surrounded, others rushed into their homes to grab their weapons, but many of the men found themselves struggling with their wives who wanted them to surrender without a fight, terrified that if they were armed and resisted, there'd be a massacre.

And suddenly there was silence. The villagers of Tel Mahmood stood still, realizing the English had come in overwhelming force, and waited for the disaster which was about to happen to them. They were rounded up at rifle point by the English soldiers, and forced to stand in the center of the village.

The young English commander stood on top of his vehicle and unrolled a document which looked horribly and frighteningly official. Beside him stood an Arab, dressed in the uniform of an army sergeant. These men, translators, informers, spies, and mercenaries for the British, were amongst the most hated of turncoats by the Iraqis.

The Englishman began to read to the assembled villages, and after a few moments, the Arab translated. "Residents of Tel Mahmood, because of your participation in the senseless and bloody murder of six English civilians, the Military Commander of Iraq, Lieutenant General Sir Aylmer Haldane has decreed the men of the village will be arrested and tried in a military court for murder, and the entire village, including every house and public building, will be razed to the ground, and will never be rebuilt. Your fields are to be sown with salt and your livestock slaughtered. Further, all women and children of the village will be deported from Iraq to a location to be determined. You have half of an hour to collect your personal possessions from your homes before they are destroyed. By order of the Military Command of Iraq."

Several women fainted when he finished the translation.

~

British Residency, Baghdad, Iraq
Four days later, when the news was common knowledge in the mess halls of the Military High Command and the Political

Residency, Gertrude, still feeling sick from hearing of what had happened in the north of Iraq, was called to a meeting with Wilson.

"We have a situation which has occurred, and I need your advice, Miss Bell," he said without according her the usual greeting. "I'm aware you and I are in a serious and irreparable conflict, but this is an issue from which we both will suffer if it remains unresolved, and so two heads are better than one."

She looked at him in disgust, but it was so unusual to be sitting in his office these days she decided to remain silent.

"The fact is, despite the dire circumstances in which we find ourselves, when it's quite possible there'll be outright full-scale war between Britain and the local tribesman, General Haldane has decided now is an appropriate moment to take his entire High Command on holiday to Persia."

Gertrude burst out laughing, but suddenly realized she was the only one who found the remark witty. The blood drained from her face when she understood Wilson was being totally serious.

Wilson continued, "He's due for leave, apparently, and so are many of his senior officers, and so he's taking them for some recreation time in Teheran. I have forbidden him to leave because of the desperate urgency of the situation, but he says he isn't answerable to me, and he and his officers' leave was granted by the War Office three months ago. He can see no reason whatsoever to defer or cancel his leave, and he intends to leave immediately. His mind is made up, and he appears to be quite content to leave the situation we find ourselves in at the present moment in the hands of his junior officers. He informs me he isn't intent upon returning here for three months. It's unbelievable."

She could hardly speak. "But—"

"I know. I can barely bring myself to look at the idiot. To leave us now, to leave his tens of thousands of men without a senior commander . . . it's . . ."

"But what did he say?" she asked. She was simply too flabbergasted to think clearly.

"He said he didn't feel any responsibility for what happened here while he was away. He said if the situation worsens, then his junior officers will benefit from the experience of making their own decisions. He also informs me he's quite willing for me to order the deployment of his troops. It's not just monstrous, it's the most unprecedented dereliction of duty I think I've ever encountered."

"How dare he?" she said. "What kind of a military officer would do such a thing? The man needs to be brought to book. He has to be censured in the very highest tribunal of England. I'll make him suffer in the House of Commons or the House of Lords. I'll have my friends in government ask questions, and that'll force the War Office to do something about it."

Wilson nodded. "I have to say I've always objected to your contacting your many friends in high places, but on this occasion, you do so with my blessing. The higher, the better. Do you happen to know the king?"

"Not personally, but I know somebody who under these circumstances will be of much greater value to us than the king. I'm thinking of writing to Winston Churchill."

Wilson suddenly beamed a smile. "I don't have much time for Mr. Churchill, but yes, if anybody can pillory this idiot and make things happen, one couldn't do better than having him on our side."

She stood and nodded to him. "Don't worry, Captain Wilson, I'll send a cable to Winston. That'll bring the wayward general back here in no time."

He called her back, "Before you go, Miss Bell, this incident at Tel Mahmood . . . it had to happen, you know. I couldn't allow the murder of six Englishmen to go unpunished."

"No, of course you couldn't, Captain Wilson. Murderers must be punished. But maybe these poor souls wouldn't have been murdered in the first place if you hadn't adopted such a vigorous attitude towards the question of nationalism. It's British government policy to form an accord with these people, not to own and control their land."

He let the remark pass without comment. "While you're here, there's another matter I wish to discuss. I know we are following different pathways, but may I have your opinion on a plan I've been thinking about putting into effect. We can't have all these murders, and then retaliations, because the cycle of violence will have no end. We need some mechanism to break the chain."

She looked at him in interest. It was what she'd been proposing in letters and memos for weeks and weeks. Now he was acknowledging that perhaps she was correct. "What if I were to call all the leaders together, from all the different factions, as well as the Christians and the Jews, and just talk to them? Tell them about England's intention, tell them they only have death to look forward to if they follow their current path? If I tell them Britain is entering into a mandate to create a smooth transition to self-government, do you think that would help to solve our difficulties?"

"Frankly, while General Haldane is on leave, I think it's the wisest thing to do. I'll willingly act to put such a meeting of community leaders together. It might be too late, but it has to be done, Captain Wilson. Now, if you'll excuse me, I have to compose a telegram to Winston which will induce him to act."

The response to her telegram took a week to arrive, by which time the entire senior command of General Headquarters in Iraq was on leave in Persia. Winston said he simply couldn't believe such an act of self-centred stupidity could have been conducted by such a senior officer, and promised to raise it at his earliest opportunity.

But solving one problem didn't assist Gertrude in all of her difficulties, as the situation between Britons and Arabs intensified and the distance and animosity between Wilson and Gertrude grew even more intense as the mood of nationalism increased. Despite the meeting which took place and the agreements for seeking calm which had been made by the leaders of the Sunni, the Shi'ite and all the other stakeholders in the country, the people were inflamed with the prospect of self-rule, and wanted the British out of Iraq as quickly as possible.

During the following weeks, the situation devolved into a nightmare. Captain Wilson was forced to organize aerial bombing of villages, which caused the situation to worsen considerably. Gertrude wrote to Thomas Lawrence that Wilson was like a man out of control, and his tactics were certain to lead to even more unpleasantness. She told him life in Iraq was doubly intolerable for her, and explained about the ridicule she was suffering under Wilson's regime.

Within a few days, she received a cable from her friend that he had taken her situation to heart, and he had asked a mutual friend to intervene. The cable was signed Lawrence of Arabia.

One morning, she came into her office, opened the copy of *The Times* and read the first few inside pages carefully. Suddenly, when she got to page four, she read an item, and burst into uproarious peals of laughter, so much so some of her colleagues looked in to see what the commotion was all about.

She ignored them, they would see for themselves when *The Times* was passed around the mess.

When she was completely alone again, she re-read the glorious words of the report of the trouble in Iraq. In it, the *Times'* correspondent, doubtless fed the line from Winston, had written an article in which he'd called Captain Wilson 'a sun-dried bureaucrat set on Indianizing Mesopotamia'.

It was, perhaps, the most glorious revenge she could ever have encompassed. She thanked God for her friendship with Winston Churchill, and for Thomas Lawrence's intervention, and she marvelled yet again at Winston's malicious sense of fun.

~

Palais Wilson, League of Nations, Geneva, 1920

For an organization formed to promote international cooperation and to achieve peace and security in the world, the League of Nations began its life with a breathtaking enigma. Headquartered in the magnificent edifice of Palais Wilson, a building renamed after the American president whose health was destroyed in his efforts to make the world come to its senses, the first General Assembly of all the signatories sat in the glaring absence of America, which refused to ratify its charter.

As the delegates of the fifty-four member nations of the League walked through the labyrinthine corridors of the Palais during the first days of its existence, many trying to remember how to return to their offices, many just sitting and talking to other delegates in relative privacy, the question uppermost on their minds was how to make the League work without America. There was so much to be done since the Paris Peace Conference, so many mandates to be agreed upon, and so many issues and disputes to be sorted out. But the single greatest issue on which all delegates agreed was the need to convince their governments that armed force was not the way to solve problems and that nobody ultimately won anything through war.

The problem wasn't the twenty nine Allied powers which had ratified the Peace Treaties of Paris, and thus become founding members of the League of Nations, nor was it the thirteen neutral nations which became members of the League in 1920. Indeed, many throughout the world keenly believed that following the war, which was now being called The War to End All Wars, an era of peace would break out, that leaders would realize the world couldn't sustain millions of its finest young men being slaughtered, and that swords would at last be turned into plough shears.

But a group of United States Senators, principally Henry Cabot Lodge, William Borah, and Hiram Johnson were vehemently opposed to ratifying the Covenant of the League, and led a tirade against President Wilson in the media, in the Senate, and on the hustings.

They were incensed that Article 10 would undermine American sovereignty and violate George Washington's last message to Congress to keep free of foreign entanglements. Their concern was that Article 10 would keep the United States permanently involved in international disputes and wars. The article allowed the Council of the League to determine how a threat to a member nation should be countered, and could commit the other members to going to war on behalf of a member under attack.

The absence of the United States was particularly upsetting for the first President of the League of Nations, the Belgian diplomat and former foreign secretary of his country, Paul Hymans. The suave and canny European statesman had been at the Paris Peace Conference, and had done much to boost the prestige and participation of the world's smaller nations in the putative League. But he, and everyone else, had assumed the president of America could carry his nation forward to sit with all other nations to determine the future of the world. Now, it appeared, the League would have to survive without the wealth and vitality of the United States.

Hyams took his fob watch out of his waistcoat pocket, opened the silver face and stared at the time. He wound it up, clicked it shut, and replaced it in his pocket. It was a nervous act he repeated a dozen times an hour, and one day, his granddaughter had assured him, he would over-wind it, and break it.

He picked up his gavel, and banged it on the oak desk set high on the plinth so he could oversee all the countries of the world.

"Gentlemen," he shouted. "Gentlemen, will the nations of the world please come to order."

He waited for ten minutes for the delegates to find their seats and to stop their negotiations and hurried conversations. Then he banged his gavel again, saw that it was precisely twelve o'clock midday, and shouted, "Gentlemen of the world, I have the honor of opening this tenth meeting of the General Assembly of the League of Nations. We begin with a prayer, and I call upon His Eminence, the Catholic Cardinal of Switzerland, to lead the Assembly. Will all delegates please be upstanding?"

Everybody stood and bowed their head while the cardinal said a non-denominational blessing for the League and its work. Yesterday, a Lutheran had made a similar prayer, the day before an Anglican. Soon, he would have to deal with the vexed question of a

394

mullah saying prayers for the assembly to assuage the sensitivities of the Muslim nations. What next, he wondered, a Rabbi and a witchdoctor?

"Gentlemen, today on our order papers, we are to deal with the question of the allocation of League of Nations mandates to the governments of Great Britain and France for their control, in our name, of the territories of Lebanon, Syria, Palestine, Iraq, and other parts of the dismantled former Ottoman Empire. I have ten speakers listed. The first speaker is the Honorable representative of the government of France."

After four hours of argument, disputes, debates, name calling, and bitter innuendo, Paul Hymans took out his watch, and checked the time. There was so much to debate, and the Middle East had taken up too much time already. Yet under the rules of debate, he wasn't entitled to prevent any member nation from having its say . . . except for a little-known clause which he intended to exercise now, if the assembly was to have any hope of considering other topics before the day was out.

He banged his gavel yet again, and shouted, "Gentlemen, under the emergency powers entrusted to the president of the Assembly, specifically those dealing with the Assembly's powers to instigate an urgency motion within four hours of the close of business on any one day, I hereby bring this debate on the mandates of France and Great Britain to a close and refuse the right of any other country to enter into the discussion. I shall now call for a vote on the granting of mandates to these two member nations."

~

Damascus, Syria, July 1920

It had been the pride of the Arabs, the first independent Arab government in centuries, a reason to convince the new League of Nations and the major powers of the world that Arabs were capable of ruling themselves.

And now it was all over.

Despite two years of begging, negotiations, threats, boycotts, violence, and consultations with anybody who would listen, the Arabic government of Syria was about to be ousted.

The dream of an independent Syria had all begun with such promise. Prince Faisal had entered Damascus as a conqueror, earning his kingship in the way of past ages. He had held his head high while Damascenes cheered his progress through the streets of Arabia's most revered capital. He used to enjoy telling people that as he rode through the ancient gates to claim the city, he could almost see the dust of the Turks running away.

And the first few chaotic months had been nothing but inspirational, full of ambassadors from the Great Powers coming to pay homage to the world's newest king, tribal chiefs promising him their undying loyalty, and religious leaders blessing his present and his future.

He and those advisors he brought from Hejaz and Mesopotamia had to deal with issues of civil administration which were foreign to them—water, sewage, roads, education, defense, housing, street lights, the marketplace—the list of things was endless. And yes, there'd been many mistakes along the way. But nobody, no visitor or resident, could deny the country was being run as efficiently and effectively as it had been run by the Turkish administration, and unlike the Beys and absentee landlords who raped the country and sucked its finances into Constantinople, Faisal and his administrators were everywhere, listening to problems, attempting to find solutions, and building structures which, they hoped, would last.

Everyone in the world, it seemed, had hoped his government would be able to learn how to run the country. Everyone except the French. Despite Faisal's pleas with Clemenceau, the French adamantly refused to recognize his regime. And despite the pressure which the British had brought to bear, the old fox in the Elysee Palace stood firm and resolute and declared Syria was French, and no upstart regime from an Offenbach operetta would prevent France from claiming what was rightfully hers.

Clemenceau had ordered further troops be sent to Beirut, and the expanded army, commanded by General Henri Gouraud began its march towards Damascus to oust the puppet of Britain who called himself king, and to rule the land as it was meant to be ruled, by the French and for the French.

King Faisal sat on his throne, and read the ultimatum. He shook his head, looking at his young brother Zeid, and shrugged his shoulders. It was July 14th, one hundred and thirty one years to the day since an outraged mob of Parisians, seeking arms to fight the government, had stormed the Bastille and released the prisoners of influence. Now the government was storming Faisal's stronghold. What irony.

"Well," said Zeid. "Do we fight or run?"

"How can we fight? They're marching with artillery and rifles and we're out-gunned and our forces are out-manned."

"And no word from your wonderful friends, Great Britain?" he asked scornfully.

Faisal shook his head.

The two men remained silent. As did all their advisors who had run out of advice.

"What does the ultimatum ask?" asked Nuri al-Sa'id, Faisal's most trusted counsellor.

"What you would expect," he said curtly. "The general presents his respects, and informs me he and his army will shortly be in Damascus to take the city and to enforce the League of Nation's mandate. He says because of the mandate, France is now in command of Syria and Lebanon, and he will take over immediate control of all Arabic armies in the countries, the economy, the railroads, and all instruments of government control. He informs me I may remain in Damascus if I wish, and I am entitled to call myself Sir or The Honorable, anything but king.'

Faisal threw down the ultimatum document in disgust. Nuri al-Sa'id bent down to pick it up, recognizing its importance to the history of his people.

"We have guns, we have artillery! Why don't we fight?" asked Zeid. "What did the fight against the Ottomans show if not that the Arabs are a brave and courageous people who will no longer tolerate an overlord? I say we close the gates to these men who would be our masters, post guards on the city walls, and fight them."

Faisal breathed deeply. "And how many of my people will die before we're forced to come to terms with the harsh reality which is the modern world? My government lasted only as long as the British were willing to allow it to last. Once the British withdrew their support and placed our future in the League of Nations, we were lost. Britain has its mandate over Iraq and Palestine. It has the oil it needs for its ships and motorcars and its industry. So why should it waste its time with supporting Syria and Faisal? Why should it alienate the French when it can hide behind the League of Nations? I tell you, my brothers, this is a black day for the Arabic people."

"Will you and Zeid go to London?" asked Nuri

Faisal nodded. "Yes, I will try to persuade the British government the Arabic people need its support, despite the League. Britain has let me down badly, but I can't see it abrogating its responsibilities in the region. There's just too much wealth for it to plunder, and without Britain, Arabia will descend into chaos and anarchy."

Zeid shook his head in disgust. "And where's your Lawrence of Arabia now, when you need him most? Performing like a puppet in New York."

The young man turned and walked out of the Throne Room. King Faisal looked at the assembly, not knowing what to say, when his defence minister, General Yusuf al-Azmah stepped forward. Only in his mid-thirties, he was one of the younger men who advised Faisal.

"Highness," he said, his voice strong and confident, "We cannot defeat the French, and you are right to go to London to seek British support; but as your Minister, I cannot allow General Gouraud simply to walk into Damascus and take what is ours, what we have fought for so valiantly. Neither history, nor our Arab brethren, will forgive us. So I will lead a force of men from Damascus, even if it means our death, and fight them. My commanders have been working on a plan to halt the invasion of the French at Maysalun Pass, a day's march to the West. There, Sire, we will fight and die for Syria's honor."

King Faisal felt tears welling up in his eyes. Just as he had fought the Turks beside Colonel Lawrence, every fibre of his body told him he should join his young minister in this glorious battle. But he knew that as a king, he had to go to Britain and use his diplomatic skills for the greater glory. He looked at the young man, and nodded slowly.

SEVENTEEN

Baghdad, October 1920

Gertrude ensured her pearls were not crossed, but arrayed in neat rows cascading down her bosom. She spent a lot of time changing her hats and shoes to ensure a perfect look, nearly driving her maid to distraction. Even the cook was instructed to prepare three lunches because the first two had gone cold as Gertrude changed and then re-changed her outfit until she was perfectly dressed for the occasion.

It was the end of her nightmare. Yes, it had only lasted a relatively short time, but it was without question the worst time of her life. And now it was all over. Sir Percy Cox had been ordered to leave Persia, and sort out the problems which had grown so horribly during the administration of the hideous little Arnold Wilson. The awful, execrable, nasty, mean-spirited, officious, rotten little man had gone. He was no longer in Iraq. He was out, ousted, removed, sent packing. Gone! And her dear, dear Sir Percy was returning. It was like a dream come true.

Even when Wilson told her of his departure, she hadn't quite taken in the fact that it was Sir Percy who would be returning to take charge. She'd been so stunned by his appearance in her office on the evening before his departure she could barely say a word. Indeed, there had been virtually no conversation between them in weeks, apart from curt notes and overheard snide and superficial comments in the corridors.

"I fear, Miss Bell, that I leave Mesopotamia as a failure. This damnable insurrection has cost Great Britain £50 million and many hundreds of British citizens have lost their lives . . ."

"Not to mention ten thousand Arab lives," she said curtly.

"Indeed," he replied. "But I don't feel the failure is all mine. This mandate which the government insisted upon, the planting of this idea the Arabs could govern themselves, is what has led to the uprising and caused so much pain and suffering. Under the Turks, the Arabs were quiescent, as they would have been under British rule had we not held out the promise of nationalism.

"But that's another argument for another day. I've come to say goodbye, and to say how much I regret not having formed a better working relationship with you. Sir Percy told me when I took this position you were a woman of great intellect and knowledge. Had we not taken opposite sides on this issue, I'm sure we could have worked well together."

He shook her hand formally. She looked him in the eye. It was a strange moment, she a middle-aged lady, he a straight-laced imperialist, rigid and pompous. Yet they were of the same coin. "I too, regret our relationship, Captain Wilson. And I too see my last year here as a failure. Indeed, I'm feeling more deeply discouraged about the future of Mesopotamia than at any time in the past. I regret acutely that we couldn't have done a better job, between ourselves and with this country. But I wish you success in whatever your career holds in store for you."

She prayed it would be the last time in her life she'd have to talk to him, but life often took unusual turns and she no longer tried to guess what would happen when matters were outside of her control. A man like Wilson would probably pop up somewhere unexpected. And she'd vowed whatever happened in the future, she would never ever work for or with him again. She would rather retire to obscurity and write her books, than suffer the isolation, the humiliation, which his rule had caused her. She felt spent, as though there was nothing left inside her. And she continued to feel so until she was told the man replacing him was her dear friend Percy. Suddenly the light had been rekindled in her life and she had purpose, direction and hope.

And now she was rushing out of the house to the central train station of Iraq in anticipation of the arrival of the man she adored, admired, and revered. Percy Cox was a figure of respect and popularity with the Arabs. If anybody could calm the situation in the country, it was he. She had finally selected a new royal blue silk dress which her mother had sent out from Harrods, her hair was tied into a topknot bun which was surreptitiously hidden beneath her hat, and she chose her coat more for its fashion than for the warmth it would provide from the cool afternoon winds of the late autumn.

When Gertrude arrived at the railway station the band of the Royal Warwickshire Fusiliers, recently arrived from Persia, had already assembled and were tuning their instruments in anticipation of the arrival of Sir Percy and Lady Cox. Other dignitaries were also beginning to step out of their carriages to be greeted by the Station Master and his staff. She noted Sayid Talib and other members of the Constitutional Assembly, Anwar Ibrahim, the mayor, Sir Edgar Bonham Carter, Iraq's judicial officer, as well as leaders of the Shi'ite, Sunni, Kurdish, Christian, and Jewish communities. Junior members of the political and military staff were also present, as was General Sir Aylmer Haldane, still smarting from the dressing down he'd received from Winston Churchill, the newly appointed colonial secretary, who'd ordered his immediate return from his holidays. It was a reprimand which ensured Haldane would never rise above his present rank, and once his tour of duty was over, he would not be given this level of responsibility again.

Gertrude anxiously looked northwards along the railway line to see if there was any tell-tale sign of smoke from a distant engine. But Sir Percy's train wouldn't arrive for another half an hour, and she was being girlish and silly, but it was because of the joy that now she would have his wise head and his gentlemanly demeanor around again to support her and her plans for the Middle East.

She loved this area with all her heart and soul. Ever since she was a girl, she'd loved Arabia, but it wasn't until the regime of Wilson, when so many of her hopes and ambitions for the nation had been dashed on the rocks of imperial arrogance, that she understood just how much she loved the desert and the people. Before him and the misery he'd brought, she'd always viewed herself as an archetypal English woman, a bit eccentric in the best traditions of the rich English, but English through and through. Now, having been in danger of being sacked and dismissed from the land, or having seriously considered resigning and retiring to a life of indolence in London, she realized she yearned to stay. If there was a metaphor for her life, then it was Arabia. Internally riven by struggles and strife for independence and recognition, externally oppressed by the imperialism and patriality of men, Arabia was more Gertrude than she had realized, until this moment. She'd been accused of being more Arab than English. She'd dismissed the barbs. But as she waited for Percy Cox to return, it dawned on Gertrude that she was, indeed, Arabia.

Under Wilson, her title of Oriental Secretary, the most senior person with regard to the entire Middle Eastern theater, had been an unutterable joke. Despite her being such a pre-eminent expert on the Arabic peoples, she was the very last person whom Wilson consulted on these matters. Percy had always called her into his office when he was the Mesopotamian high commissioner to sit beside him when some bigwig sought an audience. Then they'd talk for hours afterwards, and on the basis of their shared experiences, they'd jointly plot a future course. And now all that was to return. She beamed a smile.

Suddenly the protocol officer, an officious man from the north of England, requested the official party at the train station to assemble on the dais. Junior members of staff, their wives, and lesser locals were assembled on the periphery of the station platform, which was rapidly filling up and in danger of becoming over-crowded. Everybody, it seemed, wanted to greet the return of Percy Cox, a man known throughout the length and breadth of Arabia by locals unable to pronounce his name, as Kokus.

And then a distant whistle heralded the arrival of the Cox's train, five minutes early. It appeared on the distant horizon as a line of smoke in the sky which grew and grew until her heart was nearly exploding with excitement. She wanted to cry out with joy at seeing Percy again, but bit her tongue to prevent herself from doing anything girlish. As the train pulled into the station with steam hissing from its boiler and black coal smoke belching out of the chimney, Gertrude could barely contain her enthusiasm.

Being senior military officer and the Commander-in-Chief of British forces, General Haldane, wearing a dazzling white dress uniform and plumed helmet, stepped forward to give a crisp salute to the new high commissioner. Sir Percy stepped down, and the two men shook hands, Haldane introducing himself with pomp and ceremony. The band immediately struck up God Save the King, and all the Englishmen and women stood very still.

Gertrude couldn't take her eyes off him. He was wearing a white uniform with gold epaulettes and trimming, and looked dignified, wise, and important. General Haldane accompanied the new high commissioner down the line of dignitaries, and Gertrude ensured her eyes were held rigidly to the front, and that she didn't sneak a peek.

Eventually, Sir Percy and General Haldane arrived at the place where she was standing. "And this is our only lady on the political staff, High Commissioner, Miss Gertrude Bell."

To his surprise, Sir Percy stepped forward, and said, "Hello Gertie."

She beamed a smile, curtsied, and as she arose, he threw his arms around her and kissed her on both cheeks.

"You two know each other, do you?" asked Haldane.

Deliberately raising his voice so all The Iraq would hear him, Percy said, "Miss Bell is the most brilliant, knowledgeable and important person in this entire area. Her advice is invaluable, her knowledge encyclopaedic, her intellect has led in large measure to the successes we've enjoyed today, and her courage to overturn the stupidity of some of the decisions which have been made here in recent times has avoided further disasters. Anybody who doesn't realize that and fails to employ her precious knowledge and masterful advice is a complete idiot. Miss Bell will be my closest advisor and confidante in the fraught days ahead while the two of us attempt to repair the many egregious errors which have led to my being recalled to this theatre."

He continued meeting officials further down the line, accompanied by a very surprised and suddenly far less self-assured General Haldane. Gertrude could barely resist a smile. It was so very obvious Thomas Lawrence and Winston Churchill had been operating behind the scenes, with Percy as their willing and very enthusiastic conspirator.

~

Lady Cox emerged when her husband's introductions and formalities were completed. Protocol demanded she remain on board the train and the official ceremony proceed during the time when the new high commissioner was introduced to the indigenous guests. Only royal women were permitted to share the limelight with their spouses.

As Lady Cox stepped down, looking remarkably fresh despite the 13-hour train journey, she spied Gertrude, smiled and waved at her. She mouthed the words, 'I bought some lovely silk scarves for you in Teheran.' Gertrude blew her a kiss.

Sir Percy walked towards a raised platform, and cleared his throat to begin his address to the assembly. When the first words he uttered were in Arabic, the astonished crowd suddenly quietened and listened in rapt attention. He was known to be fluent in the language, but never used it on official occasions.

"Much has happened since I was last in The Iraq," he shouted above the wind.

Suddenly, the entire indigenous community burst into applause. It was the first time the name Iraq had been mentioned officially in public, and for such a high official to honor the local people by espousing the name of their new country, in their own language, showed this was a new beginning. Indeed, everybody knew this was the first moment of the proper transition to Arab rule, and an end to the authoritarianism and barbarism of A.T. Wilson.

He waited for the applause to die down, and continued, "I have come to Baghdad by order of His Majesty's government to enter into counsel with the people of The Iraq for the purpose of setting up an Arab government under the supervision of Great Britain. From this moment henceforth, The Iraq will belong to the Arabic people, and will be ruled by the Arabic people. The foreign secretary of Great Britain has instructed me to create stability in the Middle East, and to redeem the country from the misrule and anarchy which has cost so many lives, both English and Iraqi.

"This will not be an easy task. The road forward is strewn with the bodies of loved ones and it is natural for people of both sides to want to take revenge for their losses. But if we are to accomplish our task, we must learn to take a different path, a path which is not strewn with obstacles, but one which is to the benefit of both of our peoples.

"We British have come to realize The Iraq is incontrovertibly the land, nation, and aspiration of the Iraqi people—all people— Sunni and Shi'ite and Kurd and nomad and city dweller and Christian and Jew alike. The British presence is necessary if we are not to see The Iraq devolve into bloodshed and anarchy. We will be here to support a legitimate government and to work in partnership and cooperation with that government in establishing the framework for self-rule.

"When our work is done, and The Iraq is functioning as a modern nation whose citizens enjoy representation and all the rights which the citizens of other democratic nations enjoy, then we will depart as honored friends and partners in this cause. Until that glorious day, I ask the people of The Iraq to cooperate with me in the establishment of settled conditions so I can proceed immediately with the task in hand."

He didn't get a chance to thank everyone, because the applause and shouting and whistling and cheering overwhelmed him. Only certain of the British political officers stared at the ground, wondering how long they'd survive until Cox's broom swept them out of the desert.

~

She hadn't experienced a feeling of déjà vu like this before. It was as though the nightmare of Wilson's rule had never happened, as though the insults and abuse and hatred she'd suffered, the distancing from the other staff, the isolation in her office and being left alone to guess at what was going in the political office, simply hadn't happened.

Now she was seated in the dining hall of the residency, and her life felt as though it was all beginning again. Except for entertaining the British and Europeans who were in Baghdad, Captain Wilson hadn't had a single Arabic notable in this room since he had become high commissioner.

Now the lights of the room were blazing, a military string quartet was playing, men and women were dressed in their evening finery, Arabic men were wearing their most formal clothes, and it was as though summer had come after a particularly cruel winter.

Sir Percy had ordered his aide de camp to ensure that Gertrude sat next to him at the top table. It was a singular honor he accorded her because he knew how much her position had suffered under that fool, Wilson. It was also his way of publicly telling Wilson's cohorts and acolytes, and any in the Political Office who still wanted to follow his way of doing things, that there was a new man in the top job, and they had better be prepared to bend to his will, or they'd be out on their ears.

After the formal welcomes, as the Windsor Soup was being served, Cox turned to Gertrude, and said softly, "How bad was it? I got these repeated suggestions from Wilson that he should send you back to England, which I ignored, of course. But was it bad here?"

She decided not to spoil his dinner and downplayed her feelings. "No, not really. Just a bit lonely. I missed our friendship, our confabs, and the sharing of information. There was none of that with Captain Wilson."

"But did he behave badly towards you?"

"Let's just say you behaved better. But all that's in the past, Percy, my dear. What's important now is to make good those promises you made yesterday at the train station."

"And that's precisely what I intend to do. From tomorrow, I want to begin gathering information on forming a provisional Arab government. I want it set up immediately . . ."

She was stunned. "Tomorrow? But the uprising?"

"This rebellion will come to an end once the Iraqis see Britain is working towards their self-government. I have the assurance of Lord Curzon he'll back me to the hilt." Gertrude smiled at the mention of Curzon's name. "What's funny?" he asked.

"George Curzon. I still can't get used to the fact he was made foreign secretary last year. I know him well, Percy. He gave me my gold medal at the Royal Geographical Society. You mark my words, he'll be prime minister one day."

Sir Percy nodded in agreement. "Same can't be said for your pal Winston, I'm afraid. Are you aware just three weeks ago, he recommended the Air Force drop poison gas on the Arabic tribes. He said something to the effect that he was strongly in favor of using the gas against uncivilized tribes to spread a lively terror in Iraq. For God's sake, Gertie, the man's a lunatic."

"Winston said that?" she hissed, shocked at the news.

"I'm afraid so. Good God, wasn't there enough gas used in the trenches to put an end to its use forever. There's talk of another Geneva Convention banning the use of gas as a weapon of war, but I suppose we'll have to leave that up to the League of Nations."

He hesitated saying what was in his mind, but knew she revered honesty more than anything else. Softly, he whispered, "I'm afraid the fact is your pal Winston is probably responsible, along with Captain Wilson, for many of the problems we're suffering here today. The idea that we only needed such a small force of men for such a vast country was ludicrous. And his idea that airplanes could do the work of a battalion was nonsense. His trying to save money was the cause of much of the difficulties."

"He was instructed by the government," she said quietly. "You can't blame Winston for the problems caused by Arnold Wilson. It's not fair."

She noticed everybody else had finished their soup course, and the stewards were waiting for them to finish. They quickly emptied their plates and Sir Percy nodded to the waiters, who descended on the diners like a swarm of locust.

"Percy, almost of a third of the country is up in arms against us, and everybody else. How can you call together a provisional government if armed thugs are patrolling the roads?"

"It's not going to be easy, and I'll need every ounce of your negotiating skills to be able to do it, but the way I see it working is this—I'll appoint tribal leaders from each major area, from each major tribe, and from each part of the country to come to Baghdad and to assist in the appointment of some notable to serve as prime minister. Once that's done, they'll have one of their own as leader of the country. He'll appoint Arab ministers and they'll be advised by us. The function of the Arab ministry will be to prepare the grounds for the first general election in this country's history. If that doesn't quiet the buggers, I don't know what will."

She looked at him, and forced herself to resist throwing her arms around his neck and hugging him. It was precisely what she'd been suggesting to Wilson for months, but he'd rejected her advice out of spite or hubris; yet what Percy was proposing was so eminently sensible. The Arabs would be in charge, but the British would be showing them the way.

During the main course they discussed who would be a suitable person to act as prime minister. Someone from Basrah, from Baghdad, or from Mosul. Each had advantages and considerable disadvantages.

But it was during the desert that her next door neighbor, on the other side of her to Sir Percy, tapped her on the shoulder. It was

Ghyath Tabul, a Shi'ite leader from Basrah with whom she had often held interesting and enlightening conversations.

"I'm an old man," he began saying, "and many of my powers have failed. I am no longer able to satisfy myself with a woman, though God knows I continue to try."

She contained her laughter. It was often the way with Arabic men to say things which an English gentleman would never countenance saying.

"One of the powers which have not yet failed me, Khatun," he continued, "is my power to overhear what is being said behind my back. Forgive me, but I have been listening to what you and Kokus were discussing. You are talking about us having a prime minister and a cabinet. All of this is very good. But tell me, Khatun, in England, how is a house built?"

Now where, she wondered, was he going with this? Playing along, she said "A house, great one, is built from firm foundations. Then walls are built, then a roof is put on."

He nodded. "And that is how you wish to build a government in Iraq? You begin with the foundations of a cabinet and a prime minister, and on that, you will build consensus and a country."

She nodded. He was far too wily to have begun this conversation without a purpose.

"I don't think, Khatun, that in Iraq we should build our new houses like that."

Surprised, she asked, "And how would you build a house in Iraq, great one?"

"I would begin with the roof, Khatun. With a roof. I would support the roof with a few pillars. You see, foundations aren't easy to observe, and the householders will wonder what the builder is doing, scurrying under the ground. The house will be built too slowly for people without a home. The householders will be discouraged. They will need the shelter of a roof to protect them from the sun and the wind."

She understood what he was saying.

"Give us a roof, Khatun."

"But what of Prince Abdullah? Great one, we have suggested a roof in Prince Abdullah, son of the Kingdom of the Hejaz."

The old man shook his head. "Abdullah will not make a good king, Khatun. He is unknown in our country. He is not one of us. And his reputation does not impress. He will not rule wisely. He is a fool and a wastrel. We need a man of substance, who is acceptable to all of us in our country."

The old man's watery eyes looked upwards to the ceiling. "A roof, Khatun, a strong and safe roof which can be seen and admired throughout all of Iraq. A roof which will protect the people."

"And do you think that such a roof will be found in The Iraq?" she asked.

The old man shook his head. "No, Khatun. There is too much jealousy, too many men who want to be king. But thanks to the French, Syria has lost it's roof. I'm wondering whether the discarded roof of Syria will fit the new house of Iraq."

She looked at him in amazement, but all he did was smile, and continue eating his food.

~

Whitehall, London, January 1921

"I have to admit, Lawrence, I'm somewhat surprised, and not unduly gratified, that you accepted my invitation. We only seem to have corresponded with each other of late, and haven't met since Paris. Frankly, I'd have thought I'm the last person a chap like you would have wanted to see."

Colonel Lawrence looked at the prematurely balding head of Winston Churchill, standing as though his feet were tree trunks growing out of the carpet, hands on hips as though he was about to address a political rally. His parliamentary opponents were starting to call him bulldog, and Lawrence could easily see why.

The two men were alone in the cavernous meeting room of the Colonial Office in Whitehall. It was only 11:30 in the morning, and already Churchill had a huge cigar stuck in his mouth. Every time he drew on it and exhaled, his upper half seemed to disappear in a cloud of blue smoke.

"I'm here, Winston, because you invited me. If for nothing else, you've got a reputation for serving the best single malt in London."

"Good God, I didn't think you drank," Churchill exclaimed. "If you're still here at lunch time, we'll break open a bottle and I'll take you to lunch at The Travellers Club. During our lives, I believe we've both traveled more than five hundred miles from London, so we're eligible."

Lawrence settled into the chair, and asked, "Why did you send for me?"

"I didn't send for you, my dear chap. I respectfully asked if you'd be kind enough to visit me. One doesn't send for Lawrence of Arabia."

Lawrence scowled. "You know I hate that name."

"If I were you, I'd wear it with pride. It was one of the high points of Great Britain's experience in the Middle East."

"So that's why you've invited me. Iraq!"

"Precisely. I'm getting a bollocking in the press over Iraq. I've put Percy Cox back in charge, and he seems to be calming the situation down somewhat, but that buffoon Wilson let things get out of hand, as did General Haldane, but now the criticism's come home to roost."

"And what can I do about it?" asked Lawrence.

"My standing with the British public has slipped a bit as a result. Nothing permanent, of course—the public's memory is notoriously fickle—but the criticism in the press and in parliament isn't doing the government much good, and its deflecting us from concentrating on more serious issues."

"And why should that interest me?" asked Lawrence.

"Because you can help the government. I'd like you to issue a statement to the media that government policy in regard to the Middle East has been right all along, that mistakes were made as a result of misunderstandings, and that the Arabs are notoriously hard to deal with. Further, that this uprising and the deaths which

412

have been caused were the result of them demanding too much, too soon."

Again, Churchill puffed on his cigar. His eyes searched Lawrence's face for a reaction.

"Again I ask the question, Winston, why should I? You've never liked me. You've been caustic about my adventures, you've said publicly the work we did in the Hejaz and Yenbo and Aqaba were nothing more than sideshows and had little effect on the war, you've made horrible remarks about my demeanor, you've excluded me and ridiculed me. In Paris, you were positively beastly towards me, fawning over Gertrude Bell, and treating me like a disease, like a pariah. Why should I concern myself with your fate?"

"One reason, my dear chap, is you're a particular friend of Gertrude Bell, and her judgement is sounder than anybody else's I know. More than that, she was looking at you as some sort of latter-day Saladin. She saw you as a leader of the Arab world. Perhaps she was wrong, or perhaps events in that capricious and benighted land moved in the wrong direction, but she saw in you much that others fail to see, and because I trust her judgement so greatly, I'm inclined to look beyond the obvious when I see you."

Lawrence squirmed in his chair. "Gertie's idea that I could lead Arabia was nonsense. It could never have happened."

"Not so," said Churchill. "In many ways she was right. Because there are so many little men vying for the role of pan-Arab leader, not one of whom will find a follower in a different tribe, and all of whom will be opposed through jealousy, she saw an opportunity for an outsider to come in and scoop the pool. And she damn near pulled it off, as well. After your victories against the Turks, many Arabs saw you as a leader. But you followed that bloody American newsman's cart and horse and instead of devoting your life to leadership, you became a circus freak, a show pony. And that's why you're becoming more and more obscure. Had you followed Gertie's advice, I might be calling you Your Royal Highness at this very minute."

Lawrence burst out laughing. "So you think I'm obscure, do you Winston. Why?"

"Because, Lawrence, now peace has erupted, you and those like you have become an irrelevance. All the generals and colonels are rushing hither and thither to have their memoirs and campaigns published, as though the great British public wants to be reminded about the war! And you can't bear being irrelevant, can you? Until another war comes along, Lawrence, you've missed your chance for greatness. You're extraneous to the needs of England. You'll shrivel and dry up, and all you can look forward to is half a dozen lines in a *Times* obituary.

"But not if I lift my little finger and sign a scrap of paper. I can rescue you from the nightmares that are swirling around in your head. I can do you a great big favor. How long do you think the public's going to queue up to hear about the marvellous adventures of Lawrence of Arabia? I hear you're writing your memoirs. If you want them to sell well, you've got to be uppermost in peoples' minds. No publisher will want your work if, in another six months, a year maybe, you'll be yesterday's hero, just another soldier from a distant war."

It was now Lawrence's turn to search Churchill's demeanor for signs of meaning.

"And what's this great favor you can do me?" he asked.

"As colonial Secretary, it's in my power to elevate you to the very highest place which this country can provide."

Lawrence laughed. "I'm not interested in medals or ennoblement. I didn't want to lead the Arabs after the war and become king, and I certainly don't want to be Sir Thomas or Lord Lawrence of Kings Cross Railway Station. I'm not after that sort of glory."

"That's not the sort I'm offering. I'm creating a new office within my department specifically to look after the Middle East. I'm planning a major conference on Iraq and Palestine in Cairo. The entire world's media will be there. All the important people from this department and experts from the Middle East theater. It'll be a reprise of the Paris Peace Conference, only without the distraction of that old warhorse Clemenceau. Do this small thing for me, get the monkey off my back, and I'll include you in the conference. You'll be the center of attention again. You can guide British policy in Iraq and Palestine and the rest of the theater. Unlike blowing up a few trains on some unheard of railway track, you can have a real influence on the future."

"You'll include Gertrude?" he asked.

"Of course. Regardless of what you decide, Gertrude is essential to my planning strategy."

"And you'll treat me with respect?" he asked.

Churchill smiled. "As though you were my brother."

Lawrence sighed. He'd love to be involved in the Middle East again, but being out of the limelight had been so comforting.

"You know, Winston, you're completely wrong about me. Oh, certainly, most of the generals can't stand being at home and only having command of the kitchen staff and the gardeners. But not me. I love it. I love being obscure. I crave obscurity."

"We all crave obscurity when we're famous, Lawrence. But wait until you really are obscure. You'll sell your soul to be noticed."

"I'm thinking of re-enlisting," said Lawrence. Churchill looked at him in shock. "Not as Colonel Lawrence, but by another name, so I don't carry any baggage with me. I just want to be ordinary again, and not this *Boy's Own* adventurer. I'll enlist in the engineers or something. Or maybe this new air force you're so excited about. I have to get away from being Lawrence of Arabia. It's driving me mad."

Churchill nodded. "Why not put that decision off until after Cairo. Then you can decide."

There was a respectful knock on the door. It opened, and a woman's head poked through. She nodded at Churchill who nodded back. Lawrence wondered what was going on, until a familiar dapper figure, dressed in an immaculate dark blue three-piece suit walked in through the door.

Lawrence stood immediately, and bowed. "My dear chap," he said, beaming a smile. "What are you doing in London?"

Churchill had a mischievous glint in his eye. Yet another Churchillian *coup de grace*. "Welcome, Faisal. What a pity I can't call you king anymore."

Faisal beamed. "I think the expression is ex-king, Mr. Churchill. My friend, Thomas Lawrence," he said, walking across the room to hug his friend, "Colonel Lawrence, it's so very good to see you. How are you?"

The two men held each other's shoulders, and beamed. "My God, Faisal, but I've missed you. How often have I thought of going over to Syria and being with you."

"Too late, Lawrence. Too late. I've been ousted by the French. Driven out of my kingdom."

Lawrence nodded. He'd heard the news from friends in London and was preparing to write Faisal a letter of regret and sympathy when he'd received the invitation to come to Whitehall to meet with Churchill.

Faisal walked to the other side of the room, and shook hands gravely with the Colonial Secretary. "Is your visit a coincidence, or did you know I was going to be here?" asked Lawrence.

"Nothing I ever organize is a coincidence, Lawrence," boomed Churchill. "I've asked His ex-Majesty here to try to find a solution to his particular problem. And I see the difficulties he's having with the French as part and parcel of the difficulties we're going to be having with the tribesmen and Jews and Christians and Assyrians and Druze and Kurds all the other factions in that difficult area."

Churchill led the way through the inner doors to a private sitting room, where the three men sat in armchairs. On the table was a setting of morning tea, cakes, and biscuits. Lawrence poured for the other two.

As he sipped his tea, Faisal mused, "I suppose the problem we find ourselves in now is the difference between expectation and reality. You Europeans have an expectation that because you defeated the Turks, you have the right to ownership of your conquered territory, regardless of the people who live within it. But for some reason, you don't feel that same impulse in Europe.

You beat the Germans, but I see no move to station troops permanently in Germany and make Berlin or Hamburg into British or French cities. Why, then, should Damascus be French, and Jerusalem and Baghdad British?"

"Sometimes, Faisal, the most complex problems have the simplest of causes. Germany has no oil. It has lots of coal in the Ruhr, but then we in England have lots of coal. The Middle East is a sandpit floating on a sea of oil. We need that oil, but we don't need coal. Simple," said Lawrence.

"And Palestine? What oil is there in Palestine?" he asked.

Churchill shifted his bulk in the armchair. "Much of our policy towards Palestine comes from advice drawn up for us by the late Sir Mark Sykes. You see, back in the middle of the war, it was vital for Britain to win support of the Jewish community for the fight against the Hun. Sykes knew we needed vast amounts of money and we were already bleeding the British public dry with increased taxes and austerity. Don't forget America didn't enter the war until very late.

"Sykes thought, as the Rothschilds and other wealthy Jewish banking families in the past had bankrolled governments like the French and the Germans in their military aspirations, the time for Great Britain might have come when we would have to go to them and ask them for assistance. So in order to smooth the path to their door, he persuaded Arthur Balfour to make a declaration that Britain should support a Jewish homeland in Palestine. Suddenly we were heroes with the Jewish community and with many English intellectuals. Even that crusty old bugger, H.G. Wells thought it a wonderful idea that Judea should be re-created for the Jews."

Faisal nodded. "And as you know, I support the return of the Jewish people. But I am not in the majority. There are already street fights between Arabs and Jews, and they are set to get much worse. The fact is, Mr. Churchill, Great Britain has got itself into a mess, and we are all adversely affected. And now that the French have taken military control over Syria and Lebanon and blended them into one country, the situation is even more complex."

"Which is precisely why I've asked Colonel Lawrence to join us in the new Middle East Office I'm setting up. Real experts for real solutions. We'll no longer leave it up to the military men and the politicians. We'll get proper advice and make decisions in the best interests of all concerned."

Lawrence shook his head. "Look Winston, before I agree to join this little shindig of yours, I have to know who else is in there. I've never exactly been popular with the Whitehall mandarins. They've opposed every policy I've ever tried to carry out when it comes to the Middle East. Why do you think they'll suddenly start to listen to me?"

Churchill smiled. "Because I'm listening to you, Lawrence. And when I listen, everybody else hears what I hear. The first thing I want you to do is plan the agenda for the Cairo Conference in March."

EIGHTEEN

Cairo, March 1921

She wore a resplendent dress, deep crimson with slender vertical strips of the very finest silver thread. The silver was hardly noticeable, except when her dress caught the light, and then it positively gleamed. Around her neck was a silver fox boa and on her head was her ubiquitous feathered hat.

It was so thrilling to be in Cairo. More so than being in than Paris, where she'd played a far less important role. In Paris, she'd been the oil on troubled waters, seamlessly moving from delegation to delegation and trying to steer the Great Powers on a particularly British course. She had been a behind-the-scenes diplomat, out of the limelight—essential to British interests, more unnoticed than regarded.

But here in Cairo, things would be different. Her opinion would be sought by Churchill, Lawrence, Sir Percy Cox, Sir Herbert Samuel who was the new high commissioner in Palestine, Sir Geoffrey Archer from Somalia, General Scott from Aden, and of course all the experts Churchill had brought out from England.

Gertrude and Sir Percy already knew what Churchill had in mind. He was under phenomenal pressure to save the British taxpayer money by withdrawing troops from Iraq, and as he left England to come to Cairo, he'd made public what was going through his mind. He'd stepped on board the boat train and told the assembled press he was going to Egypt to save the working man millions of pounds, while at the same time protecting British interests in the Middle East and ensuring the legacy of so many dead British soldiers would be remembered and respected.

But the public image he tried to portray was very different from the private correspondence which Percy had received. Churchill was being crucified in the press and in Parliament because

Mesopotamia had so far cost the British government a fortune, and that was just to fight the recent Arab insurrection.

And now Churchill was intent on only having troops remain in Basrah in order to protect Britain's Persian oil interests and its route from Egypt to India. He had made the decision to pull them out from the rest of the country in order to return them to England and de-mobilise them. For Gertrude and Percy, this decision was rampant insanity. Percy had written a brilliant diplomatic response to Churchill's cable, explaining that while Churchill might want to retain troops in Basrah, without the other troops to protect them they'd be massacred by millions of irate anarchic Iraqis. He assured Churchill withdrawal would sound the death knell for the new country.

And supported by the insistence of Gertrude, he said that in view of the uprising and the demand for accelerated nationalism, Prince Abdullah was the wrong choice to be made King of Iraq. Instead Faisal, who had recently and unexpectedly been forced to vacate his throne in Syria, might be looking for another seat and would be a far better choice. Percy said Faisal had the experience of kingship, the experience of government, and the ability to lead a large Arab army. Abdullah, on the other hand, had no such experience, and the anarchy and resentment which his reign would create would be catastrophic to British and Arab interests.

Both Percy and Gertrude blamed A.T. Wilson for the problems which they were facing, but now that they were in Cairo, there was a chance, a slim chance, that with all the experts advising Churchill, he might be persuaded to take a longer-term view of the situation, instead of being driven only by money and pressure.

She was so looking forward to seeing Colonel Lawrence again. Since Lowell Thomas' lectures had become so popular in America and England, and since the American's book, *With Lawrence in Arabia,* had become such a phenomenal sensation, Lawrence was today a world-famous character. He was everything about which the new American film industry created fantasies—a genuine hero in an utterly romantic and unknowable location, dashing about on a camel and killing the enemy of Western Civilization. He was a man who took the quixotic nomads of the desert by hand and unilaterally made them into a nation. It was cinema and penny dreadfuls at their very best. It was far more fiction than truth, but truth and fiction in war were blood brothers, and so long as Gertrude had expression in her painstakingly honest articles in *The Times* and in her books, she didn't really care if Lawrence played the role of an Othello or an Iago, just so long as she wasn't cast by history as a female Caliban, or worse, as A.T. Wilson had tried to invent her, Lady Macbeth.

She and Percy took a carriage along the edge of the Nile towards their hotel, the Semiramis, in a particularly fashionable part of Cairo. And as they passed a Mosque, they could clearly hear the prayers inside, interspersed with the chanting of anti-British shouting and yelling. It was frightening how much hatred there was towards Britain in Egypt. She was alarmed at the prospect of serious unrest during their conference.

The hotel was archetypal British colonialism—tall ceilings, vast interiors, lazily wafting straw fans to circulate the air, pulled by indolent natives sitting cross-legged on the floor, obsequious porters, fawning servants, and submissive waiters, all of them outfitted in gaudy uniforms of red and gold, with black fez hats, making them look like performing monkeys, and the ubiquitous all-knowing reception and management staff bowing and scraping to ensure the English ladies and gentlemen were totally comfortable and had every wish satisfied.

Gertrude found it nauseating, perhaps because she had been brought up with such privilege, or perhaps because in all her years in Arabia, she had come to dislike so intensely this attitude of the British towards themselves, and how they expected to be treated as Englishmen and women while abroad.

As she and Sir Percy entered the lobby, she spied the diminutive figure of Colonel Lawrence standing there, reading a newspaper.

"Dear boy," she called out, striding across the thick carpet to the pillar which was supporting him. He folded the newspaper, and beamed a smile. She hugged him, and said, "I have to know all the gossip. Who's here, who wasn't invited, who's got what agenda . . ."

"More importantly, Mother darling, is who's got who's ear, if that's the correct grammatical syntax," Lawrence said mischievously, linking his arm through hers and beginning to walk her into the bar.

"Just a minute," she said, "I can't leave Sir Percy . . ."

She asked Percy if he'd like to join them, but he smiled and said he'd leave them alone and go to his room.

They entered the bar area, and like an over-excited schoolboy, Lawrence said breathlessly, "I've got Churchill's ear. It's all so different from Paris. Now that I'm suddenly so famous, the British Bulldog considers me worthy of being listened to. It's quite odd, really. I can't get used to all this fame and I certainly can't get used to politicians taking me seriously. But it's all so exciting. I remember when generals like Allenby and Haig were making decisions above my head and decisions I made in Palestine and the Hejaz were suddenly reversed by invisible forces beyond my control, but now I'm one of those forces, and it's terribly thrilling."

They sat at a table holding hands, and a waiter immediately appeared. "I feel badly about excluding Sir Percy. I really should include him in our conversation. I'm concerned he'll be miffed if I don't," she warned.

"Invite him tomorrow. I've got so much to tell you, so much personal stuff he wouldn't be interested in. Let's just be alone for a bit."

She looked into the main hall, but Sir Percy was already disappearing behind porters who were carrying their bags to the central staircase. She so greatly appreciated his understanding of her need to be alone with Lawrence.

They ordered drinks, and Gertrude asked, "What's the real agenda for this conference? Does Churchill really want advice, or just a rubber stamp on withdrawal of British troops and handing over much of the country to the Arabs?"

"I think he genuinely wants advice. He certainly wants to canvass as many opinions as possible. That's why he's invited Arnold Wilson—"

"WHAT!!!" she yelled.

People stopped what they were doing and looked around at them. She smiled politely, and nodded.

"Wilson?" she hissed. "Here? But that's insane. Wilson's the one who created all the problems for Britain in the first place. That's why we have to clean up his mess. He was the one who—"

"I'm well aware of what Captain Wilson did. So is Winston. He's got Wilson here because he's currently representing British interests in the Anglo-Persian Oil Company. And I think Churchill's hoping Wilson will play his cards in front of the gathering of experts, saying we should send more troops to Mesopotamia to keep control and ownership, and teach the Arab's a lesson they'll never forget. If and when he does, Churchill will descend on him like the proverbial ton of bricks, and distance himself. In that way, it'll show the problems in Iraq were not created by you and Percy Cox and Churchill and Lloyd George, but by Wilson and all the other buggers opposed to Arabic nationalism. Very clever."

"Very devious," said Gertrude.

"Oh, Winston is nothing if not devious."

The waiter arrived with their drinks.

As he deposited them and left their table, Gertrude said softly, trying to sound as casual as possible, "You know what we're going to have to do, don't you, dear boy?"

He sipped his lemon water, and scrutinized her. "Are you asking me or telling me?"

"I'm trying to discuss the future," she quipped.

"And are you including me in your monologue as your acolyte, or the beneficiary of your knowledge and experience, or the callow youth you found digging in Carchemish, or the soldier of fortune to whom you gave such welcome advice when he was leading the Arab revolt, or the middle-aged gentleman advisor to Winston Churchill, Colonial Secretary?"

She looked at him, but he hadn't finished. "Or the man you wanted to become your Saladin and the ruler of a Greater Arabia? Well, Gertie, which is it?"

"I'm talking to you as friend . . . and hopefully still as your mentor. You've always taken my advice, and I don't think you've suffered as a result."

"What is it, Gertie? What do you think we are going to have to do?"

"Convince Winston to swap horses mid-stream."

"Faisal rather than Abdullah?"

She nodded. "Sir Percy's already written to him, but he seems reluctant."

"I know," said Lawrence. "He wants to know why the younger son would make a better king than his older brother. And if so, what do we offer the older brother?"

"You, more than anybody, should know why Faisal rather than Abdullah. He's a natural leader, and is much more inclined to Britain than Abdullah would be. But even if he'd make a good king, he'll never become the leader of the Arabs. He's just not up to fighting some bullying bastard like ibn Sa'ud. Still, as to what to offer Abdullah, we'll create another Arab nation to the west of Iraq. One which will run to the east bank of the Jordan River. And perhaps a little bit across it to border on the west bank of the Jordan so he'll have a good water course running through his land."

"A country spanning the Jordan? But isn't that supposed to be Palestine?"

"Doesn't have to be," she said. "We could call it TransJordan. Make Abdullah the first king."

"But it's just desert. There's nothing there except a few biblical towns, and I'm sure the Jews will want those."

"Don't forget Amman."

"Amman? But it's a hovel. And full of Circassian refugees from Russia. There's nothing there. You'll be offering the poor man a handful of houses surrounded by an ocean of sand."

"You forget its history," said Gertrude. "It was the Royal City captured by King David's general Joab. We're in control of the whole area under the League of Nation's mandate. We can split off that part from the Palestine mandated area, and create a whole new country. Wouldn't it be exciting?"

Lawrence shook his head. "But what's there for Abdullah to rule? There's nobody there but Bedouin and bugger all in the place except desert."

"And the wonderful ruins at Petra. And the Dead Sea. And with proper agriculture, within a few years it could become another Iraq. All that's needed is good management and irrigation from the Jordan."

Lawrence shrugged. "But while you're inventing countries like Iraq and TransJordan, the real issue is how we're going to protect what we've already got in Mesopotamia. How are we going to withdraw our troops, save the good old British taxpayer some money, and not get our arses kicked? That's what Churchill wants to know."

~

The seven days were spent in general sessions for all the experts and in closed sessions where teams worked on particular problems. Winston Churchill wandered the halls and corridors of the hotel, dropping in on meetings and advising, cajoling, and energising the participants. His energy was boundless, his understanding prodigious. When people needed to get out of the smoke-filled rooms and go for a walk in the fresh air of the hotel's gardens, Churchill would wander with them, talking non-stop about the job they had been set. His memory was remarkable, his understanding of the complexities encyclopaedic, and his perceptions of the political realities more sophisticated than anybody believed possible.

In the time which she spent with him, Gertrude changed her opinion dramatically. She used to consider him a likeable, devious, and somewhat untrustworthy politician. Now she realized she was in the company of greatness. While she knew more of the details of the Middle East than he did, he had a universal view which encompassed the past, present, and future of the region, and the potential involvement of all the Great Powers, especially America and its growing understanding of the mining of oil. Churchill was more impressive than any other politician she'd ever met, and she'd met most of them.

During one long and lazy walk on the banks of the Nile, he asked her, "So, m'dear, this interest of yours in wogs and such. How did an upper crust English woman become fascinated by the camel riders?"

"Many years ago—many, many years ago—when I was little more than a girl down from Oxford, I was staying in Bucharest with my Uncle who was the ambassador. A certain Arab came to his home to seek his advice and from that moment onwards, I've been fascinated."

Churchill walked on, remaining quiet until he asked, "You're much more than a civil servant, aren't you Gertie? Civil servants simply do what political masters like me dictate. But you're different. When you're giving advice about your Middle East, your eyes light up and I can see the fire in your belly. More than anybody here, you have a mission in life. Do you want to share it?"

"If you read my reports, Winston my dear, you'll have seen my mission. It's to create a single, united Arabic people, an Arabia for all the Arabs so they are one, and not a hundred different tribes, all with their petty jealousies and quarrels. That would be the making of them, like it was in the days of the Caliphate."

"But isn't there a danger in that? Joining groups of little people together will create one big people, much less easy to control. Unlike a lot of small nations, a big nation could turn around and bite us."

"True, Winston, but if Arabia isn't joined as one nation, then Sunni will continuously fight Shi'ite, both will fight the Kurds, the Jews will be massacred, the Christians will be forced out of Bethlehem, and it'll be a continuous irritant on the body politic.

But with one big people, like the Swiss Federation, or the different States in America joining into a United States, there's be one voice, one government, one set of principles, and the many will become the one," she said.

Churchill smiled and said mischievously "*E Pluribus Unum*. So which are you, Miss Bell? Adams, Jefferson, or Franklin?"

Just as mischievously, she said softly, "Whichever rings the Liberty Bell."

"And does your friend Lawrence the Saladin still fit into your plans?" he asked.

"Sadly, no. Lawrence was riding high in my estimation, but unfortunately, that camel has bolted. I'm hoping somebody like Faisal could become the man."

"Or ibn Sa'ud?" he asked.

"God help us if he does," she replied softly. "God help us all."

~

It was at the general session of all the experts on the seventh day of the conference that Gertrude's fondness blossomed into deep-seated admiration for Winston. He had convened the morning meeting of all forty experts—diplomatic, military, ambassadorial and consular, Iraqi, and others—in order to assess the progress of the previous day's accomplishments by the working parties. As she walked into the room which was guarded by soldiers of the British army in Egypt, she felt there was a different look on Winston's face. It was nothing she could positively identify, but his open candour of the previous week had been replaced by the face of the wily politician. He smelt blood, and she had no idea what he was about to do.

Individual group leaders presented what their people had analyzed the previous day, and the entire group was allowed fifteen minutes of general discussion before moving on to the next group. And she could swear Winston was shuffling about in restrained anxiety as he waited impatiently for Captain Wilson to present what his group had concluded.

The moustachioed Wilson, wearing a heavy three-piece suit, stood and began to speak. "Looking at the situation in Mesopotamia today, I believe—"

"I feel, Captain Wilson," Churchill interrupted, his voice booming over the conference hall, "That we would all be better served if we were to refer to the country as The Iraq."

Wilson looked at him stonily. "You may feel that, sir, but there are those of us who believe that calling it Iraq makes it, *de facto*, into an Arabic nation, and Great Britain has a moral and blood-right to maintaining our position. We are an imperial power, Mr. Churchill, whose men fought and died for that country, and provided we rule with dignity and consideration—"

"Do not presume to address me, sir, on Great Britain's imperial status or the losses we sustained, especially in Iraq and most particularly in the time of your administration" boomed Churchill. The room immediately became still. Gertrude had not anticipated something would happen so suddenly. Nobody else had perceived anything would happen, other than a continuation of the working parties and the tasks which they'd been given.

Wilson looked at Churchill in shock. Nobody had shouted at him or addressed in that manner for decades. He immediately understood that there was far more to Churchill's sudden show of aggression than the politician's normal irascibility. Wilson looked around the table to see what might be behind the sudden onslaught. All eyes were on him, except those of Gertrude Bell, who was staring into her lap. It was then that he realized what was happening.

"Perhaps, Mr. Churchill, the discussion of such issues could be left for a private meeting between ourselves," he said sharply.

"On the contrary, sir," said Churchill, rising to greater heights of restrained fury. "These are things which must be aired and exposed to the harsh light of scrutiny, especially by those of your colleagues who were forced to serve under you and suffer the many egregious errors you made."

"I assume that you're speaking of Miss Bell. May I say, then . . ."

"No sir, you may not say; for I assume that you are going to slander Miss Bell at this table in the same way as you undermined her during your rule. But might I point out that were it not for Miss Bell, the situation in Iraq would have been infinitely worse than you left it. It was Miss Bell, Miss Gertrude Bell, who has managed to rescue both Great Britain's reputation and her standing in the eyes of Iraq."

This was too much for Wilson, who shouted, "Are you mad? Are you completely unaware of how that woman tried to undermine British interests in Iraq? Do you have no understanding of . . . ."

Sir Percy and Thomas Lawrence both were about to shout at Wilson, but Churchill put up his hand for silence, and boomed across the room, "That woman," he said, pointing to Gertrude, "as you so rudely call her, is as patriotic and noble a lady as Great Britain has ever produced. She is the woman who invented Iraq. Out of the dust of aeons, she has almost single handed carved a new nation, a future ally of Great Britain, and through her genius and diplomatic skills, she will bring this new nation together under a government which will partner our own into the future. And you're a fool and a ninny for failing to see what was there before you."

~

"I beg your pardon!" said Wilson, about to storm out of the room.

"And well may you beg the pardon of all England, Captain Wilson. I have been here for the past week, listening to all the combined talents of all the experts in England whose minds have been brought to bear on the question of the future of the Middle East. And it has become patently obvious to me that much of our problem must be deposited upon the doorstep of the High Commissioner's Office during your tenure. Your imperiousness, your high-handed manner of dealing with the indigenes, your arrogance towards the real experts in your staff . . ." he looked again at Gertrude who stared at the green baize tablecloth, terrified of meeting anybody's eye, ". . . especially Miss Gertrude Bell, have cost Great Britain millions and millions of pounds and many dead, all of which could have been avoided had you listened to the advice of those on your staff who knew better, instead of driving your own agenda so ruthlessly."

Now there was no longer silence, but audible gasps in the room. Captain Wilson's face drained of blood. He stood facing Churchill like they were two pugilists in a ring.

"Mr. Churchill," he said slowly, his voice deep with resentment and bitterness, "May I remind you it was you who wanted to drop bombs on the revolting Arabs? May I remind you that it was you who was considering the use of poison gas?"

Churchill paced down the room as though he was going to attack, "Only after the revolt had begun. Only when hundreds of thousands of Arabs were taking up arms to kill British lads. Had you not instigated your reign of terror, Captain Wilson, none of this would have been necessary."

He stood his ground half-way down the table. "Look at what's happened since Sir Percy has taken control. We are witnessing the outbreak of peace. Guns are being silenced. Men are talking. None of the past six months of hell on Earth need have happened if you'd only listened to wiser voices than your own, and be under no illusions that I refer, of course, to Miss Gertrude Bell."

Unbowed, Wilson shouted back, "But you're giving away one of the most valuable countries in the possession of the British crown. Don't you understand what you're doing? Are you so reckless, so antipathetic to the needs of our nation?" he asked. "If we continue to follow your course of action, you'll be giving Mesopotamia to the Arabs. We'll be out in a year. Then we'll lose Persia, then India, then Africa, and then all our other possessions. You will go down in history, Mr. Churchill, as the man who ruined England."

Gertrude could barely restrain herself from joining in the scrap. She glanced over to Sir Percy, who looked at her urgently, and shook his head, ordering her to remain silent. Many others were also deeply shocked someone as senior as Wilson could be treated like some miscreant schoolboy. But Gertrude was well aware of the subtext behind the assault. She glanced at Lawrence. He was the only one whose hawk-like eyes were watching everything that was going on. She knew he felt profound satisfaction. She caught his eye. His face gave nothing away, but his eyes told her he was enjoying every moment of Wilson's crucifixion.

Everybody in the room heard Churchill take a deep breath. "Captain Wilson, British government policy will be formulated by the British government. Functionaries, even highly-placed functionaries such as yourself, will conduct that policy in accord with the orders which we utter. We have been given mandates by the League of Nations to guide our Middle East possessions to a point where native governments can be formed which can take over the reins of government and rule themselves. Whether or not you agree is of no interest to me or my government. And may I remind you Great Britain is quite capable of purchasing the oil which will soon be bubbling out of the Arabian desert. We don't need to spend a fortune on a military force to protect it."

"And Russia? France? What of those nations, Mr. Churchill. If we don't have a military presence, what's to stop these or other nations from sweeping down and conquering Mesopotamia? What's to stop ibn Sa'ud from marauding north from Arabia and taking over the whole of Mesopotamia? What's to stop him from conquering Kuwait or the Hejaz? If we withdraw our troops, there's nobody who'll defend these countries, and then we very well could find our source of oil suddenly cut off."

"You may have been too preoccupied recently to have noticed, but that's precisely the reason the League of Nations has been created, Captain Wilson. To prevent such occurrences," said Churchill.

Despite herself, Gertrude let out a chortle.

~

It was lunchtime before Gertrude could talk to Lawrence. "Well?" she demanded, her urgency apparent from the way in which she walked over to him the moment he emerged from the room designated as the command center.

"It was perfect," said Lawrence. "Churchill's delighted. He's sent a telegram to Whitehall saying mission accomplished, so there must have been more to it than met the eye. I think he was probably under instruction from the prime minister to deflect criticism from the government and to find a scapegoat. With *The Times* snooping about here, doubtless it'll find its way into tomorrow's paper. Churchill, of course, will deny everything, but you can bet the bowler hat brigade will read between the lines. From now onwards, the mandarins of Whitehall will be silent, the newspapers will carry the right approach to the situation, and the government won't face nearly as much of a backlash from the loyal opposition. Captain Wilson and his cronies will privately carry much of the blame and the government will urgently whisper in the corridors of power it was misled and ill-advised. The whole thing will blow over in a couple of months. Mission accomplished."

She shook her head. "I don't understand why the necessity for all the subterfuge. Why couldn't Churchill just have made a statement to Parliament?"

"He couldn't be seen publicly to be criticising a man who used to be as senior as Wilson. It'd put the wind up too many people. After all, he was our man in Baghdad, ostensibly carrying out our orders. If we'd hung, drawn, and quartered him in Parliament, every other high commissioner would have been too afraid to act on his own initiative. And any public execution of Wilson would have brought the opposition out on the rampage. So destroying him in private and defending him in pubic is the way to do it."

She shook her head in wonder at all the artifice which was going on. She was a strategist of considerable note, but these political shenanigans were something far beyond her league.

"How are you feeling now we're half-way through?" asked Lawrence.

They walked outside of the hotel and were immediately assailed by the smells of Cairo—the stench of poverty intermingling with the perfumes of the orient—spices and herbs and the heady scents of the many extravagant flowers in the gardens.

"I'm feeling hopelessly optimistic. I've come through a war unscathed, I've battled with a hideous man whom I've just seen cut down to size, and all my plans for the best solution to Iraq are coming to fruition. Faisal is to be offered the kingship, there's to be a representative democracy replacing the provisional government, I've had all my plans approved to create a country called Iraq, which brings together the Kurds in Mosul with the Sunni around Baghdad with the Shi'ite in the south. Churchill will push for the creation of a kingdom for Abdullah across the Jordan. I feel exultant."

"And so you should, Gertie dear. Even the great Churchill called you . . . what was it . . . the woman who invented Iraq. Quite an accolade. Almost as potent as Lawrence of Arabia. Yes, dear, you should be feeling exultant. But why stop at Iraq? Now you've created one nation, what about your dream of a vast, united pan-Arab nation . . . no tribes or borders or sects . . . just one big Arabia? It's what we talked about all those years ago. It's what you've always wanted."

She smiled. Perhaps it was little more than a girlish dream. "Oh, it'll happen. Not today and not tomorrow. But when Arabia is more mature, when there's democracy in many of the new countries. When the warlords and the mullahs begin to realize the futility of war and death and mayhem, and start to understand the beauty of peace. And when the women of Arabia find their voice and come out from behind the veils that hide their identity, that's when they'll be a united Arabia, Thomas. Maybe not in my lifetime, but I have no doubt it'll happen."

She walked with Lawrence of Arabia to the banks of the River Nile. Because of the dangers of the area, he told her he should go first, and she should follow. She accepted his advice. There were many unsavoury characters looking at them in ways which were discomforting.

Cairo was a bustling, cacophonous place. It was full of black Sudanese, Ethiopians, Egyptians, Jews, Christians, Copts, and a hundred other nationalities and religions. It was a melting pot of all humanity, from the monotheists to the polytheists, from the very wealthy to the indescribably poor, from ultra-nationalists who would kill to achieve self-rule to those who saw the League of Nations as a body which would dissolve divisions between people and create one peaceful world without war. It was a place in which women like her paraded their European fineries in dresses which would cost ten year's income to an Egyptian worker, yet they walked side-by-side with women who were veiled from head to toe to prevent any part of them being seen by men.

The Middle East was a land of such extraordinary contrasts. Just as she was such a contrast in the British political service. She had reached the highest position any woman had ever reached in the civil service, she had published numerous books about her travels and archaeological discoveries which made her into one of the most lionised women in London, she had climbed unclimbable mountains in Switzerland, and a formerly-unconquered peak had been named after her, she had directed British policy in the Great War, she was fluent in six languages, had befriended and advised the most important men in England and the Middle East, she had been imprisoned by a tribal war-lord, and she would now be known as the woman who invented Iraq, and was well on the way to creating another called Transjordan.

And because she was a woman, she was still walking in the footsteps of Lawrence of Arabia.

NINETEEN

Baghdad, Iraq, July, 1921

The day, finally, had arrived. To reach this day had taken months of preparation and traveling all over Iraq, months of fear and anxiety that her carefully wrought plans would be nullified in an instant in the volatile world of Arabia by some act of jealousy, revenge, or resentment' and months of negotiations between London and Baghdad to ensure the subtle balance between the need for Faisal's independence as a new monarch of an autonomous country, and Britain's desire for a strong trading relationship, all under the suzerainty of the League of Nations and its mandate. But eventually, the day of his coronation arrived.

Faisal, soon to be His Serene Majesty Faisal I of Iraq, was preparing to be crowned by approbation of the majority of his new countrymen. Few who would be at the ceremony, important representatives from London and neighbouring countries, were aware of the road Gertrude and Faisal had had to travel to reach this point.

There were times on the roads which criss-crossed Iraq when the thermometer reached 120 degrees in the shade, not that there was any shade in the Iraqi countryside. Nor was there the prospect of comfort and convenience, because they had a huge amount of territory to cover in a short period of time. Faisal had never seen Iraq before, and so Gertrude decided to take him by the hand, and lead him from place to place, both as a guide and a teacher.

She knew it would be a strain, but she had been on terrible desert journeys before, and believed she could cope with the discomfort. But she found it unbelievably arduous, and after seven days Gertrude was forced to admit she wasn't the same person as the young, adventurous woman who had ridden on camel back, dressed in the finest Parisian fashions, into sandy hills where no white woman had ever set foot.

She felt the strain, but was determined not to allow Faisal to know how tiring she found the journey.

She was expecting to enjoy the caravan, the old-fashioned progress so similar to those which the English Queen Elizabeth I had popularised four hundred years earlier, so she could be seen by her subjects. Gertrude and Faisal were a traveling circus. Their show came to town and village, the excitement spread, and she almost expected to see posters on village walls announcing their arrival

The British Empire presents

That daredevil duo

Faisal and Gertrude

Who will perform the breathtaking magical music hall trick

of turning sceptics and enemies into friends.

And it had worked. Faisal had gained support from nearly one hundred percent of all the leaders of Iraq.

Once they'd traveled beyond the irrigated verdant lands between the Tigris and the Euphrates, all vegetation seemed to wither, then die, then disappear. No trees or shrubs provided shade from the merciless sun, just mile after mile after mile of unrelenting rocks and stone and sand and dust. Just desert.

Never had Gertrude felt more torpid, less feminine, than when she and Faisal were driving from town to town, city to city, paying respectful visits on important people, answering their questions, and wishing them well. And before they departed on yet another visit to another important tribal leader in another town, neither Gertrude nor Faisal had any opportunity to attend to their toilet. They both left and arrived in a state of dishevelment, despite hasty repair work as the cars drove along the bumpy and dusty roads and tracks.

As they left the Anazeh tribe and drove towards the east in search of a Bedouin tribe which was last reported near the oasis of Quoom, she wondered just how many more people they would have to meet and greet.

Dear God, she thought, but it was unbearably hot. Even when she had been riding through the Arabian or the Syrian Desert years earlier, even when she had been knee-deep in archaeological explorations, or imprisoned in Hayil, even in those times, Gertrude had always managed to retain something of her English upbringing, her feminine nature. But the heat of the Iraqi Desert and the unremitting sun drained her of her heritage, her gender, and simply overwhelmed her with the need to survive from one visit to the next.

Were it not for the requirement to win over so many tribal leaders, emirs, sheiks, and other notables of the Iraqi community to the reality of Faisal becoming king in the forthcoming election, she would have instructed her driver to return to Baghdad where there was the prospect of a swim in the Tigris, cool drinks, shady rooms, fans wafted by servants and baths . . . oh, what she would have given to be able to immerse her body in a huge bath of cold, perfumed water with rose petals floating on top.

At night, they had slept in tents under the freezing sky of the desert. They had spoken about Paris, about Cairo, about the prospect of a becoming a king over a country he had never previously set foot in, about Lawrence and how his new-found fame might alter him, about Sir Percy Cox and the ways in which Faisal might work him and the British government, and much more.

But what had returned to Faisal's mind, time and again, were the ideas which Gertrude had put to him very early on, when she had first suggested to him that he become king of Iraq. At first, still bruised from his forced abdication from the throne of Syria, Faisal had resisted the idea that he might become king of another land. He had gone to London trying to gain British support to remove the French.

But when Gertrude first contacted him, she assured him that, rather than Iraq being a second prize, it would instead be an historical completion of the circle which had begun one thousand, three hundred years earlier, with Faisal's ancestor, Hussein, the grandson of the Prophet Mohammad. The martyrdom of Hussein in Karbala in 680AD had caused the eruption of Shi'ism, and as the first king of a united Iraq, it would be incumbent on Faisal to mend the wounds, to complete the circle and to rule for all his people, whether they were Shi'ite, Sunni, Jewish, Christian, Assyrian, Turkoman, or Kurd.

Slowly, cautiously, the idea began to grow in his mind, especially when she'd told him his elder brother, Abdullah, was to be made emir of a new country to the west of Iraq to be called Transjordan.

Their progress had cemented Faisal in the minds of the Iraqi tribal leadership, and the Iraqi people in Faisal's mind. The caravan had been an overwhelming success, despite the exhaustion it had caused her. But now was the time for the Coronation, and all the difficulties which had nearly prevented them reaching this point were distant memories. Indeed, the caravan had been a triumph of such outstanding proportions that, just months after her seduction of him to the throne of Iraq, he had managed to seduce all the officials, leaders, and demagogues into voting for him to be their king.

And now, at six in the morning on August 23rd, in the twenty-first year of the century, Faisal, Sir Percy Cox, his advisors, aides-de-camp, and cabinet were standing on Persian carpets before a glittering crowd of almost two thousand people, ceremoniously establishing not just the king, but the kingdom.

Faisal swallowed nervously, and scanned the crowd looking for a familiar face. He saw Gertrude, and instinctively began to smile, but he immediately realized he had to behave like a king—a King of Iraq—and smiling at an English woman, even one who was his friend, mentor, and partner in this new adventure, would not be appreciated by the many Arab dignitaries in the audience. So he looked away.

But from the corner of his eye, Faisal allowed himself a surreptitious glance at her, and saw she was wearing an immaculate white dress, an ostrich feathered hat, a set of pearls, and standing proudly in the front row as the Dorset Regiment struck up an anthem. Although there had been time to create an Iraqi flag, there had been no time at all to write the music for an anthem, and so the band struck up the only tune which seemed appropriate, God Save the King. The newly designed Iraqi flag was raised, and as it ascended to the top of the flagpole, Faisal, Percy Cox, and Gertrude all saluted.

Gertrude looked closely at Faisal's face, an image she knew so well. They had worked together, cemented a nation together, traveled highways and byways of that nation together, relaxed and played together, and if she knew the mind and aspirations of any man, it was Faisal's. She wanted to wish him strength and fortune, God's speed and the very best of British luck. She wanted to tell him that now Iraq was a nation, a country whose creation owed itself to Gertrude Bell, she had decided to become one of its citizens. She wanted to tell him the conviction had been growing in her, stronger and stronger by the day, that just as much as the new nation of Iraq was a part of her, so she would be a part of it. She wanted to tell him she would ask to become its first convert, its first British subject to claim dual nationality. She wanted to tell him that just as Iraq now had a present, and would have a prosperous and secure future, it would be Gertrude Bell who would be the custodian of its past . . . that she would quit the British civil service, become a resident of Baghdad, and gather together all the archaeological wonders from the very earliest moments of mankind. That she would create the Baghdad Museum of Ancient Archaeology, a marvellous collection of artefacts which would make the entire world look in awe, not just at the present Iraq, but at the eight thousand year history on which the new country was built. She wanted to run over to His Serene Majesty, her friend and acolyte, Faisal I, and tell him all of these things.

But he wasn't looking at her. She couldn't seem to catch his eye. Instead, Faisal was staring over her head and over the heads of the assembled company who had journeyed to this newest of new kingdoms. There was a look of certainty, of determination, on his face, something which had been missing as they'd journeyed around. Faisal seemed to be looking towards some point she couldn't see. Some point in the far distance. Some point in the future.

EPILOGUE

Baghdad, July 1926

For four years, she had journeyed back and forth to England, Paris, and Teheran. She had cajoled wealthy men to give up the priceless artefacts they'd collected during their expeditions into Iraq so she could create a national museum as homage to the nation's past, just as she was donating 3000 of her own priceless treasures from the archaeological digs she'd conducted for the past thirty years.

She had been hosted at grand receptions by universities and noble institutions in England and Scotland and most recently she was wined and dined at a magnificent banquet to celebrate the signing of a treaty with Turkey. Everybody, it seemed, wanted to add the stellar Gertrude Bell to their invitation list. Everybody, that is, except those whom she most cared about. Her access to the British government was so limited she had to console herself with occasional meetings with parliamentary private secretaries or junior ministers, men whose chests were puffed out with self-importance but who carried no weight, and in Iraq her meetings with the king were all about teaching him Bridge and Chess, but when the subject of Iraq's future or its politics came up, it was as though Faisal's ears were closed to her.

As the years progressed, life held fewer and fewer prospects for her. Gertrude was increasingly excluded from the orbits of power. Despite her lifetime of diplomacy, much of it spend in the epicentre of world events, she found herself caught between Faisal's need to overcome accusations that he was a puppet of Great Britain, and England's desire to prove to the world that their relationship with Iraq wasn't that of puppet master.

~

So she threw herself into the creation of an Iraqi museum which would be her legacy to the nation she had adopted as her own. Iraq was smaller and less impressive than the pan-Arab continent she had wanted to create. Once she had dreamed a dream of a mighty nation of Arabs led by a Saladin, but this had disappeared like a sandstorm which had blown itself out. So Gertrude had been forced herself to narrow her focus. Despite a lifetime of involvement, of shaping the new world, she had to eschew politics because politics had expunged her.

And so she put all her energies into making hers into a small but imaginative replica of the British Museum. She worked there every day, and today she was filthy from dusting the exhibits. Her hair, normally spotlessly clean, gray tinged with white and shining in the sun, was dulled by the grime of the ancient antiquities, relics of a dozen ancient civilizations whose rulers had once commanded the lives of countless millions of men and women.

Arrayed in front of her on the table were artefacts from Sumer and Akkad, from Babylonia and Ur, from the banks of the Euphrates and the fertile stretches of the Tigris. Potsherds, idols of different gods and goddesses, and wine and perfume jars which had adorned the home of some rich potentate or merchant who had been dead for four thousand years, were laid out like exhibits in a courtroom. Here were mirrors made of bronze, dull now but once shining bright in the desert sun to reflect the image of a wife or priestess or daughter, or perhaps a prostitute who was dressing to please a man. Here were incense burners and combs and jewellery in enormous profusion. All things were there, all arrayed on her table, and all in dire need of cataloging. And Gertrude was the only one capable of cataloging them.

Some months ago, she'd been joined by a couple of eager anthropologists from the Smithsonian Museum in America who had heard about the establishment of the Baghdad Museum, and decided to spend their summer vacation helping out. And some junior common room people from Baliol and Magdalene had come out from Oxford because Lawrence of Arabia had been trumpeting Gertrude's virtues on his recent speech to the Oxford Union. But aside from those times of community with European experts, she was the only true intellectual in an Iraqi staff of willing but uneducated helpers.

Gertrude Bell, First Director of the Baghdad Museum of Archaeology, surveyed the enormous building in which her exhibits would be placed, artefacts which she herself had dug and brought back to life, as well as material from the digs of other archaeologists. The exhibit cases had been constructed by local artisans according to her instructions, the floor had been wax-coated, the panels of instruction had been written in calligraphy in English, Arabic, French, and Italian, and signs had been erected at the entrance to the different halls signifying the ages of the growth of human development.

She'd checked the signs carefully herself. They registered mankind's ascent from pre-agricultural times to the earliest record of his settlement, and onwards towards his current supremacy, from the very earliest Stone Age discoveries through the Copper Age, the Bronze Age, the Age of Kings and Tyrants, then the Age of Iron, the Biblical Age of the Patriarchs, the Rise of Islam, ending at the Crusades. Her interest in humankind ended with the Crusades. That record could be safely left in the hands of historians, not archaeologists.

With the rapidly approaching official opening the following week, Gertrude was instructing her staff as to where and how to place the newly dusted and cataloged exhibits in the cases.

She heard a commotion at the front entrance of the museum. Frowning at the thought of visitors a week before the museum was due to open, she walked along an upper corridor, and stopped in her tracks, stunned by the appearance of a Rolls Royce outside the front door.

Hurrying down, she saw the king of Iraq's chauffeur enter the front portals, bearing a letter. He bowed as he handed it to her. It read simply,

My dear Gertrude,

I have something which I would like you to place on a plinth at the entrance to the museum when I open it in a few days' time. Would you be kind enough to come to the palace tomorrow, and I will give it to you. It is an important artefact celebrating one of the great personages who is a part of Iraq's history.

Your friend,

Faisal I

She told the chauffeur she would be happy to visit the king tomorrow after four in the afternoon.

Late that night, when her servants had left and she was alone in her house, she was again gripped by a splitting headache. Normally several whiskeys and sodas did the trick until she fell into a comatose sleep, aided by sleeping pills, but for some reason, four whiskeys hadn't dulled the pain.

She picked up the king's note and re-read it. She was an expert in Mesopotamian history, but for the life of her, wracking her brains, she couldn't think which artefact Faisal could possibly have and which personage was so great he must take pride of place in the entrance.

Her desk was full of other correspondence. She picked up the letter from her father and re-read it for the tenth time. He was selling Rounton Grange following the death earlier in the year of her brother Hugo from typhoid. The long-running coal strike had devastated the family fortunes, and economies were forced on her father, who found them impossible to accept. Yet the bankers were in and clutching at his throat and they were insisting that she sell her jewellery and repatriate the money to England.

Servants were being put out onto the street, houses sold, plans shelved. People whom she'd known all her life, who'd served her and her family with honor and distinction for decades, were suddenly expendable. And in his last letter, the one which had made her cry bitter tears, her aging father had begged her to return, to leave Iraq, to leave her friends and her museum, so she could be there for him and help him overcome the grief which Hugo's death had caused.

But what about her? What about her needs? Was her elderly father considering her in his grief, she wondered. And how could she leave Iraq now, after she had become a citizen and when her glorious museum was about to open? Just to return to England to become her father's nursemaid? Great Britain was no longer the land of her youth. Since the war, it had changed beyond her recognition. Once-impenetrable barriers had broken and the class to which she'd been born was rapidly becoming an anachronism. And she had changed, because she could no longer be the daughter whom her father wanted her to be. She was a daughter of the desert, of Iraq, of an ancient and new people. Her home was the desert, and out of this desert and its people, she had created a nation.

She looked at other letters arrayed over the desk. All through her life, her correspondence had been meticulously ordered and answered, but in the past year or more, she had allowed it to become haphazard and she knew many letters from old friends in England had gone unreciprocated. It was her shame pile, and looking at it through bloodshot eyes, she began to weep at the way she was allowing her new circumstances to undermine the rigid structure in which her entire life had been led. For without structure, without boundaries within which she could act, what was there for her?

In a pile on the top left hand corner of her desk, were six letters from Winston Churchill's secretary. Each one a rejection of her and of their friendship.

~

The Chancellor of the Exchequer has asked me to thank you for your note, and sends you his warmest personal regards, but the pressure of his timetable during the General Strike and Labor Emergency necessitates his having to concentrate all of his energies on the settlement of the industrial disputes affecting Great Britain at this present moment. He trusts you understand why he is unable to answer you personally.

Not Winston Churchill, not Thomas Lawrence, her Saladin who was now signing his letters as Lawrence of Arabia, nor even Faisal, was any longer in regular touch with her. She was pushing constantly for recognition, but being rejected. Just like almost every man had rejected her. She felt for the idol Arinnitti which she'd once worn constantly around her neck, but it wasn't there. To whom had she given it? She couldn't remember, but as she tried to think, she saw Henry's face, smiling at her. She opened her eyes, and his youthful image disappeared. She closed her eyes, but he was gone from her darkness.

Her head was pounding. She poured another glass of whiskey and soda and spilled some down her dress. She giggled. Why was it funny? Now her servant would have to wash the damn thing. The drums thumped in her forehead. She opened her bottle of sleeping pills. It was the only way she'd be able to get some sleep. Tomorrow was . . . what was tomorrow? And what did it matter?

~

The Royal Palace, Iraq

Faisal listened to what the doctor was saying, and nodded. He swallowed and fought back tears. Was he responsible? Could he have done more?

"Did she do it deliberately?" he asked, his soft voice quivering, as he tried not to cry

"It's impossible to say, Highness. But her breath smelled heavily of alcohol, and the bottle of sleeping pills was empty. In my report, I will say it was an accidental overdose, brought on by stress."

The king nodded, and smiled, dismissing the doctor with a wave of his hand. He looked at the bronze bust which he was going to give to her in just a few hours. He had been imagining her face as he unveiled it and she read the inscription. Tears welled up in his eyes. But it was all too late.

446

He beckoned to his chauffeur, who stepped forward, and lifted the heavy bust from the table.

"Have this placed at the very entrance to the museum, so it's the first thing visitors see when they enter," he ordered.

The chauffeur nodded, and looked at the severe face of the statue. He covered it again with the cloth, bowed to the king, and carried it out to the car. It sat next to him on the front bench of the Rolls Royce as he drove through the frenetic streets of Baghdad. Before him were Arabs and English, French and Germans, Shi'ite and Sunni, Jews and Christians, Assyrians and Turkomen and Kurds. All were walking or running, laughing or arguing, cursing or blessing.

Here were men and women and children from many different parts of the world, some dressed in clothes which defined their ancestry, some dressed as citizens of a modern world. It was a cauldron of humanity, as it had been in the days of the bible, in the days of the rise of Islam, and at the time of the Crusaders. And now again, with Arabic nationalism, Baghdad was a centre of Arab pride.

It was approaching midday and the sun was high in the sky, scorching the newly tarmacadamed roads along which he drove. Above his head, electricity lines carried energy to all the newly constructed buildings. And before he could turn right to where the museum was located, a policeman, bringing order to the chaos, held up his hand and stopped the flow of carts and horses and donkeys and the occasional car to allow a party of school children to cross towards the river. The delay enabled the chauffeur to pick up the bust and read the inscription written on its base. In English and Arabic, it said, simply,

Gertrude Bell. A Woman of Iraq.
First Director of the National Museum.
Presented by a grateful King and People.

447

ACKNOWLEDGEMENTS

Gertrude Bell is just one of countless numbers of women throughout the ages whose names and deeds have been expunged from history. Some of these women are remembered by historians and other academics, but most are rarely if even mentioned by name.

I often pose a question to an audience . . . name just a couple of women who lived before the nineteenth century, and who were famous in their own right for their own deeds, and not because they were the family or consorts of famous men. The silence in almost all audiences is something of a revelation.

To bring Gertrude back to life, I was joined on the journey by the invaluable help of my wife Eva, many distant friends found in academic and other sites on the internet, and long-suffering librarians

Peter and Sandra Riva, of International Transactions, my literary agents, have been a wellspring of ideas and advice as well as persistence; they are experts at guiding and encouraging and suggesting changes which reveal landscapes in a manuscript that the author might never have known were there. I have followed their advice with considerable gratitude.

ALAN GOLD

For many years, Alan has specialized in bringing back from obscurity those fabulous but forgotten women who changed the course of their societies.

When not writing novels, Alan is an opinion columnist and a literary critic for major newspapers, and an occasional lecturer in creative writing at universities.

He has also been a human rights orator and represented a leading NGO at United Nations Forums and Conferences dealing with racism and human rights.